RECIPEARIUM

COSTI GURGU

White Cat Publications

RecipeArium is published by White Cat Publications, LLC.

This book is copyright © 2017 White Cat Publications, LLC.
Cover art copyright © 2017 Costi Gurgu
Cover design copyright © Scott Wilson

Edited by Charles P. Zaglanis

FIRST EDITION Book
ISBN 978-0-692-87945-0

Published in April 2017

Published by White Cat Publications, LLC.
2750 Oakwood Blvd.
Melvindale, MI 48122
www.whitecatpublications.com

For Vali Gurgu,
whose love and support have made this possible.
(We did it, my Angel!)

"Costi Gurgu — the top Romanian science-fiction writer — finally breaks through into the English-language market with *RecipeArium*, a brilliant, haunting tale. Move over China Miéville — this is the *new* new weird, a fabulous book with a distinctive, compelling voice."

— Robert J. Sawyer, Hugo Award-winning author of *FlashForward*

"Not for the faint of heart or imagination, Gurgu's *RecipeArium* reveals an alien realm where sex, politics, and a species' history are fused into terrible yet vital acts of consumption. Intense and unforgettable."

— Julie E. Czerneda, author of *This Gulf of Time and Stars*

"*RecipeArium* is a startling, even provocative book, yet it's written in such clear luminous prose and peopled with such sympathetic characters that you'll be pulled right in. Like the finest cuisine, it will leave you satisfied yet wanting more."

— Karl Schroeder, author of the *Virga* series

"Gurgu delivers a full course meal of epic transcendence in an alien landscape that is at once grotesque and wondrously compelling.

From the vast and forgotten lands of the Edge of the World to the corrupt decadence and intrigue of the nobility who dwell inside the monstrous Carami, Gurgu's *RecipeArium* unveils a fascinating world in transformation. *RecipeArium* is a sensual metaphoric tale that explores the dialectic quest of duality to realize itself as whole.

Imaginative. Outrageous. Original. Gurgu subverts traditional fantasy and SF with the promise of new heights in storytelling."

— Nina Munteanu, author of the *Splintered Universe trilogy*

"*RecipeArium* is a sumptuous chronicle of alien culture and cutthroat intrigue, set in a city in the belly of a gargantuan beast. Gurgu's novel gives you an exotic, daring banquet that you will not soon forget."

— Tony Pi, Finalist, John W. Campbell Award for Best New Writer

"*RecipeArium* is uniquely captivating, intriguing, and compelling. Costi Gurgu engages all the senses, tears the envelope to ribbons, and triggers the deepest erogenous crevices of the mind. The story lingers, long after you finish the book, enticing you to question the existential boundaries of hunger. Costi Gurgu accomplishes what all great science fiction authors aim to do—look at something commonplace (eating a meal) in a primal and ultramodern way. *RecipeArium* drops nouveau cuisine and lust in a blender and presses liquify."

— Suzanne Church, Aurora Award winning author of *Elements: A Collection of Speculative Fiction* and *Soul Larcenist*

"In Costi Gurgu's world, everybody eats a lot, many sorts of things and not necessarily tasty. Or at least, not tasty according to the classic olfactory-organoleptic canons. The Kingdom's reason for existence derives from the number of novel recipes proposed to the Sovereign. Becoming a member of the Royal Recipears Council is the favorite target of social careerism. They kill, they cheat, and they betray for this. Intrigues, cabals, monstrous coalitions formed only to become one of the very few super-gastronomes of the kingdom…

In the *RecipeArium* world, everybody dreams, loves, or build their career from an apotheosis of gastronomic obsession invested with the rank of lifestyle.

Pushed to its last consequences, the concept cannibalizes itself subtly, figuratively, as well as literally."

— Dan-Silviu Boerescu (literary critic), *Fantasy Fastfood*
(The Word Magazine)

"*RecipeArium's* reading is a delight. The book reads like a tasting of a Course unheard of, unbelievable. A novel like no other in our literature. A test of imagination—the recipes, the customs, the rituals, the laws—perfectly balanced, serving entirely the story.

I was saying last week that to write good science fiction or fantasy means to create a functional world filled with everything the real world has. Well, the Green Kingdom works. In a world in which life's supreme goal, the fundamental art, is to invent recipes, everything that happens in this novel, its characters, their lives, everything is integrated perfectly. It's a seamless part of the mechanism. It works!"

— Michael Haulica (editor), *Costi Gurgu: RecipeArium*
(The Cultural Observer Magazine)

"Costi Gurgu is a unique writer in the Science Fiction genre and one who belongs to a very limited group of writers in the whole world. Even from *The Wonderful Asaara* he proved that he can credibly imagine a non-human world. With *RecipeArium* he demonstrates that it hasn't been an accident, that he has this capacity of conceiving societies in which the rules are completely different than those around us—a very rare capability indeed."

— Liviu Radu (Eurocon and Romcon Award winner), *Recipes, Recipears and Palace Coups* (Pro-Scris Magazine)

CONTENTS

ADVICE.   *A Course must look so nauseating that a bitter taste comes immediately to your tongue and activates your acidular glands; a jugular spasm should precede the feeling that your stomach is turning and rising in your throat. Only then can you say, "Yes, this so piques my appetite that I could not live one more second without Tasting this Course."*

(from The Recipearium Teachings of Master Recipear Plabos)

I. HITISSH LEOMI

It was hot outside the wagon, the sun shining too brightly for his sensitive eyes, so Morminiu decided he'd rather spend the day inside, in the restful shade beneath the wagon's awning. He sat on a chest, listening to Yd, the apprentice cartographer, a well-educated phril who was eager to tell stories of his adventures and show off his knowledge. And, being a member of the legendary Edge of the World Brotherhood, the world's most appreciated scholars, he had enough stories to fill entire tomes. Right now he was showing his guest the caravan's route to the world's end on the map.

Yd paused and took a deep breath, then raised the water skin to his mouth and swallowed noisily. He was a hairy, savage-looking phril of massive build, like all of the Edge brothers. They originated in a northern kingdom, long gone, and never trimmed their hair, which varied from a dark red to an almost white blonde. Morminiu was a taller phril than most of the caravan's members and had a suppler constitution but, although well built, he looked thin in comparison to his brawny travelling companions. His shiny black hair was trimmed short on his head, not only to counter the scorching humidity in the Swamps, but also because Plabos, his master, had taught him that long hair could be an impediment in the art of Recipearium.

Morminiu leaned forward to take the water skin Yd

offered, but stopped halfway and cocked his head, listening. He'd heard a strange whistling, and then a few screams. Before he could react to that, the heavy thunk of arrows penetrated the wagon's wood, a popping rip as they pierced the fabric awning followed. An arrow passed through the water skin Yd still held and skittered along the wooden floor.

The apprentice cartographer gasped and dropped the water skin when another arrow scratched his thigh. He grabbed his leg with both hands. Around them rose the screams of the wounded and the alarmed shouts of the caravan, mixed with the bellowing of injured beasts.

"Out. Now!" Morminiu told Yd.

Yd nodded and rose from the bench. Morminiu dragged him to the exit. Outside, the noise had risen, but Morminiu did not see the chaos he expected. The Brotherhood was well trained. It had centuries of ambush experience.

They scrambled under the wagon and hid behind one of the wheels. Some more phrils hid there, taking care of each other's wounds. Morminiu shut his eyes. Tears streamed down his cheeks. The sun was much too bright for him. He'd trained for years to live in the filtered light of the cities, far away from day brightness. As Yd took care of his leg, working to stop the bleeding, Morminiu opened the rucksack that held his few possessions and located by touch the smoky crystalline lenses specially prepared for those situations when he'd have to face the daylight. Panting now, he covered his eyes with them, wiped away the tears, then looked around, blinking. The noise level had dropped. There hadn't been a second arrow salvo.

"Don't worry," groaned Yd, his hair soaked in sweat, "we have probably been ambushed by a rival caravan. We've met them before and survived." He hesitated. "Although . . . there's something strange."

"What?"

"Too many arrows. Plus we're very close to the Royal Carami. There are a lot of travellers around here. Usually the fights between rivals happen in remote places, away from possible witnesses."

"We're close to the capital?" Morminiu couldn't hide his excitement.

His leg bandaged, Yd crawled out from under the wagon. Morminiu followed and leaned against the huge wheel, blinking dizzily. The caravan had stopped on a wide and dusty road that crossed an endless plain of water. On either side stretched a muddy green lake, broken by clusters of rusty reeds and white stones cracked by the sun.

"We're very close," the apprentice cartographer finally answered. "We are at the edge of Hung Water-plain. We only cut one of its corners this morning, but in the other directions this desert of salty water stretches for days." He gasped in pain and leaned against the wagon.

Morminiu licked dry lips and looked around in confusion.

"Do you see there, in front of the caravan?" Yd pointed that way. "There is the desert's edge. Beyond that line of rocks are the Salty Falls. The desert's water falls down through hundreds of passages along the bank, from terrace to terrace, to the bottom of the valley. There it joins the rivers coming from that mountain you see at the far edge, and flows in the Mureci River, two days from here in the direction of the rising sun. Between that mountain and the Hung Water-plain is the Royal Carami. That brownish surface is the monster's back."

"We're so close," murmured Morminiu. He had prepared for this his whole life. He'd daydreamed about the moment when he'd stare at the monster that sheltered in its bowels the Green Kingdom's capital, when he'd be face to face with the famous Royal Carami. He was so close! Yet, between him and the behemoth were the Brotherhood's rivals. "Why don't the royal guards come to stop this conflict?"

"They can't see us here," Yd replied. "Anyway, the guards never leave the Carami. They have to protect what's in the city, not what's outside."

Morminiu looked around, saw nothing but the unrelenting landscape. "So, what are they waiting for? Why don't they attack?"

"I think there will be some negotiations. I told you not to worry."

The apprentice clambered up a wheel and, groaning with pain, gripped the awning to keep his balance. Once he'd anchored himself, he looked over the tops of the wagons toward the front of the caravan. Morminiu looked that way. Less than a hundred steps away, a cluster of rocks rose above the surface of the water. They were not on the route to the Waterfalls and Carami, but the attackers' arrows could easily cover the distance.

"Yes, two of our messengers are on their way to meet their representative," Yd confirmed.

Morminiu climbed onto the second wheel and looked toward the place of the meeting. One of the rivals was waiting for the Brotherhood's envoy in the middle of the road. He was armed like a professional and looked more like a mercenary than a simple traveller or merchant. Not to mention that the supposedly rival caravan was nowhere to be seen. Nearly one hundred warriors appeared on the rocks, their longbows drawn. They were clad in black, their faces covered with cloth hoods that revealed only their eyes. Each had a white scarf tied around his left arm.

Morminiu studied their weaponry. Each had three daggers of various sizes on his belt and two curved short swords strapped to his back, the most efficient weapons for gutting in a close fight. Their arms were covered with bone spikes. No shields to hinder their movements, he noted.

A flash of blue drew Morminiu's eye to the phril standing behind their line. He wore a blue cape and his face was uncovered, meaning he wasn't part of the group, but the one paying the group. He was perched on top of one of the rocks, carefully studying the Brotherhood's wagons.

Morminiu lowered himself to sit on the wheel, deciding

it was best not to be seen by anybody outside the caravan. "It looks more like a small army," he murmured. "It doesn't seem to be another caravan."

"You're right," the apprentice cartographer agreed.

"What noble House wears blue?"

"There are several. I would have to consult the Book of Houses to identify him."

"No House is allowed to wear black, though," Morminiu said, remembering Plabos' lessons.

"That's right. Those are not soldiers," Yd said with conviction. "They're the Moths."

"The what?"

"The black assassins of the Hish House."

"Ah, that changes things," admitted Morminiu.

Morminiu looked around—they were not the only ones to have noticed all these things; members of the Edge caravan were donning battle gear. The elders had gathered behind one of the wagons for an impromptu council.

"It is said that the mere touch of a Moth is enough to kill," the apprentice whispered. He was breathing heavily and sweating. He gazed back to the meeting place. Morminiu tried to see too, but without being visible to anyone beyond their caravan.

The two envoys from the Brotherhood stopped in front of the warrior, one standing facing him, the second one with his back turned, facing the caravan. He started transmitting the negotiations through sign language. Morminiu wasn't surprised. Back home in the Southern Swamps, everybody knew sign language. It helped them survive in a hostile environment.

The apprentice cartographer began translating, not knowing that Morminiu could understand the language. Morminiu preferred to leave it like that.

"They say they have nothing against the Edge Brotherhood."

"Ha, nice way of showing it!" Morminiu blurted.

"They're looking for a recipear. They know with certainty that we shelter him. This one is a fugitive. He is wanted, has a reward on his head in the Southern Swamps. The lord to whom the fugitive recipear is bound has put a high price on his head. They are willing to share the reward with us. They only want him and they'll leave us in peace."

Morminiu felt the eyes of those around him turning his way. Yd grimaced in pain, then asked him, "Is this true?"

"No. I'm not a fugitive and there's no reward on my head. But otherwise yes, I'm a recipear."

"If you're not a fugitive, why did you lie about your identity?"

"I didn't want to put you in danger. It was safer if you didn't know who I am."

"Which means you're actually wanted."

"No," Morminiu insisted. "I have the accreditation letters from my lord and master, Plabos. He is one of the most powerful lords in the Southern Swamps. He actually warned me that no recipear is welcome in the Royal Carami. There are political forces there, such as the Master Recipear of the Kingdom, who would want to prevent any new recipear from getting into the court. I didn't want to bring any harm to you. I'm sorry. That's why I need to know who wears that blue."

"I'd like to make sure you're telling the truth. I wouldn't want to risk my brothers' life for a lie," one of the elders interjected. Morminiu recognized him as one of the members of the Edge Council.

Morminiu had joined the Edge of the World Brotherhood a few weeks back, being in need of travelling companions who knew the roads and with whom he could mount a defense against robbers. Like Morminiu, the Brotherhood was going to the Royal Carami, the capital of the Green Kingdom and the seat of not only the royal court, but also most of the kingdom's noble Houses. In exchange for meals and a place to sleep during the journey, he'd offered everything he knew on the isolated Southern Swamps, his native region—maps, details of the area, information on tribes and customs. The Edge Council, happy to get the information, had welcomed him with open arms.

Morminiu opened his rucksack and pulled out a roll of documents. "These are my travelling papers and my accreditations, given to me by Hitissh Plabos, my master and former Master Recipear of the Kingdom. I have to get to the Royal Carami and enter the service of Hitissh Leomi, Lormont House." He passed the documents over to be checked.

The old phril studied them for a few moments. As he did, many of the caravan's phrils gathered around, among them the members of the Council. "It's good," the old phril finally said.

"I'm going to leave the caravan. I hope you agree with this," Morminiu told them.

"We could protect you," offered Yd.

"Yes, but at what price? The Moths want my head. They're not easy to kill. It's much too dangerous. You have children, and your mission is too important to risk it for me. You owe me nothing." Morminiu paused. "If you can delay them a bit, I'll try to get to the Hung Water-plain's bank and from there, reach the Carami before them."

The elders nodded their approval and returned to their wagons. Morminiu heard them spreading the news. A phril climbed onto a wheel and started sending the two envoys the message that there was no recipear in the caravan. *We shelter no stranger,* they signed. *Who gave you that information?*

Keeping the wagons between himself and the Moths, Morminiu crept along the caravan. To the left, the Hung Water-plain's bank rose like a stone wall. Wide canals ran through it, funnelling the water beyond the bank. The road split, one branch running through the rocks that had hidden the assassins, the other climbing over the bank and passing beyond the plain. It was only one of several passages. Other travellers and caravans approached from different directions.

He gave his lenses and the rucksack a final check. The

rucksack was made of water-proof spider leather and held his most precious possessions—three metacrystalidic fulguses, the new technology for storing information, containing his and Plabos' recipe book. The rucksack was tightly sealed, so the water wouldn't damage his treasure. He skulked off the road and through the reeds to the water. It was bright green and opaque, its bottom invisible. Realizing the Water-plain was deeper than he'd thought, he dove noiselessly and swam toward the bank, trying to stay deep enough not to disturb the water's surface. His gills started to work, and he gagged on the salty taste. He advanced through a wall of green slime. The currents were pretty strong, but he was sure they carried him in the right direction, toward the falls.

After a while his gills began burning—the saline concentration was too high. It was as if he were swimming through brine. He would suffocate soon, he realized with a flash of panic. Much to his relief, his hands touched a rocky wall. He rose carefully to the surface and breathed greedily.

He'd reached the bank and was only a few steps away from the road. Behind him, the Brotherhood was still talking to the mercenaries. He looked along the bank. He could get out of the water and make a run to the road, but he would be exposed, and the Moths would bring him down with their longbows within minutes. He studied his surroundings again and grinned. The only chance, albeit a crazy one, was to let himself be carried by the currents into the closest of the falls. Even if they spotted him, he would have the advantage.

He didn't have any idea how tall the waterfall was. It could be so high that his body would be smashed when it struck the surface of the water down in the valley. Or he could be battered on the rocks on his way down. Yd had said something about terraces—that the water fell from terrace to terrace to the bottom of the valley. That could be his salvation. On the other hand, the first terrace could be only two or three steps below the waterfall's crest, meaning that he'd be seen before he could put a good distance between them and him.

Yet, there was no other chance.

Drawing a steadying breath, he let himself be pulled along with the strong current to the bank's lip, where the water frothed ominously. He emptied his mind as the water pulled him over the edge and threw him out into nothingness.

He fell for what seemed only a moment before he plunged into a deep pool. His feet touched bottom and he pushed off, shooting back to the surface. He floated there, feeling a little dizzy, and looked up. Seen from this angle, the first step of the waterfall looked terribly high. To his relief, he saw that the waterfall did indeed fall from terrace to terrace, from pool to pool, to the bottom of the valley. Where the biggest and most beautiful Carami lay—the Royal Carami, wherein lay the swallowed capital of the Green Kingdom.

Its body covered a huge area, guarded on one side by a mountain chain with peaks buried in the clouds. On the other side, the behemoth sprawled over a dry wasteland crisscrossed by commercial roads cutting their way to the north. The monster holding the city was like a mountain itself.

Morminiu trembled in delight, relishing the view with a greed he had never imagined possible. Then he heard shouts and realized that his fascination had left him exposed.

Lunging forward, he let himself be carried toward the second step of the waterfall. Again the torrent threw him into the next pool, and he surfaced a little dizzy. He looked upward immediately, toward the road that wound down among the waterfalls and trees in tight switchbacks from the Hung-plain's bank. He'd just crossed half the distance in two mad moments of free fall. The Moths ran down toward him, their bows nocked. They were covering the distance quickly. He looked for the outlet to the terrace below and swam toward it, pausing only to ensure that the next pool was as deep as the first two. Again he plunged forward.

He sank, then burst back to the surface. His head and ears hurt. His gills stung from the salty water. He didn't waste any time in hurling himself down the fourth step of the waterfall. It wasn't as high, its pool not as deep. He sank like a rock and hit the stony bottom. The impact made him swallow salt water and he gagged. The strong current grabbed him and tugged him toward the fifth terrace of the waterfall. He caught a rock, stopping his forward momentum, then— muscles tensed with the effort—he clambered out of the pool onto the dusty road.

He immediately bent over and puked. His body ached like it had been beaten with rods. He hadn't broken anything, but his legs shook and his sight was blurry. Squinting upward, he glimpsed the assassins among the trees, shortening the distance between them and their prey.

In the opposite direction, the monster waited.

Shining green-gray, the Carami's body rose from the murky water of the lake at the lower end of the valley, a mass of moist flesh under which stretched muscles and pulsating veins. Its rear wasn't visible, and what did lie exposed didn't have any definite shape, no symmetry to its form. A bony belt wrapped its body right above the mouths. Tentacles waved in the strong currents of the lake that surrounded it.

When his breath came back and his vision cleared, he ran toward the closest entrance. Already, he ran in the Carami's shadow, so he removed the smoky lenses to better see the details of the road. After a while he reached the bottom of the valley, where he stopped, gasping for air. His lungs burned and his arms and ribs hurt terribly. He remembered the rough treatment Plabos had given him in the Swamps and silently thanked him—that was probably what was keeping him still standing, still running, still alive.

The Moths had reduced the distance and were getting closer by the moment.

A few hundred steps in front of him, the entrance-mouth into the Carami waited, gaping hideously, ready to gulp up travellers. Morminiu had mixed feelings, fear mingling with hope. He swallowed the knot in his throat and ran.

Total darkness waited beyond the entrance. A cold

breeze brought the sweet reek of fermented plants to him. Morminiu's mind balked in horror, but he couldn't hesitate. He could feel the silent assassins behind him, getting closer. He trembled violently, yet kept on running.

Arrows whistled through the air. Gathering the last of his energy, Morminiu jumped through the slick and toothless mouth. Icy saliva splattered onto his head. He continued forward, but slowed to a trot, blind in the darkness. As his eyes adjusted, he discerned a bone bridge in front of him, illuminated by a faint glow that also threw the walls' deformities into relief. He crossed it at a fast walk, breathing rapidly.

A few seconds later he heard his pursuers stepping onto the bridge. Morminiu broke into a run.

Two soldiers intercepted him as he approached the city checkpoint. "Hey, hey, you didn't pay the offering to the Carami!" they shouted.

Nobody had told him of any offering! Morminiu fought panic. He couldn't turn back—he'd be walking into the arms of his enemies. He feinted right then darted left past the guards, but one caught his cape, pulling him up short. He fell to the bone floor, made to rise, then dropped as arrows whistled along the passage. The two soldiers fell dead, arrows piercing their backs. Morminiu rolled, jumped to his feet, and ran.

The checkpoint was in front of him. "We're under attack! We're under attack!" screamed Morminiu.

The whole checkpoint garrison was alert now. Soldiers took up position across the passage, shields locked and spears ready. A cacophony of whistles rose as more arrows slashed the air. Morminiu passed behind the shields and dropped to his knees. Behind him, the massed arrows struck the bone shields with a noise like thunder.

More whistling. Morminiu scrambled forward on all fours. When he'd put some distance between him and the soldiers, he looked back. The assassins had no intention of stopping or turning back. They attacked silently and with lethal speed. They outnumbered the checkpoint garrison five to one.

Morminiu rose and ran toward a stronger light ahead—toward the city sheltered inside the monstrous organism called the Carami. This wasn't the way he'd imagined his entrance into the capital.

❖◦❖◦❖◦❖Ξ❤Ξ❖◦❖◦❖◦❖

With the Black Assassins delayed by the battle at the Carami's mouth, Morminiu had no trouble losing them as soon as he entered the city. Passersby guided him to one of the central plazas, a very elegant and well-kept one with three majestic fountains surrounded by the grand mansions of the nobility. Here, they told him, he should find Waterbone, the palace of the Hitissh Leomi.

He looked around at the palaces lining the plaza's perimeter and finally stopped at one that looked like a great wounded beast, a real giant among giants. The palace was old, its body heavy and spiky. Age had blackened the bone of the walls, and the windows and vents were stuffed with shells. The entrance was an open maw framed with curved fangs. A pink tongue unfurled down the steps onto the street.

"When asked, say that you've been sent by the Master Recipear Plabos," Morminiu's master had instructed him. *"Address the Hitissh with noble titles and with courtier flattery. Under no circumstances should you brag about having the Master Book. Everything you know is here."* And Plabos had knocked his forehead.

Morminiu opened the gate for only a few seconds before two white brop-hounds appeared from behind the building, hopping from one paw to the other. Slamming the gate closed, he quickly retreated a few steps and observed them from this cautious distance. Sharp fangs surrounded their small, red eyes, and long, thin thorns protruded from their backs, running like fine threads of hair all the way down to the tips of their tails. The detachable thorns delivered venom famous for the festering sores it provoked and sometimes even paralysed. The beasts stopped on the other side of the gate, scratching the pavement with their two paws.

Morminiu reached out carefully, keeping his eyes on the two beasts, and stroked the bell ornamented with the Lormont family's coat of arms that hung near the gate. He looked at the palace, dark and quiet. It had an air of abandonment, even dereliction, that froze the recipear's heart. He stroked the bell once more. The two guardians of the palace trembled with anticipation, their saliva dripping in thick gobs onto the bone paving of the path.

Finally, the palace portal opened. A middle-aged phril wearing the Lormont coat of arms on his chest stepped outside. He could be a servant or a palace guard; Morminiu had no idea. The phril stayed at the top of the steps and looked down on Morminiu with a thoughtful air.

After a few moments, Morminiu started to examine himself as well. His travel clothes were rumpled after the adventure at the waterfalls, but they had dried. They were simple and unadorned, rough travel clothes and rugged boots. Salt stains from the water had left ragged white traceries here and there on the fabric and leather. He didn't look good, he had to admit. But he would not let this stop him. Raising his eyes, he straightened his back. "I've just rung the bell. Intentionally." He tried to keep the irony from his voice, but until he knew who he was dealing with . . .

"Indeed," the other replied, moving slowly toward the gate. "I hope it's something important, otherwise—"

"Tell the great Hitissh that I've come from Master Plabos."

Looking disgusted, the Hitissh's phril meticulously pressed the knob in the gate.

"Haven't you heard of great Plabos?" Morminiu

exclaimed.

"Haven't you heard of appointments?"

The gate started to open and the two brop-hounds rushed forward.

"Be careful," Morminiu warned, sweating abundantly. He unsheathed his sword from his back, its velvety hilt and the familiar vibration of its blade restoring some of his self-control. He took two steps back. "Tell him only the name Plabos, and see his reaction."

"Aaall right!" the phril drawled, closing the gate, to the frustration of the brop-hounds. "Remember, the gate is unlatched. If the brops see you fleeing, they'll tear you apart. So you'd better wait for my return." He trudged back into the palace.

Morminiu leaned on his sword and looked around, trying to admire the city's architecture, the majestic air of the plaza. The other two palaces facing the plaza were newer, their bones shining with green and yellow iridescence. Phrils walked purposefully through their front yards. No one paid any attention to him.

He would admire anything, if only to avoid the baleful red eyes of the beasts. They growled and scraped at the pavement with their paws. How could he have made an appointment? He hadn't imagined that it would be so difficult to get into a noble house. Where he came from, it was different. He studied his clothes again. Yes, he surely looked like a country phril. He surely looked disgusting, with the salt stains and the mud dried into dust on his clothes. He had succeeded in washing his face and hands before presenting himself at the palace, but he'd had no solution for the other things.

In the end, he couldn't avoid the two slavering animals; their claws scratching on the bone path grated on his nerves. He glared at them. After several long minutes, just when he was thinking he would drop from exhaustion in front of the gate under a cascade of saliva from the two brops, he saw the

Hitissh's phril returning with a little more haste than when he'd left.

"Come on in, but be aware that I will be watching you," he warned, both his expression and his tone broadcasting his displeasure. "And leave that sword at the entrance."

Morminiu swallowed the phril's insolence, turning his gaze to the ground. He sheathed the blade in the scabbard on his back, intending to show that the subject was closed, then entered with his hair ruffled, trying to walk with dignity past the two animal guardians of Waterbone. The servant stretched his hand toward the sword, but the recipear caught it in a flash and looked him in the eyes. The animals growled in anticipation; he could feel their breath on his feet. He was shorter and thinner than the other phril, but he made himself as big as he could and tightened his grip, viselike, on the other's hand. He was not a servant, he was a recipear, and no matter what this phril's role was in the House of Lormont, he was behaving way above his station.

"It would be your last move!" Morminiu said through his teeth. "Keep your place, I'm warning you."

The phril surrendered. He stepped back, shaking—with fury, Morminiu recognized. He was obviously not afraid, only frustrated that he wasn't in a position to make such a decision. Morminiu watched him for a few more seconds before continuing into the palace. Eventually, the other phril directed him into a room where an older phril sprawled on a couch made of bent bone that grew from the floor, its horizontal surface covered by a thick layer of flesh. "The Hitissh Leomi," the door phril murmured.

Without even glancing at him, the Hitissh addressed Morminiu in a thick, hoarse voice. "I understand that Plabos sent you." He paused to sip carefully and noisily at some awful-smelling liquor. He was fat—it was clear that pleasure had turned into vice. Still, under the layers of fat, some hint of the muscles that had once made him a fearsome warrior remained. He was like a beast in its lair. His personal smell, the perspiration on his flesh, the last meal he'd had, all hung heavily in the air, choking in their intensity.

Morminiu read all these things and many others in the first moments of their meeting, as he studied the noble's movements, his breathing, his reactions. "Yes, Your Highness," he answered.

Leomi set the glass of liquor on a bone plate close to him and reached for a bowl filled with candies. As he stirred them with his fingers, he said, "We are talking about the same Plabos, are we not?"

"No doubt, Your Highness," Morminiu replied in a voice hearty with confidence.

"And what business would you have with me?"

"I have been sent to ask for your help."

The noble finally extracted a jelly cube from the bowl, examined it, then thrust it into his mouth. He licked his fingers, leaving them glistening with saliva, and smacked his lips lustily. Despite all this, he also managed to talk. "Hmm, this is not a very good start. I don't like helping anybody."

"You are the master's only friend. He thought he could turn to Your Grace for support for his one and only disciple."

"You are a recipear?"

"Exactly, My Lord."

"And you're also a liar!" the Hitissh thundered.

The couch moved quicker than expected, bringing Leomi face to face with Morminiu. They looked at each other for the first time. The sweet juice of the candy leaked from the corner of the noble's mouth, trickling toward his chin, then dripping onto his chest. The recipear lowered his eyes, remembering Plabos' advice. He could sense Leomi's phril standing behind him, ready to stab him at the slightest sign from the noble. Morminiu could feel his breath on his neck.

Only then did Leomi notice the private tokens of a Grand Master that Plabos had applied to Morminiu's left cuff. "Maybe you aren't a liar," Leomi mused with a gentle grunt. "What do you want, exactly?"

"First of all, if you could order the brute behind me to step away . . . " Morminiu suggested, his voice honey.

The noble roared with laughter, then said to the phril behind Morminiu, "It is all right, Babon."

He dropped his fingers back amongst the candies and stirred them for a few seconds before extracting another sticky cube and throwing it cheerfully into his mouth. He smacked his lips loudly, then said, "Babon is my trusted phril, my personal servant, my guard, the executioner in my service, my eyes and my ears, so you must forgive him; this is his job."

Morminiu bowed respectfully before saying, "Plabos makes an appeal to the love that once united you as adventuring companions, to ask that I, the only pursuer of his art, receive Your Highness's protection and the freedom of ascent."

Leomi smacked with more enthusiasm. "But you know what that means—you have to serve me. How do you expect to ascend if you've come to serve?"

"Respectfully, My Lord, I am a recipear," Morminiu began, and noticed the noble studying him from head to feet. *These clothes!* he groaned mentally. Plabos hadn't prepared him properly. He had shown him the manners, but hadn't paid any attention to the dress code. Or were even his gestures, his movements, wrong? *Peasant gestures!*

"And Plabos," he resumed, keeping his voice steady, "was the Grand Master of the Kingdom and His Majesty's Counsellor."

"What's this, threats?" the Hitissh growled, sputtering saliva thickened with sugar. "Boy, you're only a peasant here! Maybe you should go directly to the King with your request, before I give you to my brops!"

Morminiu ignored the sticky spittle; he made not the slightest gesture to indicate he had noticed anything, or that he cared about the heavy liquid staining his sleeve. He strove to exude calm and strength. "I didn't mean to upset you, Great Hitissh, but my noble profession doesn't allow me total obedience. I thought that offering my master's experience and mine would be enough for the small thing requested in exchange—protection and support in the ascent."

"Hmm." Leomi chewed his third candy. "You have a sharp tongue and it's possible you'll lose it, boy. How do I know you're a recipear, and not a simple cook? And especially that you're the master's successor," he murmured, and licked his fleshy lips. Saliva continued to ooze from the corner of his mouth. He studied Morminiu with his bulging eyes before moving his couch back into its initial position. He turned toward the interior court, exposing his profile in the darkened office. Morminiu looked around, calculating a hasty retreat, if necessary.

"I'll tell you my rule: he who promises and doesn't deliver dies brutally before the five-hundredth Course. Understand well, boy—I never forgive!"

"Master told me, Your Grace."

"You know how many recipears' skulls lie in this court?" The noble waved toward the interior court.

"No, Your Highness."

"More than twenty. Unsatisfactory! Amateurs!"

"Your Lordship won't be disappointed. Allow me to offer Your Grace my humble present, with profound gratitude." Morminiu proffered his gift without even breathing.

The lure waited innocently between them on Morminiu's outstretched hand. The bulging eyes of the noble fish swung toward it.

"Ah, Leomi, I am sorry for interrupting you!"

The shrill, sweet voice broke the tension. The lure remained extended. The bulging eyes swung away from it.

Morminiu turned, surprised by the interruption. He saw a phrilira standing in a doorway in the far corner of the room, awaiting the Hitissh's consent to enter.

"Donasa, it is all right, come in. We were just ending this meeting. You said something about a gift?" The bulging eyes returned to Morminiu, measuring, distrustful. But his breathing was heavy with curiosity. He was ready to take the lure.

"One of the finest teas that ever spread its aroma under the light of the Three Daughters of the Sky," Morminiu assured him.

"The light of the Three Daughters of the Sky?"

"And never in a Carami, Your Highness. Prepared from underwater plants known only to me. It's an absolute secret. I call it the Green of the Gods," Morminiu said off the top of his head.

"One of Plabos' secrets?" the Hitissh grunted, spraying the recipear again with sweet, sticky saliva.

Donasa started. "Plabos?"

"Not even he knew it, Your Greatness. It's my first gift. I know all the secrets of Plabos and a thousand more, to make you happy. I'm here to offer you pleasures no one has ever tasted."

"Pleasures, secret Recipes, underwater plants, yes. Who gave them to you?"

"No one, Great Hitissh. I know underwater life and that offers me a great advantage over any recipear, including Plabos."

"An underwater tea!"

"Made from underwater plants, Your Highness," Morminiu corrected him with a studious air.

"You have to make it right away, boy . . . what did you say your name was?"

The recipear suppressed a relieved sigh and said in a strong voice, "Morminiu, My Lord."

"A name worthy of your profession. Morminiu, boy, go quickly and prepare that tea. Then come and tell me the Recipe. But hurry, I don't like waiting. Babon," he grunted to the servant, "show him the kitchen and give him everything he needs."

"I don't trust him, M'Lord."

"Hmm! We shall see, Babon. Now, do what I say."

"Yes, M'Lord. This way, boy," Babon muttered.

"Morminiu, servant."

Babon stopped, surprised, blocking the doorway with his huge frame. Morminiu stopped right behind him, his lips turned down in displeasure.

"All right, calm down. I want that tea quickly," the Hitissh said in a voice made shrill by irritation. He stepped between them. "Babon, don't forget he's a recipear. And Morminiu, don't forget he's my right hand. Behave, you two, and everything will be all right!"

<hr />

Leomi watched the two of them exit quickly, clearly unhappy at the equal treatment he gave them.

"Plabos, Leo? Plabos?" the phrilira said when the door closed behind the pair. She strode toward the couch. "I smell revenge!"

"Revenge?" Leomi spat indignantly. "Plabos was my friend! I loved that phril!"

MORMINIU

I stop on the fourth floor and listen. I hear Totin, the new guard, climbing the stairs, breathing heavily. The left corridor is dark. I slip noiselessly down it, passing the first door, the second, and stopping at the third. I open it carefully, enter the room beyond, and pull the door closed behind me. Within, a greenish light filters through tall windows. I stay by the entrance, listening. Totin has not yet reached this floor.

The palace of the Hitissh is a labyrinthine fortress in the middle of the city. Traces of previous generations are everywhere—most speaking of more prosperous, more shining, more opulent lifestyles. Now, much of it is derelict. The atmosphere is tense. More than half a year has passed since I arrived and I'm still a prisoner in my protector's house. Partly because of his lady, Donasa, partly because of Babon, not the least because of the mouldering atmosphere that sickens not only Leomi's residence but its inhabitants, as well.

Babon, the Hitissh's chief of security, constantly breathes down my neck. I'm not allowed to leave the palace; if it were his decision, I wouldn't be allowed to leave my room. Initially, he set one of his trusted phrils to guard me day and night. I tried to befriend him, but it didn't work. He wouldn't open his mouth. Then I started playing hide and seek. I "accidentally" got lost a few times. After the fifth or sixth time I went missing, Babon released him from Leomi's service and put a different guard on me. It didn't take long to trick this one, too. A few months later, Babon released him as well and hired an outside phril—Totin, a young mercenary, full of himself. I befriended Totin. We talk, eat together, spend time together. Since he also didn't know anybody from the Hitissh's household and he spent most of his time around me anyway, he probably didn't see any reason to suffer boredom on the assignment.

Today is the first time I'm "accidentally" trying to lose

my way. Babon doesn't like to see me wandering through the palace. Neither does he want to lose me for good and anger Hitissh Leomi.

Totin has finally reached the fourth floor. I hear him panting and stifle laughter. He's a chubby mercenary, soft like a pie. He doesn't have a future in Babon's guard, just as he doesn't have any chance of a career in armed service. I pity him. For a moment I'm tempted to go out and call him, but I stop. Befriending him wasn't supposed to soften me, but him. I hear his footsteps moving along the corridor, then a door opening. After that, a second door opens, followed by a frightened shout. Hmm, what could the second room hide? Totin's footsteps move away toward the stairs, and I hear him climbing them to the tower's top floor. I smile, satisfied, and turn my back to the door.

The two windows in the opposite wall frame one of the sky-lightning towers, the source of the greenish light illuminates the room. I draw a glow-worm from my pocket and fix it atop a stick mounted in the wall. The glow-worm doesn't produce strong light, but it's enough to pick out details.

A hearth is embedded in the middle of the floor, covered by a lattice. I still myself and listen. Yes, I hear heavy panting, like that of a sweating phrilira. A thrill tickles my back and soles. What's going on in the next room, the one that scared poor Totin? Or is there something weird in this one? I smell a sour scent, like crushed fruits. Movement to my right makes me turn. Nobody. Just tapestries on the walls, moving in a draft.

More panting, heavier, like that of a stabbed brop, joins the first, which is coming faster, shriller. It's easy to imagine a giant phril, his long hair thick and shaggy, clutching the feebler body of a phrilira in his arms. Slobber leaks from his mouth onto her delicate skin. She writhes, her eyes open wide in demented pleasure, her soles resting on the burning-hot lattice above the fire in the central hearth.

I jump away as if burned, though the hearth is extinguished, and see a feeble phrilira in one of the tapestries staring into my eyes with a diabolical grin, teeth bared in ecstasy. She's familiar to me. No! It's just my imagination, my hungry mind playing tricks. A new sound filters through the room, a rhythmic moan, emanating from jerky movements I see from the corner of my eye, in a space suddenly animated with sounds and images.

I pant. I try to control my reactions. The sour smell is stronger now. Two steps bring me to the window, to the light. I try to control my vulbas' trembling and the chills discharging into my spine; I fight to coordinate my body and my mind. But I retract my hand with a nervous start when I feel the cold moisture on the couch under the window, and wipe it hurriedly on my clothes. I hear the profound gurgle of a phril in orgasm, choking on his own saliva, superimposed over the moan and the hysterical pant of—I deny it one more time. How could a room have such an influence on me?

It's terribly hot. It's just my imagination, I tell myself—but everything seems so real! I fall on the couch. It shudders in a muscular spasm, like a warm and hairy tongue, red, humid and soft, undulating under my weight, trying to massage my back and buttock muscles. I breathe with difficulty, unable to control my reactions. My instincts float me on waves of sensuality.

There's something more here . . . I look around. On all the walls, on the tapestries covering them, colossal, fiery-eyed phrils with savage, foaming mouths, their rock-hard muscles visible under their taned skin, possess with a beastly violence the feeble yet voluptuous body of Donasa. I see her back, her face, her mouth, and ecstatic, evil eyes. The tapestries—the tapestries are creating the illusion of real sensations, with their sick imagery and the air drafts moving them. But why can't I control my vulbas, my sexual drive?

Something smacks greedily next to my ear and my fingers scramble to remove my clothes. My body twitches on the tongue-couch. I look to the left, where two spider-tailors are copulating grotesquely in a foamy, sticky mound on a pedestal in the corner, in the putrid green light from the tower. A sweet-sour taste curls my tongue. I remain still, staring at the bestial scene, my muscles unresponsive. I feel as if I'm in a dream, witnessing the whole orgy with Donasa, watching her share herself wantonly with all the Lormont phrils descending from the very first Lormont—probably a Leomi, only much bigger and hairier. One of the two spiders starts to bite at its partner, while translucent blisters grow on its back. Within, small, agitated shapes throb.

The door opens suddenly. Totin looks at me, eyes furious. Then he smiles. First amused, then curious, he enters, eyes shining. An explosive splash wakes me from my numbness. Dozens of tiny spiders spill from the breached blisters, from the dead body of their parent, falling into the puddle of its lover's entrails.

I jump up, screaming, and push Totin aside. I have to get out of the room. I throw open the door and retreat backward, face to the room, into the corridor. I'm shaking. My clothes are undone, untied, hanging in disarray; my vulbas still tremble and my spikes are in erection. The sweat on my body becomes sticky. On the Sathali's spheres, what is wrong with me? I could have destroyed so many months of effort.

There is still a sour taste in my mouth.

It was an erotosiac! A drug produced by the spiders, I know it! I'm sure now. "It wasn't me, it wasn't me . . . " I murmur, like an incantation. I sit down on a bench, breathing deeply to calm myself.

Totin is still in there. Should I go back and pull him out? No, I can't go back into that horrible room! Totin is on his own. I head for the stairs, stumble down the steps, repeating, "It wasn't me!"

I'm scared, but I keep my mouth clamped shut over any fear rising in my throat. I kick aside a tailor-spider crossing my path; the creature is one I don't want to see now, or for a very long time. This one is a bloated specimen, way over the normal size, probably living forgotten here since more prosperous times. The two tailor-spiders in the love-room were also obese, I remember. The swollen body, the size of a phril's head, rolls down the stairs. Just when I think it will splatter against a wall, it rises quickly on a thread caught in a vent. I avoid it as I continue my descent.

One level down, I stop again to catch my breath. I'm feeling much better, now that I'm away from that room. Plabos told me of such rooms, and the pleasure they mean to bring, of the spiders used to erotically stimulate observers through their copulation, and sometimes even through physical contact between the phrilira and the repulsive creatures. Normally I have exceptional control over my body—what could have provoked such a reaction in me? Definitely the erotosiac, but something else, too. Something I'm afraid to think of.

More importantly, what was Donasa doing in those tapestries?

Plabos? I try to invoke the spirit of my master, but it doesn't care to respond. I don't like the possibilities, so I put them aside for the moment, trying to drive the demented face of Donasa from my mind. I only hope it's not Plabos playing tricks on me! I don't need uncontrollable bursts of desire for a phrilira who could be my mother.

I don't think Leomi had anything to do with all this, I think, determined to believe it. Then I feel the tension that my master creates behind my forehead every time he's displeased or worse, furious. A foreign thought is taking shape: *Leomi is guilty.*

I deny it loudly: "We don't know if Leomi is guilty!"

Leomi is guilty, the thought persists. I look up the stairs, but Totin isn't there. Probably nobody heard me talking to myself.

I need something to keep my mind occupied, but that's enough exploration for one day. Totin isn't half as bad as those before him. That miserable Babon has proven more tenacious than I thought, which is why I hate him—he is devoted, body and soul, to the old Hitissh.

I'm interested in mapping the palace after a fashion, though I haven't covered much of it yet, being more preoccupied with losing my guards than studying the building and its treasures. The towers are the most attractive features—the connection towers, the venting and lightning towers, and the habitation towers form the skeleton of the labyrinthine structure. From their crystalline cupolas, I admired the dizzying panorama of the city for the first time.

The buildings of House Lormont possess the highest and most numerous towers. Perhaps only those of the Royal Palace are higher, but there are not as many. I believe they are of the oldest style. From their top I can see the greater part of the first level of the city and vast portions of the next two levels. As for those above, the ones immediately under the monster's back, in everyone's opinion, they aren't worth the effort. They are the domain of the socially unfit, the starved, the thieves and criminals.

From up here, the city looks cleaner and tidier, but what saves it, in fact, are the monumental buildings and the luxurious commercial quarters of the wealthy who come from across the seas and over the land. Most of them arrived in the last two centuries, so their residences are newer than the Hitissh's. Even the Royal Palace has been extended and largely rebuilt, retaining only the holy core from the old palace. The last edifices raised in the business area of the city distinguish themselves from all others by being neotoists, with miraculous superpositions and joints of transparent or vividly coloured crystalline, the bones long and thin, bent into impossible configurations.

They're supplied from the bone crops—yes, bone crops have become a reality! Some say that, in fact, they're not crops, but new spaces that grew in the last centuries and discovered accidentally. They stretch all the way to the north of the Carami itself, to somewhere near the hypothetical head.

The spaces have a special structure and are rich in a particular sort of bone, as well as other new construction materials.

The Royal Carami may be, truly, the oldest in the world. It has grown and developed for thousands of years. It evolves. The nomads say that it is still in its infancy. I wonder how it will look at maturity, and when that will be. Perhaps then it will start a new evolutionary phase and go somewhere else. What would that mean for its inhabitants? But to understand it better, it must be thoroughly explored. And first I have to understand it for me, to avoid reliving those terrifying moments at the city entrance when I first arrived. I climb down a few more steps, and smile. Carami, tame animal. Carami, tame house!

Then my smile vanishes and I clench my teeth, whispering with determination, "We still don't know if Leomi is guilty! We don't know . . . "

But the idea flies freely through my mind and I have no way to stop it: *Leomi is guilty!*

GOURMET RECIPE: VERMIH IN PLABOS SAUCE

There are three complementary sides that determine a phril personality: gastronomy, politics, and romance. The rest represents salads or pickles to fill the mundane.

I will start naturally, with food for the gourmet side of the phrilic spirit, presenting to you an absolutely genuine Recipe.

INGREDIENTS:

MATURE VERMIH – a crawler from the land-worm family, having its vital organ—the sufleida—in the middle of its spindle-shaped body. This in turn is protected by a circular stomach layer, where the ingested food is stored, preparatory to being assimilated after fermentation.

SWAMP PLABOS SAUCE – for plant and insect broths, in a suckitori base.

SEQU-TULAPA FLAVOURED OIL – with hot spices, preferably from Blood-Moth's wings.

PREPARATION:

The fragrant vermih should be left to rot alive only under the light of the Three Daughters of the Sky. The diffuse light drives it mad and the cool night air makes its stomach layer tremble. The trembling forces its membrane to enlarge to several times its usual size, preparing for future storage. If it doesn't scream for mercy, it means it has not putrefied enough. However, while it is rotting, ensure it is protected from fright, to avoid wrinkling its flesh.

When it has reached the desired level of putrefaction, immediately place the gluttonous and shivering animal on the sweet maidenly leaf of the moamoam. The two beings will intertwine and the juice of pleasure will flow from the vermih, imbuing the fluffy layer of the maiden moamoam. The vermih, driven by overwhelming hunger, will then devour the leaf. Because its stomach membrane is enlarged, it will not be satisfied with only one leaf. Continue this process with another leaf, luring it by way of the gnawed stem to where the Swamp Plabos Sauce boils vigorously.

I have specified that the sauce be flavoured with suckitori. The steam from the boiling sauce will penetrate the vermih's stomach wall, moistening the ingested moamoam leaves before the vermih throws itself into the sauce, simultaneously ejecting one last fresh spurt of the bittersweet pleasure liquid.

The vermih will sink to the bottom of the pot of boiling sauce, allowing the Plabos liquor to penetrate it just short of its core. It is very important that the depth the crawler will sink and the thickness of the sauce be calculated exactly. Otherwise, the slightest contamination of its vital core with the liquor will cause a hideous death, which would thicken the vermih's flesh.

As its stomach membrane tenderizes to a suitable degree of sponginess, and with its flesh flavoured by the Swamp Plabos Sauce, the crawler should fall free from the orifice in the pot's bottom straight onto your plate, where it will spread into a well blended and sparkling stew surrounding the sufleida, still pulsing within the protective layer of the bitter crystalline coating.

Combine the sequ-tulapa flavoured oil with hot spices, preferably brown butterfly wings, and heat it to boiling. Pour the hot oil over the crystalline coating of the sufleida. This will melt the covering and evaporate all trace of bitterness. Flavor to taste with a sprinkling of Night Daughters Flower pollen and serve with red wine for a truly gourmet meal.

(*from* The Gastronomic Teachings of Master Recipear Plabos)

II. THE STENCH

She looked cautiously up and down the road, then knocked on the door. Within, the rattle of weapons and rapid footsteps before a voice on the other side of the door demanded, "Who's disturbing us?"

"In a Carami, there isn't a place for both of us," answered Donasa, then waited.

Silence for several seconds. She hadn't called here, on this kind of visit, for a very long time. Years had passed since she'd used the password. If the sellswords guarding the house were new, they probably wouldn't know it.

Finally, the door opened with a creak, and the phrilira slipped into the darkness of the house. Somebody lit a glow-worm, and she saw that the room was packed with soldiers, all eyeing her suspiciously. The one holding the light beckoned her to follow him. They stepped up to the first floor and he told her to sit on a bench in the waiting room while the guard announced her.

Donasa breathed deeply and smiled. She recognized the smell of the place, the rotten reek that probably impregnated the very walls and furniture bones. She shivered and looked around. Nothing had changed.

The soldier came back and jerked his head, indicating that she was expected, and could enter. She rose, tidied her dress, inhaled deeply, and passed through the doorway. The room beyond was dim, lit only by the fire in the hearth. In the middle of the wall to her right was an immense bed, covered with rumpled sheets. Erotic scenes covered the walls, permanently activated by the air-streams so that the murmurs, sighs, and groans never ceased. Scattered on the floor was an array of instruments one could barely classify—for torture or erotic stimulation?

Somehow, the bedroom had remained as she'd known it for years and years. It was only a bit darker, the stench a bit heavier, the atmosphere perhaps a little more terrible, with all those horrible tools gathered in a single room.

She noticed him at last, almost hidden in the shadows near the window, caressing a pair of home-spiders. He was wrapped in a gray blanket woven of soft, long hair. He smiled broadly, looking a little curious. She bowed in front of him, but he raised her and kissed her hair. Then he led her to the leather chairs next to the hearth. He had grown older, thinner; he had become haggard, his smell had become more obvious, yet he retained his arrogant and demanding demeanour. Butterfly flower petals burned in blackened bone pots on either side of the hearth. Their sweet fragrance failed to cover the stench.

"It's been a long time," Donasa started timidly.

"That means we have been smarter and we have succeeded," he answered, and laughed sadly, more an obscene bleating.

Donasa shuddered and closed her eyes. She remembered everything now, and didn't regret any of it. She shook with pleasure and looked at him again. "Have you heard of a recipear called Morminiu?"

"Yes, vaguely, but you should know more than I!"

"That's why I'm here," she answered, feigning disinterest by looking around, at the fire, the burning petals, the floor.

He remained silent. He was good at these kinds of things. One couldn't surprise him easily; she knew of no one who had ever caught him off guard. He was the best.

"Plabos is back!" she blurted, then fell quiet. She could feel his tension. Then she heard again his bleating laugh.

"And where could the old bastard hide?"

"In my house."

"Have you welcomed him back?"

"Not me. Leo."

"Leo! Ever the glutton, but he has never been stupid."

"Morminiu is Plabos' disciple and I'm absolutely sure he has his master in his soul. He hasn't come alone. I smell revenge, no doubt about it."

"No, dear, you smell my stench." He laughed again and she couldn't keep herself from smiling with admiration.

Indeed, his stench was stronger than any revenge she could smell in the Lormont palace. And, amazingly, she loved it! She hadn't thought that, after so many years, returning would provoke her pleasure—and more. She was aroused.

"Now that you've said so much, I won't be able to let them go." He waved toward the bed, and she saw for the first time the three phrils there, crouched in their own tatters, shaking with fear.

Donasa started. She'd thought they were alone. She looked at him questioningly.

"Don't be afraid. They won't talk anymore." He smiled and rose. "Pick one," he told her, and turned his back.

She started to undress slowly, weighing the beggars. They had dirty skin, and she could smell the stink of rotten teeth released by their open mouths. They were weak, but otherwise whole and relatively attractive. "I want all three of them," she said, breathless with excitement. "Let's have them in turns."

"You haven't changed a bit!" He smiled and she could guess at the pleasure behind the smile. He remembered too, and it was clear that he didn't dislike the memories.

"What about Morminiu?" she asked one more time, looking him in the eyes.

"I had my phrils in the Southern Swamps watching Plabos. They were supposed to keep me up to date with his status and also act when ordered. You know what I mean. I've known of Morminiu for years. Never thought he'd get this far. He somehow slipped past my phrils there, then amazed me again when he escaped the Black Assassins waiting for him at the Carami's entrance. And now, the boy's fame grows rapidly. The Master Recipear of the Kingdom doesn't like it. He has to take care of it."

TAHMIMH

"My dear Hitissh Tahmimh . . . "

One of the guests approaches me. I smile and shush him to silence, then return to the ritual. The storyteller is good. When one cannot have the recipear, one must be happy with a storyteller. His voice passes rapidly from gravity to irony, he knows when to stop, when to increase the tension. And the chosen music is exactly what it should be. I haven't experienced such a prelude for too long. I look around and see my guests transformed. Some of them have started to undress; others, their eyes shut, are barely mastering their convulsions.

Ah, this Recipe is divine. I shut my eyes too. I shudder. My vulbas are trembling. I feel the excitement taking over my body. I sweat abundantly. The fragrances of the Course that is being prepared along with the story have already filled the entire room. I breathe in deeply and fall back on the pillows, exhausted. Incredible!

I roll to one side, out of the pile of pillows, but I remain lying on the floor, panting. I feel my skin wrinkling in terror. The story pauses at a suspenseful point. The storyteller has finished his line in a staccato voice, and remains silent. I hear only the bubbling from the contents boiling in the pot. The sweat cools on my skin. The entire room has sunk into the most absolute silence. All the guests wait, tense, with wide, fearful eyes, not even a breath is uttered. The music has stopped, too.

The meat roasting in the tray cracks along the split made in its flesh, releasing steam with a whistle that sounds loud in the heavy silence. We all start, and a few listeners utter small cries. All eyes are now on the huge hunk of meat. My eyes bulge with enchantment and I barely restrain my tears of pleasure. Through the tear in the meat, the contents spill. First a shiny green mass overflows over the lips of the wound, resembling the moss and algae growing on the Carami's bone, only at an accelerated speed, as if a year has passed in a second.

The whole party sighs, then we jerk, groan, some start weeping in satisfaction. Most go directly into the jugular spasm, and the room fills with snorting and panting. Through the green blanket, vegetables emerge, along with fat red flesh worms, driven out by the roasting. They try to escape the Course trap, but the cold outer air dizzies them and for a few seconds they lie half out of the green mass, like red branches. Moments later, because of the temperature difference, their bodies explode into small flowers of vermin guts that decorate the Course's surface.

Holy Carami! The show is really divine! More than anyone could expect from any kind of Tasting Course. This is recipearing at a royal level! The juice of the worms drains over the vegetables, and then through them, into the meat, softening it, fragrancing it with their pungent, sweet perfume.

At this moment, the storyteller resumes. Already the whole room is trembling on the brink of orgasm. There's no more music, only the boiling, bubbling, and sizzling in the cooking tray. The servants are executing the last of the recipear's instructions and the Course is perfect!

I fall back among the pillows, shaken by my climax. I don't feel anything else, only the ecstasy that climbs up to my brain and the Course's fragrance as it transports my senses up to heaven. I close my eyes and let my instincts run free, prolonging the first orgasm to its greatest limit.

The servants cut the Course into portions, then start to serve the guests, who are crawling, salivating, toward the serving point. There are no more titles, there is no more dignity, only this satisfaction provided by the Recipearium. After such a Course, anyone could die happily. I have never been so close to heaven.

I get my plate and eat slowly, savouring the entire range of tastes and aromas. I'm crying! The Course slides down into my stomach, and from there to my solar belt, then the jugular spasms climb upward again. I'm feeling the Course as I've never felt it before! I prolong this second prelude as much as I can. Finally, I tremble so hard that I have to put my plate on the floor and collect the last crumbs directly with my tongue. I jerk violently, going on a little bit longer, trembling, nearly choking on the jugular spasm. I moan without shame. My vulbas are wide open. I fall down crying and snorting, my body in convulsions.

The last orgasm lasts almost ten minutes. The happiest among us are still shaking under the shock. The others rise, trembling and limp, looking around dizzily. The servants have cleaned up the room and now there are only guests here.

I'm the first, as host, to walk to the pool. I signal to the others. The water is warm, bubbling calmly. It is clear and fragranced with relaxing scents. I dive in, touch the bottom, then come back to the surface and float. The guests are entering the pool.

My muscles loosen, my body relaxes, my blood resumes its leisurely pace. I'm happier than I've been in a while. The others splash in the water, playing and laughing, but gently—nobody wants to spoil the post-orgasmic feeling.

"Who is this marvellous recipear?"

"His name is Morminiu," I answer. "I don't know him personally yet, but I look forward to it."

I get out of the pool after a few minutes, my body and mind relaxed, my skin and hair cleansed of sweat. I smile at my guests. "Friends, our ladies are waiting for us!"

They all burst into laughter and follow me. I open a pair of doors and reveal another, larger room, its rounded walls covered by red algae tapestry embroidered directly on the bone. My guests' wives, their number doubled by escort phriliras, have so far enjoyed a little wine, music, and the green bone pool. As I expected, they tired of waiting, and have already started their prelude with the young escorts. I read the lust in their eyes andm although they're not as happy as we are; I recognize the tense appetite in their bodies, their skin, their trembling and stirring vulbas.

We rush in, hungry for their touch. A few succeed in finding their wives, the others topple down with random phriliras. In a few minutes, the room is full of sighs. I walk among the groups rolling on the floor, heading to the armchair on the far side where my lady waits with an expectant smile. I sink into her arms and kiss her. Behind me, from every corner of the room, the guests are shouting cheerfully, "Long live Hitissh Tahmimh!"

"Seems it has been a success, Tahi," my love whispers to me.

"It's been wonderful," I answer, lifting my head from her chest. I look into her eyes and amend my opinion: "No, divine! The recipear who creates such Recipes is not an ordinary phril."

I turn to the others and shout, "Long live Recipear Morminiu!"

ADVICE.   *The greatest insult that can be delivered to a phril is to tell him the story of a Recipe and allow him to enjoy the preparation, or the presentation, being aware that it will arouse his gastrophiza, and then not serve him—refuse him the pleasure, the need, of Tasting. An unsatisfied phril's stomach will remain in his throat, leaving a bitter taste on his tongue, because of the jugular spasm. The bile will then rise to his brain and his blood instincts will take over. Your insult will reach a new level— crisis—and the insult will be irreparable.*

(*from* The Gastronomic Teachings by Master Recipear Plabos)

III. BABON AND THE BROPS

Sensing that something wasn't right, Morminiu swore shortly, choking. He checked the food one more time, but couldn't find anything wrong. He was tense, and he didn't like it. He returned the tray to the oven and leaned against the table. For a few moments he tried to define his state of discomfort, then he turned his attention to a platter and began to garnish it. The Course had to not only taste perfect, but look perfect. He froze. He forced himself not look up from the dish. He realized what was going on—he was being spied upon! Somebody was with him inside the locked kitchens!

A Recipe was worth something only if it was a savoury secret creation. And the secret was usually in the preparation, not the ingredients. But now, the mystery had been violated, somebody had dared to steal his art. He felt the presence of the thief somewhere behind him. Trying to remain casual, he resumed garnishing the platter. He sprinkled a few red berries, tossed one into his mouth, and chewed it with simulated cheerfulness. It tasted sweet and sour, like a cool morning after a night of love. More and more certain of the presence inside the kitchen, he moved carelessly toward the spy's hiding place.

. . . Leomi opened his eyes and tried to figure out where he was. He looked up, saw a seated phril—a noble, judging by his clothes. When he was better able to distinguish the noble's face, fear overwhelmed him. It was Plabos! Young and powerful, as he'd looked when he had been banished from the court. He was sitting in a chaise longue, his attention focused on something round and hairy on the floor. Leomi could see the grin on the master recipear's face, and an endless cruelty in his eyes. Hate darkened the face of his former friend. Plabos kicked the hairy ball, and Leomi heard the dull crunch of crushed flesh and breaking bones, and watched it roll to the wall, then bounce back to come to rest under its master's sole. It was swollen and bloody; coagulated blood clung to the lips of the open wound in its neck and around its mouth. And when Plabos kicked it again, hurling it toward the wall, Leomi screamed in terror—it was his decapitated head, and his former friend was playing with it, crushing its bones bit by bit, pounding its brain and eyes into a juicy porridge. Leomi screamed like a maniac, until he choked on his own tongue and started to cough and spray saliva . . .

Morminiu bent toward the tools on the sideboard and heard the unmistakable rustle. Then another one, then silence. He grabbed a skewer and straightened with the apparent intention of returning to the table.

In one smooth motion, he whirled and thrust the spike into the wall. Its pointed tip penetrated the wall's flesh much more easily than it would normally. Blood gurgled through the wall in foamy bubbles. Behind it, invisible, something was writhing uncontrollably, nailed to the Carami's bone. A bitter scent spoiled his Recipe's fragrance. Morminiu heard labored wheezing.

He drew his sword and tested the wall with its tip until he succeeded in discovering the hidden edge of the flesh curtain. He pulled it aside and revealed the intruder. It was short and reptilian, with leathery wings that ended in bent claws, and big, round eyes. A buhuta! Morminiu shook with indignation. The magical animal was also shaking, but uncontrollably, as its life drained away along the spike, the blood dripping into a puddle beneath it.

The recipear had learned that the dark creature from the Carami's innermost depths could be captured and tamed, and was used by the phriliras for ritual purposes, and by the phrils for espionage. Skilled phrils could implant a nervous appendix, obtained through cropping. With it, the buhuta recorded voluntarily what it saw and heard. He had thought they were only fairy tales. Now he knew they were real.

He left the animal nailed to the wall and went back to his Course.

⬧◈⬧⬧⬧◈⬧⬧◈◈◈⬧⬧◈⬧⬧◈◈⬧

Leomi's eyes opened wide, and he found himself transported from his nightmare, though the vengeful face of Plabos was still imprinted on his retinas. He was panting. Sweat trickled through strands of hair down his face. He became aware of the panting of another, close by, and other movement joining his. He rose and looked anxiously to the right side of the bed. His lady, raised on the pillows, gazed at him with a mixture of fascination and terror while continuing to masturbate madly. Like him, she was covered in sweat. They looked at each other in a sort of trance for a few minutes, and Leomi realized that what had excited Donasa was his nightmare and the torments he suffered while asleep.

Finally the phrilira started to shake violently, emitting a high-pitched mewing. She rolled on the pillows in a terrorized ecstasy. Though in the middle of her orgasm, she could not take her eyes from his. The Hitissh rose, wrapped himself in a blanket, and left the bedroom.

◆◆◆◆◆◆◆◆◆◆◆◆◆

Trying not to inhale the smoke thickening in the kitchens, Morminiu approached the packing system and unrolled the thin, transparent membrane that grew on the kitchen wall. It was the best insulation, obtained through methods that had lasted for hundreds of years. He packed the first platter with sure, long-practiced gestures, cutting, then turning the package to position it under the blood that trickled from the membrane's cut to drop exactly on the spot where the ends of the material joined. As soon as they touched the material, the drops started to coagulate. The recipear only had time to quickly apply the signet before the blood seal hardened. He repeated the operation with the other two platters, after which he detached the buhuta from the wall, placed it under the serving table, put the Course on top of it as if everything were normal, covered everything with a cloth, then left it near the door.

Dizzy now, he gathered all the remaining ingredients and threw them into the burner. Only then did he slide open the ceiling vent, letting in a cold, humid breeze that quickly cooled the kitchen. The smoke and the steam were exhaled through the fleshy tube and drawn upward to the lungs and the external vents of the Carami.

After one last look around to make sure he hadn't forgotten anything, he retrieved his table on wheels and exited the kitchen. The two brops made their appearance, their eyes under their fanged mouths narrowed. Morminiu tried to ignore them, though he felt uncomfortable every time they were around.

He advanced to the Hitissh's cabinet as naturally as

possible, unable to shake the feeling that he might be attacked from behind. *In thirty seconds they'll devour a phril as big as Babon,* Leomi had told him. Remembering, Morminiu felt his stomach tighten even more. "Damn, I wouldn't even have time to scream," he whispered. "And Babon would probably come, dragging his feet, to save me. Ten seconds one step, ten seconds the next step. 'How much farther? Aha, ten seconds left, and I still have five steps to go. What a shame!'" Morminiu snorted. "He had a real talent!"

He entered the cabinet with a relieved sigh, then immediately wrinkled his lips in respect. "Good morning, Great Hitissh. Have you slept well?"

"He slept very well because you haven't been around," Donasa interjected acidly. "Why don't you just send your delivery? Why do you have to always bother us?"

"This is his will, Graceful Lady. It's business. Anyway, the biggest part of the profit goes into the Lordship's treasure house and I have—"

"And if you had dealt properly with your own business, the biggest part of the profit wouldn't go to the same treasure house? He needs rest, Recipear, and from now on you won't visit him without my approval."

Leomi looked harshly at Donasa and frowned. Silence fell and with it a tension between the two, similar to the one between Morminiu and the brops that sniffed excitedly at the service table and the traces of blood he'd left behind.

"Morminiu, I want a Gods Green," the noble suddenly told him.

Donasa scowled and bit her lips in anger. The recipear stepped forward and bent protectively over the Hitissh. "Your Highness, we agreed only to one tea a day."

"Yes, and you should give up that as well, sleep more, and restart the treatment with the red plants," Donasa said, then she retreated, pale and shaking.

"What is it, Morminiu? Do you have no more underwater plants?" Leomi blinked tired eyes, ignoring her.

"I do have them, Your Highness, but—"

"Then make me a tea. I need an underwater tea."

Morminiu straightened triumphantly, but with an expression of consternation for Donasa. She had crouched on an armchair in the dark shadows of the cabinet. The recipear went to his service table and touched the packages he'd prepared.

"Later, Morminiu, later. Now, I want the tea."

"Yes, Your Highness."

"In fact, send them away and tell me later what it was all about."

Morminiu bent in a gesture of obedience, then lifted from the table a bottle made of river greenstone, carved with thousands of facets.

"You had it ready! You always guess my wishes." Leomi sighed, satisfied.

"Always to serve you better." And as he turned with the bottle to the Hitissh's couch, he added in a cold voice, "Babon, take what is under the table and show it to His Lordship."

"You show it, don't tell me to," the servant blustered, irritated.

Morminiu stopped theatrically with the greenstone sphere held in mid-air, a few fingers from the Hitissh's nose, close enough for the sweet steam to tickle his nostrils. "I regret to inform you that I have to quit your service, Your Highness. Living with this thick-skinned intriguer and traitor has become impossible for me. I am a recipear, an artist who offers you pleasure daily, and I'm to do menial chores for a servant who is too lazy and cocky? And recently, we have almost been stolen from, right here, where he assures security. And he still has the nerve to talk."

The Hitissh froze in surprise. He tried to say something, but failed.

"Your Highness, I'm sorry. It's me, or him," Morminiu finished, turning back to place the sphere on the table.

"Whooff," moaned Leomi.

"Your Greatness," Babon intervened vehemently, "fire him. This lickspittle plots against you."

"Yes, Leomi." The cold voice of Donasa insinuated itself as stealthily as a snake. "I don't like this Morminiu, whose coming stirs up memories. I smell revenge. Banish him before it is too late."

Morminiu bent and pulled the buhuta out from underneath the table. He heard the other three gasp. The brops growled low and licked the blood that dripped from the carcass. "If somebody's plotting in this house, it is not I," he said. "And this is the evidence! Who could sneak a buhuta into the kitchen to steal the Recipearium's secrets, if not the phril who's in charge of security? And for whom is he working, My Lord? Your Lordship has all my Recipes at your beck and call. Somebody from outside must have bribed your faithful advisor, guardian, and servant, who now requests my head!"

"Take him!" ordered Babon. The brops hesitated a second, then pounced on the recipear with their circular mouths open wide.

"Harshh—Babon." Leomi spat the command programmed into their small brains, which could be used only once in a lifetime.

The brops changed direction and a bewildered Babon fell under their fangs. They killed him while he was falling to the floor. Then started eating with no pause or concern that Babon had taken care of them personally since they were small pups. No bonds to anybody. Only possible food.

"Thirty seconds exactly," Morminiu noted admiringly, hiding his fear and nausea.

"How could you?" screamed Donasa.

"How could you have believed that I would kill my recipear?" groaned an exhausted Leomi. "Morminiu, give me that tea, or I'll die here. Donasa, leave us alone."

The Hitissha left the cabinet, trembling with horror and frustration. The brops had finished and, licking the last drops of Babon from their muzzles, they also left. The recipear sent away the table with its packages, then quietly closed the door and came back to the noble, carrying the little bottle. He lifted its lid and inserted the straw, close enough that Leomi could glimpse the magical sheen of the liquid inside.

"Let me see it just once," the Hitissh begged childishly.

"Forgive him, gods, for his foolishness," Morminiu said in a surprised voice, but he was watching the noble's every reaction.

"I don't think I can resist the temptation anymore," Leomi moaned as he accepted the small bottle and reached for the straw. Suddenly he tried to open the lid, without success; it now seemed to have melded with the bottle. "What's the secret, boy? These traps are driving me crazy!"

"They're not traps, My Lord, but what kind of secret would it be, if it wasn't well guarded? Plus, it's ill-fated for the drinker to see his tea. It's ceremony!"

Leomi sipped feverishly and closed his eyes. Slowly, his body relaxed. "Tell me, for whom have you prepared the Recipe today?"

"Harissh Mim. He celebrates his hundredth Course."

"Old fool," huffed Leomi with a superior air. "I'd reached the three hundred and fiftieth Course when Plabos left. I've always missed his friendship," he sighed.

Morminiu remained silent. Three hundred and fifty Courses when Plabos left. Courses celebrated in only five or six years and since then, in more than twenty years with Donasa, he had added no more than seven to his list. That said a lot.

"And you, boy, how many Courses do you have?"

"Me, My Lord? It's not important; I'm the recipear."

"No, no, no, I was always shy to ask Plabos, but now I want to know. The lives of master recipears are always shrouded in mystery."

"Your Highness, as for the title of master recipear . . . " Morminiu spoke with a vaguely intimidated air, because despite all the fame he had gained since coming to the capital, he was still the simple recipear of the Lormont House. One of several thousand recipears in the Royal Carami.

"Oh, no, Morminiu. Don't play modest. You know well that you deserve it, and next week I want to introduce you to the court and name you with all ceremony the Master Recipear of Lormont House. Then I want to elevate you to nobility. It would be an honor to me."

"Thank you, Your Lordship! I'll always be grateful."

"Tell me now—how many Courses?"

"Two thousand three hundred, approximately—"

Leomi burst into laughter. The recipear tried to smile, though he was full of rage. He knew that he had reached an artistic level that had never been attained in history. Plabos himself, still considered the greatest artist of all time, had to his credit only fourteen or fifteen hundred Courses. He, Morminiu, had revolutionized the art of Recipes. Soon he would be known and recognized as the most absolute artist.

"And when I think," Leomi hesitated, struggling to translate his joy, "when I think how, at the beginning, I threatened you that I'd feed you to my brops before your five hundredth Course . . . !"

Morminiu was confused for a few seconds, then realized the true meaning of what the noble said, and shared in his cheerfulness. He even felt a little bit of compassion for the aged, outdated Hitissh, who would have sold himself to feed his vice, not to mention Babon, or Donasa—or even his best friend.

The Hitissh finished laughing and panted, tired. "What's the hundredth Course for the Harissh?"

"Stone-fish in Gods Green Root Sauce."

"Oh, no. I can't stand knowing that what I have tasted will be tasted by others too."

"Yes, but only Your Lordship could have watched the Preparation Story, especially the last part, where the greed showed and the lead character led them into the troubled waters of politics . . . "

"I know, Morminiu, I know." Leomi trembled with greed himself. "Still, sometimes it comes to me that I should lock you up here, allow you to create only for me . . . "

The recipear's back stiffened and his expression shifted between fear and the calm he wanted to display. The noble noticed his embarrassment and grunted, amused.

"Don't worry, boy. Your future is much brighter than that, and it's already written."

Morminiu puckered his lips thoughtfully and adopted a position of polite waiting.

"We're talking now like father to son," Leomi insisted and the recipear opened his gills and took a deep breath, preparing to give Leomi all his attention.

"Right; come and sit here, next to me. Get comfortable."

Leomi gathered the blanket around his body and revealed to him the high, noble chair near his couch, a gesture that imposed on Morminiu a need for utter attention. The chair was made from two shells, carved with detailed scenes from Leomi's family history. The shells were joined with bent bones similar to those used throughout the palace, brought from the west side of the Carami, Morminiu had learned. The chair was lined with a muscular layer cultivated right on the shells, which was supposed to soften or harden according to the tension of the phril seated in it. The recipear settled himself carefully, avoiding the curling bone tips that almost created a capsule of the chair. He didn't dare ask their purpose. More important right now was his future.

"My boy, I have thought carefully. We can make a beautiful couple."

The recipear bent his head approvingly, but avoided completing the idea.

"The first step is very important and needs to be carefully designed. Your introduction to the court and being named the Master Recipear of the House Lormont needs to be perfect."

Morminiu approved once more, still keeping his

silence.

"After a while, the inevitable next step will be my death."

"But, Your Highness—"

"Listen to the end. One could say it's family business! As my master recipear, I command you to make me a princely Recipe. As much 'underwater' as possible. We will go to the court and we will tell them its story. Then, after the festivities, I'll name you heir of House Lormont."

Leomi paused, his breath whistling, waiting for the recipear's reaction. But Morminiu remained still, digesting the information. He made a tremendous effort to hide his enthusiasm.

"Well, what do you say?" Leomi asked impatiently.

"Your Lordship, I'm speechless. Actually, I was asking myself if it is a good thing for me, a simple recipear from the countryside . . . I mean, I know I'm the best, but suddenly—"

"Stop this lamentation," the noble barked with false harshness. "Since your arrival, the whole city has fallen at your feet. Half the noble houses' recipears have been fired. You've received dozens of offers. The King himself is interested in you!"

He paused again, this time for effect before continuing in a honeyed voice. "But, I have two reasons to do it. First, the interesting one, as I've told you. You become the heir of House Lormont with only one condition."

"Anything, Your Highness."

"I knew you were a smart boy. Plabos would have refused me, but he was stupid. That's why he ended up like that—"

"Your lordship, please." Morminiu rose suddenly, scratching himself on the high chair's sharp tips. "No matter what Your Highness feels, Plabos is my master and . . ."

"Yes, boy, forgive me. After all, I cared for that fool too. Anyway, do you accept?"

"And the condition, what is it?" the recipear said from

the tip of his lips peaked in a polite curiosity.

"Well, it's just a formality. You have to completely agree to my will."

"Aha, and the will says I get the title that will help me in my ascent. I understand, Your Highness, and I will always be grateful—"

"Not at all; you're my rightful heir, from the title to the paving-bones in the courtyard. My first interest though, and duty to you, is that my fulfillment Recipe will be tasted by you; this is a very important aspect, Morminiu. I want to transmigrate into you. My second interest is that Lady Donasa will stay in this house as Lady Mistress till she dies. The two brops will guard her; three, the cook, the servants, and the gardener, will remain in their positions. They have served this house since my grandfather's time. As for the head servant, we must hire another one."

"I'll see to it myself, Your Lordship. Totin, the new guard hired by Babon could be a good choice."

"Then, are we in total agreement?"

"Totally, My Lord. It is exactly what I would have done, even if it wasn't written in the will."

"And also, from today on, you're free to go wherever you might want. I'm happy you want to know so many things. Soon, I'll know as much as you. Two thousand three hundred Courses? It's unbelievable!"

"I'm grateful for my freedom, Your Highness."

"Don't mention it, boy. I mentioned two reasons. The second one is a bit more personal." He panted, fatigued, then resumed, "You're the son I never had, Morminiu. Plabos has been more than a friend to me; he was like my brother. I feel something of Plabos in you. I believe you've been like his child and that makes me consider you my son."

He blinked faded eyes and waited a few seconds. Morminiu dared to speak in a low and trembling voice. "Your Highness, I'm proud and honored by the feelings you nurture for me. I don't know how I may be able to repay you—"

"You don't have to, Morminiu. A child doesn't repay his father for being loved. He only should stay by his side and love him in return."

Morminiu could sense the bitterness in his voice. He didn't dare interrupt again. He waited politely for the noble to continue, if he was still in the mood for confession. He didn't wait long.

"When I was very young, like you are now, boy, I loved a phrilira as nobody has ever loved. I had a daughter too, but both were taken from me. I haven't seen them since. They are in the House of Phriliras, but I was denied access because . . . I . . . I haven't had a son. I had a daughter, but I don't know her . . ."

He bit his lip and gave up telling the story. Morminiu hadn't heard of this. So, there had been another phrilira before Donasa. What happened to her? He didn't wish to stir up Leomi's pain, so he kept silent.

"You can have my signet, on my desk. Take it with you so nobody can stop you. And before you go," Leomi mumbled with difficulty, showing that the tea had begun to take effect, "turn on the heat. It's damn cold in my old cave. Boy, take care of yourself. I'm interested . . . in the way . . . you preserve yourself . . ."

His head slumped and he fell asleep wearing a pained smile. Morminiu rose slowly, took the small bottle from his sleep-softened grip, and placed it on the table. Then he corked the top of the horn-couch, so that it would heat and radiate warmth into the muscular layer on which the noble rested.

MORMINIU

I climb the last tread and stop near the parapet, breathing deeply to stabilize my respiration. I have finally reached Celesthe. Unfortunately, it being evening, I can't see my surroundings clearly, though the darkness is a little less deep here than in Burtheste, farther down. To my left there is a structure made of bones, like a labyrinthine scaffold that supports the cupola and loses itself in the depths at its base. Its recesses swarm with phrils—of the lowest kind, I've heard. *A sort of sub-phril,* I add to myself, smiling inwardly.

Farther along the parapet, on the right, a ramshackle construction of overlapped shells holds a tavern. I advance up the street toward it, noticing more and more stares cast my way, at the mask I've pulled partway down over my face, in fact, so nobody would recognize me on my way here. I forgot it still covered my face! There is no point wearing it here, where no one knows me, yet now there is no point in taking it off. Everybody is staring at me anyway; removing the mask will just make my face more memorable.

It's an awkward situation, one of those I alone can attract, I think ruefully. I can't turn and go back with so many eyes measuring my footsteps, but neither will I be able to explore too deeply. I turn right, trying to keep my expression calm, and enter the tavern.

Inside, I catch my breath—it's so dark in here, I could never attract anybody's attention. I walk to the counter, where curiosity urges me to buy the house specialty, Crevex. A hand, its skin darkened by dirt, pushes my order in front of me. The receptacle is a mummified butterfly as big as a fist. A rough hole has been cut in its head between its antennas, from which protrudes a straw.

I sniff discreetly and draw back immediately, overcome by nausea. I recognize the slop as a concoction made from the excreta of the bone butterfly, thousands of which reside in the Carami's caves, gnawing at the external layer of the skeleton; they are a real nuisance. I recognized another odor in that whiff, too: the Crevex stinks of the lowest quality hallucinogen. If I drink that, I will probably crawl into bed and remain there, out of my head, for two days. That is, if I could even reach my bed!

I look around, worried. Realizing everybody is too drunk to take notice of me, I grab the bloated receptacle and exit to the terrace, an area so crowded I can hardly find a free space for myself.

This level, called by the locals Celesthe, is completely devoid of any artificial light source. I've heard that they must continuously clean the monster's back to maintain a translucent arc of flesh overhead that will let in natural light. I see that night has fallen, the sky filled with stars that look like smudges. From here, I see all three Daughters of the Sky, like a puddle trembling on the ceiling. The sight of this night sky wakes no memories in me, but it does reveal something new. Here, on the last level of the Carami, in the hovels of the outcasts and scoundrels, life gains new meaning.

I rise, feeling empty inside, and a little dizzy after gazing upward for so long. I'm shaking; the cold wind that blows up here wipes me like a moist cloth over the flabby edges of my vulba. I walk a few steps to the railing and sit down there at the top of the chasm, my feet hanging over the city. I feel like a dizzy bug hovering over a field of little lights.

"What's up, wacky, no mood for butterflying?"

I turn, surprised. A drunkard has sat down a few steps away from me. He's banging his shoeless feet carelessly against the ledge, watching me with eyes nearly hidden under greasy strands of uncombed hair. *Down there,* I think, glancing over the edge, *he would be just another beggar; but here, he's right at home.* "What do you want?" I ask him.

He nods toward the butterfly. "It would be a pity to drop that over the railing. It could break somebody's head down there!" He stares meaningfully at me and I barely suppress laughter.

After the first temptation to simply offer it to him, I hold it up and ask him, driven by a strange impulse, "What would you give me for it?"

"What would you like?"

"What do you have to offer?"

"On the mother's skin!" he blurts, exasperated. "Just spill it out, tell me everything you'd like, and we'll see. You know how the market works here. Or—I have uncertain eyes at this hour, but your clothes are too new for a place like Celesthe," he says thoughtfully, then says slowly, explaining, "I give you information, and you give me the pretty thing."

"The pretty thing?"

He blinks toward the butterfly receptacle and I nod my understanding.

"Shake hands, old phril?"

I sigh. "What is it you can tell me?"

"I don't know what you're looking for here, but next time you come, dress more commonly. Some of the more alert phrils have spotted you. I hope you don't have full pockets." He shrugs, looking into the crowd. "Anyway, those guys don't know anything useful."

I give him time to focus back on me, then ask, "What would I find useful? What would I want here?"

"You playing smart with me?" He peers closely at me, studying my mask, intrigued. Then he shakes his head. "No, you're serious. You really did just come here for a walk!"

"Still, what could there be here for me?"

"Everything!" He avoids looking directly at me. "Give me that stinkin' thing."

"In a moment."

"We shook hands, wacky," he warns.

"We may be able to do some business together," I tell him quickly, to calm him down. "I don't want you to fall asleep before you tell me what I want to know."

"Meaning?"

I hesitate. "I don't know . . . "

"Come on, spill it out. What's the catch?" This time he turns his eyes straight on me. He's curious, I can tell, but he's hiding it, presenting an indifferent face.

"Other people like me, why would they come here? What sort of business do they do here?"

"I told you, anything. Antiquities, works of art, Recipes, information, drugs, crystalidic swarms, easy babes—anything."

"What's the most valuable merchandise you know of?"

"The Recipes, in mother's vulbas! The newer a Recipe is, the more valuable it is. And if it's unknown—and I mean everywhere, not even His Shitness the King knows about it—then you can make yourself truly powerful here—build an army, buy all the babes in Celesthe." He drops his voice. "You can even have access to the royal database."

"How's that?"

"Simple. Smack, pop, it's ready. But it costs, big time." Again his voice falls. "Some even have sacrificed phrils—if you pay, they'll do it. Better butterfly'n Celesthe, than a rimshi in Burtheste!" he finishes, his voice now high-pitched as he raises his empty receptacle.

In response, all the drinkers, less the ones already passed out, roar like maniacs and lift their drinks.

"Do the same, you moron!" he exclaims, smiling.

I keep any comments to myself and raise my own butterfly, roaring. I realize that, as I'd thought, the guy's more alert than he seems. I also realize that—on the Sathali's spheres!—a whole new world, full of unsuspected opportunities, is opening to me.

One of the unconscious phrils jerks awake, startled by the noise, and jumps to his feet. He stands face to face with another drunkard, who still has his drink hoisted over his head while yelling, the effect quite menacing close up, I suppose. I almost don't notice, in the commotion, as two shiny objects burst from the level of the revived phril's lungs, or perhaps even from his lungs, arrowing directly toward the cheering phril, who drops dead immediately. Nobody pays attention to them as the party continues. One corpse in the middle of the room and nobody cares, no guards come in to established order. Somebody takes over the dead guy's butterfly and moves to the next room.

"What was that?" I blurt.

"Basai. Circular blades, this small." He displays his fingernail. "His gills are destroyed and replaced by a blade loader, which projects the basai through incisions in the lungs."

"Extraordinary!"

"Just a bloody graft." When I remain silent he adds, "Now, give me the butterfly, big boy, and beat it while everyone's still distracted. Tempers are very hot here right now, and you wouldn't want to burn yourself, wouldn't you? I'll cover you; stay in the shadows. Here, this is my vorb code. You have a problem, come here at night and ask for Mahop. If it's an emergency, you call me at this code."

"Vorb, here? I haven't seen any nerve network—"

"I handle it. You want to know more, pay. It's been a pleasure," he finishes abruptly, his tone mocking, and puts the straw to his mouth.

I rise carefully and walk away. I try to follow his advice because indeed, I don't feel safe here anymore, after all I've seen. When I reach the lower levels I slow down, waiting for my heartbeat to slow down as well. From here, it's an easy, short road to Hitissh Leomi's palace.

Only now do I realize the danger I was in, due to my ignorance. But a wave of satisfaction fills me, and I draw a deep, contented breath into my lungs. My life has gained a new dimension. I haven't waited a year and half for nothing, after all.

A few days ago, I was introduced at the royal court. It is the second most important step I've taken. The King is old and rotten, thirsty for power and life, and this is important to know. He was already impressed by my fame, and I was no longer treated like a provincial. The most interesting moment came when, despite Leomi's jealous protest, I offered the King, amidst the greedy murmurs of the audience, a sphere of Green of the Gods.

When I'd prepared this for the Hitissh when I first arrived, I made it in triple concentration, fearing he wouldn't like it, even though no land plant can produce such exquisite sensations. Thus, Leomi was the first one to discover the true world of dreams and pleasures, the escapism available in "Gods Green," as the Hitissh calls it. How could I, in these circumstances, deny the sovereign such an experience? After all, wasn't it the King who banished Plabos? I feel a wave of tranquil approval; the master is present, still supervising me.

I made it for him in the normal dose—no point in hurrying, and revealing its addictive effect; who knows when I'll need him? And doesn't he deserve such a side effect? When I noticed he had slavered enough, exactly before he was in danger of losing his temper, I asked his permission to offer him the tea myself. This allowed me to see the Master Recipear of the Court, Harissh Tathar, for the first time. An idiot lacking originality, Plabos had told me, one who is satisfied, I had learned myself, to continuously use the few hundred Recipes created by past master recipears.

The moment I opened the sphere before the King, Tathar shuddered and made to step forward, but those around him restrained him. I knew I had instantly made an enemy.

Like Leomi, the King tried immediately to learn the secret ingredients of the tea. How rude! More diplomatic than Hitissh Leomi, he apologized graciously, explaining that he understood how sacred were the secrets of the master recipears. Father Sky, protect him!

I stop and remove the mask—it's pointless to continue concealing my face here, where I'm expected to be. At the entrance to the city's ground level, I present the House Lormont signet to the guards on duty. They bow silently and allow me to pass. My feet automatically choose the right roads without my having to concentrate. Down here, the air is warmer. I open my cloak and leave it to wave in time with my stride.

During the ritual of the Story—this was the first time I revealed such an extravaganza to such a large audience—Tathar left the court in a poorly concealed rage. That perfected my first victory over the Court Recipear. He realized—and soon everyone else will realize—that I'm the only one who can pull off such a feat.

Another character present who, if not interesting, is at least as important, is Taharissh Chathu, the closest relative of the King, who is childless. Chathu's potential relationship with the King—that of heir—was obvious in the way he was looking almost continuously at the sovereign as if he were a gourmet feast. Certainly, Chathu is a character to watch, one with whom I should take care, because rumor has it that Tathar has a great influence over him.

On the King's left was a dark phril, very quiet and wearing a severe expression. He stood still almost all evening. A few times I bumped into him, and he gave me an interrogative glare. I didn't like that at all. Merely approaching him gave me shivers, even without the alarmed whispers coming from Plabos! I found out that he is the King's counsellor, the closest phril to the monarch. The dark side of the sovereignty, in my opinion.

My naming as Master Recipear of House Lormont was, Leomi later told me, the grandest naming celebration in the last one hundred years. The Hitissh spared nothing, and now, thanks to the two new Recipes and their Stories that I told and offered to the court, I am riding a wave of appreciation and popularity that not even the heir Chathu enjoyed. But I am careful to remind myself, *Watch it, boy; now is the time to retreat behind modesty and flatter the heir as well.* I have no wish to fall into the trap I myself have set.

Master Recipear of House Lormont. That doesn't sound bad! I smile.

POLITICAL RECIPE: STONE-FISH IN GODS' GREEN ROOT SAUCE

INGREDIENTS:

AN ADULT STONEFISH.

CEROPTES BUDS.

CRAWLING LIANAS from the lake bottom.

A PINK-BLOSSOMING DUSK FLOWER.

GODS GREEN ROOT.

FIVE TO SIX PUDDLE AND LAND REPTILES, ranging in size from tadpole to silver lizard.

SWAMP RED WINE.

PREPARATION STORY:

Take the stonefish, still alive, and clean up its fat layer, but slowly and with delicacy, as if you were combing it, so its road to death is gentle, as if gliding into a deep sleep. The fish is, in fact, a senseless mountain of fat surrounding its spine, which is surrounded by a muscular layer. Work carefully so you do not scratch this layer.

The wrinkled muscular layer will now be aged by the pain and cruelty. Attempt to make peace in your sorrowed soul, then plunge it into a bath of hot oil fragranced with sequ-tulapa to shorten its torments. This will melt any remaining fat, leaving the muscle clean. You will notice that it relaxes and its wrinkles smooth as it is satisfied by a welcome bath. Remove it from the oil and immediately wrap it in a towel imbued with cave flower smoke.

While it is resting, prepare the hot sand bed and the sauce.

For the sauce, pour swamp red wine into an oiled tray dusted with sugar and place this on a small fire. When the "swamp" begins to bubble, releasing from the wine the unique essences of its source, and the sugar is about to fall from the tray's walls, add crushed Gods Green root. Allow the mixture to boil, adding swamp spices and sequ to taste.

As the sauce boils, prick the stonefish's muscular layer deeply in many places. Gently insert ceroptes buds into the holes, then, because we know how it is with the sleeping political spirits, tie it up with crawling lianas from the lake bottom, which have been well marinated in advance, and place it carefully in the sand bed. Cover it with an even layer of sand, a palm thick, and leave it there for half an hour, or until well cooked.

The sauce should be done by the time the featured ingredient has been put into the bed. Now deal quickly with the supporters of the opposition, as well. Feed a green frog tadpole the pink-blossomed dusk flower it craves while singing patriotic songs. After it has swallowed it all with its usual greed, as it is digesting the meal, pour hot animal oil over it and let it pass into posterity. Immediately offer it as prey to the next reptile in size. This one will swallow it greedily, probably be contaminated, and should be coated in hot oil as well. Withdraw a bit of the tadpole's head from within the throat of the second reptile and leave it as ornamentation.

Repeat the process with the third reptile, and so on, until there is a spiral of immortalized reptiles, each one protruding from the previous one's mouth.

Finally, the last step! Remove the muscle, now well done, from the hot sand and add it to the prepared sauce, arranging it in a circular position. This will, as it is called, "clear the waters," in our case the sauce, which will turn clear yellow and crystallize instantly around the centrepiece. This crystallized sauce will turn brown and take on a crunchy consistency on the surface.

Place the opposition, reduced as well to a respectful silence, in the middle of the circle formed by the centrepiece. It too will have a similar reaction when it comes into contact with the sauce of truth, and will be covered by a jelly-like crust.

To be served chilled, with the acid of icy lichens, preferably after a tumultuous speech, for a Political Meal.

(from The Gastronomic Teachings of Master Recipear Plabos)

IV. THE ROYAL NET

Morminiu stretched his limbs and rose from the hammock. He was in a good mood. Grabbing the rucksack that was still writing, albeit more weakly, he placed it on the table, smiling as he remembered Leomi's greedy curiosity when he had returned from the expedition with the load on his shoulder. The Hitissh had tried to restrain himself, but in the end, he'd approached Morminiu with saliva moistening his chin.

"What do you have in the rucksack, Morminiu?"

"Small discoveries, Your Highness."

"Hmm ... show me quickly, just a bit," he'd wheedled. "Open the rucksack's mouth, just a little."

"I humbly apologize, My Lord, but that is impossible. My secrets are my only fortune, and at the moment, until they're turned into a Recipe, everything in here is secret."

"I know. But I'd really like to feel whatever's that secret."

"You'll soon have them all, My Lord," Morminiu told him with a cunning smile. "You have to prepare yourself for such knowledge."

"Oooh!" the old noble exclaimed, then jerked back as the sack writhed on the recipear's back. "Oh-ho, Master Recipear, I do believe that I really don't want to know all your secrets right now. Maybe it is not so healthy."

"Wise thoughts, Your Highness. It's better for both of us if some things stay as they are."

The sack twitched slowly, for the creature inside was exhausted. Morminiu lifted a cage waiting near the wall, put it on the table, and opened its lid. Then, lifting the sack by its corners, he upended it over the cage and shook it sharply to dislodge the creature within. It tumbled into the cage and Morminiu banged the lid shut, jumping back in time to avoid one of the creature's claws. It was as big as his palm, with thin, telescoping legs and three pairs of claws emerging from between a clam-like red shell. Its head rolled furiously from one side to the other within the shell, revealing a constellation of phosphorous-green eyes.

"Hmm, you look pretty, brute. I think there's

something different about you, though," Morminiu mused. "You look like the clawers from the swamp, only smaller and prettier," he said, referring to similar creatures outside the Carami, "a flaw that should be remedied. I'll keep you for a while to see how you behave."

Morminiu looked around the room. The walls were lined with stands full of flowerpots exposed to diverse light sources. Leafy stems covered almost all the walls. He cleared a stand and placed the cage near a vent, then flung himself back into the hammock. He stretched his lips in a smile and started to smack them noisily, translating his satisfaction into something more physical.

Then he rose, remembering something. He stepped out into the hall and glanced up and down its length. No movement. Not surprising; the room he had made his own was in one of the abandoned wings of the palace. Morminiu crept back toward the main body of the building, then ducked into an unused room. Crossing to an empty wall, he pushed on a small protrusion of bone. The wall's skin opened with a soft swish and Morminiu stepped into the dark passage beyond.

Some time ago, he had discovered accidentally that the structure of the wall in the central body of the palace was, in fact, a tight network of passages from which he could spy on what was happening in any of several key rooms. He also discovered trace evidence that the network was being used by others, though he never encountered anyone else in the passages. Over time, he mapped the secret labyrinth. Now, following that mental map, he moved quickly to the vantage point he sought within the network.

Cautiously lifting the leather patch that covered the peephole into the Hitissh's cabinet, he put his eye to it. Exactly as he suspected, following his departure, Donasa rushed into Leomi's office and started one of the arguments they'd been having so often lately; her words revealing that she knew everything discussed in private. Morminiu knew how; he could still smell her perfume in the close air of the passage around this observation point.

"Show me the will!" the Hitissha demanded.

"I repeat, that is of no concern to you," Leomi retorted. "Stop this nonsense and return to your quarters."

"Are you mad, Leo? You don't sleep in the bedroom anymore, you don't allow me in the cabinet in your absence, you go out only to salute that stinking bastard, Morminiu!"

"I've told you before that you have no business here in my absence. My business is not a phrilira's concern."

She studied him. "That tea . . . That tea, Leomi, is killing you! You're weaker and skinnier than you have ever been. The life is draining from you with every day that passes. That tea is pure poison." She paused and narrowed her eyes. "Is that why you've done your will? You feel the end is near? But think, Leo: don't you suspect that all of this has something to do with Plabos?"

"I suspect nothing, Donasa," the Hitissh snapped. "I decide everything. Starting tomorrow, I'll begin to take three doses of happiness a day. And in a week, two at most, I'll die. This week I'm making the official statement at the court and setting a date for the Story."

The Hitissha made a muffled sound that Morminiu suspected would have been a scream of surprise, but her expression revealed her horror. She tried to hide her shaking hands by squeezing the back of an armchair. "Leomi, it's over," she said. "Tomorrow, I'll seek an audience with the King and I'll denounce this bastard for poisoning you—and for his intention to poison His Majesty himself with that tea. This has gone too far!"

The noble swung a heavy palm, knocking the phrilira to the floor. "You're not in a position to threaten me," he grated. The hair on his head was like a mane. "If I hear this drivel coming from your mouth again, I'll reveal everything. The Guild has been watching you for a long time," he warned, then his voice grew imploring. "Don't make me do it; don't spoil everything between us in these last days; don't throw away all those beautiful years we shared. You can still have many more such years, if you keep your place and your common sense."

The Hitissh turned his back on her and leaned, panting, against his desk. Donasa rose, crying silently, and stumbled toward the door. After a few steps she stopped, looking uncertain. Then she retraced her steps and looked at him. Leomi was trembling with the effort of standing, his face a stubborn mask, as if he were determined to remain upright until she left the room. She burst into tears and held him, lovingly caressing his back. Then she helped him walk to the couch.

Morminiu pulled silently back from the peephole and dropped the leather flap back over it. What he had witnessed left a bitter taste in his mouth. As he made his way back through the narrow passage, he remembered a similar scene, during his childhood in the Southern Swamps. Hidden behind a door with the innocent intention of surprising his mother, he had instead witnessed another argument, this one between her and Plabos. They were talking about him, but at that time he hadn't understood what exactly they were arguing about.

The master had slapped her, and when the phrilira fought back, he flung her to the floor. She had risen and lunged toward him and he slapped her again, then he grabbed her by her hair and dragged her across the room to the opposite door. He locked her in that room, packed up his possessions, then helped Morminiu pack as well. That evening they left the house and the village of his childhood.

That day had been the last time he'd ever seen his mother, and the last day he'd been allowed to enjoy the daylight hours. Plabos had taken him to his fortified mansion, the House of the Tree, and Morminiu had entered into the most rigorous training period of his entire life—his preparation for life in the Royal Carami. When he left for the capital city many years later, he passed through his village to see his mother, but the phrils there told him she perished a short time after he left with Plabos.

Now Leomi was perishing. He'd been astonished by Donasa's compassion for the old noble, because he could sense her wickedness and cruelty. Love and affection weren't in her character. But Leomi was different . . .

He leaned against the tunnel wall and tried to repress the black thoughts that surged within him. He rubbed his forehead, swallowed to moisten a suddenly dry throat, and saw in his mind's eye a proud Leomi, trembling with effort, announcing the will he had made to Donasa. He heard again the Hitissh's breath whistling as he argued.

They are both guilty! Leomi and Donasa must die! The words rolled furiously through his head.

Morminiu had a holy duty to his master. *True, but Leomi* . . . The master rolled furiously through his brain, manipulating his thoughts. He had to do it; he had a holy duty . . . he had to do it faster, and regain his freedom. Yes!

He went back to his quarters, packed a few things in the rucksack, and sat down on the couch to pull on his shoes. Morminiu felt a tickle on his neck but ignored the sensation, focusing on lacing up his shoes. As he grabbed the rucksack and made to stand, though, a sharp pain lashed through his brain. A scream reverberated behind his forehead as he fell forward and crouched on the floor, bewildered. Subconsciously, reflexively, he blocked access to his terminal lobe. The screaming pain stopped. He remained on the floor for a few seconds longer, recovering. Then, realizing what was going on, he jumped to his feet and ran to the wall.

He folded back the little door that concealed the fake memoric store and spat. When the saliva touched the membrane it instantly reacted, pushing forward from its depths the processing unit, which contained not only one, but three real, sophisticated memoric stores. In all of Lormont palace there were only two such stores, both of small capacity and based on crystalidic swarms. Leomi hadn't much information to store, or to traffic. He was an old-fashioned noble, used to trafficking information with his sword and later, recording it in written documents and locking them in a safe.

Morminiu brought with him three metacrystalidic fulguses, obtained in trade for ten Recipes—a veritable fortune—from a merchant from Deep South. Such technology was unknown in the Green Kingdom. What made fulguses superior was their eight-crystalidic swarm capacity, the eight units all working together as a single unit. They didn't need replacement, as they could replicate themselves very easily. Practically speaking, it was an immortal processing unit.

When the system had fully emerged from its hiding place, he examined the whole ensemble. He saw no obvious damage, and the stores looked untouched. He asked for details, then breathed a relieved sigh. Still, further examination revealed that one of the fulguses was prostrate, and the other two were connected in the resistance position. Somebody had attacked them, probably trying to penetrate to the stores. Swarms were passive—they had no survival instinct. But a fulgus protected the information entrusted to it with its life.

Whoever had tried to break into Morminiu's system had failed in the first attempt and withdrawn. But surely, after the surprise at the system's sophistication had worn off, the invader would return to try again. The attempt revealed a serious problem: despite the Carami's built-in security system, there were phrils capable of moving along the information circuits without being detected by the city-monster's nerves.

Morminiu kicked off his shoes and locked the door before extracting the wounded fulgus and placing it on the table. Filling a basin with water, he put it in the cold drawer to chill it and then poured the cold liquid on the nervous receptors of the wall. He waited. In a few minutes, the temperature had dropped twenty degrees.

He connected the fulgus's umbilical to his terminal lobe and initiated the reproduction command. It was the only way to save it—the fulgus would access its primary information and rebuild the original equation in as many copies as it wished, ignoring its damaged state for the moment. When the operation finished, Morminiu disconnected the fulgus's umbilical and placed it carefully in the freezing box. Reproduction would take twenty-four hours.

He walked across the room, feeling annoyed that he was being forced to use the security measure provided by the trader from Deep South along with the fulguses: he had to install an alarm that would alert the Carami's security system every time somebody entered his unit perimeter. This would then trigger an energy field around the unit that would burn any intruder—and a good part of the nervous network—to ash. At least his unit would be safe until the healing of the information system.

He stretched, as satisfied as he could be with the solution, and, his lips puckered in concentration, he started working.

MORMINIU

The road is becoming more difficult, the path steeper and steeper. I don't know where it might end, how high it could climb. The crumbling bone rolls underfoot, unbalancing me. And worse, the glow-worm weakens with every step I take, and the darkness presses in, making my exploration of the Carami's subterranean levels more difficult.

"What on mother's skin—!" I exclaim, too loud. I stop, giggle, and repeat in a quieter voice, savouring the words, "What on mother's skin has brought me this bad luck? I will never finish this arm."

The drunkard Mahop's words have stuck in my mind. Still, I have to be cautious. When you move in noble circles, they watch you like predators. The first mistake, and you're food. A thoughtless gesture, a mistimed sidelong glance, a look that is too daring for some or too weak for others, a commoner's word or expression, and they burn you. In my case, I must be careful not to speak if Leomi might hear me! He seems old and doddering, but his spirit is still vigorous. Only the tea has softened him a little, but I wouldn't count on that softening his instincts. Only the moment of death will eliminate all this tension.

Leomi postponed everything at the last minute, probably at Donasa's urging. I don't think he's afraid—the Hitissh is no coward.

A thick bone beam lies across my path. As I look beyond it to the far side I notice with some surprise that the steep slope I've been climbing levels out just ahead. I decide to see what waits there and then return before the glow-worm expires completely and I am plunged into darkness. Lying on my belly, I crawl under the beam.

On Sathali's spheres! What beauty! I look around eagerly. I am on a ledge partway up the wall of a huge circular cave, at least three hundred steps across, and much higher.

Somewhere above, very high above, a window has been cut; light spills through it in an almost liquid stream to become a blue-white spot on the surface of a pool on the cave's floor. I can distinguish shiny white spots in the circle of illuminated water.

I glance around, see what looks like a chute descending from my ledge to the cave floor. Settling on its smooth surface, I slide down to the bottom. I rise and, staring fascinated at the traceries of light on the walls, I move closer to the pool. The threads of blue light on the walls mingle with the water trickling over them to become works of sculptural beauty beyond imagination.

The white spots I saw from above are, in fact, huge white flowers, their gracefully arched petals as big as a phril's head. I lean out over the pool for a closer look. Surprised, I realize the petals are covered in fur, a thick down of gleaming white, soft as silk. The corolla of one is filled with a red liquid and I notice that a reddish net of veins runs across the petals.

I sprawl on the edge of the pool and look around, enchanted, at this fairy-tale place. In moments like this, I feel the need to share my enthusiasm with somebody, but I tell myself to be patient; now is not the time to allow myself a friend.

I rise and arrange the glow-worm on the rucksack so it can recharge itself in the spotlight of sunshine. Then, impulsively, I undress hastily. As I'm about to plunge into the pool, though, I stop as my training urges caution. I pull a chunk of meat I'd brought for a meal from the rucksack and throw it into the water. There is no movement; the lure floats languidly to the bottom of the pool. I wait a bit longer, but still there is nothing. Only silence.

I take a few steps back, then run forward and jump in among the flowers, the move plunging me underwater. The pool is not too deep, only about the height of three phrils, so I reach the bottom quickly and linger, my gills working. The water is warm and crystal-blue; I feel as if I'm in a bath of liquid light. I swim along the bottom, which is even, and formed of bone plates of uniform size.

Something catches my eye and I swim toward it. A skeleton! *So,* I think wryly, *I'm not the first one to discover this cave.* As I draw closer I see that it is phrilic. Beyond it lie more bones, scattered, probably older, the sinews that once held them together long since rotted away. Belatedly I realize, as more bones become distinct, no longer blending with the white bones of the pool's bottom, that the entire pool is a cemetery.

Something bumps into me from behind. I turn, see a swollen corpse bobbing within the tangled flower roots, and panic, gulping water. That one has been dead not more than two weeks, maybe not even a week and half! And suddenly, in a moment of lucidity that overcomes the fear, I see that every plant has its roots wrapped around a body from which it sucked, or is still sucking—

I visualize the red liquid in the flowers' corollas, the red veins in the white petals, and now the water seems deadly; I see roots wriggling greedily toward me, feel something scratch at my skin, and I put my foot down to kick off the bottom plates toward the surface.

I feel the skin on my foot sticking to the bottom of the pool, the plates now burning hot, as if the water is boiling, yet it now feels ice cold on my flesh . . . Panic overworks my lungs and I begin to hallucinate, now resting my cheek on a velvety petal . . . Its down smells of blossoming sequ forests, sweet and harsh, lascivious and old, inebriating, raw, putrid . . .

I burst from the water, wanting to scream, but I haven't the strength. A flower touches me softly. I scramble up the bank then crumple, vomiting. My stomach feels as if it will pump itself right up my throat and out my mouth; my tongue is swollen, and the sick-sweet smell of carrion fills my nostrils. I throw up again, wondering how much more there could possibly be in my stomach to regurgitate.

I fling myself onto my back, then roll away from the pool and clench my nostrils with my fingers to escape the smell. Gods help me, I swam through a carrion soup! I throw up again. I feel as if I'm choking. I breathe in gusts, and I realize with abstract shame that my vulbas are wrinkled with cold and fear, puckered into small, disgraceful rolls of flesh. I squeeze my lungs like they're sponges, pressing them with the backs of my palms, feeling as if they're dirty, tainted, smeared with—

Breath whistling, sobbing uncontrollably, I crawl to my clothes, dressing in whatever comes to hand first. I grab the glow-worm, fix it again to the top of my bone walking-stick, and stride quickly away from the pool, muttering as if possessed, "This is a sign! This is a sign!"

In my subconscious, though, Plabos and his rational lessons are fighting to drain my brain of the soup of fear; I hear his voice very clear in my head and at last I sigh deeply, and only now notice that my body is shaking. My mind now clear, I begin to relax.

I feel very alone. Sometimes it's terrible to be alone.

"How in mother's skin could I have come here alone?" I say. Speaking aloud seems to warm me, so I continue. "Here, everything is upside down: the underworld is above, in Celesthe, and heaven is below, in Burtheste. What can be lower than the places of the favored? I mean, if the upper level is the underworld, what could be lower?"

I'm me again, I think, *I'm back. What in the spheres could've scared me so? I'll think of it when I'm home, but only after a good sleep. And that's it, time to take a break from expeditions!*

ADVICE.   *The ritual is exclusively a male practice. Spiritually, phriliras are unable to transmigrate or, even more importantly, inherit a soul. In this sense, phriliras are hermetic beings, having evolved along a completely different path from phrils. That is why Father Sky has left the Law for his sons: "It is suicidal sacrilege for a phril's soul to transmigrate into a phrilira."*

The ritual is meant to prepare the soul of the phril to die, to enter into the phril who will taste him. It comes from an age older than that of our Holy Royal Carami.

First of all, the Recipe has to be conceived in minute detail, in concordance with the appropriate phril. It has to stir the appetite, first in the soul's heir, then in the prepared one, pushing him into a spiritual self-eating, as it were, that will help him to transmigrate.

Second, the preparations must be performed with the dying phril aware of his evolution only as far as he can bear it, because we cannot allow a soul to go mad before entering his heir. Note, however, that the longer the preparation period, the more efficient the transmigration will be. Finally, it is compulsory that the Tasting take place within the limits of the ritual, the head offered as a gift only after the whole body has been served by the heir.

Feel it fully, and transmigration will be successful! You will be at peace with your brother in your soul!

(*from* The Teachings of the Recipearium Revolution, by Grand Master
Recipear Morminiu)

V. GASTROFEST

The great, living snake of the Gastronomic Festival wove along the main boulevards, stretching almost the entire length of the city and back in a vast circular route. Hundreds of thousands of phrils were on the streets, dancing, laughing, jostling along in the parades. Most of the participants were fat, a great many obese, their bodies jiggling to the rhythm of the music. Most would make the trip more than once, as the various parades would be repeated a few dozen times, at a snail's pace, during the three days of Gastrofest.

And thus the Recipearium slides from fine art to vice, Morminiu thought as he walked among the revellers, trying to keep the mask on his face. *What other art form could turn itself so easily into a vice? One can read as many books as it is possible to read, listen to as much music as one likes, contemplate as many paintings as one can, and none of these will ever have a harmful effect. But the Recipearium contains both good and evil in its essence; it is this that makes it divine. It cannot be good without evil. Any ecstasy is the consequence of suffering.*

He stopped and looked in disgust at the thousands of repulsive, greedy phrils streaming past, their joy and appreciation of the entertainment based on nothing more than getting their free portions. The Festival's brightness, its ideals, were tarnished by this obsessed herd of commoners, by the tons of sticky fat around him, all swaying and undulating, prepared to suffer blindly if suffering in its turn led to the continuation of ecstasy. *This is what happens when the Master Recipear of the Kingdom is an incompetent with a putrid soul. The people lose their ideals and let themselves slide into the mud. We are a sick people,* Morminiu concluded bitterly, and continued on his way.

Banners, coats of arms, and garlands of flowers brought in from the Carami's exterior adorned the streets, and the natural light had been augmented with skin-lanterns containing swarms of glow-worms. Here and there along the route, brightly colored terraces had been installed, their dozens of bone-stump tables and chairs filled by those lucky or determined enough to snatch them up. The musicians sharing the terraces stopped playing only to wolf down some food, otherwise playing to exhaustion. The music was constant during the three days of the Festival, with musicians from all corners of the kingdom working in shifts.

The populace had the Royal House to thank for the

constant supply of food and beverages made available at trifling prices, and the terraces with their non-stop music; even so, there were frequent fights over seating, or the served food. Most didn't get and didn't try to take a seat, but remained standing, dancing, or joined the processions that represented their chosen House.

Each parade entry was preceded by the coat of arms of its House. The Royal House had opened the festivities, the snake's head in the undulating body of participating Houses. Now the Royal House had become only one more link in the continuous chain. The Houses' recipears occupied places of honor in each procession, and directed the preparations of the Courses, much to the people's delight. When a Course was ready, it was served to those who had followed closest to their respective House.

Morminiu managed to reach his own caravan, waiting in a side street. He had been invited by the King himself to participate for House Lormont, alongside the other noble Houses. Neither he nor Leomi could refuse such an invitation, so the Hitissh had dipped into his coffers and provided Morminiu with the money to assemble a bright caravan to proudly carry the Lormont coat of arms. The old noble was more excited about participating than Morminiu. House Lormont had not entered the Festival since his father was alive, when House Lormont was at the peak of its glory, with recipears and hundreds of servitors in its employ.

Morminiu climbed into his place on the central platform, where everything he would need for the Recipes he had designed especially for the Festival was arranged for him and the other two recipears hired to assist him during the event. Hundreds of recipears had presented themselves in answer to the Hitissh's summons, eager to assist a recipear of Morminiu's standing. Morminiu smiled at the memory. Already, his fame had surpassed the Royal Carami's boundaries.

In front of the platform, on a small dais, were the musicians. They, like Morminiu and his two assistants, wore the Lormont colors and the coat of arms. Supplies of foodstuffs for the three days were stored behind the platform on his cart and in the three carts that would accompany it, one on each side and one following; these also served to keep the masses away from Morminiu's cart.

Morminiu drew a deep breath to calm his stomach's nervous trembling, then bowed toward the balcony where Donasa and Leomi sat watching the preparations. The Hitissh's eyes were bright with pride. He had wanted to participate himself, but his deteriorating health would not allow it. Leaning forward so the coach-phrils driving the lead cart in his caravan would hear him, Morminiu shouted the order to proceed.

A moment later, the cart lurched gently as it rolled forward. Exiting the side street, it bumped over the bone curb and moved directly into the carnival atmosphere of the passing parade. The crowd cheered and sang constantly, all around them, the dizzying uproar rippling forward and aft from Morminiu's caravan in waves of sound that burst from the throats of thousands of enthusiastic phrils.

Morminiu had planned his caravan's music step by step for the whole three-day period; now he and his two assistants focused, preparing to synchronize their movements with every change of rhythm, an essential part of the Recipes he had chosen. All were spectacular Recipes, but all contained only simple developments that could be told during their preparation. He knew that for three days he would be more a magician, a juggler relying on special effects, than a real recipear. Even so, he had created new Recipes, using unique combinations of ingredients to make them taste as spectacular as possible. Now was the time to conquer the people!

His caravan paused until the next procession in the parade slowed to make room for it, then entered the river of bodies on the main route. The crowd swirled around them like a river surging around a rock in its midst, and for a moment panic raised the hair on Morminiu's head and wrinkled his skin. The fear passed quickly, however, and Morminiu became caught up in the extravagant show.

His musicians started playing a joyful tune and the phrils around them cheered. Morminiu looked around at the raised hands, the undulating bodies, the upturned faces of phrils searching for pleasure. He remembered Plabos, who had trained him especially for these kinds of events. He'd learned the choreography of Recipearium, practicing some movements for months, until he was able to instinctively guide the movements and progression of the Recipes according to the tunes.

He snatched up a tray, twirled it, at the same time launching a pellet of butter into the air by flipping it from a spoon; at the moment the tray returned to the horizontal, the butter landed in the tray with a moist thud. The audience howled enthusiastically. He smiled, gaining confidence. Spinning around, he placed the tray on the fire and whirled around it, casting a sprinkling of spice toward the fire. When the particles contacted the flames, they burst into a wreath of sparks. The phrils around them went wild.

He signalled to the assistants, who began their work as well, tossing vegetables cut in all sorts of fantastic forms from one side of the preparation table to the other before the tidbits reached the woks prepared for them. Then, together with Morminiu, they started the knives ballet. The trio threw the sharp utensils into the air, caught them, flipped them to their fingertips, and cut vegetables in mid-air, letting the slices land in the bone trenchers below; then they passed the blades between one another and hurled them at targets for a quarter of an hour in a dazzling dance to the rhythm of the music. The performance held the phril audience in a tense, rapt silence, the thousands of eyes following the flashing blades. Then, all at once, they caught and thrust the nine knives they'd been juggling into the bone trenchers with a penetrating thump, accompanied by a dramatic riff from the musicians. The cheering of the crowd was so loud it overwhelmed the music of the processions before and behind Morminiu's, the applause seeming to reverberate from one side of the Carami's body to the other. Their caravan had to stop for a few minutes until the phrils stopped jumping up and down and started to move forward again.

A tear trickled onto Morminiu's cheek and he whispered, "For you, Master." Then he took a deep breath, smiled gratefully at those around him, and resumed the choreography.

This was but the first of three days of intense effort. But if his performances were successful, he knew—in that moment he knew—he could rely on the people's loyalty. Somewhere in the back of his mind, he heard Plabos laughing happily. And from time to time during the rest of the day he heard Plabos' distinctive voice, guiding him. Plabos had been a charismatic manipulator with a deep knowledge of mass psychology. It was reassuring to know that his master was watching with approval.

By nightfall, they were only at the fifth Recipe. They gathered around them the greatest number of phrils a procession could and still keep moving. The distance between them and the processions behind and in front of them had grown considerably, held back by the crowds around Morminiu's. Only their music and the cheers of their audience could be heard. For more than half an hour, their music first calmed, then impregnated imperceptibly the phrils' souls with a lugubrious mood that resonated with the darkness that had settled around them, despite the thousands of glow-worms that flew in bright swarms above, the sight of their numbers against the black night festive and threatening at once.

The preparation was bloody and cruel. A heavy silence had fallen over the audience. This was a truly horrifying story. Morminiu took care to ensure that droplets of blood splattered occasionally on the cheeks and clothes of those watching. Sometimes he even added bone splinters, which drained marrow on the cheek of an unsuspecting spectator, startling him and those around him into releasing shocked shouts. Here and there, sighs and despairing moans rose from the crowd to mingle with the musicians' special acoustic effects.

Suddenly, a great roar of fright rose from the audience. Alarmed, the neighboring processions stopped both their advancement and their music. Morminiu smiled to himself as an unnatural silence seemed to settle over the entire city—in the middle of the Gastrofest, yet! Even Morminiu's assistants had run terrified to the other side of the platform when the huge chunk of meat Morminiu had been chopping rose and transformed into a monster; they watched, just as paralyzed by fear as the audience, as the monster swallowed him.

A shocked, waiting silence fell. Then a new roar broke the silence as Morminiu rose, shaken by invisible hands, his skull crushed in by huge, unseen fangs that left his pink and steaming brains exposed. Cries went up—their idol had been mutilated!

Morminiu rose completely to his feet, climbed onto the preparation table, and thrust a trembling hand toward the bloody mass of brain. The phrils went quiet, their jugular spasms shaking their bodies. He knew what they were thinking: could this somehow be a live Tasting? An auto-Tasting? Something never before dreamed of?

But the recipear displayed a spoon filled with brain matter, which took them by surprise. Without waiting for them to recover, he threw the spoonful to the first row of admirers, who, astonished, caught the pink meat but, for a moment, could only gape at it. Morminiu threw them a second spoonful of brain. The music crept back in, unnoticed, casting further shadows on their souls. They blinked, disoriented.

He noticed a phril pushing his way through the viewers. When the phril reached one of those who had caught the first portion of brain matter, but who had not yet dared to taste it, he snatched it from the phril's hand, stuffed it into his mouth, chewed it a bit, then spat it out, clearly disgusted.

Morminiu froze. His eyes scanned the suddenly quiet crowd. Nobody stretched his hands up for a sampling and the second spoonful had fallen to the bone of the street.

"What is this crap?" The stranger's voice rose above the nervous shifting and the music from the distant processions. He threw down what remained in his hand, his face twisted in revulsion, and shouted at Morminiu, "Do you think you can fool us with your peasant fireworks? Go back where you came from and leave the real recipears to do their job. Imposter!"

Numb with disbelief, Morminiu took off his fake skull full of prepared brain and placed it on the table. Who was this phril? He noticed something emblazoned on the phril's clothing, but it was too dark for him to see, and the device was partially blocked by the crowd.

Scattered boos rose from the silent crowd. Could it be that easy? Could they be so fickle? All day they had sampled and adored his Recipes! Yes, a part of him said; people didn't need proof, they did not have long or accurate memories. All it took was an initial impulse and they could lionize you on the spot, or hate you violently.

Something caught his eye and he looked up, noticed a silhouette in the shadows of a balcony. He stared at the figure until it focused into a noble, smiling happily and waving at him. Morminiu instantly identified him—Taharissh Tathar, the Court's Recipear. So, his rival had done this to him!

Others followed the example of the troublemaker who had boycotted his brains and insulted Morminiu. The crowd began to thin. Morminiu glanced around, saw no supporters in their hard faces, saw nobody there who might defend him. Even his assistants were gone; he was alone, only him and his Courses—about which nobody was curious anymore.

And over it all, he could hear Tathar's triumphant peal of laughter.

Mastering the nervous tremble in his hands, he took off his apron, then concentrated on washing his hands, hiding his dismay—no, panic! It was over for him. He could probably get away alive, he told himself cynically. From the corner of his eye, he watched more and more spectators melting away, moving to the other processions.

"Stop him! He is a fraud!"

Morminiu stopped too, this time shaken by terror. Wasn't it enough for them that they had dishonoured him; now they wanted his head, too? He scanned the remaining spectators and noticed a phril dressed in rich clothes—it was unusual for individuals possessed of the wealth that such clothing implied to walk alone in a crowd.

The well-dressed phril made a show of stopping and studying a blob of the brain that Morminiu had flung a second time into the crowd, then bent and lifted it from the street, and tasted it in front of everyone. Licking his lips expansively, he raised the remainder of the sample above his head and cried, "You are so easily fooled? Are you not even curious enough to taste it yourself? This Course is delicious! I have never tasted anything as good. Morminiu, give them some, let them see for themselves. *Give them some,* Morminiu, don't just stand there!" he urged when Morminiu stood staring.

His two assistants reappeared and immediately thrust spoons into the skull, then moved to pass samples around. In a short time, an appreciative murmur rose from the tasters, and the crowd around the Lormont caravan grew. The instigator had disappeared, but Tathar still stood on the balcony, watching Morminiu. The kingdom's Master Recipear smiled without warmth and drew his finger across his throat. Morminiu instantly knew the significance of that: the war had begun.

The well-dressed phril who had rescued him climbed onto the platform. "I'm Tahmimh," he said to Morminiu. "Harissh Tahmimh. A great admirer of yours."

"I haven't the words to thank you enough, Your Highness," Morminiu said with feeling.

"Just Tahmimh, please. Your friendship would be enough for me."

Morminiu held out his hand. "With the greatest pleasure, my friend."

MORMINIU

The Silence Plaza is the most sensitive area in the city. Formerly the site of a bazaar and popular festivals, it is now a place of utter quiet, where one could only speak in whispers, and running or loud footsteps are banned. The palaces and estates surrounding the plaza have long-since been abandoned, for life under such conditions is impossible. The once lively circle has become a graveyard of the past, the most unpleasant place in the lower city—which makes it the safest place for the social outcasts to conduct business.

I enter the Silence Plaza zone, and then the court itself, shivering with growing excitement. It has been a long time since I've seen such an explosion of vegetation; the area around the checkerboard circle of the plaza is a veritable jungle. Here and there, dwarf palms have erupted through the black, green, and white paving bones. But seeping in from the plaza's outskirts is a brownish-gray slime, the color of porridge. The plants have a carrion aspect and the air smells of putrefaction. I am reminded of a corpse.

As I approach the place where I'm supposed to meet Mahop, I see that the drunkard is already there, and has been there long enough to lie down to wait in comfort. As I wade through the slime toward his island of vegetation, I wonder how anyone can be comfortable here. The air is hot and humid, like that in a greenhouse. Indeed, the palms seem to be thriving, their huge leaves sprouting in dense masses from the thick and knotted trunks that grow more horizontal than vertical—they have no reason to grow upward, not being dependent on sunlight. I recall the peasant name for them: "the plants that feed on shadows." When I once asked why, I was told, "They absorb the forgotten shadows, the ones found over the ground of the dead."

I pass under leaves like skin stretched over bones and arrive at the bower where the stone-bushes grow, in the middle of the plaza. The space is densely packed with the small plants, more pocked and porous monoliths than what one expects of flora. These are the only plant that blossoms in the deep shadows of the Carami—just once, the large flower covering its entire surface, like a swollen disk marked with deep scratches and full of what looks like shiny beads. I have never been a botany enthusiast, so I look at these oddities with the eyes of ignorance.

Curiosity convinces me to touch a leaf. Blech! I withdraw my hand quickly, disgusted, and wipe the thick and stinking sap on my cloak. Only now do I notice the moisture that drips from the vaulted ceiling—but just over the islands of vegetation that have broken the smooth expanse of the plaza. I tell myself that only acid could possibly drip from the cavernous walls of the Carami, but—acid? How, then, do the plants survive? I look closely at the palms around me, see that dozens of seedlings have sprouted at their bases, where the tender young plants are temporarily protected by the foliage of the parent plants—which are already dead, or dying.

After the cacophony and madness of the Gastrofest, the terrible silence here seems surreal. It presses on my spine, makes me want to lie down and sleep, and let the plants steal my shadow, and never wake again. The Festival has left me fatigued, and this silence wraps around my brain, making me drowsy.

I skirt the other areas of vegetation as I draw closer to Mahop, who waves at me. He rises and leans against an isolated stone-bush.

"Hello, Mahop," I whisper when I'm within his range of hearing.

"Hello!" he replies, his tone civil, even obsequious. I suspect that he has noticed during our other meetings that I'm not into foul language, and is tempering his usually colorful speech to accommodate me.

I sit down on the ground next to him and give him the Recipe. He hands me the hunters—small and twinkling insects of a species unknown to me. I ask him where he got them and he laughs as if amused, but he seems nervous—no, anxious, for this is not the nervous behavior someone might display before performing some action, but that of someone who has already done something and cannot bear to keep it to himself. The silence stretches, so I ask him what's new, to make him feel comfortable.

"I discovered something, bigwig. Something that would . . . that if . . . How in the mother's skin can I put it? Something like . . . "

"Like what?" I prompt.

"How much?" he counters, his tone again sure.

This is our relationship—a neverending bargain. I think it over, and I realize that I have already decided what to barter with, had decided even as I entered Silence Plaza. Still, I don't know what urges me to tell him.

"I have some exciting information," I begin. "There is even the possibility of . . . an association, a partnership, if you will."

His eyes shine, but he doesn't try to negotiate. His information burns within him, the need to share it stronger than the need for the poison from Celesthe that he keeps sucking from those butterflies' skulls. "I've discovered something, in the new parts of the Carami," he says. "It is a thing, a phenomenon, that defies any law of nature."

Suddenly I'm alert. I'm not interested in anything else. My educational conditioning whispers, but I keep quiet and let him speak.

"It's like . . . an aura. It's a—how can I describe it?" He pauses in thought. "It is an aura that protects everything inside it from any external aggression." I blink, bewildered, and he grimaces his frustration. "Look, I put a turd inside, in the area within that aura, and seal it. Then, if you were to step on it—you know, like if you enjoy stepping in shit—your foot would slip aside. Don't ask me from what, because it's invisible. The point is, the shit inside remains untouched. Or if you try to hit it with a bone or something—you know, to splatter it," he smiles mischievously, "the aura protects it. It doesn't matter what you try to do, it will protect what's inside; what's inside stays *untouched*."

I'm still looking at him in blank confusion. The silence of the plaza feels heavy around us. "Ugh!" He waves his hand in disgust, realizing I didn't understand a word of what he said.

"It's all right, I'll think about it," I say, hoping to mollify him.

He pulls out his panpipes and holds them to his mouth. I don't immediately react, but when the implication of what he intends to do sinks in, my eyes widen in terror. The plants in the plaza are sticky with dripped acid. But why is it dripping like that, without reason, when there isn't any noise? Not because the protective mechanisms in the plaza are broken and drip unexpectedly, but because this area has become too sensitive, and even the noise of the growing vegetation disturbs it. And if that is the case, how will it react to the whistles of panpipes?

Clarity has come too late—Mahop is playing joyfully, laughter in his eyes. And then I hear the swish of a deluge of acid, and scream as the flood is unleashed.

He lowers the panpipes and laughs, saying, "Come, get under my cover with me!"

"I'll smash your—" I hiss, lunging for him.

He jumps on me at the last second, covering me with his body. Then he puts the pipes to his mouth and resumes playing joyfully.

It rains acid. The plaza's bone pavers sizzle, the stone-bushes liquefy, and I scream, maddened by fear. Then I shut up and close my eyes. And he laughs. Laughs!

The rain stops. It is quiet again. Mahop is still. The bitter taste of vomit rises in my throat. *Why did he do that?*

"What's up, bigwig? You shit your pants?"

I push him off me and scramble back from him on my

elbows. He is alive, whole, untouched.

"Do you get it now?" he asks. "The aura! It's around me!"

I can only gape in terror. Then I calm down as his words penetrate my brain: the aura! It's around him! "Hey—hey—hey, what do you mean?" I babble. "It didn't touch you. You're . . . "

"Whole? Alive? Yes. Nothing happened to me."

"All right," I concede, then squint at him. "So where is it?"

"I told you—around me. On me."

"Where? I can't see it."

"*I told you*—it's invisible. If you touch it slowly, and if you don't have the same properties as acid," he laughs at his little joke, "then it doesn't react. You just can't see it or feel it."

"That's impossible," I snap. "Now really, what *is* it?" I press.

"A Carami defence mechanism against various attacks, I assume," he replies, his tone conversational. "Against bone butterflies, for instance."

"A Carami product—phenomenal! How did you discover it?"

He shrugs. "That's it, big boy. That's all the information I have to give you." He leans toward me, implying confidentiality, though no one is around. "We still don't know everything. We're still researching."

I keep quiet and chew over the ideas he has implanted in my mind. There are even more questions. I choose the easiest one: "Who is we?"

"None of your business."

The calm reply leaves me open-mouthed. I deserved that if I'm an idiot, but— As I prepare an indignant response, he blurts, "The payment, bigwig. I want my payment. Tell me."

I think feverishly. Should I tell him? Who is 'we'? Should I get mixed up with them?

"Hellooo, anybody there?" Mahop drawls impatiently.

"All right. The information is that I go outside. And my

proposal is, you can come with me if you want."

He laughs. I don't know why.

"Come on, get down to business," he says.

"I admit it is not of the same calibre as your information, but how could I have known what you had? You agreed to it," I remind him.

"All right, wait. Wait a second. You really mean it? You really go outside? Why's that, have you been exiled?"

"No. I just go on my own. On little expeditions," I add with an important air. He's confused and looks at me askance. "Tell me," I say. "Do you want to come?"

"I don't know," he says slowly.

"What's the problem? It's just a walk. You do that frequently."

"We have never gone out," he admits. "We are afraid of the exterior, like everybody else."

I release a disbelieving chuckle. "Then who cleans the cupola? The phrils from the lower city say you do."

"It isn't us. On mother's vulbas, I don't know who's doing it, or even if it's a somebody doing it."

"Aren't you the people who never adapted fully to the city atmosphere? Isn't that why you've stayed closer to the light that filters inside? So what's the problem? Come outside, into the daylight."

He doesn't say anything. Then he smiles broadly and says with false heartiness, "Mother's skin, let's go outside, Morminiu! When are we going?"

"Let's meet in three hours at the West Mouth."

"Deal. The West Mouth."

⁂

As I expected, he hasn't shown up. And I'm telling myself that these unadapted phrils have a problem for sure, but it's not life on the Carami's outer level.

SIDE RECIPE: RIMSHI PICKLES

When preparing pickles or salads, we must keep in mind that firstly, their role is to stimulate and emphasize the gastric reactions, to provide a new perspective to the Course, and complete the spasm palette. Therefore, for the rimshi pickles, we need the following.

INGREDIENTS:

RIMSHI – blindworms from the shore of the subterranean lakes.

RED ALGAE – found only on the water pouches from the inferior zone of the Carami.

MUCUS OF CARAMI – collected from the subterranean fleshy zones.

WATER – from the depths of the lakes.

PREPARATION STORY:

Store the rimshi, together with the soil from which they have been gathered, in a bone box, the walls of which have been lined with red algae. Close the top of the box, which must at all costs have holes in it for ventilation—not for the rimshi, because they are insensitive beings, but for attaining the result described in the Recipe—and immerse the box in warm mucus of Carami. Leave the box there for at least a week, but no more than two weeks.

After the appropriate period has passed, extract the box and open it. Of course your senses will be hit immediately by the overwhelming but inviting reek of dead rimshi, fermented in their own juices and now encased in a greenish slime. No matter how enticing they will now appear, you must not serve them at this stage.

Pour the contents of the box into a sieve and pick the rimshi from the soil. Discard the soil. At the bottom of the box you will notice a thick layer of small, plump, whitish worms—grasela. Do not be influenced by the name; the reality surpasses any fantasy.

No matter what opinion you may have, crush the grasela through the sieve to extract the juice from the skin. Mix the resulting whitish liquid with the water from the subterranean lakes. The combination will instantly produce a reaction that creates an effervescent effect.

Wash the rimshi picked from the soil and combine them with the grasela's juice in a jar. Seal the jar and allow the contents to ferment for a month. During this time you will notice that the liquid becomes murky, and that thick fibres have grown from the rimshi's bodies; these have a sweetish taste.

Add pieces of bitterish wood and tsetser bark to taste and allow to ferment one more week. The pickles are best served with hot gourmet meals.

(from The Teachings of the Recipearium Revolution by Grand Master Recipear of the Green Kingdom, Morminiu)

VI. DEATH TALE

"This was the Death Tale of the great Hitissh Leomi," Morminiu finished in a grave voice, his eyes fixed on the nobles gathered to celebrate the important event. The music faded as he finished speaking.

It had been a long time since a phril had last been afforded such a ceremony; in more glorious times, a gastronomic festivity had taken place at least once a month.

The last phrase had been repeated, broadcast from the balcony, to the mass of phrils gathered on the streets that ran alongside the Royal Palace—the fanatic admirers who had been following Morminiu's every move since the Gastrofest. After a few moments of respectful silence for the dead, they burst into applause and shouted accolades.

Hearing the reaction on the street, the King smiled and nodded silent approval, and the anxious courtiers felt free to show their own enthusiasm. The Recipear watched them, wearing a smug smile of victory. All the great Houses were participating, and he knew it wasn't because of the title and the importance of the Hitissh Leomi, but because of his—Morminiu's—fame. In subsequent days he would probably receive countless requests for mortuary Recipes—the court was full of old phrils with one foot in the grave.

The nobles, dressed lavishly in their finest silks brought from the Fever Swamps and garnished with heirloom jewels, shifted restlessly. The servitors entered, dozens of them, bringing platters piled with exquisite food. The court bustled with a pomp and polish that had not been seen since the practice of Recipearium in Plabos' time.

The Hitissh began to shiver. He clenched his jaw, making an effort to stay upright, but the strength was leaving him. His teeth started to chatter, and his hair hung damp with sweat. Morminiu knew what was happening. Most phrils, at this moment before the most important event in their life, realized only during the Death Tale the terrible thing that was going to happen to them. And, despite everything they had learned, they couldn't overcome their fear.

The audience did not pay any attention to him, did not think less of him for revealing his fear or sympathize with his embarrassment; they thought of him as already dead, and celebrated his memory, not his presence. Only Morminiu stared at him for a few intense moments, then rose. He was the only one who knew that fear was not the cause of the old noble's reaction; it was the tea—or more accurately, symptoms of withdrawal from it. Leomi had not had any that morning because Morminiu had told him it would spoil the Recipe.

❖❖❖❖❖❖❖❖❖

Tathar, the Master Recipear of the Court, remained seated in his armchair, ignoring the joy and greedy anticipation around him. His fist clenched the pommel of his sword and his eyes were shut. After Plabos' banishment, there had remained just one candidate for the position—Scanthum, the master's only student. A child—a talented child, but a child nonetheless. The King, his chief counsellor the King's Trust, and several advisors had hotly argued the wisdom of giving the position to a child. There were dark aspects in the Recipearium, as well as highly spiritual ones, and to expect a child to fully understand their significance, let alone apply them, seemed too much to ask.

There were other possible successors, two of whom were practicing in provincial courts; they had quickly travelled to the Royal Carami in hope of a competition for the position that would allow them to prove their skills. Another two were found at the royal court, at the Table of the Six: an old Recipear who was bright in his own way, but who always found himself in second place, burning with frustration in the shadow of the giants; and Tathar, young at that time, labelled as mediocre by Plabos and therefore ignored by the King. These were the alternatives to placing Scanthum on the High Chair of Master Recipear of the Green Kingdom. Possessed of the same creativity, the same pomp, the same exotic flair as his tutor, Scanthum had presented the best option. With only one concern: his youth.

The King's Trust, in his wisdom, had proposed a compromise—a guardianship of sorts. One of the four adults would hold the position of Protector Recipear until Scanthum reached adulthood himself.

The two provincial masters never made it to the capital city. After a long time the remains of one were found in the Southern Swamps; the other's body was found in the mountains. Their deaths remained a mystery. A few days after their disappearance, the old court Recipear withdrew his candidature without explanation. Under no circumstances could he be persuaded to reconsider, and he left the royal court a short time later, retreating to one of the provincial courts.

Forced to the decision by circumstances, the King and his counsellors designated the least probable nominee, Tathar, as Protector Recipear. The child Scanthum had grown fond of him anyway, and thus things could quickly return to normal. Nobody could have forgotten Plabos, but the Green Kingdom Court had succeeded in maintaining the status quo.

A year later Scanthum was found dead in the gardens of the Royal Palace; he had choked to death on a fish bone. This unhappy accident put Tathar in the much longed-for position of Master Recipear of the Kingdom.

He could still remember the child's eyes, bulging with terror, when the fish bone had been inserted in his throat in something akin to a very delicate surgical operation. The youngster had writhed in agony for a very long time, but he could not make a sound.

Tathar smiled and opened his eyes. The Master Plabos' shadow was threatening the position he had worked so hard to obtain two decades ago. As impetuous as their master, Plabos' disciples, though geniuses in the art of Recipearium, proved lacking in political sense when they crossed into his territory. He would take care of this one. With that thought, he turned his eyes, now seemingly gentle and magnanimous, toward Morminiu.

✦❈✦❈✦❈✦❈✦

The King's Trust, a massive phril who looked more warrior than advisor, approached Morminiu with a courteous smile. "His Majesty invites you, illustrious Master, for a meeting to exchange Recipes," he whispered. "He is sure you will be interested in new experiences."

"Tell His Majesty that I'm honored, and convinced that the royal experience will enrich and enlighten my spirit. As a matter of fact, I had in mind to reserve for His Grace a whole chapter in my book."

"Oh!" the Trust exclaimed, impressed, then quickly continued in a lower voice, "Tomorrow evening, then, my carriers will convey you to the palace."

Morminiu bowed respectfully, trying to temper his emotions. The future was bright indeed, and approaching at full speed.

❖❖❖❖❖❖❖❖❖❖

When they entered the palace and the door shut behind them, the raucous street noises now muffled by the thick old walls, they breathed their relief. The Hitissh had held up well until that moment; now he collapsed to the shiny floor, exhausted.

"Take him to the Ritual Room," Morminiu directed the new house servant before hurrying to his quarters.

He locked the door behind him and quickly started to undress. The long-awaited moment was getting closer. Emotion overwhelmed him as he draped the cloak of the Master Recipear of House Lormont over his shoulders. Made especially for this event, the dark blue algae fabric had been hand-stitched with green silk thread. On its back was embroidered, also with green silk, the symbol of House Lormont: a snake coiled on a sword with the motto *Cunning Enforces Bravery*. The C and the B were entwined around an L in the ancient written language—L for Lormont.

"Bravery drowned by Corruption," Morminiu mistranslated disdainfully, his hand tracing the embroidered sword's hilt. "I have inherited the name Lormont, but I swear to found a new House, one worthy of all respect, a House that will rise from the ruin and the shame of the Lormonts. It will be House Mormont, and thus I will not upset the overly conservative spirits," he added, smiling his delight.

He opened the fake memoric store, spat, and watched the processing unit emerge from its hiding place. The alarm was untouched, but the cage was still sparking in the aftermath of attack. The five fulguses were visibly irritated and writhing in a manner understood only by their kind.

He connected the vorb to his terminal lobe and dialed the net code to access the main unit, then examined the data pertaining to this latest attack. The infiltrators were still in the area, waiting for the branch-circuit to be unlocked by the Carami's immune system before they were detected by the royal hunters. Time to personally intervene, Morminiu decided.

Withdrawing from their place of concealment the little bugs he'd bought from Mahop, the stealthy hunters processed in Celesthe, he first programmed them to protect his own unit, then to lock onto the traces left by the would-be thieves and track them down. That should end once and for all any attempts to hack into his memoric store.

Relaxed in that knowledge, Morminiu disconnected the vorb and sent the unit back behind the camouflage of the fake store. Then he donned his cloak, unlocked the door, and left the room.

And encountered Donasa.

"Bastard!" she hissed when she saw him. "You mocked him. Traitor!"

The words, though spouted hatefully, also revealed that the phrilira was at the end of her strength. Morminiu studied her carefully, noticed the tension that had accumulated under her eyes during months of abstinence, months when the Green of the Gods had robbed her of the ability to satisfy her vice. Now that the God's Green tea had definitively stolen her lover, Donasa could endure no more. The Recipear started to understand some of the things that had seemed inexplicable before.

"Was it so good, with the old phril?" He could not hold back the question.

"How dare you?" she shrieked. "Scoundrel!" She tried to slap him, but Morminiu caught her hands and squeezed them in his.

"I will denounce you! I'll fix you . . . " Her struggling

grew weaker and less willful, while Morminiu squeezed tighter. Finally she slumped and slid with lost eyes to the floor. Morminiu, still clutching her hands, landed on top of her.

The wing of the palace where Morminiu's quarters were located remained uninhabited and unrefurbished. A thick layer of slime covered the vents. The walls had not been polished, scraped, or guided in their growth in decades, so they had thickened unchecked and uncontrolled, now occupying almost half of the corridor's width, their stalactite-like protrusions sculpted by the palace's sweat running over the brittle bone layer casting eerie shadows. The air was cold, damp, and cloying, adding to the atmosphere of isolation and abandonment. Morminiu preferred it that way.

"Why did you betray Plabos?" he asked hoarsely, feeling the violent vibration of Donasa's vulbas under his body.

"I didn't betray him!"

Morminiu ignored her denial. "Was it because he wasn't as vicious as you? Why didn't you tell him the truth?"

"I didn't betray him," she muttered, her trembling becoming more pronounced. "And he was almost impotent," she added. "I would've gone mad next to him."

"And the old Hitissh?"

"Leomi? Leo is something else. He is a true force. You have no idea what powers lie hidden in that weakened body." Her voice grew vehement again. "But it wasn't me who betrayed Plabos."

Morminiu tore aside her veil to discover her vulbas already open and trembling. The wanton plateau stretching from her nervous belt to between her legs rippled eagerly, her body writhing in a lost battle with her instincts as much as with him. The Recipear felt an excitement he'd never before experienced—not pleasure; more a desire to possess. Tossing aside his cloak, he bounced as if in battle, his spikes erect. They pinned her savagely to the floor, until the moment when their vulbas joined.

Her body felt cold with fear, yet he saw in her eyes

frenzied excitement. A moment later he turned tyrant, giving in to a pure, physical, devouring pleasure—to cruelty. He tossed about, pulling her with him and making her groan in pain—until she fainted, and they lay there, covered in bruises and slime.

He thought of what had just happened, of his possession by Plabos. In the middle of the lovemaking, he'd known it was more than mere possession, something far from a soul revisiting his love for a phrilira through the vessel of his protégé. He'd felt all of Plabos' sexual anxiety, his frustration, and the impotence he'd hidden behind his art, all bursting out through Morminiu's artificially induced potency, through, in fact, a double possession.

With this new insight, Morminiu was suddenly ashamed by Plabos' famous Recipes—the Wanton Plateau, the Spiky Plateau, the Vulbian Chill, to name but three—all worshiped in ignorance by his Master's admirers and tasted with feigned bashfulness by the courtiers at almost every party. Now he truly understood. How many great works of art— not just Recipes—actually hid obsessions, frustrations, and anxieties, all admirably masked by the label of art, or science? How much of the recorded story of Plabos was actually true? How truly great was the Great Recipear, and how much of him was really worth remembering?

Morminiu concentrated on stilling his trembling. The shadows on the neglected walls around them seemed to be reliving forgotten times, scenes of long-past fornications waving across the walls; the palace itself seemed to groan as if aroused by the touch of their bodies. Despair became a palpable weight on his body and he started to cry, begging Donasa for forgiveness. But Donasa was still unconscious.

He started violently when he heard footsteps approaching.

"Master . . . " a tentative voice called. It belonged to Totin, the new house servant.

"Stay there; wait in the other corridor," Morminiu

barked, revolted by the thought of anyone seeing him this way.

He anxiously awaited the decoupling, and when it came, he rose and drew a deep breath, turning his back on the body lying on the floor. He entered his room and cleaned himself quickly, then dressed in fresh clothes. Swinging his cloak back over his shoulders, he called hoarsely, "Totin."

"Yes, master?" The servant appeared, stepping timidly from behind the supporting columns at the corridor's end.

Morminiu nodded toward Donasa. "Take her into one of the rooms nearby and tie her up—I want no possibility of escape," he warned. "Then put the brops in the interior courtyard, below the windows that open on the courtyard from the Ritual Room. Lock them in there. After that, send the cook and the gardener to their quarters."

Without a word, Totin bent over Donasa. He drew her veil over her body and lifted her gently into his arms, then carried her down the corridor toward one of the vacant rooms.

His footsteps heavy, Morminiu entered the Ritual Room and closed the door behind him. Now he could no longer hear the rumble of excited murmurs from the crowd waiting on a side street adjacent to the palace.

Hitissh Leomi had seated himself on a couch-horn that radiated heat into his aged body. When he heard Morminiu's entrance, he turned and watched him closely. "It took you a long time," he said.

"I beg forgiveness, My Lord, but at certain moments my preparation is even more difficult than yours. As a matter of fact, you will suffer only a change of corporeality, while I . . ."

"All right, boy, I understand." The old phril sighed. "Do as you think best, but . . . it's getting harder for me . . ." He stopped and breathed in with difficulty, then sobbed,

"I miss the tea."

Morminiu bowed and began the preparations. He lit the fire in the huge hearth and placed the grill above it. The handful of dry, aromatic woods he threw on the flames burst into glittering sparks, spreading the scents of rotting swamp vegetation and decomposing corpses throughout the room.

Moving to the table grown from the floor bone and carved over three generations with the portraits, the mortuary Recipes, and the names of all the nobles of House Lormont, Morminiu unfurled a seqolosal leaf like a green eiderdown over its surface. He lubricated it well with liquid sugar and sequ-tulapa-fragranced oil, spreading the mixture with a wide, thick brush. His movements were rhythmic, as if he were in a trance, his gestures ritualized and balanced between sober and ridiculous.

Putting the brush aside, Morminiu wiped his hands, then chose the plumpest, most muscular crawling lianas and measured them before cutting them carefully on the diagonal. He stirred the coals, adjusted the grill to ensure an even temperature, and turned solemnly toward the Hitissh.

Leomi offered what he no doubt considered a careless smile, though to Morminiu it looked tortured. The old phril rose, trembling, and took a step, then he bent suddenly, mouth agape, his gill slits working spasmodically several times. Recovering, he straightened and began undressing, his breath whistling through his mouth, his lungs heaving. Morminiu turned his eyes away from the naked phril, from the fat layers hanging in vulgar display, the monstrously thickened vulbas.

Leomi jerked sharply, his teeth clenching so violently Morminiu heard them crack. Saliva dripped from his mouth when he opened it to say, "I didn't eat . . . as you told me."

"That's very good, My Lord," Morminiu said. "You've done what the Ritual requires." He stepped out of the old phril's way, waiting in an attitude of respect as Leomi used the last of his strength to totter over to the table. The Hitissh collapsed beside it, exhausted. The hair on his head hung limp and gray with dampness.

Now the Recipear had the right to approach and help the old phril climb onto the table. With gentle hands, he arranged the noble on the huge seqolosal leaf, then wrapped it around his body, leaving only his head exposed. He bound the leaf around Leomi's body with lianas, winding up each leg and out to each hand. When he was done, Morminiu straightened. "Your Highness, there is a limit . . . "

"I know, Morminiu; just do what it takes—I know my part." He paused before chanting, "Heavenly Beings, may you help us pass the threshold, and may the Ritual be received."

Straining, Morminiu lifted Leomi in his arms and set him carefully on the oiled grill, now glowing a dull red. Protected by the seqolosal leaf, Leomi showed no discomfort. The leaf started to singe, then it swelled until its external layer burst. White smoke wound slowly toward the ceiling. When the tendrils of white smoke grew denser, Morminiu turned the bundle containing Leomi, so the other side would roast while he sprinkled the singed upper surface with swamp wine and a spice made from ground brown butterfly wings.

Leomi's reddened face glistened with sweat. Yet his teeth chattered, clattering like a bucket of broken bones. He was face down, looking straight into the flames, watching how they ate into the leaf, slowly but surely advancing toward his body which, so far, was just simmering in the hot oil brushed on the leaf.

Morminiu again turned the leaf-wrapped Hitissh on the grill, and now the skin on his cheeks were burned, crusty, and split, as blood dripped from his mouth. The visible portions of his body were puffed out, forming sacks along his ears and neck as his lungs swelled.

"Now, Morminiu," Leomi said clearly, mastering the pain.

The Recipear blinked, admiring the phril's endurance. He stepped closer, watching the old phril closely.

"I said *now*, Morminiu," Leomi said louder.

"Immediately, My Lord." Morminiu moved even closer, leaning forward so Leomi could see him. "But first, I have a message for you."

Leomi's eyes bulged in surprise. He gasped, as if he were losing his strength of will under the pressure of the heat. His breathing came heavier, more labored as it passed through his split and bloody lungs.

"First, I want you to know that Plabos is here with us," Morminiu said through clenched teeth. "Therefore, to perform the Ritual, we must have his consent as well—and he doesn't consent. He will not, after your betrayal. He thinks that you, together with the Master Recipear Tathar and Donasa, plotted against him, to defame him and have him banished from court. I believe that there is somebody else behind this plot, somebody important, and that Your Lordship played only a minor role. But Plabos is not in the mood to forgive you. I am truly sorry, but I have a holy duty toward my master, even if I don't always agree with his conclusions."

He waited for a few seconds, watching Leomi writhing in pain, then he concluded, his voice calm, "Plabos has remained convinced of your guilt after the mocking letters sent by the actual Master Recipear of the Court, Tathar. Now I, Morminiu, considering Plabos' revenge sufficient, will take away the pain of the Ritual. But I don't intend to serve you, Hitissh. You will have no place in my soul. Your wonderful Recipe will be served to your beloved brop-hounds, and I will remain only with Plabos' soul. Goodbye!"

He lifted the sword he held and brought it swiftly down, severing Leomi's head from his body. It rolled to the wall and stopped, the mouth stretched open in terror, its wide eyes staring toward Morminiu.

Morminiu stumbled to the couch and sat down to recover. He had discharged his duty; his master had been avenged. From now on he was free, completely free. From now on, he alone would decide the course of his life.

Working quickly, he cooked Leomi's head as the

Ritual required, muttering continuous prayers to be forgiven for his deed. While he waited for the head to cool, he lifted the body from the grill and hung it on the pulley just outside the window, mounted there especially for this moment. He lowered the body slowly into the courtyard and tied it off within reach of the brops penned inside so they could devour it. Then he placed the cooked head on a tray and carried it from the room. He stepped out onto one of the side balconies and held up the tray. The crowd waiting in the street below burst into cheers.

"Good rising to the new Hitissh!" they chanted. "May he be at peace in his soul with his brother!"

Morminiu waited for the cheers to die down. Then he said, "The Recipe went straight to my soul. The tale has been told, and Death has been delivered. I'm fed now, and a new spirit haunts me, at the moment striving to find his balance. May Leomi enjoy my experiences, as I enjoy his presence. And this," Morminiu finished in a lower voice, "this is my gift."

He threw the head into the sea of lifted hands, and then he withdrew.

He shouted for Totin. The servant appeared immediately. "Totin, I denounced Donasa to the Perpetuation Guild. The priestesses should be here any minute now. Give them all the assistance they require. I have an urgent problem to resolve. And get rid of those brops," he added.

"Yes, My Lord."

Morminiu hurried back to his quarters in the abandoned wing of the palace, anxious to follow the progress of the hunters he'd obtained from Mahop.

PLABOS

When I'm troubled, I fly through Darkness. Saying that I fly is not quite accurate. In fact, I throw myself upon it and float. Sometimes I float for a long time, stopping only when I tire of it. I never move in the true sense of the word, though my actions are practically unlimited. When I don't want anymore constraints, I fly. I have no aim, no landmarks, no departure point or arrival.

Different again are those times when I dive into the subconscious. There are places there where known and unknown mingle. They are generations old and hidden to the waking mind, and nobody knows what obscure reasons, or new things, have arrived since last time. Yet all of them are connected to the external reality. They are existences. Not thought, not feelings, not even an idea; they are not connected to possibility or imagination, or who knows what. The art . . . the Recipes, for instance, arrive here as stony realities. They fall pure and simple, stirring up dust, and settle on the bottom. They are the foulest and heaviest things, the works of art. In time, to make room for the new, they become lighter and start mingling too.

There is also a barrier. On the other side, like carmine smoke, is a thick, obscuring fog that hides . . . the forbidden zone! Every time I try to pass beyond the barrier I awake still here, my back to the barrier as if I've just escaped it. I'm tortured by the stupid curiosity of mortals—even without knowing whether anything is here, I want to know what is there.

In fact, there is no curiosity, there is no carmine fog, there are no heavy things and light things mingling, no barrier; everything is something else. I mean, they look as if they are something recognizable, but they're something else. They look different. They look . . . !

The first time they, the others, appeared, I was

afraid—if that was fear. In Upwards, in the utter Darkness, in the place-of-practically-unlimited-action, a meeting area was created, where the darkness inside me and inside the one that dwells inside me, and the ones that dwell inside the one that dwells inside me—everyone in my existence—merged, and everything was one. I felt as if my ego were slashed apart and blended into a giant ball of souls, and I panicked. There they were, the ones residing in me, entire generations, led by the last entrant—my master.

I remember his mortuary Recipe; I didn't like it at all and I barely finished it. Plus, he was old, his flesh tough. But afterward, we went together very well; his presence made me happy. His was a gentle soul, one I always thought of as akin to that of a phrilira.

Their visits are known only to me. They are very vague, more a knowing than a definite feeling. They come from another other side, after all, wherever that is. I'm afraid to follow them—I'm still connected to the outside world.

There is a boy, Morminiu, whom I need to help. Now we are two souls in one body. It's a pity I can't cross the barrier. Maybe on the other side, where his thoughts are born, I could be there for him in hard times, act as mediator. I'm still not sure what I want more—for him to succeed, or to avenge me. I mean, I invested almost two decades in his education . . . But what else could I have done? The highest level of success is when one transfers one's logic and intellect, one's emotions and accomplishments, into his heir. Or so I thought. I wish I could free him from my revenge, but I don't know . . .

Plabos is my name and I'm not afraid of you!

They think to beat my vulbas with rods, that they might be aroused at last. The flocks giggle in the Darkness. But I have no vulbas, not anymore. Plabos is my name and I'm not afraid of you!

I saw her through his eyes, standing next to the traitor, and I went crazy. I mistook ... I was mistaken in grooming the boy to go into that damned place. Since then I've seen her again, in the Darkness, flying here and there, when I don't expect it—flocks of Donasas. They are not truly flocks of Donasas, but I have no other name for them.

I refrain with difficulty from doing anything stupid, anything that would compromise Morminiu. I'm proud of him—he's a cunning and wise young phril, very animated. I don't know anymore what this is, but I remember the meaning, the comparison, the essence . . . Sometimes I feel pity for him, for I torment him with shameful urges, and I have burdened him with my problems.

Flocks of Donasas giggle and cane me with rods where my vulbas should be, hoping to be aroused at last. Plabos is my name and I'm not afraid of you. Damn you to Sathali!

I have discovered something interesting, in the subconscious, when flying very high, up where the air is thin, almost gone. I tell myself that I have to start my research from the top and work downward, so I will not miss any useful information. Useful? The kid's system is still influencing me.

I have discovered that Morminiu is of royal lineage, on the maternal side. This explains his more developed gills, his taller stature and reddish skin.

Almost a millennium ago, Chathron the Conqueror invaded the Royal Carami with his army, defeating the inhabitants, the red-headed phrils, and either banished them from the city or enslaving them. The red-headed phrils had been the first inhabitants of the Carami when the monster was still full of water. Chathron was the first Green King. The red-headed phrils not enslaved fled to the farthest reaches of the swamps, where they mingled and intermarried with the people of the invading army.

From the upper limits I have learned that Morminiu is the direct descendant of Bartrabar, the king of the red-headed phrils who was beheaded as punishment for opposing Chathron. For the history of his family since that time, I have to research the levels in the Darkness in descending order.

Where does life take you, Morminiu? Even as late as yesterday—yesterday?—his system still influenced me. Morminiu has been introduced to the royal court. The two direct descendants of the two ancient foes have been brought face to face. One old, impotent, and barren, the other young, arrogant, a rising star. And neither one knows it!

⚜ ⚜ ⚜ ⚜ ⚜ ⚜ ⚜

When I'm troubled I fly through Darkness and I see her through his eyes. But now the Darkness is deeper, thicker—it enters my mouth and chokes me. I'm growing, getting larger; I try to float, but my body struggles. Body? Not my body, but two big vulbas. I am two big, thick vulbas—immense, gigantic, huge, immeasurable—that barely conceal a spike field, a monstrous spike field; monstrous in its virility and fury.

I am a spike field as large as a city, full of towers and palaces with dented roofs, seething with fauna, awaiting the flock of Donasas. Now Plabos' vulbas cannot be caned anymore, because there are no rods huge enough. Now Plabos will pierce you, will rip you, will tear you . . . Look there—Donasas!

I prey upon them; I hear their groans. Another flock comes and again I hear the groans. And another flock comes . . .

The Darkness is at its highest. I have no more reasons to go downward; the subconscious is Morminiu's, not mine, and I will not poke my nose into somebody else's affairs.

The Darkness is higher than it has . . . ever been? When did all these limits start? And what does—*when* does—

it mean?

I have no meaning here. My Soul Brothers call me from the other side. I'm not interested anymore in revenge, but I don't have the strength to make myself heard to Morminiu. My brothers called me . . . call me . . . And yet, if it was not just Leomi and Donasa, who conspired with them? I cannot believe that Comtap would lift a hand against me.

I think I will cross over to the other side, but I will come back to see how my protégé is doing. I feel content; I have made peace with myself—myself?—the one I was . . . The Darkness was . . . is higher than ever, and I have to climb up to . . . what does "up to" mean?

Plabos, self-consciousness

ADVICE. *The fundamental difference between a phril and a phrilira is not of gender, as it is considered lately, but indeed, it is as our ancestors said: the difference is gastrophilic. The phriliras lack the gastrophiza, the paired lobes that hang on either side of the pleasure center, just above the neck. During the last centuries the gastrophiza has partially replaced the pleasure center, taking over some of its functions. That is why pleasure is differently perceived and understood by phrils and phriliras.*
Lacking the gastrophiza, phriliras have nothing that can be activated by a Course's stimuli. These stimuli act upon some organs (the salivary gland, for instance) at the primary level, without creating the cascade of emotional states experienced by a phril that end in gastric orgasm. Thus the eating process has been and remains a simple physiological necessity for phriliras, an experience that is impossible to translate to a spiritual level.

(from The Teachings of the Recipearium Revolution by Grand Master
Recipear of the Green Kingdom, Morminiu)

VII. THE BLACK VISIT

The return to the subterranean ponds, last vestiges of the great lake that one thousand years ago covered three-quarters of the Royal Carami, meant travelling a road walked hundreds of times before. The route signs affixed to the pipes and tunnels were difficult to maintain, usually needing replacement monthly because the directions printed in the ink of phosphorescent lichens were, slowly but surely, eaten away by the thick slime that crawled blindly over the bone at these levels.

Morminiu entered the last and widest tunnel, where he succeeded in affixing some glow-worms to the walls, encasing them within protective bone guards. He stretched conductor nerves obtained in trade for a Recipe from Mahop to them, thus ensuring that they would function permanently.

He even asked the black marketeer where he might extract the nerves himself, but Mahop answered with a derisive laugh. The unadapted were certainly a force to be reckoned with.

In the tunnel's stronger light, he could observe the Carami's skeletal structure, always aware that this small section did not represent the whole, but rather a specific zone. The walls were formed by thousands of thin bones connected by dense cartilage, looking like a fence of deformed and bent poles held together with mud. Arteries as thick as his arm or bigger snaked through the wall, pulsing without rhythm under the elastic skin. Here and there muscles bulged, free of the dripping slime due to their continuous expansion and contraction. In other places, bone spoiled the geometry of the wall by curving without visible reason over the point where wall met mud-colored muscular surface. Some of these bones had been broken, by what, Morminiu did not know. Through the gaps he saw that the marrow had settled into masses that pulsated under the pressure of some internal force.

He stumbled and barely kept his footing, his lips parting in surprise. He breathed deeply, overcoming the brief moment of panic, then fell still, listening. Had it been his imagination, or had he truly heard a strange sound? His gills, folded over his lungs, hung limply on either side of his head.

He could hear something, but what held him still was that he was also seeing something: a breach in the wall to his right—an entrance, or a large opening, anyway, protected by a flesh curtain. It was not an illusion, but he was certain that it had not been there before. He jerked back, both excited and disgusted, though it was not the delicious disgust so appealing to the gastrophiza, but horrified disgust. The curtain looked like a vagit—or, more precisely, like a wanton plateau missing its vulbas.

The hair on his head rose and fell in time to the waves of fear and curiosity coursing through him. The horn plates on his shoulders finally glided over his stomach and his digestive system, their pressure dissipating some of the nausea stirring up his bowels. He spat bitter saliva, then drew his sword and took a step toward the entrance, cursing the education that always urged him to research rather than run.

He pushed aside the fleshy curtain with the tip of his sword, unwilling to touch it, and entered cautiously. He froze on the threshold, prey to new waves of horror. The room beyond was bathed in a reddish light that made the raw flesh of the walls look as though they were streaming with blood. On the wall directly across from him, a phrilira hung suspended, her vulbas open to their limits—beyond their limits: open from her neck to the area between the legs splayed on the wall, as if her wanton plateau was in a grotesque coupling with an oversized spike field growing directly from the Carami.

The phrilira's body was relaxed, her white skin stretched smooth across her back, softer than silk. Her lithe legs were buried to her ankles in slime. A swollen vein wound from her groin up to her armpit, where it circled her arm several times. The walls themselves groaned, heavily; in the background Morminiu heard a sound like liquid bubbling from an immense wound. The phrilira slowly contorted, clearly trying to turn her head.

Panting, his hair damp with sweat, Morminiu sprang backward, pushing through the fleshy curtain, which seemed to cling to him like a warm, moist tongue. He stumbled free and ran toward the end of the tunnel, his emotions oscillating between horror and relief that he'd had the presence of mind to affix glow-worms to the walls for precious, precious, light.

Scrambling up the ladder made of smooth, gnarled bones, he flung himself through the trapdoor at the top, rolling onto the floor of the palace before turning to bang the trapdoor shut. He sat on top of it, his breathing harsh and rapid, and looked around at the gloomy abandoned wing he called home, with its bulging walls and the light, the weak, greenish, blessed, light that filtered through the dirty vents.

He blinked, bewildered, his relief so palpable he thought he would vomit, and rose. Only then did he notice that he still clutched his sword and the rucksack he habitually carried. Tottering on trembling legs, he moved toward his quarters, unlocked the door clumsily, and entered. He crossed to the fake memoric store and removed it, but his mouth was so dry that it took him several tries to find enough saliva to spit on the identification membrane.

At last the processing unit emerged. He caught the functioning fulgus and connected it to his terminal lobe, then concentrated, striving to record everything he had seen, heard, smelled, and touched while his impressions were still fresh, unaltered by subjectivity. He would analyze what had happened later, when he was ready to face this discovery.

His mental voice, which in time had taken on the cadences of Plabos' voice, warned him that every being had its secrets, and the more complex the being, the more incomprehensible its secrets. Who, then, could resist the horrible mysteries of a Carami?

Finally he disconnected, returned the unit to its hiding place, and flung himself on the hammock, emotionally exhausted. He quickly fell into a deep sleep.

He woke with a heavy head and nausea, which muted his mood. The memory of what he'd seen along the subterranean route still hovered in his fatigue-numbed mind; he willed himself to forget it, at least for the moment.

He left the laboratory for his bedroom, taking with him his sword, held on his back in a harness of plaited leather. It had been Plabos' sword, which he'd named Donasa the Faithful, and his mentor had given it to a young Morminiu as was the custom among nobles; Morminiu carried it for so long it was like a body part, an extension of his arm, and he no longer noticed the weapon's weight.

So it was that his hand slipped automatically to the sword when a blade sliced the air near his nose, arcing away after it failed to connect but recovering quickly to swing in on a horizontal plane. Dizzied by the flash of steel before his eyes,

Morminiu fell on his back, but reflexively tensed his muscles to turn the fall into a somersault. He bounced to his feet, weapon in hand, and had his first glimpse of his opponent— the attacker was wearing a costume he didn't immediately recognize, through the exhaustion and nausea fogging his brain.

His opponent again attacked; Morminiu parried the two blows without difficulty, the violence of the impact that jarred down his arm bringing him fully awake. Though he was indeed in danger, Morminiu realized as he parried for the second and third time that the phril was clearly a novice who had not passed the first level of swordsphrilship, relying solely on the classic moves taught to beginners. He avoided a thrust, parried the next, then turned the other's blade upward, far from the phril's body. Morminiu's sword slithered into the opening and penetrated just below his opponent's stomach, the blade plunging easily into the nervous belt where there were no bones or even muscles to impede it. With a smooth twist, Morminiu sliced along the belt, splitting his opponent's body in two.

He pushed aside the corpse with his foot, noting the absence of a coat of arms or identifiable colors, and continued toward the central area of the palace, all his senses alert. He encountered no one else.

The grand salon's tall, round, doors of intricately carved, yellowed bone were wide open. He stopped in the doorway. Harissh Tathar was waiting for him within, leaning against a twisted column upholstered in sphere-fish's wool. Morminiu immediately made the connection between the dead assassin's costume and the house colors Tathar wore.

"Great Tathar, how glad I am of your presence in my house," the Recipear said, his face and tone emotionless. "But, where is that rude servant, to make you wait without refreshment?"

"Do not worry, my dear Morminiu. I managed on my own without the imbecile, although I've been waiting for you for quite a while now, and I have to admit that what I hate most is waiting. But never mind that; why do you stay there in the doorway, conversing from such a distance?" Tathar asked, his tone oily.

Morminiu heard footsteps behind him a moment before the shadows of six of Tathar's soldiers fell over him. Morminiu glanced at them; they stood poised, their swords ready to strike. "Well, you really honor me!" Morminiu hedged.

But Tathar was already walking toward him with his sword in hand, followed by five more soldiers who emerged from the corners of the room.

One of the six behind Morminiu attacked. Morminiu whirled, slipped beneath his outstretched sword, and straightened behind his attacker, his sword red. The imprudent mercenary fell to the floor and lay still. His fellows swooped down upon Morminiu, forcing him back a few steps. He counterattacked, sword flashing, and two more adversaries dropped to the floor.

Tathar, with his five soldiers, paused in the salon, watching as the last three soldiers in the hall attacked. Blocking and parrying their blows, Morminiu had no choice but to back into the salon, coming dangerously close to the second group. Before he could deal with either group, though, a heavy net fell upon him, dragging him to the floor. The soldiers leaped forward. In a few minutes he was tied hand and foot, and thrown to the floor near a column. From this vantage point Morminiu saw Totin, lying unconscious behind a settee.

"I think the time has come to thank you for your hospitality, usurper," Tathar said. "But it will be a longer thank you than usual, and do not think I intend to avenge Leomi. He was stupid to let himself be eaten by you, a stinking peasant," Tathar sneered, stressing the word "eaten." Morminiu gritted his teeth at the offence Tathar intended by calling the Tasting of a Course, and even more, a transmigration, mere eating.

"Therefore, let Leomi hear—when I kill you, I'll do it with double satisfaction, knowing I'll be killing him, too. And now—" Tathar stepped to one side and addressed his soldiers. "Thank them, boys."

Two soldiers grabbed his legs and pulled him away from the column. Back pressed against the warm floor, Morminiu stared at the ceiling, searching his mind desperately for a solution to his dilemma. He was bound tightly; no chance of escaping the ties. He noticed that Totin was lying bound as well, probably after receiving his own round of "thanks." That left the cook and the gardener, neither of whom he had seen. Had they been overcome and bound too? Even if they were still free somewhere in the palace, he could not rely on them coming to his rescue; they might not even know there was danger.

Movement made Morminiu turn his head. A phril approached, one he had not noticed until he rose from an armchair in the shadows. He was wrapped in a cloak made of an expensive vegetal material, the black cloth embroidered with black silk. Tathar's soldiers fell back respectfully, while the Harissh grinned in satisfaction. The stranger bent over Morminiu and seemed to study him for several long minutes, then extended a hand smelling strongly of dusk flower and touched Morminiu's face. The hand caressed his lungs as if weighing Morminiu's gills in his palm, then moved lower, the fingers trailing delicately over his neck and then gently massaging his stomach. The hand stopped short of Morminiu's vulbas, and the stranger shivered and withdrew his hand.

As the phril straightened, Morminiu tried to identify the phril behind his mask. The only clue to his identity was the strong perfume, which was clearly hiding something else. The phril turned and walked back to the armchair in the shadows, the air in his wake heavy with that perfume.

Tathar stepped forward, withdrawing a bottle from within his cloak. He shook it vigorously, then opened the top and tipped the receptacle. There came a whistling as the contents made contact with the air, then two drops of the liquid fell directly on one of Morminiu's swollen lungs. As the drops sizzled into his flesh the Recipear screamed in pain and tried to roll away, but the soldiers kicked him onto his back. Two more drops fell on his other lung, making Morminiu writhe in agony. In the shadows, the dark phril started panting in excitement.

"Morminiu, my boy," Tathar drawled, "I have thought this over, and I believe I can be a little bit rude and retract a few of my thanks, if you tell me where you keep your Recipes."

"You'd need ten lives to read them," Morminiu blurted. "And anyway, a talentless recipear like you wouldn't understand a thing." In the next instant Morminiu regretted his proud stupidity, realizing it would not help in postponing his death, or hasten a miraculous rescue. Two more drops burned into his chest. He groaned through clenched teeth, his pain eliciting a deep sigh from the occupant of the hidden armchair.

Then the Court's Master Recipear refined his procedure—he ever so slowly tipped the bottle, the movement sometimes lasting minutes, leaving Morminiu to jerk and spasm in anticipation of pain. Whenever Morminiu relaxed, Tathar would tip the bottle farther, letting a drip fall, and the shock would rip screams of pain from his victim and excited groans from the masked phril. The groans grew so quick that they became panting, as each new pain for Morminiu built up the masked phril's excitement and pleasure. The strong floral scent mixed with the stench of burnt flesh and hair that hung thick in the air.

Suddenly, a boom echoed through the room, followed by a deep rumble, as of thunder. Morminiu recognized the first sound as the palace gates being slammed shut and barred, but it took him a moment to identify the thunder as the shouting of many voices, the words muffled by the thick walls.

One of Tathar's soldiers entered the grand salon and trotted over to his master. "Your Highness," he gasped, "the crowd has surrounded the palace. They have already occupied the courtyard and they demand to see Morminiu."

The Harissh's face darkened. He looked around, bewildered. "Are there many?"

"Several thousand."

"How did they learn we were here?" Tathar demanded.

The soldier shrugged. "Perhaps one cannot come to visit a Hitissh with so many soldiers without being noticed, My Lord."

"You're right," a frowning Tathar muttered, too preoccupied to comment on the soldier's impudence. He puckered his lips in concentration and a respectful silence fell over the salon as those present awaited his decision. In the quiet, the roar from outside seemed louder. "Check out the other exits from the palace!" Tathar decided.

As the soldier nodded and strode off to execute the order, the Harissh turned toward the dark corner. "We kill him and run," he said. The masked phril rose and approached Tathar. He whispered something in the Harissh's ear, then they left the room.

At least for the moment, Morminiu could breathe easy. He looked around, searching for a solution to his predicament. The cords binding him had not loosened despite his twisting and tossing, and the place was still crowded with soldiers. Plus, the torture had weakened him; he could not plan too adventurous or vigorous an escape.

One of the Harissh's soldiers hurried to a vent that opened on the courtyard and peered out at the crowd. The rumble of angry voices came loud through the vent, shouting and chanting slogans, though Morminiu couldn't make out the words. Suddenly, a great roar assaulted their eardrums and the noise from the crowd amplified considerably before an absolute silence fell. The soldiers looked at each other, their eyes wide with terror.

Shocked momentarily by the terrible roar, his pain momentarily forgotten, Morminiu listened, eyes round and his lips stretched in a rictus of hope, his breathing a staccato rhythm. Then, abruptly, he relaxed and closed his eyes as he realized what had happened. For the first time in years, his eyes filled with tears, and he didn't try to keep them from falling. He had forgotten why phrils never gathered in the plazas of the nobles' palaces. He had forgotten that, when the Carami detected a disturbance, it released an acid rain meant to banish troublemakers and restore the phonic balance. The same sonic balance that had been broken decades ago in the Silence Plaza, leaving a place so sensitive, silence was imperative. He just hoped that not many phrils had been caught in the open plaza.

Tathar returned at that moment. "Shall we party some more, my peasant friend?" he asked Morminiu. He beamed with satisfaction. His lungs, from a point behind his ears down to his neck, had swollen, straining against their protective membrane as if ready to burst.

The phril in the black cloak stepped up beside him. He trembled with excitement. At that moment, Morminiu's stomach climbed into his mouth and emptied its contents on the nicely polished shoes of the masked phril. "Chap your vulbas!" the masked one exclaimed, at once furious and surprised. He stalked angrily away, back to the shadows.

Recognition tickled Morminiu's memory, making him alert. The voice seemed familiar, but he could not place it. He waited, but, the masked phril didn't say anything else, only muttered to himself. He turned his attention back to Tathar when the Court Recipear said something to him, but not in time to be sure of what he heard.

"You're in big trouble now, peasant," the Harissh said cheerfully. "I believe he is quite angry with you. You've been very, very, naughty."

"Look," Morminiu tried, "if I tell you where to find the Recipes, will you promise to kill me quickly?"

The noble stared at him in surprise. After a moment he asked, "Where?"

"Untie my legs so I can lead you."

"No. Tell me. We can find them ourselves."

"You'll never find them." Morminiu lightened his tone, as if indifferent. "Suit yourself." He settled back on the floor, breathing heavily.

Tathar cast an anxious glance his way as he moved over to whisper with the masked phril. But before they'd reached any decision, the same soldier who had brought news before, interrupted them again.

"Your Highnesses, Taharissh Comtap is coming to the palace. He is accompanied by a troop of the Royal Guard and wears the green ribbon."

"He comes as the King's Trust?" Tathar asked, astonished.

The announcement launched a flurry of activity. Tathar and the black-cloaked phril conferred in whispers for a few seconds, then the masked phril took a few soldiers and left in a hurry. The Harissh left four soldiers to guard Morminiu, then also walked from the room and closed the doors behind him.

<hr />

Tathar waved his people through the rooms and the halls, then he entered the guest salon, leaving the doors wide open behind him. A short time later the palace gates resounded with knocks like thunderclaps. Tathar had instructed his soldiers to unlock them and admit the Taharissh; he waited until Taharissh Comtap, the King's Trust and the Counsellor of the Throne, entered the entrance hall and demanded loudly, "Where is Hitissh Morminiu?"

As Comtap strode straight to the closed grand salon doors, Tathar hurried out to the hall, then came up short and exclaimed as if surprised, "Ah, My Lord Comtap!"

"Yes, Tathar. I have a message from the King for the Hitissh, and I want to speak with him. Now."

"Leave it to me," Tathar said smoothly. "I'll tell him you were here when he gets back. I have been waiting for him for quite a while now. He's out walking, I was told."

"The King wishes to speak to him *now*, Harissh Tathar," Comtap replied, pushing past Tathar and walking toward the grand salon.

Tathar cut in front of him, smiling benignly. "Your Lordship doesn't trust that I will give him the message?"

"If he's dead, you'll follow him!" the Taharissh growled, and gestured at the royal guards behind him.

"All right, all right." Tathar raised his arms, stopping them. Then he added sourly, "But be quick, because I was just cutting a deal with him."

Comtap shrugged and strode past him to throw open the tall doors of the salon.

⁂

Morminiu tried to rise and lean against a column as the door burst open. "Your Highness," he began, but the Taharissh signalled him to keep quiet. Two royal soldiers approached him, cut his bonds, and lifted him from the floor. They held his arms, supporting him a few moments, but he pushed them away.

"Your Highness—" Morminiu began.

"He's lying," Tathar blurted, entering the room behind Comtap.

"I—" Morminiu tried again, glancing in confusion at Tathar.

"He's lying again, Your Highness," the Harissh interjected, then went on dryly. "Tell him the message from His Majesty and leave us, please, to continue our negotiations."

The Taharissh threw a disparaging look toward Tathar, then something in the air distracted him and he sniffed the scent in the room for a few seconds before wrinkling his nose and peering into the dark corners of the chamber. Finally, he returned to the matter at hand and lifted the sheet on which was written the royal message. The grand salon fell silent as all present listened.

"By our Great Sovereign's will, the Wise and Mighty Green King Chathron Chat the Sixteenth, named also the Recipear-King—" Comtap paused and looked around. "Hitissh Morminiu, Master Recipear of the Mormont House, is appointed today Master Recipear of the Royal Court, full member of the Table of the Six."

"No!" Tathar shouted, shaking with anger.

"Your Lordship Harissh, you talk too much in the presence of His Majesty's Word," Comtap said smoothly, and Tathar shivered in fear. Comtap was an extension of the royal authority; the King spoke through the Taharissh's mouth, and the Taharissh through the King's mouth—no one dared defy him.

"I beg forgiveness," muttered Tathar.

"Tomorrow, Your Lordship Morminiu, you are invited to come to the court and assume your position. You will be under the supervision of Harissh Tathar, Master Recipear of the Court, yet will obey *only* the King's word. Harissh Tathar, you are ordered by the King to prepare the ceremony of appointment for tomorrow. You will name the recipear who is guilty of failure to execute his function, thus making available a place at the Table of the Six. The guilty one will be banished to a provincial court."

Failing to hide his rage, Tathar bowed shortly and left, followed by his soldiers.

Morminiu waited until they were gone before saying simply, "I thank you, Your Highness. You arrived just in time."

"Do not thank me, thank the King. He wants you alive. Starting from tomorrow, you'll begin teaching him Recipearium. I hope for your sake that you will meet his highest expectations."

"No worries; the King will be satisfied."

"Tomorrow we will be awaiting you at court," Comtap

ended coolly, and withdrew.

The Palace remained silent, its gates still wide open. The contents of all the rooms had been turned upside down by Tathar's soldiers as they searched for his Recipes. Totin was still lying behind the settee, though he was regaining consciousness, and moaning faintly. Morminiu did not know how badly the servant was hurt. He experienced the silence and solitude for a moment, then—

He was Royal Recipear!

He savored the moment, then sighed and went to Totin.

He was Royal Recipear.

MORMINIU

The acid ripples in the Silence Plaza. I breathe deeply, inflating my lungs. This is not a tranquil place, but I was longing for solitude. I inhale the silence through all my pores and relax. I have a deal with Mahop. The exchange is to take place in the Silence Plaza. Any moment now he should arrive with the merchandise.

My eyes fall on a rat lying upside down in the gutter, dissolved down to its bones. I turn my eyes away, disgusted, and see shadows moving among the derelict buildings—Mahop followed by twenty . . . something. They walk in a rigidly aligned column. I rise, fighting a thrill of panic at the sight.

The black marketeer presents them as if directing a parade; they march past in a conspiratorial silence. They are under average height and completely camouflaged, if indeed we are talking camouflage here, because I cannot distinguish where the body armor ends and the flesh begins. On their heads, they wear yellow-gray bone helmets. From the center of their face masks hang thin, wrinkled hoses that disappear somewhere under their cloaks; ribbed lenses protect their eyes. I look closely at what I've called cloaks, because I'm not sure if they ar,e in fac,t skin; they seem to join smoothly the legs of . . . trousers? Or a thick, gray-white skin, covered by a complex net of nerves? I can see only from their knees downward.

"Armored skin, wacky," Mahop tells me, seeing me squinting. "More resistant than any other type of shitty armor."

I remain silent, both impressed and overwhelmed by the fierce appearance of the mercenaries.

"What the—mother's vulbas, are you scared? You shit your pants when you saw them, didn't you?" He laughs, in a good mood.

I force a smile and ask, "Are they . . . ?" I stop, knowing

it sounds foolish, but he answers me.

"Yes, they are: the best mercenaries in the kingdom. Professionals."

I stare at them, mistrustful. There have been no truly professional mercenaries for centuries. Currently, the military schools train pupils at the minimum level of expertise, pushing them through as quickly as possible. For, as is obvious in a country where the right to retaliate, the right to revenge exists, at least half of them die quickly, and must constantly be replaced. Which makes me wonder where they have been trained as professionals, and for what purpose? Questions to which Mahop just shakes his head.

"Old boy, you pay and the merchandise is delivered. That's all you need to know. They're good for what you want, but they're expensive. Disgustingly expensive. The contract is for two years."

"We talked about five years."

"That's the deal; you take it or you don't. But better sathalists than these you won't find."

"I'm sure," I mutter. "What can they do?" I ask, more to gain time for thinking than out of curiosity.

"You'll see for yourself." He smiles devilishly. "Oh, I'm sorry I forgot to bring you the instructions for use." He laughs—silently, of course.

I sit down slowly, as if deep in thought. I slip a bone splinter into my hand, then suddenly throw it at one of the sathalists. It hits him pretty hard on his shoulder, but he doesn't flinch.

"Hey, hey, what was that for?" Mahop exclaims.

I glare at him. "He doesn't have reflexes!"

"Let me finish my spiel," he says in exasperation. "You didn't give me a chance to tell you: I conditioned them for you. They can never act against you. You can even kill them and they won't resist, although that wouldn't be a very smart thing to do, if you ask me."

"But, don't they have a self-preservation instinct?"

"No."

"For such conditioning to be successful, they must not be phrils," I observe.

Mahop shrugs. "Believe what you want about the merchandise. My job is to make it available to you; if it meets your requirements, you pay. You can have shit in your house and call it a brops, if that's what satisfies you—it doesn't bother me, as long as I don't step in it." He laughs again, heartily. This time he is laughing at me. He can be such an idiot sometimes!

He sobers abruptly and offers me his hand. "Do we have a deal?"

"All right. But I want a trial period first."

"That's it, old phril—the deal I spelled out to you; you won't regret it. There are a few more minor details: you pay a Recipe between five and ten years old for each one that dies. And don't pester them for information. They're like newborns, with no memories, only their professional training. That means they can't give you any details about their past. And last, see that they eat only sequ soup with suckitori. Nothing else."

This information makes me uncomfortable; it also makes me certain that these mercenaries are not phrils. No phril can live on sequ soup with suckitori; it's like drinking the most potent, intoxicating liquor. Sequ is the strongest spice known, with an extraordinary palette of gastrophilic nuances, impossible to perceive fully by the uninitiated. It is very similar to a narcotic, though more powerful than anything on the market, and is sometimes used for that purpose. And the suckitori are insectoid spices often added to hot sauces—alive, after they have ingested great quantities of herbivore blood (so that the vibrations sent through its blood do not disturb the gastrophilic perception). They are also a strong aphrodisiac.

Still, I hand over the Recipe required for payment, and Mahop tucks it carefully within his ragged clothes and turns to leave.

"Take care, old phril," he says, then glances at me and my new purchases and laughs as he leaves.

I stare at my personal guard. Uncertainty rummages through my stomach.

The acid ripples in the Silence Plaza.

DIPLOMATIC RECIPE: BAT WINGS SOUP

This is a most refined soup, meant for diplomatic, political, or artistic Tasting. Before serving, one can give a patriotic speech or a welcoming speech, which the soup will accentuate, adding unimaginable philosophical depths.

INGREDIENTS:

4 RED BATS, fully grown
3 SWAMP CARROTS
4 YELLOWS OF CORA, juicy and sweet
1 RED SWAMP POTATO
3 SWAMP-SNAKE'S EGGS
1 SHEAF OF MANARIN

PREPARATION STORY:

Bring a pot of water to boiling. Clean and grate the carrots and place them in a deep bowl. Peel the red swamp potato and slice thinly, directly over the bowl, so as not to lose any of its sweet and murky juice. Those whose vulbas do not tremble with the vigor of youth should pay great attention to the red potato's juice. (More information on this can be found in a later chapter.)

Break the snake eggs and separate the yolk from the white. Set aside the white and stir the yolk into the bowl to coat the grated carrot and sliced potato. Place a pan on the fire to heat. Beat the egg whites with a bit of vegetable oil and pour into the hot pan; leave them to heat through.

Using a hatchet, remove the wings from the bats at the point where they join the body. Thoroughly drain the marrow from their bones, wash them, and dry them well before adding them to the pan to fry.

When the the water in the pot has begun to boil, add the contents of the bowl and raise the grate over the fire; leave the carrots and potatoes to simmer until the water has partially evaporated, about one hour. The resulting soup should be thick and creamy. Cut the yellows of Cora into small pieces over the pot, and stir them into the soup. Leave the soup on the fire not more than ten minutes to prevent the yellows from boiling.

The bat wings should now be well done, the egg white and oil mixture now permeating the fragile bones where the marrow was. Remove the wings from the pan and add them to the soup. Cook for five more minutes.

Remove the pot from the fire. The soup should now be thickened and creamy, the consistency of jelly; the wings softened and their egg-white permeated bones crunchy and delicious.

Serve the soup in small portions at room temperature in white bowls. Garnish each with a bit of chopped manarin for a fresh and exotic aroma suggesting Southern Courses.

(from The Teachings of the Recipearium Revolution by Grand Master Recipear of the Green Kingdom, Morminiu)

VIII. BLOOD ON THE STREETS

After being in a Carami for a long period of time, one started to perceive the nuances and the subtleties of the light filtering through the translucent back of the monster. Morminiu knew it was a clear morning, because the greenish light shining through had a special, spring-like purity. It was one of those rare days when one could distinguish all the details of the walls and the cobblebones in Burtheste, the lowest level of the city, without the added light of glow-worms.

Morminiu left the avenue and entered the narrower streets, walking under the bone-balconies grown directly from the entanglement of the caramic skeleton that acted as walls. Actually, this was the beautiful part of a city—the inhabitants did not build it, but grew it. Only the initial space was expensive; the buildings, the dwellings, required only craftsphrilship and the imagination of the owners.

The Royal Carami was not the most beautiful or the cleanest city, but because it was the capital city it was surely the biggest. And the richest. And thus a city of contrasts—from opulent, well-tended palace plazas one could pass into quaint neighborhoods full of imagination, or even directly into slum zones, chaotically grown, with sewage systems dripping pus and a nervous system scarred in so many places, there were surely great parched areas, or areas withering from neglect.

Morminiu liked to walk the narrow streets. Often, disguised, he slipped out the back door of his palace to spend a few hours in the crowded streets, looking in the windows of the lithographers' and the armorers' shops, mingling with the buyers in a junk market, or even simply sitting on a bench and watching the phrils around him.

Now, though, he was walking down a narrow street surrounded by his new guard of mercenaries, before which all phrils parted fearfully. His sellswords surrounded him, sides and back, like a living wall. He was not in a hurry, for he had left early enough to enjoy a walk into this part of the city. It was a well-tended, elegant area grown by architects who flocked to the Royal Carami from other kingdoms. It was the merchant and small manufacturing district; a flourishing, cosmopolitan neighborhood with powerful cultural and artistic overtones.

A flash of movement in the corner of his eye surprised him, and he turned to see the soldier beside him grasping a small ambush-arrow in his upraised hand. He froze as he glimpsed two more flashes of motion, much too quick for his reflexes to react to, and he realized that somebody had just tried to kill him. He was suddenly very grateful for his sathalists; with most phril mercenaries, he would now be bleeding out his life on the cobblebones, if not instantly dead.

Several of his bodyguards moved in front of him, instantly engaging in a sword fight with unseen assailants, metal striking metal, the noise bouncing from the walls on either side of the street. Three more, one on each side and one behind, were still busy snatching arrows in mid-flight before they could strike Morminiu. He had never encountered an ambush of such proportions. Had he become so predictable in his movements, he asked himself while retreating to the protection of a nearby wall. He looked around, from behind his wall of bodyguards. The first arrows had emptied all pedestrians from the street.

He unsheathed Donasa the Faithful and entered the battle. The attackers were at least as numerous as his guard, excluding the bowphrils firing from buildings and cross streets. They filled the street and pressed forward, relying on sheer numbers to overcome Morminiu's guard. Who could hire so many assassins for an ambush?

His mercenaries wielded their long, broad blades with tremendous swiftness and strength. What they lacked in finesse, they made up for in force and speed. *Real killing machines,* Morminiu thought with a small thrill of pride. With just a few blows, they struck the swords from their opponents' hands, then stabbed them in the blink of an eye, or cut them down like they were scything reeds. Some closed in and slashed the attackers with basai, the hair-thin disks glinting as they whistled through the air before embedding themselves in the necks or chests of the assassins. The victims, bearing what looked like only a thin red scratch, crumpled to their knees, then toppled to one side, dying without even knowing what had hit them.

Morminiu engaged only one adversary, whom he overcame quickly enough. Not as fast as his guardians, he noted wryly as he realized the fight was over, but faster than most of the swordphrils in the Royal Carami. He had seen two of his mercenaries disappear during the skirmish but now he saw them emerging from between the buildings on either side of the street, each dragging the limp body of a phril. They dropped them next to the other dead assassins as if they were merely animal skins.

Morminiu was tempted to lean against the wall until his legs stopped trembling and he'd overcome the urge to vomit, but he suddenly remembered that he was downtown, wearing his House's coat of arms—he must not reveal the slightest sign of weakness. He looked around at the carnage on the street—over thirty phrils lay massacred, their bodies bent in grotesque positions, gaping wounds oozing greenish-red blood. He had never been to a slaughterhouse, but he imagined it would look similar to this.

For the sake of appearances he composed himself, assuming an indifferent expression and forcing himself to study the tableau for several minutes. He sensed eyes watching him from behind closed shutters and through doors opened merely a crack. He raised his gaze and studied every window, scanned every blood-splattered wall, peered into every shadow that could conceal an observer. The shops had closed, but he saw curious eyes staring through their windows. The phril who had hired the assassins was in the area, he knew—at that moment staring at him, hateful but for the moment unnerved. Nobody who had set over thirty swordphrils and two bowphrils on him could have expected anything but victory. It had not been a simple attempt; it had the proportions of a small war.

He stepped among the bodies and stopped in the middle of the street, continuing his meticulous inspection of the neighborhood. His guards had regrouped. Not one of them had fallen, which made the scene more ominous. Morminiu focused on shifting his expression from indifference to one of triumph and cruelty. He had to send his message very clearly to the author of this ambush, as well as to any other potential enemies. They would certainly spread the story and add details. By the end of the week the battle would have grown to legendary proportions. In a few years it would enter the city folklore, and he would become one of this age's icons. Only this way could he hope that someday, his enemies would give up trying to kill him.

He resumed his walk, his bodyguard moving with him. One of the fallen phrils caught his calf as he passed and thrust a bone dagger toward his leg. Reflexively, Morminiu thrust his sword into his attacker's neck, nailing him to the cobblebone. The sharp point of the bone dagger stopped a hairsbreadth from his flesh, then it withdrew a few fingers distant. Morminiu pushed down on the sword and twisted, feeling the blade tear through tissue and cartilage; only then did the dagger fall.

Two of his guards had stepped forward and were crushing the head of the surviving assassin—a fraction of a second too late. That delay could have cost him his life; the dagger was surely poisoned. He withdrew his sword from the body and kept it in his hand as he continued his walk, maintaining his mask of cruel victor even though, inside, he was shaken.

How much had the assassins been paid for such dedication? The surviving assassin could have remained still until they left, and lived. Yet he had chosen to complete his mission, despite sure death when he struck in the midst of Morminiu's mercenaries. Which highlighted a second concern—he had discovered a weak point and he was sure that the author of the attack, still hidden in the area, had noticed it too. Once within the perimeter of his guard, close to Morminiu, an assassin would have a good chance of success. It was not easy to get into such a position, but neither was it impossible. Morminiu shuddered involuntarily and clenched his teeth.

No longer in the mood for a walk, Morminiu travelled the rest of the road with hurried and nervous steps, mentally thanking Mahop for the mercenaries before plunging again into black thoughts.

They arrived at a small plaza, as clean and meticulously crafted as others in the area, and stopped in front of a decorative gate of carved and tightly dovetailed white wood. He had not seen carved wood since arriving in the Carami. This example was probably unique, if not exactly eccentric; others might have been able to afford it, but the only building material considered proper in a Carami was bone, especially as the city itself was providing the raw material.

Morminiu opened the gate and entered the courtyard

beyond, followed by his guard. They were immediately met by the house's servants, and Morminiu requested a room where his mercenaries could clean themselves and tend their minor wounds. He himself entered the palace, then stopped. Everything around him was shining white, the decor simple, with little furniture and only spots of color to define the space. It was an elegance and luxury he was not used to seeing.

He felt giddy and disconcerted, and asked the house phril to wait a moment before announcing him. Then he asked for the privy, where he hurried to the orifice in the floor and vomited as noiselessly as he could, not wanting to give any clues to those who were probably listening at the doors. Finally he rose, washed his mouth at the washstand, used one of the mouth fresheners displayed on the table, then rubbed his palms with scented leaves. He smoothed his clothes and studied himself in the mirror. He looked decent, no trace of trauma. He had recovered. He breathed deeply, composed his face in a friendly smile, and left the privy.

The house phril announced him with a lot of pomp, and even before he put his foot inside the salon, he was welcomed by his host, the ambassador of the Clerugia Kingdom, a solid, blackish little phril dressed in garments customary to his country. The unfamiliar clothing looked strange to Morminiu, for Clerugia was a realm far, far away, somewhere on the south shore of the Interior Sea. He did know that the kingdom maintained diplomatic relations with many other kingdoms, not particularly for political reasons, but commercial ones. Here in the Green Kingdom, their main interest was in Recipes and after that, in blue wood, swamp worm silk, and sequ oil.

"Maestro, what a joy," the ambassador greeted him effusively.

Morminiu's response was more reserved. "Your Highness. I apologize if I'm late, but I met some small difficulties on my way here."

"Do not mention it, dear Maestro," the diplomat

assured him. "I only hope that the small difficulties did not cause you big troubles. Now that would really worry me." He widened his eyes significantly.

Morminiu saw an opportunity to explain his time in the privy. "Your Lordship, everything has been resolved in my favor, but it took some time to clean the blood from my clothes, so that I might present myself decently in front of you."

"Maestro!" The ambassador feigned consternation and moved his fat, manicured hand in a delicate gesture to his mouth—which had rounded into an oval of surprise. "Shall I call the doctor? Somebody should see you, to assure us that everything is all right! But, what barbarian would make an attempt on the life of the most accomplished artist of all time? The gall!"

Morminiu stifled laughter and felt that he really had recovered from his earlier ordeal. Maintaining a concerned expression, he smiled and assured the ambassador that all was well.

They moved farther into the salon and sat down near a tea table, continuing to exchange pleasantries before the Recipearium lesson, for which the Clerugian was paying generously. One day, Morminiu decided, he would like to visit that realm. The ambassador had bragged that it was the richest and the most flourishing kingdom in the whole civilized world, a place with a long history of patronage to the arts and a culture that prospered in the absence of more brazen forms of politics. And the youngest art in Clerugia— the Recipearium—was preoccupying much of the population nowadays.

According to the ambassador, Morminiu was a god in Clerugia. Yes, he should visit them one day . . .

CHATHU

How boring! How vulbing boring! I hope I get something after this visit. Uncle Prado! Who would have thought he was still alive? And that he also has other relatives in the mountains? He has not sent any nephews to the court for more than ten years. Maybe this nephew will be special, and I'll recruit him . . . or maybe I'll recruit him anyway, special or not.

Hitissh Kramo, yet—who the spheres ennobled all these young phrils? We are a land of lords! Where will we hire our soldiers, our servants? Who will work the land, or raise up the castles? I don't care; everybody can lift a hoe, title or no, as far as I'm concerned.

Hmm, good idea. Little nephew Kramo, I have two options: either you impress me and I recruit you, or you disappoint and I send you back to your father with an annual tax owing. Hmm, yes . . . a tax for his title. Back to the hoe, false nobles!

When I'm king, the first thing I'm going to do is take a census of the nobles—who they are, when they were lifted in rank, to what rank, and by whom. Anyone without authenticated papers will also be given two options: renounce the title and all its privileges, or pay for it, for life. I'll call it the Nobility Regularization Tax. Yes, that sounds good. I'll go down in history with that. And if not, at least the royal court will flourish again, under my reign. One or the other, or both.

Ah, here we are. To what little palace has the chariot brought me? How prosperous is my nephew, Hitissh Kramo? Hmm . . . a relatively poor relative: small plaza, in one of the less fashionable neighborhoods. Palace? It is in fact a mere mansion, and not even renovated! How rude. He must hardly have arrived in the capital before buying such a shanty. He didn't even clean it up before inviting me to a Tasting. Hmph. And in two or three days he'll expect to be introduced at court—where I will likely have barely presented him before he starts making requests. Or—hah!—he will be lost among the other hangers-on at court and I will never hear of him again.

Hmph. He has not even fixed the gate properly. "You! Throw that gate into the garden."

Shall I enter, or just ignore him? What would he do? Stay a while in the Carami, no doubt, then leave when his money runs out. Or he might be a parasite, and I'd wake one morning with him on my doorstep. What—why are you staring at me, you pieces of shit, have you never seen a prince?

Hmm, let's just enter. That must be him approaching.

"Your Grace, what an honor! Welcome to my humble home."

Huh, he is a peasant! And a disgusting one, at that. What a mess! *Welcome to my miserable shanty,* he should've said. "Kramo, my dear, what a surprise to learn of your arrival in the city." Is he reddening? No, he isn't, the thick-skinned— "When did you plan to show yourself, boy? If Uncle Prado weren't around to send me letters every time relatives from the countryside visit, I wouldn't even know of their existence. Decided to drop the hoe for a while and spoil yourself in the Royal Carami, did you?"

Not even now is he blushing, the cad! And his hand has never touched a hoe in his life. What did he do up there in the mountains, all day long?

"Your Grace, you are too kind to think of us in the midst of the many state affairs. But please, do come in—my house is your house."

At least he follows etiquette. My, what a dirty little place! You animal; how rude of you to invite me into such a hovel! Bone plates on all the walls, inadequately joined; everything blackened with age—and probably covered in slime when he arrived. I can still smell its stink. Not enough glow-worms are mounted on the corridor walls; their light is sufficient only to cast monstrous shapes from the wall drains. Where is Kramo taking me? Personally, yet. Ah, the greeting salon. What's that? The light reveals it discreetly, but sufficiently enough to see the tapestry's details.

It is the coat of arms of his family. Across the bottom is emblazoned their ancestral motto: "Us for us, through us." The device is a fist clenching three or four weapons used in hand-to-hand combat. I don't recall seeing it before. But, as far as I know, Kramo's ancestors could have served as the bodyguard of a great warrior who, upon retirement, thanked them for their service by ennobling them. It is quite possible that they don't have papers. "So, Kramo, you for you and through you, eh?"

"Your Grace?" His face is blank and he leans slightly forward, uncertain of the attitude he should display.

I indicate his House's motto as I step over the threshold and walk past him. Several glow-worms are arranged around the salon, warming it with their hazy light. An assortment of shields and weapons is displayed on the walls, and there are furs on the floor. Barbaric, yet interesting, as if I've stepped back in time three hundred years. The furniture is heavy and massive, yet the lines are simple, without pretensions.

He makes excuses: "Your Highness, I haven't had time to accustom myself to life in the Royal Carami. After I've entered the court, I'll pay some visits to the city's nobles and catch up on the latest trends."

Imbecile! Does he think he can force my hand? Ah, but I'll smile, and widely, for the first time.

"Once I've made a few new acquaintances, made a few visits to their palaces, you'll come back here and it will have changed so much, you won't recognize it anymore. We of the Koros clan, we adapt quickly. But now, I have invited you here to Taste a Recipe from the mountains. I hope Your Lordship will appreciate it, even if it seems simple to you, maybe even barbarian. Next time I will hire a royal Recipear to honor you—maybe the Great Morminiu," he adds with a twinkle in his eyes.

I remove my smile. "Hmm, I don't think so . . . "

"I beg your pardon; I have misunderstood." He bows to a flattering degree, his eyes narrowed by their fat pouches.

"I don't think so," I repeat. "I don't believe you will hire him, my boy. He is much too expensive for your means." I wave around me.

"Your Grace, for Your Lordship, anything . . . "

He's spraying saliva. I quickly back away. Fat and lewd—he doesn't have a face for the court. We shall see if he has any good fortune.

I take the seat he offers—a huge skin sack so soft and comfortable, I feel as if it has swallowed me. I signal to my guard to leave us alone in the room. Through another door enters a servant dressed exactly like a peasant—fascinating. I haven't seen one in years, so I study him. He's simply dressed in coarse clothing, patched in some places. The voluminous shirt is snugged with a string belt over the trousers, I imagine so the shirt won't flutter about, and to keep the trousers in their place. He is barefoot, his soles hardened with calluses and corns. This phril has never met any peasant sandals. He walks clumsily, navigating with difficulty through the dim room. He has been brought from the mountains, not hired here. My nephew probably came with a sufficient escort, and has no intention of hiring city phrils anytime soon. There are two possible reasons for this, I decide: either he is really poor, or he is too stingy.

With a stifled grunt of effort, the peasant places a tray with two stone cups and a large, bulbous bottle on the little table in front of us. Before he straightens, I notice, his sweat drips onto the tray. Ah, good heavens! My hand trembles on the hilt of my sword. If it's like this now, what can I expect of the Course?

With effort, I turn my attention to my nephew. "Tell me, Kramo, what business has brought you into the capital?"

He freezes, confused, for a few moments. Hah! He thought he'd made his intentions clear. Did he think I would hand him the keys to the realm or something? Now he probably thinks I'm senile—or that I want to negotiate. I watch him trying to find his voice, watch his little fat fingers, full of bone rings, groping for one of the cups and the bottle. His hand trembles as he pours, and a harsh, strong smell hits my nostrils immediately. I identify it as linca, a liquor from the mountains. A strong liquor—three or four cups will put you under the table.

"Your Highness," he says, his voice quavering, "I've just moved to the Royal Carami. For Your Lordship." He offers me the filled cup.

I lean across the table to take it. I see him grimacing and holding his breath. Uncle Prado, did you forget to warn him? Are you that old and forgetful? I remain stretched over the table as I arrange my vest so the stench will be ever stronger. I encourage him with: "That's it? Tell me; there must be more."

He tries desperately to open his mouth, but that would mean breathing in my stench. He knows it is coming from me, and he doesn't dare offend me. What will you do now, fat ball?

He suddenly bursts into laughter, then throws his head back in a loud guffaw. I know he has done this way to escape the full impact of the stench; I see him release the pent breath from his lungs and adjust his breathing. I pretend surprise, though I've seen this behavior numerous times. But he abandons it and, still laughing, rises from his pillow—with difficulty, with all his fat trembling in indignation against the effort. "Your Grace, you're testing me!" he finally gasps, approaching the problem with a cheerful mien as he paces a few steps away, then turns to pace back toward me.

I look at him in unfeigned wonder.

"We have nothing up there in the mountains, nothing we can successfully commercialize in Carami, nothing to justify my presence here," he explains, still cheerful. "We are not rich enough to travel for pleasure, so naturally, there is only one conclusion. But wait—you want me to speak freely, not hide behind courtly politeness."

I barely keep from laughing—courtly politeness! This milksop would be crushed in his first five minutes in the court's intrigues. But I have to admit that he's managed well so far. Let's see his behavior when the Course comes; what other solutions he will find to avoid the smell. I smile and listen as the idiot begins his story—begins it during the time of his great-grandfather, to be sure he does not finish it too quickly, and he is forced to sit again across from me. He's lucky that I'm patient—my illness and the court's machinations have taught me patience and tolerance.

I taste the liquor and breathe deeply; it's good—flavorful and velvety on the throat, warm and soothing on the stomach. I appreciate its harshness and purity, but it is not suitable for any kind of Tasting. Unless he wants to numb my senses, so I can't tell if I'm eating boot leather or the cooked Course!

As Kramo reaches the point in his neverending story where he has just been born, two servants enter the dim room with the same clumsiness as the first servant, interrupting him.

"I hope that after this linca, aged by my father for thirty years and brought by me all the way from home, I've whetted your appetite," he tells me, his small eyes straying greedily to the bowls in the peasants' arms.

He has certainly whetted his own appetite—or worse. The contents of the bowls seem to have stimulated him. All I see is a dinner, nothing resembling a Tasting. I interrupt him, displaying my open smile. "Kramo, what happened to the Tasting you promised?"

He looks at me, bewildered. He has grown tired of telling me stories while standing, and settles his fat mass, sighing, onto his skin sack. "I do not understand, Your Grace."

It's clear he doesn't know what I'm talking about. He looks desperately to the steaming bowls on the little table, to the two servants who wait with bowed heads in my presence. His jowls shake like jelly. He tries to master his lung sacks, to prevent them from swelling and deflating spasmodically—which, instead of regulating his breathing, produces a whistle that makes him look even more panicked.

I let him stew for a few more seconds, then I explain in a soothing, patronizing voice, "Kramo, dear boy, a Tasting is supposed to be a Course accompanied by a tale. The tale of a Course alludes to its preparation. Now, don't tell me you don't have a cook, at least—that these peasants have cooked your so-called Course!"

"Ligo, Your Grace, has been our cook for as long as I can remember." He indicates one of them—the one who was sweating over my cup of linca.

His ignorance borders on stupidity. Or perhaps it is both, for I'm not very sure which one he suffers from most. He didn't notice my word choice, suggesting that his Recipe has been *cooked* and not *prepared;* a simple meal of food, without any of the quality of a Recipear Course.

I throw him another lure; maybe he is just anxious and nervousness slows his thinking. "Ligo, you say. Has he cooked any other Tasting Courses?"

"Yes, Your Highness; at home he was the only one to prepare the Tastings." His head is lowered in humility. I feel his greasy fear insinuating itself into the shadows of the room, ruffling the beastly furs on the floors.

I signal to the servers that they can go, then I drag my bowl closer and sniff. It is a kind of stew, smelling strongly of some harsh spice. Nothing here looks like a Course. It is only food. I look up, my grin frozen on my face, and invite him to serve.

I take the wooden spoon and stir in the bowl he gives me. I sniff again; I'm not hungry. What a waste of time!

Kramo also stirs his food, then he timidly tries a mouthful. He has realized how crude his manners are compared to mine and he doesn't know how he should eat. What he does know is that he is hungry. The linca has awakened in him a crazy hunger, and fear has prodded it toward ravenousness. I gesture for him not to hesitate, but to satisfy his appetite. At first he takes small tastes, conscious of my eyes, then when I pretend I'm ignoring him he starts to dip his spoon vigorously into the stew. The thick, fat-laden sauce dribbles from the corners of his mouth back into the bowl he holds close, though some splatters onto his clothes. Such a glutton, I have not seen in a long time.

I stretch my hand over the table toward the linca bottle, intentionally waving my sleeve in front of his nose. He stops shovelling the food into his mouth and he swallows laboriously, as if some is stuck in his throat. He almost frowns as he looks at me from the corner of his eye, then concentrates on relaxing his forehead, and swallows heavily to clear the morsels from his mouth. I pour linca into his cup, then withdraw my hand. He thanks me humbly and focuses on the food again, splashing sauce all over himself and greedily smacking his lips.

I wait through a few spoonfuls, then I slide closer to him and put my arm around his shoulders. He stiffens like a skewered traum and looks at me with moist eyes, as if asking for mercy. Sauce trickles down his chin. "Eat, Kramo, eat," I urge.

I can see the battle on his face. He is nearly strangling under my stench. I keep my arm over his shoulders, exposing the armpit toward him. "Now, you eat and I'll talk," I tell him in a gentle voice, but I stress my words by lightly squeezing his shoulder.

He resumes eating, with difficulty at the beginning, then greed makes him snort and again breathlessly swallow the food. He frowns. He is panting, and sweat beads on his temples and runs down to mix with the sauce already running down his neck. He tries to keep his nostrils shut, but he doesn't succeed; I can feel him trembling, on the verge of tears.

"Kramo, let me make it clear for you how things stand. The Recipearium is an art. You don't invoke it unless you master the art, or at least buy it. You do not invite a phril for a Tasting when you know you will offer only food. Do you know the difference between food and a Recipear Course, Kramo?"

He tries to say something, but I stop him by pressing the back of his neck, pushing his face toward the bowl. He continues to eat greedily, gagging on the morsels that get stuck in his throat. The pelhitza produces the most overwhelming stench in the world. If someone is not accustomed to it, it can choke him to death. I actually tested it.

I twist to look at him directly, shifting the source of the smell—my armpit—closer to his nose. The stench hits him like a frontal assault. His jaw trembles, tortured by the act of chewing and the urge to retch, to free his respiratory pathways of the obstructing quality of the stench.

"You do not know the difference, Kramo. But that is not important. The bigger mistake is that, if you should not invite even an ordinary phril without knowing the difference, under no circumstances should you invite a Taharissh to an ordinary meal. Neither should you petition a Taharissh, especially not before offering him the Tasting, before you see if he has enjoyed it. Only an animal could make such mistakes."

A resounding gurgle rises from his stomach, followed immediately by a wave of undigested food that bursts out of his mouth and spills into the stew remaining in the bowl. He drops the bowl on the table and, unable to contain his nausea, he spews vomit into the pot and all over the table.

I jump up, swearing, and back away. A few drops have splattered my cloak. Disgusting! I wipe at them with a cloth, then look at him. He is still shaking with convulsive heaves, still disgorging puke. I position myself behind him and wait.

"Your Grace . . . " he begins, shaking with the effort to raise his head.

I don't let him finish. I put my hand against his sweaty neck and push his head into the bowl filled with vomit and food. He thrashes wildly but ineffectually, taken by surprise. I prop my knee against his back and place both my hands on his neck to push him forward—he is much heavier than me, and I cannot risk losing my leverage.

He struggles for a while, then jerks, and his arms fall limply along his body. His head sinks into the bowl under its own weight. The room stinks worse than I could ever have imagined and I suddenly realize that the slob shit himself with fear in the last seconds of his life.

I walk away from the table and open the door to the hall. I signal to the captain of the guard to come to me as I exit the room, eager to breathe the fresher air of the corridor. The soldiers, specially trained to tolerate my stench, don't move a muscle when the fetid odor wafts out of the room and hits them. My warriors! They make me proud. "Captain, take your people and clear the house of all peasants. No noise. Meet me in the entrance vestibule when you are done."

He doesn't say a word, just bends his head and turns to issue orders.

ADVICE.   *Music is not more valuable than literature, but it is more direct. In a way it is more brutal. It leaves its fingerprint directly on our psyche, with no intermediaries such as letters, colors, or shapes. Nobody knows whether it is better. It is true that the essence, or meanings could be lost when passed through intermediaries.*

That is why music so resembles the Recipearium. Despite the apparent incompatibilities, it enriches the spiritual experience of the Recipes. Still, it should complement the prepared Course, because music badly chosen can generate allergies, migraines, and even an irritation of the gastrophiza. Thus I advise that you always consult a specialist.

(*from* The Teachings of the Recipearium Revolution by Grand Master
Recipear of the Green Kingdom, Morminiu)

IX. HOUSE OF PHRILIRAS

Morminiu detached himself from the crowd and entered the Fertility Plaza with heavy steps, eyes downcast as if examining the tips of his footwear as it passed over a white wave of shiny bone, a black wave of matt bone. *A step is as big as a wave,* he thought as he approached the fountain that gave the plaza its name. A few phrils sat on its edge, cooling their feet in the water. One of them was laughing heartily; he had contracted a phrilira, Morminiu overheard as he reached them. Her nose was too big and she wasn't enthusiastic at all.

He looked up at the statue in the fountain's center, its angles softened in the diffuse light filtering through the Carami's back. Frozen in the midst of a victorious scream at the moment of birth, the image of beauty and grandeur, the Phrilira-Mother rose triumphantly over a mound of squirming bodies. Her own body was dividing, revealing two radiant, newborn faces. Water streamed from the points where the body had not yet divided, filling the oval basin at the fertility statue's base. *Lies over lies,* Morminiu thought. A birth was a terrible thing. But the legend of the Phrilira-Mother was beautiful.

He breathed deeply, readjusted the cage beneath his cloak, and strode toward the gate that opened onto the plaza. At the King's insistence, he was here to obey the law and make a contract with the House of Phriliras for a wife. The answer to his request had arrived from the House the day before: an invitation to come for his wife. A formal ceremony would follow at his palace, under the Sacred Oath of Intimacy.

He had not liked the wording of the invitation: *come for your wife.* Why didn't they deliver her to her new home? And, the impression of something certain, already decided, had made him angry. He intended to speak to the Mothers Council—this was why he had brought the cage containing the clawer he'd caught in the Carami's depths. He hoped it would placate them—or force their hand.

It was the only bird in the city, though no longer a true bird; it had evolved to suit the different quality of the air, the food, and the light conditions, becoming a tree-bird. Claws once covered in a short, thick coat of hair had, after a long period of nearly total immobility, stretched into vigorous roots that had broken the cage's bone and extended beyond its confines into a fine network from which grew small, red beans. It was an air root, he realized. The beans attracted mice and insects that became caught in its stringy webbing, trapping them for the clawer to suck them dry. It had shed its hair and grown down, then feathers. Its shell had softened and wrinkled, the process deforming it until it looked like a miniature tree, its gnarled hollows filled with clusters of small, phosphorescent green eyes, its "branches" three pairs of wings. Yet it was dangerous to let this seeming inanimate object lull you into complacency, for it had not lost its claws. The red wings that swayed so gracefully could themselves become a trap. When it got bored, it sang, contorting its trunk to produce high-pitched wails. As the only bird in town, it was the most appropriate gift for the Mothers.

A low fence of fangs, their natural curves turned so that the sharp points faced outward, surrounded the gardens of the House of Phriliras. The gate was open. Beyond it he could see a wall of shrubs. It was not truly a barrier—but who would rise against the Perpetuation Guild? It did effectively hide the House from the plaza.

Suddenly feeling anxious, he walked along the bright white path that took him through the hedge, then split. He had to make a choice—take the trail to the left, which followed the line of shrubs, or continue to the right, which led to an open area, probably in front of the House. Curious, wanting to see this legendary palace in its entirety, he made to take the right path, then stopped. That seemed too simple, too obvious. Why was there a trail to the left? Where did that go? He turned and followed it.

It took him into a labyrinth, its walls high hedges too tall for him to see over. After a few turns he stepped onto a new path, this one composed of bone mosaic worked in colors of green, dark red, dull orange, black, and a lot of yellow. It told the story of the first Mother's birth from the Fertile Sky. It had been a unique multiple birth, a legend with no correspondence to reality. Only one of the Daughters had left the other Sky Daughters, climbed down to spread her offspring among the ignorant phrils, who then discovered phrilira and erotic pleasure. She had come down, too, to spread the faith.

The road ended suddenly, without finishing the story. He stumbled a few more steps, stopping before a threshold. Bewildered, he tipped his head back and looked up at a tall door so narrow, it seemed more a crack in the House's wall than an entrance, made from a single long piece of softly shining bone. He slowly climbed the steps, looking about. He could not see more than this small portion of the House of Phriliras. The rest was concealed by the wall of shrubs. It seemed very old, and he didn't recognize the architectural style. Unique, he decided as he opened the door. It was unique.

Nobody met him as he crossed the threshold. Etiquette told him to walk to the first salon and wait there for the host to appear. The same etiquette required the host to provide there all the necessary comforts for the guest, or at least have servants ready to serve him. He entered what he thought was the first salon. It was nothing more than a dark, long corridor that led steeply upward. He saw rays of light streaming from somewhere above, as if inviting him to approach. He started walking up the sloping corridor, passing myriad erotic sculptures that lined the walls, resuming the story begun in the mosaic pathway, this time teaching—again, part of the legend—all the divine love positions in phrilic images. He reached the source of the light—a vent. Here the corridor turned sharply and continued on in darkness. The statues here were darker shadows in the shaded corridor.

He perceived heavy breathing and grew anxious, feeling as if he were inside the respiratory system of a monster. Two more sharp turns brought him to an area that held the faint promise of light that grew stronger as he glimpsed ahead glow-worms, fixed on the walls, their luminescent wings illuminating the sculptures. The walls were wet, streaming with water that flowed among the carved shapes. Something fluttered nearby, agitated, and he saw the image of a bird, caught in a snake's coils, superimposed on a body contorted into a bizarre position.

He stopped, surprised. The image sent thrills through him. He concentrated, focusing his eyes, and now saw a phrilira in an ecstatic position, her head thrust forward far beyond the other statues in the row, craned over her partner's shoulder. Her face expressed an unimaginable ecstasy, pleasure bordering on madness. Morminiu shivered and tried to control the instinctive reaction of his vulbas. There was more, though; a detail that made him tremble. The unreal beauty of the phrilira and the impossible pleasure captured by the artist was tarnished by a red tongue, in stark contrast to the statue's pale bone. The tongue trembled between small, sharp, carnivorous teeth. The shock of the image pushed him to orgasm.

He stretched out his hand to break the spell, and touched the tongue. Which felt warm and moist as it licked him. He screamed and jumped backward and lost his balance.

Mastered himself with difficulty, he looked at the sculpture. The tongue had disappeared. He heard stifled giggles, mingling with increasingly agitated fluttering. The heavy breathing resumed, now whistling, then cut short, resuming as jerky moans. He tried to peer through the mouth hole to see who was on the other side and realized how silly the gesture was. The phrilira's head was far forward of the row of statues, and beyond it was the phril's shoulder—it had no point of contact with the wall. No one was on the other side of the wall, playing with him. He stepped back, embarrassed.

He hurried onward, the hair on his head standing up like a brush. He did not look at any more of the scenes on the walls. Something crossed his path some twenty steps ahead. He swallowed the knot in his throat and ran that way. There were no exits, unless there were secret doors . . . ! An image flashed into his memory and stayed there as if imprinted: a phrilira, split from her neck to her legs along her spine, the original half pulling the newborn half along with her.

As he managed to regulate his breathing he noticed that the line of sculptures had ended at two towering sculptures of Father Sky the Fertile, his organ erected, ready to receive—an image of force and vitality. The two representations of the Father framed a square doorway into a dark hall. He entered. Another, longer hall ran left, strongly lit and hung with white fabric. The floor was pale bone.

He stepped into the corridor and it was as if all sound had remained outside, as if he had sloughed it off in crossing the threshold—except for the fluttering. Realizing its source, he opened his cloak and soothed the clawer. At the end of the hall he stopped at a half-open door. He knocked, then etiquette urged him to enter and wait.

The salon was high-ceilinged and spacious, sparsely furnished with rare antiques, more treasure than furniture. The walls were covered with fabrics made by water-spiders, at one time common. Based on their texture, they seemed to date from the age of redhead phrils—a fabric now more priceless than an unknown Recipe.

A phrilira waited on the sofa. She rose when he noticed her and waited politely. She was quite thin, even frail, a child. Hesitant, yet he detected a curious mixture of intelligence and intuition in her eyes. She would be lost in the Mormont palace corridors, no more than a figurine among towering others.

He searched for something to stimulate his interest. He'd initially been curious, but only a little. She did nothing to stir his desire. He felt bad, simply staring at her as if she were for sale. This was the phrilira the Mothers Council was offering him based on his contract. But, why her? In the contract he had not specified any of the elements that would prompt them to choose her for him.

She was frail, immature. Had they believed he was attracted to children? He remembered the feel of the flesh of his first phrilira, on the moss carpeting the rocks in the swamps. They'd been the same age, still children, but she was taller and much bigger. He shivered, feeling again the initial shock when they had coupled, the thrill that had taken him by the throat and the panic when he thought they would never be able to detach again. To stop his writhing, the phrilira had rolled on top of him and immobilized him with her weight. Slowly the fear had melted into amazement, his breath had come back to him, and he started panting, this time with pleasure.

All those contrasts—the sweaty hair, her beautiful eyes, her soft, warm vulbas, the lubricating fluids flowing between them, her silky skin, soft as rose petals—all had conjured in him sensations he had not guessed existed when simply looking at the same things individually; sensations he had not dreamed of when he'd imagined coupling with a phrilira, one of those magical beings who had remained magical to him ever since that moment.

He was brought brutally back to the present, and the salon, by a voice: "She is the one for you, noble Hitissh."

He looked around, but there were only the two of them in the room. He paced a few steps while he digested the situation. Then, he said, avoiding looking at the phrilira next to the sofa, "Could I speak to the Mothers Council?"

"There is no reason for such a request."

"I cannot be obliged to take what you want to give me without first consulting with me."

"You do not like her?"

"I don't know. This is not the point."

"Then . . . ? She is exactly what you need."

"How would you know?"

"On the way here, your reactions were analyzed and your hidden desires were revealed. She is the most appropriate choice for Your Highness."

"The most appropriate choice for me is the one made by me and the one chosen. This child here is seeing me for the first time in her life. Does she know that she likes me?"

"We know, and that is enough."

"As you knew in the case of Donasa?"

Silence. The petite phrilira smiled, amused. Morminiu paced around the room for a while, then glared at her. She had tears in her eyes, yet she kept smiling. The Recipear stared, surprised, but in the end he avoided her eyes again as he said, "Look, I'm sorry . . . "

"Yes, My Lord Hitissh? How sorry are you?" a voice asked nearby.

He jerked around as if burned. Another phrilira had entered noiselessly. She made a discreet sign and the chosen phrilira left the salon, sobbing.

"I am Valiria," she said as she settled in a high-backed chair near the window. The green light streaming through gave her skin a cadaverous tint, but it did not diminish her appeal.

She was the High Priestess herself, the most revered phrilira in the kingdom, the symbol of fecundity. She wasn't yet a Mother, though she ruled the Council. The phril who would father the offspring that would make her a Mother would be chosen by mystic lottery from a large number of bachelors, and she was not permitted to know his identity beforehand.

She wasn't as beautiful, as attractive, as some other phriliras, at first glance. But she drew the eye and held it, and after a moment's study, the observer would conclude that she was indeed unimaginably, coldly, beautiful.

"What is your problem, My Lord Hitissh?"

Morminiu breathed deeply and tried to concentrate. The clawer was fluttering in agitation under his cloak. He revealed the cage and offered it to her. "For Your Highness, Valiria."

"I do not believe you brought it for me."

"But I'm offering it to you now. I would like you to have it."

Without a word she took the cage, looked at the clawer for a few seconds, then placed it behind her on a little table. Morminiu clenched his teeth, hiding his annoyance at her blasé attitude toward his gift, and withdrew a few steps, to sit down in an armchair across from her. The chair's layer of flesh stiffened, sensing his tension.

"So? What was unsatisfactory to you?"

"I cannot accept somebody else deciding my fate."

She sat calmly, emotionless in her high-backed chair. "We have specialists. We have studied your reactions to different stimuli. We have created a profile of your personality and we have chosen the most appropriate phrilira based on that."

"That's absurd!" Morminiu exclaimed. "Do you really think what you observed of me on the way up here revealed every important aspect of me? You can't possibly know what's hiding in here!" He tapped his forehead as he rose. "Nobody makes such decisions about my life. This is a decision I'll make myself, without the help of those 'specialists' who so wrongly assessed Donasa. How accurate a profile can they develop in half an hour?" He drew himself up. "If allowing me to make my own choice does not suit you, we can cancel the contract."

"You'd be forced to pay damages."

"I would not. Review the contract; you'll notice a number of small changes to your standard form. I accepted the profiling only as advice. Based on our deal, I have full freedom to choose my own wife."

Valiria flushed, her lips tightening in indignation. "That is impossible; such changes are not permitted!"

"The King arranged this; I was assured of the right to negotiate."

"Only the price!"

"Apparently I have found other loopholes in your contract—a contract to which the Mothers Council agreed. I am entitled to choose my wife or to cancel the contract. After this reception, I believe I should withdraw and think before I make my decision."

The priestess rose, the window's light silhouetting her tall, slender figure as if limning her in power. Morminiu was impressed; Valiria did indeed embody power and strength of will. She looked at him, her gaze penetrating. "I remind you where you are and to whom you speak," she said in a level voice. Her lips curled in disdain. "In fact, you are new in the city."

She did not give him a chance to respond. "You do not know yet our customs, here in the city. You are not aware that the Perpetuation Guild rules. When you have learned what you must know, when you are familiar with all these things, then we will approach you with a proposition." She finished in an off-handed tone and turned away, a signal that the audience was over.

She had offended him purposely, Morminiu knew. Ignoring her dismissal, he walked into her field of vision and brought himself to his full height, torso thrust proudly forward. "High Priestess, I invite you to dinner in a week, that we may further discuss the contract which, despite your protestations, still remains a valid contract. At six o'clock, in exactly a week, a carriage will arrive to carry you to my abode. In this matter, with the King's blessing, I have decided; I do hope you won't contest a royal . . . suggestion."

He withdrew quickly, without giving her a chance to respond. At the door, he glanced back, not hiding his smile at her bewildered expression. "As for the city and its rules, we will continue that subject at dinner."

He immediately closed the door behind him and went straight to the main entrance. It was time to see the front door, too.

"Did she study all those statues?" he asked himself, his laughter drawing bewildered stares from the phriliras he passed.

MORMINIU

I am anxious to get to know the beautiful priestess. Because of that, the week seemed to pass slowly when I was idle, and waiting; yet at the same time, quickly, when I was busy with preparations.

Only one thing happened all week to draw my attention. This morning the gardener interrupted my preparations, trying to tell me something in a stammering, incoherent stream. He usually stays mute for days, but this time he was very agitated. I managed to get from him that the craftsphrils had finished cleaning and reshaping the south side of the main palace and had moved to one of the four abandoned wings to work. He said something about a locked room they couldn't find the key for, and tried to tell me that something will happen if I don't make things right. Lord Leomi had been reckless, he said, then muttered something about the Hark.

"The Hark?" I asked, bewildered.

"Hark of the House Lormont!" he exclaimed, obviously surprised at my ignorance, then he plunged on. "We finally found it!"

I kept quiet, realizing it was the only way I would learn enough facts to understand what he was mumbling about; distracting him with questions did no good. The locked room they couldn't find the key to turned out to be the one I discovered three years ago, during my first wanderings through the palace. Curiosity and the thrill of a mystery excited me this morning, as they did in the past. For a long time we looked for the key, searching in all the cabinets and in the former apartments of Leomi and Donasa, but with no result.

"Now I'm sure," the gardener declared with a solemn face. "It is the Hark." Saying there was left only one place where the key might be, he urged me to follow him. Realizing that otherwise, we would have to break down the door, I obeyed.

We went to the north side of the palace, the one I've been in no hurry to restore, as it contains only a round ballroom with grand exits onto two stepped terraces overlooking the garden. A dense living fence flanks the terraces, rising as high as the second-floor windows and then veering off across the north expanse of the property to run along the palace walls. Thus, the only entrance to the garden remains the round ballroom, excepting, of course, the personnel entrance.

The old gardener stopped in the corridor that ran around the outside perimeter of the ballroom and asked me if I intend to refurbish this side of the palace, too. I haven't been attracted to the idea, because I don't like the plants that feed on shadows that comprise the garden; it seems a morbid place. I told him that I'm still thinking about it, but I will probably repair things there, too. I was thinking of his feelings, this old gardener fated to the pagan death, a phril nobody will ever taste, whose life's work is being ignored, forgotten behind the derelict condition of that side of the palace. Leomi had never shown an interest, either. Still, though no one ever admired his artistry, he tended the estate, especially the garden.

"Yes, I will surely restore here as well," I eventually concluded.

"Then you don't need this anymore," he said, and attacked the corridor wall with his big gardening shears before I could do more than shout. He tore away the leather-paper that covered the yellowed bone studs. I hadn't noticed till then that the wall was only leather-paper, so I fell quiet, curious.

After he'd finished tearing away a pretty big expanse, he gestured victoriously at two tall salon doors that had been hidden behind the leather, and I realized the round ballroom was next to a salon on the east side and probably another one on the west side, hidden as well for reasons of symmetry. In fact, the living fence wasn't there to hide the wall, but the exits of these salons onto the terraces. That side completely opened to the garden. This gave me another perspective regarding the building. I became determined to find out why the palace's north section had fallen into disfavor.

It was dark inside the salon, the air stale and damp, and everything covered by a thick layer of dust. We entered and opened the doors wide to air it out and let in some light. Then he guided me to a corner where a square, massive metal pedestal stood—a real eccentricity, I thought as I studied the empty, dusty surface. The gardener had moved past the pedestal and suddenly shouted in satisfaction. When I looked up, he pointed to a key hung on the wall over the pedestal.

I frowned. "Why here?"

"The old Hitissh, Lord Leomi's father, was killed in this salon by a paid assassin. Right here, in front of the Hark."

"Who hired him?"

"Nobody knows. They paid for his silence, too."

The gardener took the key, apparently content with the level of explanation he'd given me. But I was determined to know more—he hadn't interrupted my preparations a few hours before an important meeting, only to leave me still ignorant in the end.

"At that time, the young Hitissh," he started, clearly annoyed that I wanted to know more, "hid the Hark. He said he didn't need a powerless Hark."

"What is the Hark?" I asked, exasperated, mentally cursing Plabos for choosing to disappear from my psyche when he did, leaving me alone when I most needed him.

The gardener looked at me incredulously. "The faith of the Harkers does not exist in Your Lordship's land?"

"No."

"Then everything is in vain," he moaned. I blinked, bewildered and annoyed, and waited. Finally he felt obliged to reveal to me, "The Hark is the luck of the House. It is the spiritual core of the family. It weaves an invisible net that protects the family and the honor of the House against a cruel or shameful fate. But destiny is destiny. It can be deflected, but not controlled. The old Hitissh's death had to be understood and accepted, yet they couldn't. They banished it from their hearts and since then, misfortune has fallen over the House of Lormont, driving it to extinction. The demise has been slow, but sure. Out of 326 servants, only the cook and I have stayed to the end. We have served three generations of Lormonts. We have no place else to go."

I watched him with new understanding as he paused to control his emotions. His eyes had moistened as he spoke.

"The Hark is also a source of pride," the old phril recited in a tone that would brook no interruption. "It is the work of generations in a Family. The father conceives it, the son grows it, the grandson maintains it, and the great-grandson cherishes it. Everyone can be proud to have a hand in it, though it will never be perfect. It is created and it creates itself perpetually. But of course, during a lifetime, a phril reaches a certain level of accomplishment. It is the greatest spiritual satisfaction of a House."

I didn't contradict him. It wouldn't hurt, not reminding him of Recipearium. I patted him on the shoulder and set him to find the Hark and set it free.

It proved to be a stump of porous bone, gray with time and dust, from which had grown a fang, bent in such a way that its tip touched the other end of the stump. Multiple holes were punched in the fang, and on this frame had been stuck a small skeleton whose legs were anchored in its core.

"It is somewhere here," the gardener muttered.

"What?"

"The Harker's Klila."

"You mean this?" I asked uncertainly, pointing to the imprisoned skeleton.

"Yes."

I looked closely, but I couldn't identify the animal it had once been. "But it's long dead, probably."

"No. Its soul is immortal and it is hidden somewhere here. If you take good care of the Hark, it might come back.

But without the Klila, it remains only a decorative piece. You would never be proud of it."

I ordered that it be replaced on the pedestal and both moved into a cabinet, after they were properly cleaned.

"The High Priestess of the Perpetuation Guild, Valiria," the house phril Totin announces in a stentorian voice.

I rise and look toward the entrance. She is standing on the threshold, alone. Her companions have remained outside. She is wrapped in a white algae gown that is embroidered with designs in green and yellow silk. I realize she is waiting, and invite her to enter with a sweep of my arm, indicating that she have a seat on the couch.

Part of me wants to see her reaction to the changes I've made in the house, but common sense tells me that I'm the only one who can notice them. The salon is warmer and more welcoming, now that it's wallpapered with yellow weaver-spider fabric, and the furnishings have been rearranged. The pieces are massive, the bone carved and inlaid with dark wood, very old, though not quite from the age of the red-headed phrils; the flesh recovered in clud leather, brought all the way from the great Southern Swamps of my homeland, where the huge swamp worms have beautifully colored skin in white and yellow, thick and soft and fine. The twisted columns I left covered with sphere-fish wool, to complement the same wool in the carpet in front of the hearth, on which I've placed two huge and princely armchairs.

"You're moving quickly."

I look at her, bewildered.

"The walls," she explains. "You were quick to borrow from the fashion."

I smile sincerely, pleased that she noticed the change. She sees my pleasure and is bewildered in her turn, and that surprises me. Mothers and priestesses are special. Phriliras themselves are special, and these are their spiritual leaders—a compliment from their High Priestess is praise indeed. It is possible to live your entire life next to a phrilira and not know her fully. Maybe this is why I've postponed the moment when I'm forced to accept a phrilira as my wife—they overwhelm me.

I change the subject. "How is the bird?"

She hurries to follow the new direction of the small talk. "Very good, thank you. I took it into the garden so that the whole palace could enjoy it, and it sings all day long."

"Ah-hah! And are they enjoying it?"

"Very much."

I know she lies, to mislead me. A large number of phrilira reside there; one of them would have had her fingers caught by its claws, if it were left in a garden. And clawers don't usually sing unless they are alone, certainly never when they are the center of attention. I smile, amused. "I'm glad my gift has been appreciated."

She looks away, pretending to admire the leather on the couch. I lift two steaming cups of ceroptes bud tea from a tray on the small table beside me. It stimulates the appetite for phriliras, and the gastrophiza for phrils. I hold a cup out to her, then take a seat on the couch across from her, cradling the other cup. "Ceroptes tea; I hope you'll like it."

She lowers her head and takes a sip. "Excellent. It has a . . . smooth taste."

A disappointed shudder ripples through me, but I ignore it. Phriliras comport themselves differently from phrils and I need to be alert to these differences. Here is the first: a phril wouldn't make any comment until he had reached the bottom of the cup. Then he would make an appreciative sound, if the tea were well dosed and mixed. I realize she wants to take her time and sip the tea while conversing, so I ask her, careful to keep my voice neutral, "Have you drunk ceroptes tea before?"

"No."

I feel it's my duty to explain to her a few of the elementary notions of a Tasting, so it doesn't turn into a mere overdone dinner. Although I am also interested in her natural reaction to the gastronomic stimulus. Tonight, I'll be her Recipear guide. "The ceroptes tea is a gourmet introduction to Tasting. It is generally served for Course Tasting, and not for eating."

She watches me, curious; encouraged, I continue. "It is a kind of . . . spiritual preparation. You relax, forget your cares while you drink it, then return to reality a new phril, better prepared for Tasting."

"But, phriliras cannot Taste!" she exclaims.

"I know. Tonight, we'll make an exception. There won't be any gastrophilic arousal and you won't enjoy the gastric orgasm, but we will try to create a parallel atmosphere for you, so that you can at least have an illusion of these sensations. It would be a great honor to my House, if you accept it."

"I'm used to illusions; I think I could try," Valiria accepts graciously.

I don't know what she means, but I nod contentedly and relax; I don't intend to unleash my excitement and reach orgasm in front of her. I'll try to coordinate her feelings throughout the meal. She imitates me and relaxes herself, leaning her head back against the couch and closing her eyes.

It will be an interesting evening. There are undoubtedly some legends that began from actual events, among them the legend of the Recipear phriliras—phriliras who ruled society exclusively, with phrils being at best the lower class, if they were not enslaved outright. Their Recipear phriliras created Recipes for the Queen and her court. Which, according to legend, were Tasted and led to gastric orgasms! I don't expect Valiria to reach something like that, but if anybody can come close to experiencing these sensations, then she is the most likely, as High Priestess—the most powerful among the phriliras with powers!

After a few minutes, I invite her to the table. I clap my hands and immediately the light softens, and the waiters enter the salon and place on the table two platters of gourmet appetizers. They are meant to focus the perception and smell of the spice in a certain direction. An experienced taster is able to use this to stimulate and excite his gastrophiza, and thus feel more intense pleasure. In a hidden niche, the musicians start to play—something neutral and suggestive of nature at first, with no hint of how beautiful it will become when the Story starts.

I explain all these things to Valiria and she tries to comply with my instructions, eyes closed in intense concentration as she munches slowly on the appetizers. I take the opportunity to study her face.

She doesn't have a perfect face—her eyes droop a little bit at the corners, giving her a sad expression, and her cheeks are prominent—but she is indeed beautiful. I have noticed similar imperfections in the more beautiful phriliras before, and often wondered why they seem more beautiful than the perfect ones, whose harmonious features provide only a faint beauty, or even, in some cases, homeliness. She has sensual, plump lips, at odds with the relatively prominent nose, but the combination actually makes her face more interesting.

She opens her eyes and I smile clumsily. She smiles in return. I begin the Story; she concentrates on the narrative thread and I tell her that she has to hear the words passively, while tasting or watching the preparation of the Course, and combine the two—the spoken Story and the events happening in front of her—sensing them at a higher level of consciousness; at a spiritual level, for her. She tries, and seems to accomplish this, after a fashion. I have served this Course to quite a few phrils, but a phrilira accomplishing what is taken for granted with them, no matter how uncertainly, stirs excitement within me.

The waiters silently reappear, surprising her. They ignore her reaction and gather the remains of the appetizers, then depart, leaving the Course a few steps from the table. The light dims even further, signalling a twilight story, though she cannot know this. She probably has never seen twilight, I realize. This saddens me, to be denied this pleasant and usually common frame of reference; it's as though the natural order of things has arranged an incompatibility.

I draw the Course closer to the table, continuing my introduction. Valiria's curiosity grows visibly, as does her hunger, no doubt. I begin preparing the Course while continuing with the Story itself. The vermih has not been tenderized in the light of the Three Daughters of the Sky because I didn't have anywhere to do it, but it is good enough, as the smell confirms. She wrinkles her nose, but politely keeps any comments or gestures of displeasure to herself.

The lights go out completely, and on one wall is projected an image of the Daughters of the Sky. The music wails—Tanghshu music, from the Southern Swamps; almost unknown here in the north, but it expresses so well the southern peasant's soul.

Valiria opens her eyes, otherwise sitting so still, she seems more doll than phrilira. I can't distinguish her expression, but I sense her enchantment. My excitement blossoms. What would Plabos say of that?

Weak, clean light flickers in the chamber, imitating morning sunshine penetrating a forest canopy in playful beams. Royal marches mingle equally with the wailing Tanghshu music as the vermih climbs the moamoam leaf. At its touch, the leaf wrinkles subtly, the pink-tinged down seeming to shudder with each movement of the worm. With an abundant gush of pleasure juice, the worm starts to gnaw the center of the moamoam leaf. "Rude worm," I inject into the Story, and Valiria laughs, a bit bewildered. The tension of the music makes her uneasy, generating sensations of both rebellion and hope within her.

The vermih slides greedy toward the second pink-tinged leaf, abandoning the skeleton of the first leaf. Valiria watches with amused eyes. The worm is already plump, although its stomach bag, distended during the tenderizing period, is not yet completely full, and hangs limply, making it look like a fat little old phril with his cloak hem entangling his feet. It slides forward, stretches out, reaching toward the new leaf, then—violent music as it falls! Spurting another stream of pleasure juice as it tumbles, it splashes into the waiting pot of boiling Plabos sauce hidden behind the table. Valiria jumps, startled. I smile to myself. She didn't suspect that the second leaf was a trap. The vermih didn't, either.

I lift the pot into the air above a platter on the table. Within its transparent walls, the dark shadow of the worm writhes in the thick sauce as it sinks toward the hole in the bottom of the pot. The beat of the music has become sharp, but sad notes weave throughout. My voice softly injects into the tension, "Mistakes are not forgiven—by nature," I quickly add.

A blinding light flashes when I open the little trapdoor at the bottom of the pot and the well-done vermih falls onto the platter. Its stewed organs slosh against its flesh, which bursts. Bits of meat and fluids flow outward, cooling rapidly, leaving at the center of the platter the throbbing, bewildered souleida, as big as a fist and looking like a squinting eye.

Speechless, Valiria stares in astonishment at the souleida. I'm on top of the world.

My Story nears the end. I expertly raise the tension. Experience has taught me that this denouement will be successful. I pour sequ-tulapa, heated in oil spiced with swallow butterfly wings, over the souleida's protective crystal, and it melts, sizzling, the "eye" closing in death.

The Course is perfect, the preparation flawless.

Not that I have done a lesser job at other times, but when one is putting one's soul out there for all to see, success generates something more than mere artistic pride; there is great pleasure—and a measure of relief.

Valiria turns desperately away, putting her back to

the table. I cannot hear her over the wailing music, but her shoulders shake as if with sobs. *Why is she hiding her tears from me?* I wonder, but I keep quiet. After a moment she rises and snatches a bowl from the little service table—then vomits!

I collapse into my chair, choking with indignation and surprise. Normally, a jugular spasm followed by the climbing of the stomach into the throat, all provoked by a Course, cannot possibly provoke such a reaction, even if one forced oneself, for the gastrophiza pushes against everything and the cascade of gastric pleasure is overwhelming. There are uncontrollable chain reactions that always end in orgasm . . . Then I realize my mistake.

I rise promptly to help her, but she's already finished and withdrawn to the far side of the room, embarrassed. I offer her water to get rid of the bitterness in her mouth. I start to apologize, but the effort sounds idiotic: how does one tell the High Priestess that vomiting over the Hitissh's Course is not her fault? Yes, that sounds idiotic. I could not have been a stupider Recipear; I myself developed and set out in my book all the gastrophilic ideas and theories concerning the differences between phrils and phriliras, and yet I have made a truly ignorant mistake! Not having a gastrophiza, Valiria had nothing there to be aroused, nothing to block the gag reflex and prevent her from vomiting, no threshold to bring her to gastronomic fulfillment. I should have stopped after instigating a lower level of excitement. But I fell prey to vanity!

"I know . . . " she eventually says. She avoids looking at me. "I'm sorry!" I watch her uncertainly. "I have involved myself too much, although I could have detached myself when I felt myself slipping down this slope. Something kept saying to me that it was all right, that I'm doing exactly what I'm supposed to do. I'm sorry. I mean . . . I understand."

I know that somehow she's right and I ask myself if I should feel justified in accepting her apologies, or if I should be objective and fair. Because objectively, a big part of this is my fault. I knew how everything would happen, right down to the last detail, I could say—and still, I crossed the line.

"No, please," I say. "You should forgive me. I've been a fool."

"There's no need to be polite now."

"I'm not. You, pure and simple, lack the gastrophiza; this is the main problem. If you had it, you would have passed beyond the gag reflex and succeeded in experiencing something very interesting, even very enjoyable. I believed that everything could be experienced spiritually, vicariously; that you would have an emotional, never a physical, experience. It was my mistake. I went too far."

She looks at me, her expression a little vexed, then laughs. I laugh as well. Oh, her laugh! She has a beautiful laugh—sincere and unassuming, childlike. "I believe I'm not hungry anymore," she says, and laughs again.

I clap my palms together and the waiters appear, gliding about silently like ghosts, and minutes later all traces of the Course are gone. I regret the outcome of this one, but still, I would like to convince her that it could be different, that there are Recipes with no such risks that I would really like her to try. That I would love to show her a real twilight, a real morning in a forest, all the beauty of the world beyond the Carami. *I can communicate so easily with her,* I tell myself, then dismiss the idea. *I can exchange thoughts and feelings with her,* my mind insists, even though, up to this point, I haven't understood a thing about phriliras. I end my crazy argument with myself with a smile and: *I would love to share my secrets with her.*

WARRIOR'S RECIPE:
URSUB BLOSSOM WITH A GARNISH OF DESERT
WILD POTATOES

INGREDIENTS:
AN AVERAGE-SIZE URSUB – hunted during hibernation.
FOREST FRUITS.
GREEN VEGETABLES – gathered on the mountain;
preferably those ones with a six-month greening cycle.
DESERT WILD POTATOES – the kind with sweet, dry, black
meat.
POTATO BUGS.

PREPARATION STORY:
The ursub is a mountain carnivore that ranges tens of megasteps daily while stalking its prey, most of that time spent running. This active life has developed its muscles to a high degree, and toughened its flesh, a condition that changes only during hibernation, when its flesh relaxes completely, and toxins in its blood, normal in all carnivores, are eliminated to ensure that the months-long sleep is trouble-free. As well, the fat layer that has grown during the active feeding period diminishes drastically during hibernation, until at the end of the dormant period it is almost non-existent. It is recommended that the ursub be hunted during this hibernation period, to ensure plenty of delicious meat with very little fat, and no toxins. If you kill it before it wakes up, its muscles will remain loose and relaxed.

It is imperative that the ursub be left in its natural state for three days, to soften its flesh. At the end of this period there will be only a faint smell, which means that its preliminary preparation is not yet complete. Its fur can be now be skinned off easily, detaching from the flesh with little bleeding. In some cases, the complete lack of bleeding means that it is a young and fairly inactive ursub.

Once skinned, it should be washed well and cut into pieces. For this Recipe we need only the back of the beast. Normally, the meat should be cut upward from the waist, between the lower back limbs, along the ribs, carefully avoiding its shoulders and calves, and then slicing it apart at the neck and right under its tail. Stretched, the slab will be two phrils thick and as wide as one phril's outstretched arms.

Starting at one end, slice down through the middle of the meat, not cutting out to its edges, thus forming a sack. On its exterior, score the flesh on two sides without cutting through entirely, meaning that the two halves are still connected by a layer of skin.

Pierce the flesh at intervals on the inside and insert the forest fruits, so their sour juice will permeate the meat during baking and counteract any possibility of the taste being too heavy for the sensitive gastrophiza of some phrils. Fill the cavity itself with fresh green vegetables gathered from the natural habitat of the ursub; having the same energetic palette, they will accentuate the tastiness of the meat and prevent any danger of the meat souring or going rancid. Once the sack is filled, pour the animal's blood over the vegetables to fill and sew it tightly shut.

The next step is the second softening. Hang the prepared meat, the sewn mouth upward, in fresh air for another five days. Normally, left in fresh air for so long, the meat would become tainted and worm-infested, but when prepared with the native vegetables and the forest fruits and steeped in its own blood, it cannot possibly go bad. Instead, now field fertilized and prepared for sowing under optimal conditions, it will soften even more and self-sow.

At the end of this five-day period a crop of fat, red worms will appear, true giants of the worm world: swamp crawlers, which normally grow only in corpses so far decomposed that they are approaching a liquid state. After these five days they will be swarming by the hundreds through the interior of the meat, and through the now macerated greenery.

Finally we begin the last stage—the actual cooking of the Course.

Take down the meat carefully, because it is both very heavy and very fragile, and thus easily damaged. Place it in the heated ashes in the middle of the fire. The heat from the ashes will form a crisp crust on the meat, within which the remains of the green vegetables and the blood will boil as the meat roasts. Allow it to bake five to seven hours, occasionally sprinkling a blend of sweet red wine, the beast's blood, and sequ-tulapa flavored oil over the Course.

In the meantime, place on the fire a pot containing whole, unpeeled desert wild potatoes, completely covered with water. While the water is still cold, throw in a few handfuls of potato bugs. These insects are completely dependent on the vegetables; they are born around them, eat them, then die near them. Consequently, the only thing they will do is feed on the potatoes, munching their sweet, black meat and turning it into coarse flour that will fall to the bottom of the pot and form a paste. By the time the water begins boiling, they will have finished munching and will be sufficiently well-done, in their turn.

The most important consideration is their hard little wings. During boiling, the bugs will die and all the oil will drain from the wings, then they will detach from the body and end up floating on the water's surface. Skim these off and discard them, leaving the bodies to boil well into the potato paste. In the hours during the complete baking of the meat, the water will boil off, reducing what is left to a potatoes and bugs porridge; if necessary, add some snake milk to prevent it becoming too dry.

Baking of the meat will be complete when the layer of skin holding the two halves of the meat sack together cracks and peels back, widening the cut. The vegetables inside, now swollen, will overflow the meat's lips, covering it in a green carpet. A few minutes later, the fat red worms will emerge from the split, penetrating the vegetable layer and crawling out, seeking escape, but the cold air will make them dizzy and they will undulate groggily, waving like plant stems. Eventually, the temperature difference will produce a spectacular reaction. To the delight of your clients the worms' fragile and engorged bodies will explode, spraying the digested contents of their stomachs along with their entrails over the Course's surface, blossoming like red flowers. Their sweet and pungent juice will moisten and further spice the meat.

Remove the meat from the ashes and place it on a warm bone tray. Also remove the potatoes from the fire.

For Warriors' Gourmet Meal, the Course should be served thusly: the meat only on heated bone plates and the potato porridge only in stone bowls. The choice of beverage should be red mountain grape wine, a sparkling, cool wine that is easy on the palate, which will balance the gastric weight of the Course. To finish, serve juicy, sour fruits instead of more typical desserts.

(from The Teachings of the Recipearium Revolution by Grand Master Recipear of the Green Kingdom, Morminiu*)*

X. SCURGITON DEVERSATOR

The door opened wide and the King entered the conceptorhm unannounced. The six Royal Recipears rose in surprise, then bowed their heads. The sovereign answered their salute with a quick nod, then looked around the huge hall in delight.

One of its walls was furrowed by a bank of narrow windows that ended near the ceiling. The other wall was completely covered in shelves housing a library of treatises and ancient documents, most original. A round table sat in the hall's center, with places for twenty Recipears, though only six met here. Individual study tables were aligned under the windows. In a corner gleamed the massive metal boiler where Chathron the Conqueror, founder of the Green Kingdom and the ruling dynasty, had been prepared.

The King's roving gaze stopped on the boiler. Nobody dared speak as the sovereign stood remembering his ancestors, with whom he was probably still in contact.

"Where is Tathar?" he asked at last, his face expressionless.

"He has not come yet, Your Majesty," one of the

Recipears answered.

"Hmm . . . " The King turned and walked toward Morminiu, no longer the joyous phril who had entered the conceptorhm minutes before. His eyes looked tired, and stress has gouged heavy, dark rings around them. "Morminiu, I want to ask you a favor," he said in a low voice, pitched so that nobody else could hear him.

"I'm at your command, Majesty."

"I believe it would be better if I have two Green of the Gods tea a week. It has become almost addictive; I wait anxiously for tea day to arrive, and when it does, I have created a ritual of the moment of its arrival, as if greeting a long-lost friend. I want two such meetings a week."

"I'm flattered, Your Majesty; you've made me a happy phril. I'll see that you have two teas a week, at equal intervals."

The King smiled warmly, his joyousness restored, and strode to the door. He stopped on the threshold and gazed happily around the room as he announced, "I've decided to hold a Recipes competition. You will all compete, together with Recipears from the other noble houses in the Royal Carami. It will take place in a week, so get ready. The winner will receive the title of Master Recipear of the Kingdom. Let Tathar know that his position is the competition's prize."

He turned and exited, followed by his personal guard, but after only a few steps, recalling something else, he stopped and told them over his shoulder, "Oh, and I forgot to tell you—the top six Recipears will take positions at the Table of the Six."

The news fell like a thunderclap among the Royal Recipears. They kept quiet until the door closed, but then panic erupted.

Beyond the door, another panic had erupted. "Your

Majesty," a hoarse, panting voice called to the King, "we are under attack!"

The King stopped and stared at the chief of the War Council. "What's that supposed to mean, General?"

"We are under attack," the old general repeated. "By the SCeders."

Nomadic tribes of SCeders often flowed down from the frozen north in search of warmer lands in which to settle, but they had never ventured as far south as the Green Kingdom. Although they resembled phrils, they were much taller, more massive, and blonde hair covered their heads, which lacked gills—their lungs were completely internalized. Sharp fangs protruded from bulging, muzzle-like mouths, but despite their fierce appearance they were a thousand years behind phrils in social evolution, their tools of war and mode of fighting archaic. Because of that, and sheer distance, ever since Chathron had conquered the Green Kingdom in battles against the redheaded phrils and their neighbors centuries ago, the land had not known war. No standing army still existed, only the few thousand soldiers forming the nobles' complements of guards.

"How many?"

"Tens of thousands," the general replied, his tone ominous.

The King turned and re-entered conceptorhm, frowning. "My lords," he told the Recipears there, "our competition will be postponed indefinitely."

<hr>

Situated close to the three Southern Mouths, the broad Grand Bazaar was designed to handle the convoys of merchandise that arrived regularly. Nevertheless, the bustling crowds today were unusually heavy, swollen by the curious, when Morminiu arrived at a run. The enemy was arrayed before this, the principal and the widest entrance into the city.

With the help of his guard he pushed through the crowds in the bazaar and crossed the road on its far side. A few hundred steps behind the gates, barricades had been hurriedly thrown up. On the other side of them, everything was burning. Already the SCeders had sent forward skirmish parties, which had penetrated nearly to the bazaar. Morminiu saw numerous bodies, both dead and wounded, lying about near the burning area.

Spying a company of soldiers from the Royal Palace led by a young general, Morminiu approached him. "Are you in charge of organizing the defense?"

The officer glanced at him, his expression harried, then recognized Morminiu and smiled. "No, we're preparing to attack."

"Attack?" Morminiu blurted in surprise.

"Yes. We want to end this thing quickly. The population is already close to panic."

"But, it's pure suicide!"

A scowl replaced the smile. "Why?"

"There are tens of thousands outside!"

The officer shrugged. "They're only barbarians. They don't even know how to hold a sword properly."

"They've still got numbers. At least a hundred for each one of your soldiers."

The general shrugged again, looking bored, and turned away. He strode to the forefront of his company and barked a command, trying to be as military as possible. A curious crowd watched him. They marched toward the gate, and he called out, heartening his soldiers, "Don't be afraid, they have only clubs. We need to teach them a lesson!"

"In the name of the Green King!" the soldiers cheered, then they charged.

He died immediately. As he emerged from the Carami, ten javelins pierced him. His blood splashed the soldiers behind him, who fell back behind the barricades, their faces tight with fear.

"You asked for an audience, Hitissh. You said it is urgent. It had better be."

Morminiu bowed. "It is, Your Majesty. It is, and I thank you for receiving me."

"If it is confidential, they can leave for a few minutes." The King waved a hand toward the thirteen generals of the kingdom who formed the War Council. The fourteenth and youngest had died that morning.

"It is not confidential," Morminiu said. "I believe they should hear, as well."

The King indicated that his general should remain and looked back to Morminiu. "Then say what you've come to say. We are listening."

"Your Majesty, Sirs, we have seen the great host of SCeders and know they arrived quickly, without our detecting them. We don't know how they got here, but if they have succeeded in crossing the Great Desert and the two other kingdoms bordering us to the north, unhindered, there can be two only conclusions: either our neighbors and presumed allies have betrayed us, or the SCeders have crushed everything in their path so quickly, there was no time to warn us. In either case, we should assume that they want to do the same here—crush us quickly."

"Hitissh, we have been sitting here since morning, examining the problem. We have already reached that conclusion," one of the generals said, his expression haughty.

"I beg forgiveness," Morminiu countered, "but I noticed that your officers tend to be impatient. As was the youngest of your number this morning. And we all know what happened there."

"Do you mock us?" the general growled.

"Your Majesty, why are we wasting our time with an artist?" asked the chief of the War Council.

The King held up a placating hand and turned

to Morminiu. "Hitissh, if what you're trying to tell us is connected to the war, then say it quickly."

They were right to speak with urgency, Morminiu reflected; their only chance left was to arm the population and wait for the final attack. "Your Majesty," he began, "the SCeders have arrived so quickly and are obviously so powerful that we have no time to gather an army from the rest of the country. We need to resolve this quickly, and locally. Therefore, I propose an uncommon solution for this exceptional situation."

"And I suppose you have that solution!" one of the generals sneered, then laughed.

Morminiu kept his eyes on the King. "Yes, Majesty, I have a solution. But if you've already found one, and don't need alternatives, I can leave and come back afterward."

"What do you mean by *afterward?*" the chief growled.

"For the kind of situation we're dealing with, the classic solutions are no good anymore; the SCeders know of them, too. We must surprise them, do the unexpected. And if they have conquered the other kingdoms, overcome other Caramis—and we must suppose this is so—then it will be hard to find something they haven't seen yet, something to really surprise them. That's why we need a phril who knows the Carami very well and is able to take all eventualities into consideration when offering a solution—a solution that others have not yet found, probably because they are treating the problem as you are now . . . with pride and arrogance."

With affronted exclamations, three generals jumped up and lunged at him with unsheathed swords.

"Stop it!" the King roared, sounding surprisingly vigorous for his age.

"Your Majesty, I propose that we lock away this traitor who weakens the army's morale, until you decide what to do with him," a voice said from the other side of the room. Morminiu looked that way as Tathar rose from the armchair where he had been observing the exchange, unnoticed. The

Master Recipear moved from the shadows, a shadow himself, and stepped into the light. A stench like rotting flowers flowed through the room in an overpowering wave; Morminiu's eyes darted around the room and finally settled on the source: a second observer, standing as still as a carved bone pillar. He couldn't distinguish the faintest detail, but the stench prompted a memory: the masked phril! Morminiu clenched his teeth and turned back to the King, ignoring Tathar and the other.

"He purposely offended the War Council and, by implication, Your Majesty," Tathar continued.

"Why does this concern you, Harissh Tathar? Are you afraid he'll take your place at the Table of the Six?" The King scowled and Tathar slipped quietly behind the officers. The King looked at his generals and indicated Morminiu. "My lords, I treasure the wisdom of this phril. You are upset because he put his finger on our wound: yes, we are poorly prepared, militarily speaking. But it's not only your fault; it's ours—all of us, and especially me, because I neglected this aspect of my rule. Centuries of peace have made us lazy, and we have lost much military knowledge."

He rose from his high chair, drawing his thin body up, straight and imposing. He waved his hand at them and commanded, "Take your seats and relax." Then he returned to Morminiu. "Tell me, Hitissh: have you, an artist, ever wielded in battle the sword you wear so proudly?"

"Ask Harissh Tathar, Majesty—not if I've ever struck with it, but how efficient I am. He knows." Morminiu spoke while staring at Tathar.

The King glanced toward him, then gave his head a little shake of disgust returned to the more important subject. "Very well; tell us your solution. I promise you, we'll analyze it."

"Thank you, Majesty. I suggest we attack during the night, when they sleep, and when we will be more comfortable outside the Carami. The problem is, where should we exit?

They will certainly be guarding all of the mouths. I propose that we sally forth through Scurgiton Deversator."

"Through what?"

Morminiu smiled a little at the King's puzzlement, then explained, "That is the code name, Your Majesty."

"Explain."

"We will exit through the Carami's anus. At least, the one I know of. There are probably another two, but I haven't discovered them yet. I've calculated how far the rectum stretches and estimate that the anus surfaces about three megasteps from the Carami's body. Which would place us right behind the enemy's camp. If we leave tomorrow morning, by tomorrow night we should be in position, around two megasteps behind them. We can approach under cover of night and launch a surprise attack, which could be sustained by sending further units from the city. This could succeed if you could hold your current defensive positions in the city for one more day."

Silence fell in the hall. Then it was broken by a mocking laugh. Tathar rose, trying to take control of the situation one more time. And the black presence behind him seemed to double his stature and the force of his words. "That is the stupidest idea I've ever heard. How can somebody walk through a rectum? Imagine a detachment of soldiers marching through the rectum of any of you. In a short time they'd choke to death in feces."

The King looked at Morminiu questioningly. Morminiu retorted to Tathar, "Have you ever been there?"

"No, but I can make an analogy. If it would surely happen like that in the body of a miserable phril, then *ta forthiorium,* it will happen in a Carami's body, even if it is populated by hundreds of thousands of phrils," Tathar replied, stressing the argument of logic with conviction.

Such lessons in logic were part of Recipear training, the equations and rationales expressed in the old written language. They were valuable in manipulating listeners' minds during Recipes.

"And that's further proof of an impatient mind," Morminiu answered casually. "A phril's body is not inhabited by anything, while the Carami is inhabited by hundreds of thousands of phrils. A significant population in a symbiotic relationship; a populace that has adapted to help it survive, while it makes sure that nothing happens to us. And thus, if our bodies are not meant to host symbiotes, we must say that, *tes ta conthrarhiom,* our bodies are not in any way similar to a Carami's. Therefore, your analogy has no real basis," Morminiu concluded, applying another argument of logic with equal conviction.

He stopped for effect, then continued, exploiting the Harissh's mistake in not taking advantage of Morminiu's pause. "Actually, I would like to ask how much you do know about the Carami's anatomy, so I can keep that in mind when you argue on this subject."

"Enough to—"

"Meaning? Something concrete."

Tathar fell silent and retook his seat. Morminiu turned triumphantly toward the King. "Majesty, I believe I forgot to mention one detail. I volunteer to lead this detachment, because I don't think there is anybody else who can handle this. If the plan fails, I pay for the error with my life. I consider this preferable to waiting to be slaughtered, even if it seems crazy. Or precisely *because* of that."

"I may lose my best Recipear!" the King moaned.

"Your Majesty, I'm flattered, but this problem takes priority."

"You're right, Hitissh," the King sighed. "Tomorrow morning the detachment will be waiting for you in front of the palace. May the Holy Sky protect you!"

The muscular tube of the rectum was protected with

a thick, grayish-white, greasy skin. The waste on its bottom was ankle deep, moving slowly in the same direction as the soldiers, who had been advancing in columns of two for two hours, hunched over in the low tunnel. Only a quarter of them were using glow-worms; the others followed, ready to use their own when the first ones were exhausted.

"Do you know how much farther we still have to go, Your Highness?" the military commander of the detachment asked Morminiu.

"Probably as far again as we've already travelled."

The commander frowned his displeasure. "But, you told us this asshole was three megasteps long, and we've already been walking through its crap for two hours."

Morminiu gazed at him calmly, ignoring his crude language. "Do you have any idea how far we've already travelled, Commander?"

He shrugged. "Should be about four mega."

"Four mega at a normal pace. We've actually gone only a mega and a bit," Morminiu answered dryly.

"But, we left the city proper five hours ago! It's almost lunchtime and the soldiers will want to eat."

"Commander, nobody has his lunch until I say so." Morminiu looked forward, indicating that the discussion was over.

"I understand, Hitissh," the phril muttered.

"Watch out!" someone shouted behind them.

Immediately, all the phrils, beginning with the ones at the rear, started to curse and scream. Although they had gotten used to the smell, now a dizzyingly strong stench hit them fully. Morminiu watched soldiers clinging to walls that a minute ago they had been too disgusted to touch. A moment later a waist-high avalanche of feces rolled through the detachment. It passed them rapidly, and the tube gradually drained. After a while they heard a distant splash. Morminiu listened carefully, but heard nothing else approaching. It was quiet again.

He walked the next one hundred steps cautiously, continually testing the way ahead with a stick. At last, as he had supposed, the tunnel ended in a steep slope plunging down into a round cavity where several tubes met. Morminiu climbed down and tested the depth of the basin full of excrement with his stick. He couldn't reach its bottom. But studying the ceiling, he decided it was safe to cross; there weren't any deep pits in Carami, and most were symmetrical. This cavity was probably only a transition point, not a storage point. So he jumped in. The excrement came up to his nervous belt, just under his stomach. The span of two more palms, and he would have had feces in his mouth.

"Come along, quickly," he called. "Come in pairs and follow me."

He heard a disturbance behind him and turned to look at the gathered soldiers. The commander stood to one side, watching him with an expression of disgust. Apparently he was content to let his soldiers mutiny.

"Do you know the expression, I'm in shit up to my neck?" Morminiu called up to him.

The soldiers fell silent, surprised. One of them approached the edge of the slope, more curious than the others.

"Well, I'm in shit up to my stomach, physically speaking. But if you stay there, you'll all be in shit up to your necks." A new wave of protests arose, which Morminiu ignored. "You know why? This is the only way through this monster's ass. I'm the only one who knows the exits. So, if you don't follow me, you'll remain for the rest of your short lives up this creature's ass—shit eaters for real!"

He laughed sarcastically, then suddenly stopped and yanked the curious soldier toward him. He helped him regain his balance, then wiped a few drops of excrement off his face before he asked him, looking askance at the others, "Well, it's better to be in shit up to your stomach than to spend life as a shit-eater, isn't it?"

"Yes, M'Lord," the soldier muttered uncertainly.

"All right, then, we two are going to get out of here, and I wish you all good appetites!"

"I don't think I want to eat anymore," the commander grumbled, still looking disgusted, and climbed down the slope, slipping into the pool of excrement violently enough to make waves—happily, none big enough to add truth to Morminiu's shit-eater taunts.

"I hope there won't be any more interruptions today; otherwise we'll have to lay siege to the SCeders from inside the Carami's butt," Morminiu commented as he waded out of the basin before the whole troop climbed down into the pool of shit. The waves rose alarmingly.

He moved into the drainage tunnel that collected all the waste brought through the intestinal tubes. As a precaution, Morminiu had a soldier mark the tunnel so they would know which way they had come.

They advanced for three more hours. The route grew more difficult because they were now wading through excrement almost up to their necks. They moved slowly, both because the dense medium was difficult to move through, and out of caution. A slip in such conditions was sure death. At last, the level started to drop and the tunnel lightened ahead of them. Morminiu stopped when the level had dropped down to their knees and the light was bright enough to hurt their sensitive eyes. Gone was the filtered green light of the Carami's interior; now a bright yellow sun can illuminated a summer afternoon.

"Put on the lenses you were given," Morminiu ordered.

They all pulled the smoky goggles from the inner pockets of their uniforms, placed them over their eyes, then tied the strings behind their heads. When they were done they stood ready, breathing deeply of the fresh air blowing in to cool their abused lungs. Morminiu watched them, smiling. They looked like giant insects.

"They suit you," he congratulated them. "This way, at

least, I can't recognize you, to know later which of you ate shit and which ones didn't."

They stood on the lip of a pit into which all the feces were deposited. The light was irritating their eyes, even filtered through the dark lenses. Rivulets of sweat left wet tracks on their faces. Morminiu leaned cautiously over the edge. The exit was not at ground level, but halfway up the pit's wall. He listened carefully, but heard only the sounds of nature. If there were any phrils or SCeders, they were far away.

Still leaning out over the edge, he withdrew a clawed bone grappling hook from his pack, swung it a few times, then threw it powerfully up and over the pit's edge. He drew the attached line back and the claw caught on something. He tested it by yanking on it a couple of times, then nodded to himself and turned to the commander:

"Throw your claw, Commander, and at my order start the climb."

He turned back to the edge and jumped to hang on the rope, then began to climb cautiously upward, pausing at the pit's lip with only his head above the edge to look at the surrounding terrain. Behind him rose the bulky body of the Carami, stretching into the distance to the north; to the south rose the high bank of the Hung Water-plain. Something hit his cheek, hard, making him jerk. The skin there stung, but he saw no threat when he scanned the landscape again. Satisfied, he climbed the last few feet and rolled onto the dry soil, pausing to look around one more time. Over by the Carami, smoke rose from the many cookfires in the SCeders' camp.

A flutter tickled his cheek and he slapped at it in annoyance. A golden butterfly with a swollen midsection and small, metallic yellow wings tumbled to the ground. He lifted it between his fingers and studied it for a few seconds, then, not recognizing it, he tossed it into the pit. A thunderous roar erupted, destroying the silence. Flames rose from the pool of feces, and thousands of butterflies took flight, yellow wings flashing in the sunlight as they beat frantically to lift the insects above the pool's surface. They moved through the air in a chaos of color, whirling with incredible speed.

Movement caught Morminiu's eye and he watched, terrified, as the edges of the anus contracted spasmodically, then closed tight, sealing the exit. They opened again, and again closed. One last contraction hurled a liquid stream of excrement against the opposite wall of the pit. Morminiu glimpsed the tumbling body of a phril in the torrent. The phril slammed into the wall, then slid down to drown in the pool. For a moment he hoped it was the recalcitrant commander, then squelched the thought, shocked. Quiet settled again. The butterflies settled back onto the fetid surface of the pool. Through which, Morminiu noticed, something moved; he could not distinguish what.

"Commander, are you still there?" Morminiu called in a low voice.

"We are. What in the spheres was that?"

"I'll tell you when you're up here. Come on, get everybody out—quickly."

As the soldiers began climbing up, Morminiu felt something on his back—then another, and another—something was swarming all over his back! He screamed and dropped to roll around on the ground, trying to get them off, then rose onto his knees and waved his arms around, batting at his assailants. At last they dropped off and scuttled away he saw that they were rats, much larger than those in the city, their huge paws bearing strong claws. They disappeared into holes peppering the ground around the pit. Morminiu whistled in surprised relief, then turned to help the first soldier climbing over the edge of the pit. As he leaned forward, he glimpsed one of the rats emerging from a hole in the wall of the pit and jumping into the pool of feces. Morminiu squinted, wondering . . . who or what had dug the pit?

Dusk fell. The excrement on their clothes hardened into a stinking crust, and finally they stripped down to their undergarments and discarded the clothing. While there was still enough light, Morminiu ordered them to catch as many of the golden butterflies as they could and tie them to the tips of their arrows. Despite their scowls, this time they all obeyed, without Morminiu having to offer any explanation. The insects were easy to catch; they blanketed the area in the thousands.

When darkness ruled the land completely, they started moving stealthily toward the SCeders' camp. Big fires still burned there, in the midst of the crowded tents. As they got closer they could also hear voices raised in harsh songs, shouts, and screams. They stopped in a group of trees a short distance from the camp and waited. On this side of their camp, the SCeder sentinels were few; most were concentrated on the Carami side of the camp.

Midnight came and passed. Two of the Three Daughters of the Sky had already arisen, throwing pale light over the dark land. There were still a few fires burning in the camp, but for the most part it was silent. From time to time the sentinels exchanged murmured passwords.

Morminiu spread his soldiers in two lines parallel to the camp and they moved forward, crawling, to get as close as possible. Then, at the Recipear's sign, the first rank rose onto their knees, and the second to their feet. Bowstrings stretched, were released. From the SCeders camp came a few screams—of injury, and surprise. The alarm rose immediately. The hiss of arrows whizzing into the midst of the enemy nearly drowned out the sounds of panic. Morminiu saw an arrow slam into the neck of the sentinel that had shouted the alarm; the subsequent explosion hurled him to the ground with only half of his face intact.

A rolling chain of thunder shook the air, startling phrils and SCeders alike. The second row of archers nocked butterfly-tipped arrows and stretched their bows, preparing to cover the first row of soldiers who, at Morminiu's order, charged forward, screaming war cries. A wave of arrows exploded among the tents, turning the camp into a pyre.

Corpses littered the ground behind the first rank of charging phrils. Riding animals ran about in terror. SCeders collapsed to the ground, mortally wounded by an arrow or sword blow. The survivors of the first wave of the attack were disoriented. Taking advantage of this, the second rank of phrils, led by their commander, swept into the camp. They wove around the fires, shouting and hacking at any enemy still standing, or stabbing the wounded crawling on the ground.

Morminiu noticed the tent on the highest ground in the middle of the camp—the enemy commander's headquarters. Taking out the SCeder commander would finish the fight quickly. Beckoning the phrils' commander and nearby soldiers to follow him, he ran toward the tent, his sword whirling before him, slicing and quickly withdrawing. As he drew closer to the tent, though, the ranks of SCeders deepened, and his run slowed to walk.

At that moment, reinforcements swept into the camp from the Royal Carami, and the ranks of SCeders surrounding the central tent thinned as its defenders ran to battle this new threat. Morminiu fought toward the tent, avoiding the last few strokes from defending blades and flinging himself to the ground and rolling, to spring back to his feet inside the tent, sword in hand.

The SCeder commander stood there as if waiting for him. He was tall, massively muscled, a giant dressed in skins and gleaming bone armor. His white hair, partly hidden under a yellowed bone helmet, flowed down his back in a thick ponytail. With a flick of his hand, he signalled the guards to retreat. They obeyed, regrouping at his back. He smiled cruelly at Morminiu.

At that moment, the Green Kingdom commander burst into the tent, trailed by five soldiers. At first they saw only Morminiu. "Hitissh, we have a message from His Highness, Tathar—" the commander began.

"Not now," Morminiu snapped, but then he saw the commander's sword levelled at him, and realized that the message could only have been issued before the expedition had left, its delivery purposely delayed until this moment. "Why did you wait all this time to tell me?" he asked slowly, knowing what answer he would hear.

"I was instructed to deliver it once we had reached the SCeder forces. I'm sorry, Hitissh; it is nothing personal," the commander finished, waving his soldiers into the tent.

The recipear withdrew to the farthest corner of the tent as if fearful, allowing the traitors to enter fully before they realized the true situation—allowing the SCeder commander's guards to close the trap.

As the Green commander and his men realized they were surrounded, the SCeder commander grinned in satisfaction and drew his giant blade. With one blow he decapitated the Green commander. Then, leaving the Green Kingdom soldiers for his guards to finish, he lunged toward Morminiu.

Morminiu parried the warrior's blows, though their force nearly drove him to his knees. Now, he realized with a thrill of panic, he really was in deep shit! He went on the offensive, trying to get to the entrance to the SCeder commander's private quarters. If he could just find more space . . .

He succeeded in reaching the second room, pushed aside with his foot the items that stood in his way, and took up a position in the middle of the room. From the other room he heard the screams of pain and the shouts of fury of those locked in battle there.

The SCeder commander entered the bedroom, his sword ready, and immediately attacked Morminiu. The blows were violent and, despite the weight and length of the massive weapon, delivered with deadly speed. He focused on avoiding the blade, parrying as little as possible in an effort to conserve his strength while forcing his opponent to exert himself by moving around the room. Eventually the giant stopped the attack and stood, breathing rapidly, though he didn't seem tired, only that he had lost his initial enthusiasm.

Morminiu raised Donasa the Faithful, aiming the sword's tip at the SCeder's neck, and lunged forward just as his opponent pounced. The giant stopped just inches from the tip. Now it was the Recipear's turn to attack. In the first moments, despite the speed of the blows, the SCeder held his ground, parrying with apparent ease. Morminiu pressed the attack, feinting quickly left, then swiftly right. He continued the blinding swordplay, knowing he could not maintain this speed for too long, hoping the giant would tire before he did. He would have no other chance, he knew.

And, finally, his opponent took a step back, then another. He counterattacked, but Morminiu slipped under the other's sword and swept his own up as he passed, turning behind the enemy commander. He sliced through all the leather strings on the giant's right side, and the bone cuirass protecting his chest and abdomen, loosened, now bounced and shifted, distracting. The SCeder commander snatched off the armor and threw it at Morminiu, who ducked and again attacked. The huge sword parried the first blows, then stroked wide, tearing through the tent fabric. The SCeder tried to get back into position to prevent Donasa the Faithful from finding her mark, to no avail; the sword penetrated deep into the SCeder's side, passing between his ribs before withdrawing quickly.

The SCeder commander brought up his weapon and withdrew a few steps, glancing down at his wound as if bewildered. It wasn't lethal, but Morminiu could read the pain on his face.

Morminiu attacked one more time, swinging his blade high to force his opponent to raise his sword to parry the blow. Morminiu twisted, his blade sliding along the sharp edge of his opponent's, then turned and thrust his sword into his opponent's chest. He drew it out immediately and whirled away to again face the SCeder. Still holding the sword in his hand, his breath whistling, the enemy commander remained on his feet only with effort.

The Recipear leaped forward, thrusting his sword at the SCeder. The warrior tried to dodge it, but the weapon penetrated the SCeder's back. His massive sword fell from nerveless fingers, and Morminiu stepped in, caught his wrist, and yanked the giant off-balance. He tottered two steps before Donasa the Faithful sliced off his head.

Thrusting the SCeder commander's head onto the tip of his sword, Morminiu stepped out of the tent holding it high for the enemy to recognize their master's white mane, stained with blood.

The carnage lasted till dawn, when the phrils, unused to the sun, withdrew to rest.

MORMINIU

Yesterday I attended a dinner party given by the King in honor of the victory over the SCeders. The whole evening I smiled widely, to satisfy all my well-wishers. My mouth still hurts. At least ten times I was asked to tell the story of the battle and I refused every time. I have nothing to tell. The only words I can think to say are: shit, blood, shit, fire, shit, and smoking flesh. I've eaten only fruits and raw vegetables since the battle. I can no longer tolerate noise, heat, or strong smells of any kind.

And to make the party perfect, Comtap, the King's Trust, announced that the new Master Recipear of the Kingdom will be, according to the King's decision, Hitissh Morminiu. I'm probably still too shocked from the battle to appreciate that, for I'm not feeling any enthusiasm. Master Recipear of the Kingdom—and only after one year as a Royal Recipear on the Table of the Six. Plabos would be proud of me. Maybe I will be too, eventually.

Tathar, newly relieved of that position, approached me, bowed, and smiling, congratulated me: "You won't get through this so easily, hero!" After which he left the party. I noticed that he was alone for the first time in my knowledge; the masked phril who seemed his shadow was absent.

I was invited to sit between the King and Taharissh Chathu at the head table. Taharissh Comtap sat on the King's right. Reluctantly, I took my place between the King and his heir to the throne. Several times throughout the meal I was tempted to rise and find a privy to vomit—despite being drenched in an overwhelmingly strong floral perfume, every time Chathu raised his arm the cloying stench of a decomposing corpse hit me.

Finally I rose suddenly and stepped over to the window, ostensibly for air, although I bent over behind a curtain and vomited. I noticed that the room behind me had fallen silent, then I heard the King's voice, followed by laughter as he finished a joke, probably at my expense. Nevertheless, it did the trick; the normal party banter resumed.

Afterward we all moved to another room for after dinner conversation. The heir, who hadn't addressed me even once during the dinner, settled into a high-backed armchair, surrounded by his usual company of courtiers, and observe those in the room with a bored air. One of his hangers-on, in his way to the prince, paused to whisper in my ear with a courteous smile, "Now you'll probably die sooner."

I stared after him as he continued on his way.

ADVICE. *Lately, I've been surprised by how fast things can evolve. At the beginning of my book, I wrote marked by a certain reality and a certain school of thought; now I am oriented toward a new direction, different not only from my school, but from all that has ever been thought in Recipearium since its written beginnings. I won't start denying the theory of the phriliras' incompatibility with the gastronomic art. Especially as, at the moment, it is still true. It is a certain fact that they lack the gastrophiza that is the key to the whole gastronomic art and philosophy. Still, this key could be replaced (and I mention this based on fact, not only theory) with an instrument which, handled with a lot of will and skill, may bring results closer to our spiritual experience, partially replacing the role of the gastrophiza. Look how one can rewrite history! Probably sometime in future, gastrophiza will be only the phrilic instrument in the gastronomic art, while the phriliric instrument will be an incredible imagination and psychic power.*

Before going further, I have to say that I don't have in mind to replace the chapters in which I sustain arguments to the contrary of what I will demonstrate now, because they shouldn't be interpreted as inconsistency and failure of logic, but rather as history, as evolution. This is the book that will surprise history.

(from The Teachings of the Recipearium Revolution by Grand Master Recipear of the Green Kingdom, Morminiu*)*

XI. MASTER RECIPEAR OF THE GREEN KINGDOM

The ceiling in the Royal Palace kitchen was higher than most, so the smoke would not accumulate around the food and taint it with its smell. The chimneys were permanently open and regularly cleaned, too, from the same reason. The small windows were actually vents, preventing rather than allowing in the light. The light source was in fact a row of glow-worms lining the wall like a belt.

The cooks hurriedly left the room as Morminiu entered the kitchen behind the King, whose bodyguards remained at the door. The sovereign was dragging the bruised body of a white brops. According to Recipearium conventions, a Course had to be prepared by the Recipear, start to finish, with his own hands. Therefore, the King had beaten the brops himself, in order to tenderize its flesh. He'd clenched his jaw, but hit it forcefully; it would not do for the courtiers to notice any sign of weakness or, on another level, of Recipear incompetence.

Shaking with exhaustion, the King swung the brops onto the long bone table, nicked and gouged by the sharp edges of countless hatchets and knives wielded by the royal cooks. Then he sat down to catch his breath. The door closed behind them as the guards left quietly, leaving only Morminiu and the King in the kitchen and assuring that the Recipe would remain secret.

"All right, I'm relaxed now," the King said eventually, rising.

Morminiu snapped his fingers and immediately the sound of a flute drifted through the air, exciting the hair on the King's head. He looked at Morminiu in wonder, but the Recipear smiled as a signal that everything was under control and said, "Every Course shares resonance with certain sounds, with a certain melodic tone. If you succeed in finding the proper music and tune it to the Preparation Story, it glorifies the Course; the Course preparation becomes at a certain moment a musical story. The spirit lets itself be overwhelmed by the music, experiencing levels impossible to express in any other way. That's why it is suggested that the Recipear look first for the Course's melodic tone and only after that for its Story."

The brops still breathed, blood bubbling from its mouth, its red eyes surrounded by fangs bulging from their sockets. Its skin was mottled red in spots, sweat foaming pink from it. The King avoided looking at it. The flute continued its dark tune.

"Your Highness can start now," Morminiu urged.

The King, demonstrating that he had learned the lesson well, selected a broad, sharp knife. Holding it clumsily, he tried to thrust it into the brops' belly, but too slow to pierce the brops' skin—cursing, he stepped back as the animal's reflexes reacted and it promptly kicked its two feet. It growled with the last of its strength, spraying red foam into the King's eyes.

"Can't you put on more cheerful music?" he complained.

"Not even this beast deserves that," Morminiu answered, watching the King closely. He added, "Majesty, if we put on inappropriate music, we spoil everything. We're not making food here; we're preparing a Course. We interpret art, according to Recipearium precepts."

"All right, all right," the King grumbled, intimidated.

"Look how we're doing," Morminiu explained. "Music is good because it resonates with the Course. It is good because we have been cruel. No beings should suffer this way. On the other hand, this Course becomes impossible if we don't proceed this way. What are we going to do? To satisfy our immeasurable vanity in making art, we prepare the Course by the book. Then it is the music that purifies us and punishes us—we have to somehow pay for this. It is very good that the music has upset you. That means you have started to feel the art, its secret meanings that urge us to do it that way and not otherwise."

The King listened closely, but kept quiet, waiting like a diligent student. Tension had been building in the kitchen; they both felt it, both felt tense themselves. And the flute music was accentuating this tension.

Morminiu picked up the knife and twirled it a few times in his fingers. "This time I'll show you," he said, and deftly cut the brops the length of its body, stopping just under its head. Its paws jerked once, then the animal breathed its last foaming breath. A sour smell rose from the split as the entrails bubbled out. The King wrinkled his nose and withdrew two steps.

"Art is dirty, Your Highness. Only the finished artwork is clean and beautiful, pleasant to the eye, the ears, and especially to the tongue and the gastrophiza," Morminiu said. "But the road to it is dirty, deceiving, and sometimes degrading. Like politics. An important position is beautiful, powerful, but the road to it is full of traps and dirty, degrading, dealing"

"Are you referring to a specific road and position, Morminiu?" asked the King, his face a mask.

"No; I believe that any political position requires this. But, I'm referring to art. As for position, I didn't have time to thank Your Majesty properly. I beg forgiveness and I hope it is not too late to express my gratitude."

"Do you think you deserved more?" the sovereign asked.

"It has fulfilled a dream I had since my first lessons with Plabos. The four and a half years of struggling, of slinking through the nets of political intrigue at court—for this I feel I deserved to reach this position, and only for this. I did not seek favor when I battled the SCeders. I did it for my kingdom and my king. There are things a phril does because he wants to, and things he does because he should. Most of the time they are not pleasant, but they need to be done."

The King smiled. "And the lessons here, with me—are you doing this because you want to, or because you feel you should?"

"These lessons are a pleasure and an honor, Majesty," Morminiu told him. "To be teacher to the first Recipear King; that will go down in history."

The King fell silent, looking both thoughtful and flattered. Morminiu set the knife on the table and waited. After a while, the sovereign turned to the table and started to skin the brops. Near the end of the process he became nervous, agitated, and his movements were hasty and brutal. Blood splattered his arms to the elbows. The brops looked no better, mangled in many places, blood pooling in craters gouged into its flesh. After the King cleaned out the entrails, Morminiu helped him to wash the body, and they placed it on a platter.

From the freezer, the Recipear brought a bowl containing fruits, vegetables, and greenery. The flute rhythm became more vivid, joined by the unmistakable trills of bone pipes. The King started to relax. Guided by Morminiu, he chose appropriate ingredients with which to stuff the beast, thinly slicing vegetables and tossing them with pieces of fruit and greenery before pouring fermented sequ syrup over the mixture. After filling the brops with this, he brushed honey over the exterior.

"Your guard is not very friendly," the King said offhandedly when Morminiu paused in giving advice.

"I beg for forgiveness if they have disturbed Your Grace's peace."

"Oh, no. I have not seen them yet. But I've been told that while you're in the palace, they wait for you, mute and still. They don't even partake of meals in the mess. Do they have something against my soldiers?"

"Not at all, Majesty. They have been trained to behave that way. We can all relax, knowing they are unobtrusively protecting us."

"I have also been told that they look odd, even terrifying. They are completely covered, and masked. One cannot see the smallest area of their bodies. And they don't have the Mormont House's coat of arms on their cloaks."

"Indeed, Your Majesty. They're not, in fact, my soldiers. They are hired through contract as sell-swords. As part of the deal, they have the right to wear the uniform of their caste and not display my device."

"But, where did you find them?"

"I'd heard of them ever since I was a child in the Deep

South on the Green Kingdom's borders. Actually, I'm not very sure if they're from there, or somewhere else. In connection to this— If you'll allow me?"

"Please."

The King had finished arranging the platter. Morminiu poured vegetable oil over the brops and onto the tray around it. Then he sprinkled a few yellow dusk flower blossoms onto the oil and smiled, satisfied, and continued their conversation.

"I ask for forgiveness if I dare too much, but I consider it a pressing matter. I understand that the two kingdoms north of the Green Kingdom have fallen." Morminiu helped the sovereign lift the tray into the oven. "And now the SCeders are stronger than ever. They will probably return to the Green Kingdom. I assume their ambitions are on the same level with their military training, which they've proven is substantial— in just a few weeks they have conquered the Great Desert with its nomadic tribes, so widespread and mobile that nobody has ever succeeded in mastering them until now. And they have conquered two more kingdoms—relatively small, it's true, and not very powerful, but which have at least twenty Caramis in which they could resist attack and survive a siege, having enough of their own resources for more than a year. Yet they have fallen in just a few weeks."

"That's right, Morminiu," the King said honestly, turning a serious gaze on the Recipear. "And we probably would have shared their fate, if not for you."

"Thank you, but I'm more concerned with what preparations have been made since, to mount a better defense."

At a signal from Morminiu, the music stopped. The brops was in the oven. They only needed to prepare the pastry for the green salad that would follow the Course.

"I'm confused, Morminiu." The King slumped into a chair beside the table, no longer looking like a mighty sovereign, but merely a phril on whose shoulders rested a terrible burden. "I've been the first in many generations to face war. Others have done and undone in peace and quiet, leaving the kingdom flourishing. Now, at my age, just when I was looking forward to relinquishing total control over the realm, I have to be hit with this curse. I have a mind to announce Chathu as rightful heir next month at the Annual Ball, with the Royal Bid."

"You consider him the most appropriate to see the kingdom through its problems."

"Yes. He's young and ambitious."

"But, he's sick."

"You know that?" the King asked, surprised.

Morminiu nodded.

"So, you know! Yes, he has had pelhitza since childhood. There's no cure."

The Recipear felt his eyes bulge, but he masked his surprise immediately. The King was watching him, so he said quickly, "It seems to be getting worse."

"Ah!"

"Otherwise I wouldn't notice," Morminiu continued. "And more, think about it: if he loses control, proving that he's weak, then the realm will be invaded and he will die. Your Grace will be within him at that moment, and you'll perish together, dragging into darkness whole generations of the Green Dynasty. I think this is only a temporary solution, with no future," he concluded in a whisper, his tone humble.

"What do you mean?"

"That I believe you should stay on your throne and follow only the advice that is good for the kingdom."

"Like yours?"

Morminiu smiled. "Like mine, too. Or better, like Comtap's."

The King lowered his head to his chest and his wrinkled lungs deflated pathetically. "Comtap is sick too, my friend. Advanced senility. Only the bone's roots keep him standing in public appearances and keep his consciousness awake. My good Comtap is too old."

"Why didn't he retire?"

"The kingdom," answered the King, lifting his head to look into Morminiu's eyes. His voice trembled when he continued. "I didn't allow him to retire. I needed him." He looked away and chewed his lip nervously. The Recipear kept silent. The King's guilt was sufficient punishment.

"Before Comtap you had Plabos as counsellor. How was he?" Morminiu asked.

The King looked surprised by this. Then he sighed, looked at the floor, and answered, "Not before Comtap. They were both advisors at the same time."

Morminiu kept silent, hoping he would get more. He had not had many of these moments, in which the King was alone and willing to talk.

"That was the most rewarding time. They were the best friends I ever had, but also the best team with whom I've ever governed." The King turned to study Morminiu. "You, Morminiu, remind me a lot of Plabos. I understand that you were his disciple—Plabos' last disciple. But was there ever anything besides that?"

"I don't think I understand the question, Majesty."

"What else connected you two? Kinship, alliance? How did he find you?"

"I'm eager to know that too," Morminiu answered sadly. "He never wanted to tell me."

"Certainly, if he found you randomly, he would have told you."

"Certainly, Your Majesty." He paused so the embarrassing moment would pass, then said, "But, returning to the actual problems . . . "

"The actual problems are a great mess, Morminiu."

"To address the size of the SCeders army, I believe that all nobles should recruit soldiers from their lands and immediately begin training in specially prepared and hidden locations where the SCeder spies cannot find them. You should also order that a sack of the explosive butterflies from the cesspit at the end of the Carami anus be brought to me, alive. I'll try to set up a breeding program to assure us of more of this ammunition."

"Why not set up the breeding farm there?"

"Because now the SCeders know of their existence and they will attack there first, to eliminate that advantage. We also need to send spies into the neighboring lands and along the frontiers, so we will have ample warning when they return. At first notice, we will capture all the butterflies from the cesspit and burn all that escape. We will not leave the SCeders anything they can use against us. Begging forgiveness for my audacity, but you should suggest that the chief of the War Council retire. He is too old and inexperienced to react properly in such situations. Even now, he should've called for a general mobilization!"

VALIRIA

I stop in my prayers and try to understand what I have just felt. An indignant thrill quivers up my spine—somebody is trying to spy upon my thoughts! Somebody is trying to rape my mind!

I open my eyes and stand, hiding my rage so I don't warn the spy that I'm aware of her presence.

Around me rise the soot-stained, rough limestone walls of the Holy Temple. No window breaks their expanse; green light penetrates through a hole in the ceiling. After millennia of existence, the surrounding wood has grown right up to and over the temple, and the green light shivers with the shadowy lines of branches, so the path through the temple's central room to the altar, the Old Path we are not allowed to change, is like walking through the forest itself. In the walls are fixed torches whose smoking red flames are reflected in the shiny surface of the metal pillar that rises behind the altar. It is seamless, its sides like mirrors, and has also been there for millennia. It protects within it a stalagmite made of pure resin from "the plants that feed on shadows" which itself contains within its translucent walls the Carami's soul. The old priests of the redheaded phrils worshiped the Carami as a divinity and considered this the holiest place in the entire universe. We still believe that; none of us dares perform or agree to dirty deeds in this place. It is a holy law that all philiras obey.

There is no phril in this world able to read minds, I think. With measured steps, controlling my breathing, I walk toward the exit of the Holy Temple, which I'd believed could protect me. I don't fight the mental touch that probes me, but neither do I give it access to what it should not know. I keep the spy at a superficial level without warning her that I'm alert to her presence. As I reach the threshold and look around, another thought thrills me—what if it is not a phrilira?

The Holy Temple is in the heart of the Tormented

Forest. The thick black trunks of "the plants that feed on shadows" surround the building like an unfriendly wall. It is said that the redheaded phrils mated with the trees to give birth to the temple's guardians—trees with consciousness and mysterious powers. Moreover, the legend states that, hearing the news of the fall of the Carami at the hands of the Green phrils, the old priests left their shadows in the forest, in order to remain watching over the divine soul to whom they had sworn service forever. When the soldiers of Chathron the Conqueror found them, the bodies of the priests were empty, mindless and soulless. And from the forest depths could be heard whispers and voices, sometimes even screams—giving rise to its name. For more than half a century, nobody dared pass through the Tormented Forest. Even at this hour, only phriliras have the strength to come and pray in the Holy Temple.

That is why now, looking around me at the knotty and twisted trunks, so massive that not even ten phrils can encircle one within their joined arms, I'm asking myself who is actually trying to spy me.

I feel a nudge in my mind and then something like a stream of cool air, tickling my gray matter. I open my mouth for air and breathe greedily. It probably wasn't wise to leave my mind open, even though I've shown only what I want seen.

Inside the Temple are a few phriliras that maintain the flames and the altar, attendants without significant powers. I cannot trust them to be of any help. I don't know if even the temple building would be able to hold back the Tormented Forest's spirits. I have no choice but to pass through the darkness of the forest alone, walking to the park around the House of Phriliras. There is a bond between me and the Carami; I don't remember upsetting it with anything!

I hear a terrified scream. Invisible fingers touch my forehead and turn my head toward the left side of the temple; I feel them trying to get ahold of me and then slipping away.

I concentrate, close my eyes, and extend my mind to catch them, but they escape me, disappearing in the direction they had shown me. "Help!" I hear whispered through the foliage, the sound fading away. A terrible howl shatters the ancestral silence. It sounds close; I run toward it.

"Stay inside, hide!" I yell to the temple servants who are gathering at the exit.

The forest is not very dense, yet it takes time to dodge around the huge trunks. The soil is soft under my soles, the elastic consistency of a sticky mattress. My mind is seeking the one in need—the one spying on me, I know now. Not an apprentice—that is clear to me now, too—but more a professional spy. I perceive movement in front of me, between two trunks to my left, and I change direction toward a silhouette there.

As I get closer the silhouette resolves itself into a phrilira dressed in the colors of House Hish. She is a silver spy, not somebody from within the House of Phriliras. The silver spies are the best in mental manipulations. They're better than most of us. Only the Mothers can face them. I ask myself who could have an interest in finding out my secrets and a shiver licks my spine.

The spy is kneeling in deep obeisance with her fingers spread on the soil as if trying to catch something, or perhaps merely to keep her balance. She raises her forehead and looks at me. I stop and watch her closely—if she was sent to kill me, it is possible that the shouts were only a ploy to draw me to this clearing, away from any witnesses. Though the expression I glimpse behind the silver mask seems odd.

With a huge effort she detaches one hand from the soil and searches underneath her chin. I concentrate, ready to fight, but eventually she only loosens her mask and lets it fall. She's just a child, even younger than I! Her face is ravaged by emotion and her breathing is agitated, not that of a professional. A spasm shakes her violently and she lets free a rattling gasp followed by a moan as she fights to detach herself from the soil.

I move closer and study her. "Who sent you?"

"They... st-st . . . shhh," she gasps.

I circle her, see the straight blade of a short sword scabbarded on her back. She hadn't even tried to unsheathe it. Whoever attacked her was very fast. Though this would not be her only weapon, I remind myself; I imagine that secreted in her clothes, up her sleeves, tucked in her belt, is a whole arsenal. No wound, I note—at least, no wound visible to me. A gust of wind scatters my hair. I take another step then freeze in sudden realization and swallow dryly—in the Tormented Forest the wind never blows!

I stop in front of her and study the girl. Her face has paled even more. Carefully, alert to any movement, with all my nerves tense, I lower myself to my knees less than a step from her.

"They stole . . . " She stops and pants. Her face has lost all color, as if all that remains is the bone. " . . . my shadow," she finishes with great effort.

The impossible wind swirls gently around me. I keep my face emotionless and try to close my mind to any intrusion. The Tormented Forest has stolen the spy's shadow. It is the first time I've seen something like this. I see now that the girl's eyes are milky, frosted, as if covered in some sort of mist.

"Who sent you?" I ask when her breathing eases.

"My name is Shea," she suddenly says in a calm, coherent voice. "I probably have only a few more seconds before I'm lost completely. The forest has stolen my shadow and now it hunts her through the darkness. I can see them all . . . " She hesitates and I realize that she isn't breathing anymore; she speaks in a monotone, like an automaton. "There are a lot of shadows around, and they hunt mine. Others stay near you, like a guard escort next to its prisoner. You've been a worthy adversary, High Priestess . . . "

She rises. Her eyes are covered by that frosted veil; her hands are like blue-veined marble. She walks toward the forest's heart. I remember what my grandmother used to tell me: the ones left without their shadows follow them until the shell they have become withers and fails. Shea is no more than a shell without a core.

I rise and look around. I seem to be alone, despite what the spy told me. The wind has stopped as suddenly as it sprang up. I maintain my concentration, remembering what she said: "They stay near you, like a guard escort next to its prisoner." If this is so, I won't be allowed to leave the forest. But who can tell what they think, or how the forest's shadows will act? Who knows if they even exist?

I walk back the way I came and after a few minutes I see the Holy Temple, old and coarse, looking more like a cave in the cold shadow of the trees. In the cave's mouth flickers the red light of the torches. I reach the trail and walk toward the edge of the forest.

The House of Phriliras' park is bright and cheerful compared to the sinister darkness of the trees. Less than a hundred steps from its outskirts, I see the Mother Who Studies Development of the Echo in Our Consciousness. She notices me and smiles kindly, for she is the mother of my mother. She has trained in the development of the echo for years, but now I'm asking myself for the first time, *Is it good to do so, this close to the Tormented Forest? Have the shadows ever spied on her? Do they know what a terrible weapon she develops through her supple and repetitive movements when she's practicing her craft? Can the forest's souls read her mind and know her secrets?*

I return her smile as I continue toward the House of Phriliras, next passing the Mother Who Awaits the Leaving. She's been here for so many years, she's become a fixture of this place. Sometime in the future she will leave to colonize the newborn regions of the Carami, guiding the colonists while bringing the holy mission of the Guild into the new territories. *Will all these things happen?* I wonder. *Will the Royal Carami extend to infinity? What will the world be like when it engulfs all the others and covers the whole world? All the phrils would then be forced to live inside the universal city. Although our civilization will expand with it, in the end we will only be retreating behind a protective shell, conquered from the inside. We will have only the illusion of expansion. Then, for sure, the notion of liberty will be revised.*

A bit farther, in a clearing amidst a stand of stone-bushes that surround it like a fence, the oldest of the Mothers sits in contemplation. I approach as quietly as possible. She is the only phrilira who awakens within me a feeling of veneration. Her eyes are closed, her face relaxed, her expression revealing kindness and understanding. On her shoulders, a pair of white wings have appeared. Although they're already quite large, they're still growing. Since my last visit here, they've matured from soft, newborn down into bright feathers. I circle behind her and stop to touch her wings with my fingertips, just enough to feel their warmth and softness. I sense their tantalizing power.

"When you have erased half of my names, a stair will open between Up and Down, and the chosen will climb up it," she murmurs. "When you have discovered half of ⚠ then you will know. Because the sign will be there, clear to be seen, no longer hidden. Then things will gain new meaning, and the Light will reveal another part of the road to Truth."

I recognize this as a passage from the ⚠ Discipline. A thought startles me—what if, in erasing all of his names save the name KAVOH, we have in fact, only reached the halfway point? What will be the sign? And would that mean that the Mother Who Contemplates could be the Chosen? And conversely, if it's proven she's the Chosen, then would that mean a stairway has been opened and we've reached the halfway point of the names? *Then,* I think, *we would have a measure, a milestone. We would be halfway to the Truth!*

KAVOH is the last revealed name. The others have been erased and instantly forgotten. Which name will be revealed next? And if things will change, what will the next reality be? And what role will I, as High Priestess, have in the new order of things? A thrill shakes me and I look behind me, but no shadow has dared follow me here.

SENTIMENTAL RECIPE: THE PHRILOLIR LIQUEUR

This special Recipe opens a new chapter in my book. It doesn't assume more than two participants for the introductory portion. These need not be recipears, but it is necessary that one be male and one female. Therefore, we will move quickly to the Preparation Story.

It is dusk. On the lakeshore, water boils in the kettle. The huge solar globe, already half-hidden below the horizon, spreads fire over the sky and makes the shimmering lake look like flickering flames. Red-petaled flowers soften in the broth as you stretch your long, thin legs out on the shore.

You lean forward, watching, still as stone. Then, in a flash, you thrust your hand out, catching a snake. Its thick body encircles your arm, maddened by the red and fiery sky. Solemnly, you chop off its head with one stroke, and it falls into the kettle. You work your hands down its body, squeezing all of its blood into the kettle, then cast aside its corpse as the last of the sunlight disappears.

Don't hesitate to wipe your bloodstained hands on your tights, but don't forget that you should plunge your hands into the lake and wait for the fat, lazy, golden fishes to appear. Their flesh knows everything about love, just as the snake's blood knows everything about binding souls—once lured, the golden fishes can't escape. Catch them and toss them into the kettle. The furiously bubbling broth will tumble them about.

Don't lounge in the grass before finishing the Recipe. Your clothing, stained with the trails of your bloody fingers, will hurt your silky skin. Stay near the kettle, to continue the preparation; do not be afraid.

Velvety darkness follows the fiery sunset that covered the horizon only moments ago. You sprinkle white powder into the fire and the smoke rises, thick and stinging. You and your counterpart clasp each other's arms, your heads bent over the kettle, and let the smoke draw forth your tears. You are sweating, your flesh firm. Your hands tighten on your counterpart's arm. You still have a few tears to offer.

The evening air is getting cool; it smells of grass and flowers, warmed by the sun and crushed by your bare feet. When darkness has fully fallen, pour a small amount of gentle light nectar into the broth—this is important, if you are to see your soul! Your silhouette is now darkness on a dark background. Soon the wind will come.

Pick out a star and show it to your counterpart. Arch your back and stretch your arm as high as you can toward the farthest star. Yes, there—you see it! Show it to your counterpart again to be sure there is no mistake. Promise the star, and mix the promise into the broth, stirring well enough that you will never forget it.

Skim off the foam that forms on the surface of the broth and throw it far away. Then pour the kettle's contents into a special mug, oiled with pollen, that you've brought. It can be used only once; then it will be smashed. This is a custom; a beautiful custom whose origins are unknown.

The Sky Daughters smile upon you, promising something that makes you laugh, and your counterpart looks at you with a sight that is pure, but not naïve. Your smile is sensuous, but not perverse. The wind starts to blow. You place the mug filled with the broth on a small fire to simmer as you and your counterpart draw close to protect one another from the wind. When the air turns cold, you give your counterpart a sip from the hot mug, then your counterpart does the same for you. You face one another, stand close to one another, warming each other for you don't know how long.

Wasn't it like that in the beginning—a phril and a phrilira, joined together; a phrilolir? Yet they have been split. Will faith suffice to see what birth is, forever? And, since phriliras give birth and phrils taste each other, we return to the primordial union, to the phrilolir. You won't repeat their mistake, will you?

The broth—the liqueur—begins to take effect.

(from The Teachings of the Recipearium Revolution by Grand Master
Recipear of the Green Kingdom, Morminiu*)*

XII. THE HUNTER'S TRAP

The Silence Plaza awaited him—acidly quiet and mysterious as ever, avoided by everyone. Mahop, as usual, leaned against a stone-bush. When he saw Morminiu approaching, surrounded by his guard, he smiled wryly.

"What's up, bigwig?"

"Hi, Mahop." Morminiu sat beside him. His guard waited out of earshot. Mahop ignored them.

"For an honest citizen, you're a bit too pretentious lately. In fact, you know what? I don't even think you're an honest citizen."

Morminiu smiled broadly, but kept his silence.

Mahop continued, his tone still tinged with humor. "My phrils have discovered that you don't reside in the west, at the channels. But, of course—if you lived there, you wouldn't be able to buy all the stuff I've offered in our trades. And to be honest, you don't know where I live, either, so I need not know where you live. Anyway, that's strictly confidential— though my phrils are still digging."

"If you tell me your secret, then I'll tell you mine," Morminiu countered lightly.

Mahop grew serious. "Spill it—what do you want to know?"

"Who's behind you? For whom do you work?" Morminiu waited, trying to keep the smile on his lips.

Mahop studied him a moment. "Better leave it alone," he finally said; "my phrils will eventually find you."

"You're refusing a bargain?"

"I have my limits too," Mahop replied. "And more, it's better this way; I'll know you're safe."

Morminiu rose abruptly, annoyed, and paced for a few seconds before turning back to the black marketeer. "Mahop . . ." He stopped, then decided to try again. "We need to clear up some things. I'm not Lorminiu."

"I figured that out—I told you I knew about your home; it follows that I also discovered that you gave me a false name," answered Mahop.

The recipear dropped his eyes. "My real name is Morminiu." Silence. "I am Morminiu," he repeated, and looked up.

The red flush on the marketeer's face was obvious even in the city's green-tinged light. He rose and walked over to the recipear, then silently lifted one side of Morminiu's cloak, different from the one he usually wore to their meetings, and turned it over. He studied the House Mormont coat of arms embroidered on its silk lining for a moment, then his eyes snapped up to meet Morminiu's. "You're Hitissh Morminiu!"

Mahop sat back down, his chin trembling, his chest rapidly rising and falling as his lungs swelled and deflated spasmodically. He closed his eyes a moment, as if trying to calm himself.

Morminiu came close enough whisper to him, "Now, your turn to spill everything you know."

"I have nothing to spill." Mahop's smile looked forced. "Your Highness," he added ironically.

"We can still make some good business together. I don't see what you'd have against that."

"I'm sorry, Your Lordship, but I'm not available anymore," Mahop said, his tone wooden.

"Cut the crap. For you I'm just Morminiu."

Mahop rose. "I think I will go now, if Your Highness allows it."

"No, I don't allow it," Morminiu snapped. "Sit down, stay there, and listen to me carefully."

Mahop complied, trying to appear indifferent—but he couldn't control the trembling of his hands and his chin. The drunkard's weakness betrayed him.

"Mahop, I know almost everything about you," Morminiu said, stressing the words. "Only one detail eludes me and I hope you'll give it to me. Then, I want to stay friends. Because, you know, since I came here, you've been my only friend. And I'm sorry that, now that you know who I am, you're acting like this, trying to ignore our previous relationship. That's exactly what I want to know: why?"

Mahop stayed silent, looking blankly ahead of him.

"You're probably waiting to hear how much I know," Morminiu said, trying a different tack; "wanting to see how much you can lie to me and how much you can sell. Well, you have a net of six thousand processing units in Celesthe—more than the whole royal informational system."

Mahop jerked and looked at him, eyes wide.

"You have laboratories set up as real research centers, and you're planning more, along with expeditions into remote areas of the Carami. The breadth of your studies amazed me."

"You succeeded in breaking into our memoric stores?"

Morminiu nodded. "Yes."

"How?" Mahop blurted. "It's impossible. We're using the most advanced technology, twenty years more advanced than even that used by the royal system. There is no way." Mahop shook his head and said firmly, "It's a bluff. Or somebody up there is betraying us."

"I don't know anybody 'up there,' besides you," Morminiu told him, then asked, "Do you feel like a traitor? And by the way, how much are you paid to keep your mouth shut and steal from your friend?"

"I don't understand."

"Come on, don't play this foolish game anymore. I warned you, I know all about you! You have coordinated all three attacks on my memoric stores. You are Chief of Research and Informational Investigations for the Secret Service. At this moment, your primary mission is to break into my data store. What you don't know yet is that counter-spies have tracked you down and now they are still hunting, camouflaged within your network. So—there are three possibilities: you find them and reveal them, and they blow up your whole network, with all your memoric stores and information; I get angry with you, order your execution, and they blow up everything; I die, and they automatically kill themselves—and blow up everything. Oh, I almost forgot the last option: we cut a deal and I don't die, and then everything is all right, and everybody's happy. Questions?"

Mahop snarled, "Bluff."

"I can make a little demonstration. Are you willing to take the chance?"

No reply. Morminiu shut his eyes. After a few seconds he opened them and smiled. Mahop smiled as well. They both kept smiling at each other, until Mahop suddenly frowned and pulled from his pocket a portable vorb.

"Yes?" Mahop pressed.

Silence. His eyes bulging with distrust, Mahop rose and turned to Morminiu, who was still smiling. He pounced upon him, but the recipear's guard rushed forward and immobilized him immediately.

"Tartrrr," whistled Mahop, and tore himself away from them and stood waiting, clearly expecting the mercenaries to obey him. But they remained still. "Hey, you're mine—my babies." He whirled on Morminiu. "What the mother's skin happened?"

"I doubled their conditioning. I have to admit, you did an admirable job, but I eventually managed to untangle it. Now they're mine. Did you think I'd be stupid enough to come here armed with your weapons?"

The drunkard sagged and held up his hands, surrendering himself to the mercenaries. They left him standing unhindered. Mahop looked at them, then at Morminiu. "How did you do all this?" he asked, this time with a spark of curiosity within his angry tone. "You have destroyed a whole memoric store of ours, gone in just an eyeblink. Do you know how much data was there? Long years of research, and bang— that's it!"

"I'm sorry, my friend, but I had to convince you. By the way, you took the chance, remember? It is important for both of us to understand that we're talking about the same thing."

"Don't talk about friendship here. I was the friend of the other phril, mother's vulbas, not yours!"

"Let's see how we stand," Morminiu said calmly. "You can't get away from the hunters, so you have to consider the other option—my life. As long as I'm alive, you'll remain alive too. Therefore, I want an aura."

"A what?"

Morminiu spelled it: "An a-u-r-a. That thing you showed me that protects the Carami's walls. There are always attempts at my life. In the last month alone, there have been at least six. An aura would keep away danger, and we'd all be safer."

"You must be mad, to ask for something like this!" Mahop exclaimed.

"I'll pay for it."

"I don't need shit from you!"

Morminiu shut his eyes and started to concentrate.

"What are you doing?"

Morminiu opened his eyes and looked at him. "Are you willing to risk another memoric store?"

"I won't give you anything—hey, what are you doing, motherfucker?" Mahop tried again to jump him, but again the mercenaries immobilized him. After a few seconds they released him, and the drunkard dropped to the sticky bone paving, drained of his strength. After a moment he said, "Another store—you won't get what treasures you destroy. You're just a murderer, *a fucking shitty murderer,* to play like this with us!" He started to cry.

"I want an aura," Morminiu repeated.

"You'll get it," Mahop grated.

"Call right now; have a phril bring it. He can be here in an hour."

Mahop sat up and took out the vorb. He waited a few seconds, then said to it, "Mahop. Give me Thirty-one."

Almost immediately, he spoke again: "Yes, it's me. Bring an aura to the Silence Plaza. Now. No, I'm not mad. Yes, a fat deal." He shut down the vorb and put it back in his pocket. Then he wiped the tears from his face and breathed deeply.

"I'll give you an unknown Recipe for that aura. I want to keep our business relationship equitable."

"Go fuck yourself," Mahop muttered.

Morminiu ignored the insult. "I want to know who's behind you, and why he wants to steal from me."

"I don't know."

"Wrong answer." He made his tone friendly again. "Mahop, relax and think it through. You're not in the position you believe you are. You're just a phril who listens and judges. When I came to this city, I was welcomed into a House without disturbing anybody else. I don't interfere in anybody else's business, I just do my job. The Recipes are the meaning of my life, they're part of what I am. So when somebody tries to break me and steal my secrets, my work, my livelihood, he's stealing my life. He's trying to take away my identity, my personality, my genius."

Morminiu sighed and shrugged. "Maybe he pays you well. Maybe you've been involved in the harassment of a phril you didn't know, so you didn't care about it—you were doing it for pay, like a mercenary paid to kill. But now you've learned who I am, and you know I'm telling the truth. What side are you on, Mahop? You probably think, ignorantly, 'our stores are valuable, but his are not.' But mine are the work of centuries, not years, as yours are. The work of centuries, of whole generations of illustrious recipears, is there along with my genius, the fruits of my mind. It's a huge work, one never before seen in history. And you are calling me an ignorant criminal? I'd do anything to save it!"

Morminiu grabbed a handful of Mahop's shirt and shook him. "Who's behind this?" he hissed. "Who coordinates everything?"

The drunkard pulled free and turned his back on

Morminiu.

"Pity. Though, sincerely, it hurts me to lose access to all that science." Morminiu shut his eyes.

Mahop threw himself at Morminiu's feet and wrapped his arms around the recipear's legs. The mercenaries immediately pulled him away. He moaned through his teeth, "No Morminiu, please, don't . . . "

The recipear opened his eyes and asked in a low voice, "Who is it?"

"Taharissh Chathu—but only on the intelligence side. Otherwise, we are on our own."

"Taharissh Chathu," Morminiu repeated slowly. Certain connections started falling into place in his mind. "Who is he working for?"

"For the Green Kingdom," Mahop moaned. "He is Chief of Intelligence for the Secret Service. He is the second most powerful phril in the kingdom."

"That's true," Morminiu conceded. "As long as there is practically no army, he is the secondary power. Does the King know?"

"The King doesn't know anything. Primary power does not rest with the King, but with his counsellor, Comtap. He and Chathu have run this kingdom for the past twenty years."

"The King is a puppet," concluded Morminiu. "And Comtap is allied with Chathu." He paced slowly in front of Mahop, thinking. The conclusions were not to his liking. He stopped and looked at Mahop. "How long has this alliance existed?"

"Since the beginning."

Morminiu frowned. "Wait a minute—in the beginning it was Plabos. Comtap had no influence at that time."

"Oh yes, he did. Plabos was their puppet, too. And when they didn't need him anymore, they . . . removed him. The same thing they will probably do to you, at the right moment."

"So, Hitissh Leomi had nothing to do with Plabos'

banishment," Morminiu murmured, suddenly feeling tired.

"I don't know if he did or not."

Morminiu speared the drunkard with his gaze again. "What about Tathar, the Royal Recipear?"

"I told you all you need to know," Mahop protested.

"Who's Tathar?" Morminiu pressed, angry.

"He is Taharissh Chathu's lover!" Mahop slumped, a broken phril. Morminiu sat down next to him and embraced him. "Now, my friend, let's save what's left of our friendship. I will always stand by you."

MORMINIU

I notice I have changed. Change is hard for phrils. Among the few things that can influence them is a phrilira. A phrilira made Leomi betray his best friend without even realizing he was guilty of doing so until his very last moment of life. She made me change my plans for greatness; I gave up my political ambitions. Political ambitions are good for lonely phrils. But the Recipearium is one thing I'll never give up. Without it I'd be half dead. And even if that means I'd be half alive, from the quality of life perspective, I would be—I repeat—half dead.

She doesn't show the slightest anxiety over how deeply we have gone into the Carami's entrails. Rather, she is fascinated by this world she's discovered. Would it be due to her trust in me, or a kind of recklessness?

We have reached the passage to the Altar Hall. If there is a horrible splendor anywhere, then it should be here. I help her slide inside. She thrusts her head through to the other side and remains still for a few seconds that seem like an eternity to me. Then she exclaims, "It's superb! It's like a dream!"

I tremble with joy, glad to have shared one of my treasures with her. I can't find any words—all of the explanations I'd prepared in anticipation of her questions, all of my expectations regarding how I would handle her surprise, her every reaction, are gone. Now I know nothing other than sitting here with her, admiring the Altar Hall together. Through my new eyes, it seems more a rediscovery than a presentation.

I see her hurriedly stripping naked and gape in astonishment. I—the phril who has always believed he is used to this kind of behavior—can only stare and choke with emotion. If she were to turn toward me right now, I would turn into a statue. Almost all of the easy phriliras Mahop has supplied have undressed in front of me, but not like this! In fact, I don't know what the difference is, but this is something totally different—this is Valiria undressing!

She keeps a soft, white fabric wrapped above her nervous belt; it falls to a point two palms above her knees. She has long, slender legs, the skin as white as her arms, untouched by sunlight. When she removes the cap from her head, she seems twice as naked. The skin on her scalp shines like pale silk.

She runs toward the lake in the middle of the cave, drawn to it like a torch attracts a butterfly. It gleams like an exposed diamond in the bright beam of light flowing down from the chimney above; a diamond speckled with great white flowers, fine and graceful and furry. The Altar Hall's irresistible splendor is, first and foremost, morbid.

"Wait, Valiria! Wait!" I shout.

She stops, staring at the lake in wonder.

"Before you plunge in, I should warn you what's there. It's not what you think. The Altar Hall is a—"

She whirls toward me. "Please, Morminiu, let me do this. Don't steal my emotions."

"But, it's not what you think!"

"I want to discover it as if I were the first, as you did. You know how it is, when you discover new and wonderful things, terrifying and marvellous secrets. You told me a lot, you showed me this place, now let me experience it as you did."

I say no more, because she is already running. She wouldn't listen to me anyway. With a childish jump, her legs flung before her, she plunges into the water amongst the flowers, a divine butterfly about to be singed by the powerful flame of curiosity. How do they see these things, these strangers we share our lives with—the phriliras? I've asked myself a thousand times how two beings as different as a phril and a phrilira could form a single whole, could find unity. It has nothing to do with opposites attracting one another. If only everything weren't a myth . . . but if it is not a myth, where is the truth hiding? What keeps us blind? What keeps us so close, yet still so untouchable?

Valiria bursts through the surface of the water like an air bubble surrendering noisily to pressure: Boah! The noise reverberates around the cavern. "Oaaah, Morminiu!" she screams.

I instantly toss aside my cloak and kick off my boots. Valiria is sinking! Her breath streams up through the water as a series of bubbles, and the movement of her arms is quick, jerky—panicked. There is no time; I jump into the water and dive down after her, seize her and kick back to the surface with her in my arms. She has stopped writhing and wrapped her arms around my neck, hanging limp, making this easier. I swim toward the bank with her body a dead weight in the water, moving awkwardly; I've never swum while supporting someone.

I carry her a few steps from the edge of the water and lay her down on the bony floor of the cave. Her skin looks yellow and shrivelled. I sit next to her, my breath whistling. The bone beneath me is warm, and for a moment I feel as I did when I first arrived in the city, and a few times afterward— that it is alive, like the skin would live on a snake, its functions independent of the rest of the body. Touching it makes me feel cleansed.

Valiria is trying to catch her breath, her lungs swelling and deflating spasmodically. I rise and take off my clothes and spread them on the bone to dry, retaining only my underwear, though it is soaking wet as well. I hesitate, looking at her. What should I say, what should I do? What would comfort her the most?

I drop to my knees, bend over her, and lift her face. She's breathing easier. She opens her eyes—round, deep brown eyes, childish, erudite, frightened. She's crying. I want to taste the crystal drops, imagining them sweet and salty in my mouth. I draw her closer and try to speak, but I can't. Anything I can think to say seems stupid to me. I feel ridiculous.

She sighs, bursts into new tears. I embrace her, caressing the top of her head, her shoulders. Her skin is cold. I calm her in the most fundamental way. "It's all right," I coo. "Come on, it's over now. It's all right."

She relaxes and I fall silent, all inspiration gone. She shivers and I think, *I must cover her with something.* But she encircles my waist with her arms and hangs onto me like a phril clutching the only tree around in the middle of a windstorm. I consider making a joke, but I catch myself in time. I feel her breath on my neck, sending a frisson of pleasure through me; the hair on my nape rises with my arousal. There are moments when you're proud of this kind of thing, and moments when, even though they're normal, your body's natural reactions shame you. I don't want to let go of her, don't want to lose the sweet pleasure that overwhelms me. But it's me again who bends, breaking the spell, to kiss her on her forehead, her ear, her cheek.

We untangle ourselves. She trembles violently and avoids looking up at me. The spell is in fact stronger than I thought. I kiss her plump, moist lips. She waits, at first hesitant, then she responds, her kiss warm and sensual. I kiss her again, then I stroke the tip of my tongue over her neck, her shoulders, then back to her mouth. She answers with urgent, sinuous gestures, as if it is the end of the world, breathing as if overcome with heat.

And indeed it feels like the end of the world when she unwraps the white fabric covering her nervous belt and lets it fall to the bone floor, like a water-soaked petal. I'm in a knot around which the whole world is spinning. Here and now is when everything should begin and end. *Look! Look!* I'd like to scream, but I cannot because my hands, my tongue, my whole body is exploring her, haunted by doubt—that something so velvety and voluptuous can exist; that there can be such happiness! Because I realize with astonishment that I'm feeling more happiness than pleasure, and that the pleasure is of the purest essence. Then I realize nothing. I'm only joining with

Valiria, feeling as if it might never end. No beginning and no ending . . . my knot is endless.

※❈※❈※❈❈◇❈❈※❈※❈

The last of her tears tremble on her cheeks. She cried continuously, burning my face and neck with her hot tears. In the beam of strong sunlight and the unfiltered air, she appears more beautiful than she does in the green shadows of the city. I hold her in my arms and we lie still and quiet. How clean is the silence! Like a cold, swift-running river after a drought.

Only now have I realized that it is not about inspiration, just as it wasn't before. Because she was and is Valiria, and there is no need to communicate in words. Only now do I understand.

After a while she moves slowly, as if trying not to wake me, pushing up onto her knees, then to her feet. She stands naked, superb and uninhibited, before bending to lift her cloak from our pile of clothes and swing it around her shoulders. I glimpse something and blink in wonder, but only for a second, because in the next one, I forget.

"I'm hungry," she says, smiling faintly.

She glows with both happiness and sadness. It makes me feel guilty, and that hurts me. While she spreads our undergarments to dry, I open the rucksack and take out the snack I prepared for the trip. She settles next to me and starts to eat silently. Our eyes meet, and we smile—mine wide and happy, hers sad and kind.

"I keep wondering who could have built the Altar," I say, to break the tormenting silence surrounding the lake.

"I cannot be sure, but I think I know the answer," she replies. "It's an old story."

I raise my brows, surprised, and wait.

"It's no secret to anyone that you, the phrils, don't have religious feelings. At least not as we feel them. You're passive in this aspect. The phriliras are the chosen because we are born in faith, live in faith, and have the holy role of spreading it and maintaining it. Among you, of course, there are those who respect the faith as tradition and civic duty, but they are not pious. There are known things, though they are inexplicable.

"Two generations ago, the Mothers decided to take a bigger step—to invest some phrils as priests. They believed that doing so would more successfully spread the faith—the true faith, the one you cannot touch. A religious school was established where the chosen were educated. I don't know what the selection criteria were; they are secret, as many of the Mothers' actions are. The beginning was promising. The chosen were children who, through the years, appeared to believe—not in our faith, exactly, but they no longer doubted in their souls the existence and the truth of the faith. The phrils had been, finally, converted!

"In their turn, the priests opened places of worship where they hoped to convert other phrils. But after a while, it became apparent that the core was tainted. Something had happened to their spirit, to the priests' consciousness.

"After long interrogations and many searches, the Mothers realized the truth—phrils, too, have a faith. The existence of the mortuary tasting imposes a certain faith, a mystic experience that is deeply and subtly lived by you. But it is a faith contrary to the true one, a pagan belief ever rooted in your life and your spirit, coexisting since the beginning, or maybe even before; you only use the real faith as an adornment.

"The priests realized these things, and were aware of everything that started from there—the unrest and, foremost, their changes. They have already invented a new religion, different even from your beliefs—a religion that has at its core a primordial god, in fact a pluri-being from which phrilkind was born. They said that they had communicated with it, or with its spirit, which lies in the depths of each of you, at the root of all the spirits that dwell within you. They said it considered them the Chosen and showed them the Truth.

Their method of worship switched to cannibalism and phrilic sacrifices. That's why I believe these are their relics."

"You're telling me this story refers to things older than two generations?" Morminiu asked.

"No. The population, frightened by their atrocities, killed most of them, but a few escaped. They hid somewhere in the countryside near the Carami, and started to convert phrils to their religion. They probably have a powerful sect, if they succeed in maintaining it. There is a heavy curse on the city, since they left."

"What curse?"

Valiria glanced around, a superstitious habit, Morminiu decided. "One cannot speak the curse without attracting it," she said. "The Guild fights it even now, to keep it away from the city."

"So, in the end, that primordial being truly exists—or your converting phrils as priests has awakened unsuspected powers in them."

"Exactly."

"And what about the true faith?"

"It's hard to explain," she replied. "Because, as well, the practice of mortuary tasting has existed since the beginning. The problem is that we need to reformulate the notion of truth. Because certainly, to exist is not synonymous with 'to be true.'"

"What did you mean by cannibalism? They just eat phrils?"

"No. They believe that, through mass Tasting—for instance, a person served to fifty will dwell in all fifty, exactly like that pluri-being—they could eventually materially reconstruct that pluri-being."

"But, that's impossible!" Morminiu exclaimed. "Such mass Tasting cannot work!"

"Of course not. Still, they say it works. At least for their god."

I fall silent, impressed by what I've heard. I hadn't

known about this sect; I believe that, besides the Guild, nobody remembers it exists. How many mysteries can hide in a shell like our world? And all coming from inside it, from a point packed with existences—that primordial point where it all began. That means that beyond our world there is either nothing else, or mysteries surpassing our capacity to comprehend.

I recollect myself and look at her, curious. "What actually happened?"

"With them?"

"No, with you."

She looks about to speak, but instead remains quiet. Then she changes her mind, opens her mouth, and says quietly, "I was making peace with myself. Only after we've done the most foolish things do we think about them."

"You mean that we've done a foolish thing?"

She looks down. "Yes."

"Shall I take it that you regret what we did?"

"Yes. No." She pauses, thinks a moment before continuing. "I was just making peace with myself, my beliefs, my meaning. I don't know what to say. In a way I regret it, and that's natural. But otherwise, I'm happy we did it. Probably I wished to do it and I'd do it again, if given the choice, in spite of my purpose."

I feel the ground trembling. I look around, surprised, but nothing has changed. *Maybe it was my imagination,* I think, though she seems to have noticed it, too.

"I'm afraid I don't understand," I answer cautiously, a little disappointed by the ambiguous explanation. In my phril's pride, I would've liked to be told that she doesn't regret it, that it is the thing she wanted most, that . . . *But she is not any phrilira,* I remind myself. *She is the High Priestess, and it is my misfortune that I have forgotten this.*

"If you'd been interested in religion at least a bit, at least historically, you'd have found out a lot about us, and you would understand now," she tells me.

"Meaning?"

"I'm the High Priestess. Unique. The latest in a line of sixty-seven High Priestesses. A line which should not have ended with me. And now that I'm saying this, I desperately realize the importance and the greatness and the seriousness of the duty that rested on my shoulders, and I tremble with fear, with anger, and with shame that I betrayed my purpose. That I have been weak. I didn't live up to the promise of my birth. We are initiated and moulded to provide the most extraordinary pleasure, the supreme sensation, everything favorable for the unique moment when we mate with the chosen phril, the phril ever unknown to us; everything to give him and us the ultimate pleasure, to strive toward perfection, so that our joining will conceive the next High Priestess. With every birth, we draw one step closer to perfection. After we serve our purpose, we find the Truth and live in it. In this way, we become Mothers."

"Now I understand why I've been so happy," I quip.

She shakes her head, missing the joke. "No, I didn't use the knowledge with you. The supreme pleasure kills the phril. Between us is something else, more profound than I imagined."

My thoughts return to what she's told me. "What if it's born a phril, the product of this perfect union?"

"There has never been a phril born, just a long and uninterrupted line of phriliras. Until I broke it!"

A new ground-tremor, as faint as the last, distracts me. This time I have no doubt—something's going on. But right now I want to focus on Valiria. "Is this about some kind of religious wonder?" I ask her. "Some mystical secret, or do you master a secret science?"

"I cannot tell you. There are secrets I can never reveal, to anyone. I'm conditioned. Otherwise, the Perpetuation Guild would have disappeared a long time ago."

I nod. "You're right. But, I still cannot see the problem. Unless you should be a virgin at the moment of mating with the chosen phril?"

"Precisely. I was supposed to know a phril only once in my life, and only then achieve divine orgasm."

"All right, let's admit that you have known me. Do you think the Mothers will be upset? In the end, I'm not such a bad choice."

"I didn't use the knowledge. I didn't follow the purpose," she says vehemently. "I let myself be controlled by my feelings. Secondly, I wasn't supposed to know my partner, and you should have been dead by now, to maintain a centuries-old balance. The Mothers will sense the difference in me right away. They know everything immediately. I ruined the Guild's balance and I'll have to be punished. I'll probably be banished from the Carami, exiled into the Great Desert, where I'll be charged with finding my destiny and purifying myself. That in the best-case scenario."

"If this is your religion, no wonder phrils have never believed in it!" I exclaim. "It is absurd. I want you to be my wife."

"The Guild will not allow it."

"But the King will."

"Nor the King. Nothing in the world will prompt them to contradict one another. It's how they have maintained peace and order in the kingdom."

"This time they will. The King will do it for me," I state, aware of the road I've chosen. I would be risking everything, although I cannot believe I might lose. There are no supernatural forces pulling the strings—we phrils are doing and undoing everything. That's why this is possible. She'll stay with me, or we'll leave together.

Valiria doesn't share my determination. "What makes you so sure?"

"It is one of my secrets. You know, there are some secrets . . . " I trail off suggestively and smile, hopeful. I'm rewarded with a blossoming smile, but it fades immediately, much to my disappointment.

"It's no use; the faith is holy. The belief is well-rooted."

"I will not allow anyone to separate us," I vow. "Not the Guild, not the King, not even your religion. If we have to, we'll leave—both of us. I'll take you somewhere far to the south, where you won't hear mention of the Guild."

"The Guild is everywhere."

"Indeed, it has widespread control, but it doesn't enter into the intimate lives of phrils and phriliras, as it does here. Phriliras are free to live as they want, with whomever they want. The peasants have no money to sign contracts with the Guild; they prefer free phriliras. That's why Mothers have neither power nor influence in the far-off zones."

She is quiet, her expression confused. I ask her, "Do you love me?"

"Yes," she answers. She raises eyes unbelievably heavy with guilt toward me.

"Then you should trust me," I tell her. "Don't let anything interfere with our love. You'll come with me to my palace, and in a few days everything will be resolved."

Her eyes grow round, but she's still quiet, still watching me, unmoving. Then she draws a deep breath and the guilt vanishes from her eyes, though she still looks uncertain. She rests her head on my shoulder.

"I, Morminiu, want you, Valiria, to be my wife under the sacred oath of intimacy," I say solemnly. "I so swear."

"I too swear," she murmurs, and rises onto her knees in front of me.

Another ground tremor, stronger this time, as if sealing the oath. *The Carami,* I think, *the Carami has started to move!* But I don't have time now for such a wonder, because Valiria herself is a wonder. A sweet dizziness overwhelms me and I lie back, breathing deeply, and smile. I'm happy and more relaxed than I've ever felt. She leans over and kisses me, then she lies down next to me. I don't know what powers she has, but I know I like them. *She is the High Priestess,* I remind myself.

A terrible noise destroys our peace, and I jump up, surprised. My first reaction is to look toward the hole in the cavern ceiling, but nothing is happening there. The light from the setting sun is entering obliquely to precisely illuminate a crack in the wall. No—a crack that is forming in the wall! We watch as if watching a stage show illuminated by a spotlight as a terrible force splits and smashes the limestone deposits. They fall like white rain from splinters in the bone wall. The skin stretched over the bones tears with a deafening and obscene noise. And then silence. We look at each other, awestruck.

Tension rises rapidly. Crises lower the tension and set the blood in motion. Action doesn't give it time to accumulate. But waiting does. It freezes the action and allows the nerves to overload.

"We should run," I whisper.

"Pointless," she says. "He wouldn't allow us to escape."

I swallow my bewilderment and look at her as if she's insane. What's she relying upon? It can't be trust in me. Trust in herself, or her madness?

The crack in the wall waits like a giant vagit, torn and tattered , powdered in clouds of white dust after a centuries-long wait. Valiria rises. The cloak slips from her shoulders. Naked as a goddess, she walks toward the crack. After a few steps she stops, holds out her hand to me. Her expression is serious, preoccupied, not in any way frightened; neither is it mocking. I inhale deeply and take her hand. We enter together.

And emerge in another cave, ten times higher and wider than the one behind us. We stand on a ledge a few steps wide, like a balcony that runs around the walls, about thirty statures above the floor of the cave. The light is diffused, gloomy and gray, like an autumn morning. Here, all is gray and brown, with no trace of the city's green.

Valiria is looking straight ahead. I follow her gaze, but I don't see anything. I look higher, then lower, and a shiver runs up my spine. Cold sweat instantly beads on my body, awakening me from passivity.

Before us stands a giant sculpture of a phrilira, carved into the wall's bone, held there only by a thin membrane. It is the same kind of sculpture as those I saw in the House of Phriliras, only this one's feet rest on the floor of the cave and her forehead supports the roof; her muscles are tensed, her bottom is pressed into the wall, her body bulges in front. Her lungs are swollen to double capacity, like two balloons attached to the skin of her neck. No air moves there, but liquid. The depiction of flowing liquid is so real that I shiver. It seems to flow through the swollen veins of her arms, which are turned toward us, her palms pressed to the wall. Long, sharp nails like metal blades tip her fingers. On her feet, vulture-like claws, shine sinister in the gloom. Her legs are spread open in a vulgar posture, with her vulbas opened obscenely and with her wanton plateau aroused. Her body is perfect; a measure of all things. Her skin is smooth and taut. It shines a pleasant white in the dimness, like freshly formed bone.

It is a giant replica of the phrilira I saw under the Lormont palace. This time she faces me, with the vein writhing from her body to reconnect at her left leg, then over her body to her right armpit before coiling around her arm a few times. Now I can truly say that I've seen a horrible splendor. She is spread in a terrible ecstasy of heavenly splendor. If there really are Sky Daughters, then they must look like this!

With a shock, I suddenly remember what I glimpsed when Valiria rose and donned the cloak, something that shook me. A vein, running from her left leg across her body to her right armpit, and coiled two times around her arm. It is really there! Not swollen and horrible, but a purple tracery on her white body. But it is there! I look at the sculpture and see that it's moving. Slowly, frightfully slow, she lowers her head, which had been thrown back in ecstasy. Her eyes are big and round. Her mouth, fleshy and sensual. She is Valiria, wearing an expression of ferocity and animal pleasure. Her metal teeth gnash together, and she grins—a promising grin that is directed at us.

Valiria, the flesh and bones Valiria, is breathing rapidly. I don't know what keeps me from scooping her up, throwing her over my shoulder, and running. She turns her back to the giant and presses her palms against its wrinkled surface. A vein next to her hand pulses uncontrollably. Slime sizzles around her palms and evaporates, leaving behind an unpleasant smell.

The metal on metal gnashing of the statue's teeth and the scratching of the wall with her metal nails intensifies. I cover my ears and fall to my knees. The phrilira tries to escape the thin membrane that holds her to the wall. Her vulbas close and open wetly, like a toothless mouth. Valiria turns slowly to face the "sculpture" and it calms, the body relaxing, the arms sliding down the hips to rest beside the legs, the movement of her vulbas slowing to a stop. She looks tired. And then she cries. The statue cries!

I rise as Valiria returns to me, and we leave the balcony. Valiria's hands are burned, but she doesn't feel the pain.

I finally voice my bewilderment. "Who is 'he'?"

"The Carami," she answers, her voice heavy with fatigue.

I ask no other questions. I dress her because her burned hands are useless, and we leave.

ADVICE. *Why do phrils need the Recipearium?*

No master recipear has ever answered this question. Either nobody has asked it, or master recipears themselves have questioned it, without finding a satisfactory answer. Or perhaps it is better if no answer is given.

Why does the world need a creator? What is Father Sky doing up there? What is Master Plabos doing inside me?

Non-believers ask questions, while believers rely on faith. That's why we need the Recipearium: because we really believe! And we don't need to know "why," but rather "how" and "when."

(from The Teachings of the Recipearium Revolution by Grand Master Recipear of the Green Kingdom, Morminiu)

XIII. EXOTIC TASTING

"Your Excellencies, Harissh Bahara is waiting in the guest room."

The heir prince rose from the armchair and stretched, yawning, before telling the butler, "Let him wait."

He entered the privy and began his ablutions preparatory to the trip beyond his apartments, first submerging himself in the bone tub filled with perfumed water, scattering the strongly fragranced dusk flowers floating on the surface. After a few seconds he lifted his head above the water and remained there, floating among flowers. He smiled at Tathar, who was watching him from the door. "You go first," he told him. "Keep Bahi busy. I'll come very soon."

Chathu had found Tathar when he was still a child at his father's court where, frequently beaten and tortured by his sadistic father for his poor ability in weapons training, the young phril had been soothing his fury against his parent. Hidden in the shadows, no more than a dark silhouette, Chathu had watched him tack a writhing and squealing rat to the wall, preparatory to dissecting it alive. He had watched the youngling's every move, trying to stifle his increasingly heavy breathing as the phril methodically maimed the animal, but soon he was groaning, and Tathar had easily sensed his presence. Though he did not acknowledge it, he seemed to enjoy having an audience.

After Tathar finished with the rat, Chathu, masked even then, approached him and caressed him, feeling overwhelming affection for this kindred spirit. He could tell the youngster was unaccustomed to such treatment, having received only blows, kicks, and whippings, for years. He undressed him there in the yard, touching him and caressing him in that new and pleasant way, leaving him without power or will, his frail body trembling with pleasure and satisfaction.

Tathar returned with him to the royal court, where he educated and taught the youngling, taking care of him as if he were a little brother, becoming dear friend, lover, advisor.

So long ago, Chathu thought as Tathar left, smiling fondly. They both had taken care of Tathar's father, a few years later.

He climbed out of the tub, vigorously rubbed his fur dry, and smothed floral-scented creams into his skin, focusing on the areas that stank the most. He studied himself in the mirror—he looked well. If not for the smell, nobody would know he was ill. On the outside he looked pretty good, he decided, even a bit athletic, as he still worked out. The decay was happening inside, hidden to the eye and camouflaged by his masterful perfume-mixing. He'd studied the art for years, and now had a team of phrils who brought him from his privately organized expeditions all the plants, essences, and spices he needed to stock his secret laboratory. It had been in operation for more than ten years, and neither the King nor even the King's Trust Comtap knew about it. He puffed little clouds of fragrance over the same areas he'd rubbed with cream, then entered his bedroom and chose the clothes for his meeting.

Bahara was one of Chathu's faithful allies. They'd known each other since childhood, when they'd shared the same teachers. He was an opportunist who'd made a place for himself near the true power of the kingdom—second only to the partnership of the King and his King's Trust—by executing its commands without question. Bahara benefited from the arrangement, one that could only get better, when Chathu became the highest power in the kingdom. Bahara had become even more visible as Chathu's supporter, now that the reins of power were slipping from the aging King.

Bahara bowed courteously when Chathu entered the guest room, his eyes on the prince, waiting for the formal moment to pass. Then he turned into Chathu's best friend.

"Bahi has arranged for guards faithful to us to be on duty in the SCeders' wing for the next few hours," Tathar told him, clearly pleased.

"Then let's hurry, my dears." The prince caught them by their shoulders and pushed them toward the exit.

"Can't we wait a bit longer and, uh, entertain ourselves with them after the King's interviewed them?" Bahara looked worried, but his voice sounded false. He'd always had full trust in Chathu's plans.

Chathu laughed. "Bahi, the SCeders have waited for an audience for more than a month, and the King didn't care to honor them with his presence, or even ask about them. His Majesty doesn't know what to do with them. He doesn't have a clue what to ask them. He doesn't want to be bothered with them."

"It's not His Majesty who worries me, but His Majesty's Trust," Tathar interjected, the concern in his voice real. After the incident in Morminiu's palace, he had felt Comtap's presence in everything he did, as if the phril were breathing down his neck.

"The King's Trust is passing through a weird stage, Tathar. He hasn't emerged from his apartments since the battle with the SCeders. I still haven't been able to find out what's going on. Either he's tired and old age has caught up with him, or they are up to something. But the King is guarding him very carefully—you know how obsessed he can be. I cannot get past his guards to find out what's going on. What's certain is that they aren't even thinking of the SCeders right now."

"Have you somehow seen Morminiu entering Comtap's quarters?" asked Tathar, trying to look indifferent to hide the quaver in his voice.

Again Chathu laughed. "No, my friend. Morminiu is not involved in this. He hasn't been to the palace more than once during the whole period."

They were travelling deeper and deeper into the royal palace's basements. The guards and servants in the passages grew fewer, the light grew dimmer, and the passages themselves looked more neglected.

"You can't possibly know," Tathar insisted. "Morminiu is an intriguer, just as Plabos was. He seems to be involved in everything; wherever one turns, one sees traces of his influence."

"Now you're being paranoid," the prince reproved him softly. "Morminiu is just a peasant, one we'll take care of personally, Tathar, I promise."

They'd reached the royal dungeons, housing ranks of tiny cells from which no one had ever escaped. The identification membranes that formed the doors responded to the saliva of only a few people, and the Carami flesh here was resistant to digging. In fact, in this area, the Carami had been conditioned to launch an attack of acid rain on anything it perceived as alien—and phrilic prisoners were fed a substance that ensured they would be perceived as aliens.

Chathu wrapped his fur cloak tighter around his body and, ignoring the guards, said to Bahara, "I want to see the translator as soon as possible." He turned to Tathar. "Have them move the first five prisoners to the torture chamber and chain them there. I'd like the first five prisoners to be drawn from among their officers."

Tathar nodded to a guard commander hovering nearby, who bowed, waved for a detachment of soldiers to follow, and descended to the cells.

The prison superintendent joined them. He smiled nervously, swallowed visibly, and said to Tathar, "If His Grace wishes, he can wait for his orders to be fulfilled in my apartment. It would be an honor—"

Tathar cut him off. "His Grace wishes to go to the torture chamber right now." The superintendent retreated hastily, his eyes downcast. "His Grace also wishes not to spend all day here and would like your phrils to be more prompt," Tathar went on mercilessly.

"Of course, of course, Your Highnesses. Please, follow me."

The superintendent led them to a narrow spiral stairway and gestured to four guards to grab torches and go before them. They climbing cautiously on the slippery treads, they went down three more levels, into the Carami's depths; just as Tathar started looking alarmed at how far they were travelling, the stairs ended at a narrow, curving tunnel that in turn led to a labyrinthine passage through a series of narrow, low-ceilinged tunnels whose mold-splotched walls glistened with moisture.

"My friend," Tathar said, touching the superintendent's shoulder, "tell me: where are we?"

The whole group stopped as the big, burly superintendent turned ponderously toward the Royal Recipear and looked at him in amazement. "In the royal dungeons."

"But, where are the prisoners? Where are the cells? What are we doing in this labyrinth? *Where are the damned dungeons?*" he blurted in exasperation.

Chathu laughed, the high-pitched sound immediately absorbed by the fleshy walls. The superintendent and the guards waited silently, their eyes on the moist, twitching flesh of the walls while the prince answered, trying not to laugh,

"We are in the middle of the dungeons, Tathar." He waved to the superintendent. "Show him."

The superintendent nodded to the four guards, who surrounded him as he moved to the wall, stroked its surface, then spat against it. The Carami's flesh cracked with a noisy slurp, then tore vertically, the tattered edges spreading back with faint splashing sounds. Tathar clutched his stomach and looked nauseated, but Chathu moved closer and watched in fascination as fat white worms spewed through the layers of flesh around the cell entrance. "You see, Tathar," he said absently, eyes still riveted on the worms, "all the cell doors are merely open wounds in the city's flesh, wounds that are never allowed to heal, else they would seal the cells shut permanently." He stepped aside as the smell of putrefaction gusted past. "In a way, the dungeons are a spoiled portion of the Carami's anatomy. No one knows how it was convinced to cooperate."

Overjoyed that there were smells more fetid than the stench of his own body, the prince turned and gave Tathar a wide smile, beckoning him closer. The recipear hesitantly moved closer, grimacing with distaste, his back ramrod straight, as if he'd been commanded to march to his death. When he saw the writhing white flesh of the worms, he exhaled as forcefully as if he'd been punched in his nervous belt, the air whistling from his lungs before his mouth gaped open to suck in fresh air. Chathu caught his hand as the recipear made to step back and held him there, watching t sticky yellow pus oozing from the torn edges of flesh.

The vermin teeming through the wound wasn't just from the flesh, but from everywhere inside the cell—a tight space only a bit wider than a phril's shoulders and five paces long, more a corridor than a room. The fleshy walls were irregular, resembling mincemeat pressing against an elastic and dirty white skin. On the floor lay the curled figure, one hand thrown over the eyes to protect them from the torchlight. If it had been a phril, it had lost any phrilic characteristics long ago.

Only a skeletal husk remained, twitching with convulsions. Its patchy white hair hung in greasy tufts. The lips were gone, the sagging mouth stretched in a rictus over the facial bones like a grisly grin. A half-chewed worm was caught between the teeth, forgotten in the surprise of the opening door. The worm wriggled feebly, trying to escape and crawl along the swollen tongue to the floor.

"Can you see, Tathar?" Chathu said like a teacher instructing a pupil. Tathar turned horrified eyes to him. "We have here a case of a closed natural cycle. The Carami is forced to keep the cell's door at a level of partial healing, in order to keep them shut but ready to be opened on command—meaning reopening the wound. This state leads to a considerable level of decay, hence the worms. You were the one to teach me that these worms are very nourishing, containing a substantial amount of the nutrients necessary to a phrilic organism. Therefore they serve as the prisoners' meals, providing both the required fluids and solid food. What the prisoner's body eliminates afterward is assimilated by the Carami and recycled. Isn't it so, Superintendent?"

The superintendent was leaning against the far wall holding a perfumed handkerchief over his nose. He straightened, smiling guiltily, and nodded.

"That means . . . ?" The prince waited expectantly.

"That means we don't have to feed the prisoners, or to care for them in any way," the superintendent mumbled. "That means lower maintenance costs overall."

"How many prisoners do you have at this time?"

"Around eight, nine hundred phrils, Your Highness."

"How many of them go back to the streets?"

"At most one hundred, Your Grace. Only those who are imprisoned for less than a year. The others are left to live in the cells. We are merciful; what else can we do?"

"That means any prison sentence of more than a year automatically turns into a life sentence?" Bahara asked, horrified.

"It seems harsh," the superintendent answered him humbly, "but, look at him, Your Highness." He waved a hand toward the convict on the cell floor, who had barely moved since they'd opened the door. "How could you let someone like him back out on the streets?"

"You could send him to his family to take care of him," Bahara sputtered.

"In order to feed and care for him in his invalid state, his family would need more food than they can produce, and good doctors for which they can't possibly pay. Most of the detainees are poor—beggars, thieves. Returning them to their family would force the family to start stealing, in order to be able to pay for such care. And that would land all of them in prison."

The superintendent looked triumphant as he ended his presentation. Chathu nodded, pleased. The system was infallible, virtually free, and effective. Few systems could work so well.

Bahara swallowed laboriously and wordlessly followed Chathu as he led the way to another point on the wall, where another wound opened in the Carami's flesh to reveal the torture chamber—a round hall with walls of the same thick, elastic skin, stretched over a row of arched ribs. Here and there, other smaller, sharper bones pierced the skin, and from these hung the chained SCeder prisoners, suspended by their arms. They were naked, their glabrous bodies stretched painfully, their feet unable to touch the floor and take their body's weight off their arms. Chathu led his fellow nobles on a tour from one detainee to the next.

Bahara turned to the superintendent. "Where is the translator?"

"Surely on his way, Your Highness." He addressed the guards. "You four, stay here and guard Their Graces with your lives. Do everything they say." Then he turned back to Bahara. "I'm going to get the translator."

"Ah, no," Chathu said. "I want the guards waiting

outside, near the door. I want to remain here alone with my friends. And, of course, the translator."

While they waited for the translator, they browsed through the instruments of torture and studied the array of ominous devices in the center of the room. There were enough to allow one hundred phrils to be working here at the same time.

"Well. It's obvious we're busy." Chathu grinned.

"Those cells looked like sufficient torture," Bahara muttered.

"You haven't gone soft, have you Bahi?" The prince threw a friendly arms over his shoulders, while turning a pliers in his other hand.

Bahara mumbled an answer, then straightened his shoulders and moved off to continue his exploration of the room.

They examined crushing tables made of a single plate of thick bone, others with thinner plates positioned over fire pits to slowly detach a prisoner's skin, and still others with a latticework of holes in a whole series of shapes to admit various tools. There were racks for stretching limbs until they dislocated from their sockets, shelves full of a thousand kinds of pliers, tongs, hooks, ropes, needles, knives, files, and saws. And that was only the mechanical part of the torture chamber.

They entered a separate room as large as the main hall. Lining one wall were cages containing different animals, birds, and reptiles that could be used to bite, gnaw, sting, spit acid or venom, scratch, tear, slash, break, crush bones with their jaws, and do many other things that the three of them could only imagine. Their entrance prompted a cacophony of squeaks, barks, croaks, growls, and howls. All the beasts had been used for years and rewarded for purposes other than their natural behaviors; their origins long forgotten, they begged to be allowed to satisfy their unnatural urges. On the other wall were aquariums filled with all sorts of worms, crabs, fish, and insects, interspersed with potted plants that looked misleadingly benign.

"By Sathali's Spheres, now I know we are a sick nation," mumbled Bahara.

"What did you say, my friend?" Chathu asked him, amused.

"I think he was wondering who had the time to develop all these methods of torture," Tathar said.

"I agree," the prince said, delighted. "Do you realize the level of refinement, the subtlety that lies before us? I bet our specialists could torment a phril for years on end, and never kill him or use the same method twice."

"That's a culture in itself!" blurted Tathar.

"Culture?" Bahara shouted, shaking. "That's not—that's something—it's a . . . it's something that should remain here, underground and forever hidden."

"You're right, my friend," Chathu said calmly. "This is one of our darkest sides, one that we must keep hidden. And not for fear of our neighbors, but to make it even more ominous and frightful. And yes—this, Bahi, is a culture. I could write dozens of books about the meaning of what happens here. About the story behind every method, and the mentality of the inventors. These are the Recipears of Torture!"

The recipear trembled at that, and raised his hands. "Do you realize, Chathu," he breathed angrily, "that all the hundreds of recipears who have lived since the kingdom's birth could write only a few tens of thousands of Recipes? And they have been publicly acclaimed, encouraged, royally rewarded for their efforts."

"And in contrast, the recipears of torture, those that nobody knows of, have been much more prolific, exotic, and imaginative," the heir finished. "I understand what you feel," he added, lowering his voice in compassion. He paused before saying solemnly, "Tathar, today you have the opportunity to become Master Recipear of the Dark. Here, now, you'll be our Master of Ceremonies. I want you to release all your creativity, all your imagination, and delight us as we have never been delighted before. You're free to do whatever crosses your mind."

"Shouldn't we get some information, too?" Bahara interrupted.

"Bahi." Chathu looked at him, a bit hurt. "The information will come. The informants will beg to provide it." He clenched his fist and waved it in front of Bahara. "This is, Bahi, an act of power. You don't ask, but everything is offered to you. Even then, you're not obliged to reward for the offering. You can merely say, 'Go on,' until they are dry of information, and still you could continue, for only the refinement of the game."

"Chath, do you know whom I'd like to have here, roped to one of those tables?" Tathar said breathlessly, his eyes bulging with visions of what he'd do.

"I know, Tathar." Chathu grinned, then broke into merry laughter.

"I'd like to have him here and every day prepare him in another Recipe," Tathar continued eagerly. "Prepare him and make him taste himself alone. Then the next day do it again—bring him here alive and aware, and start everything from the beginning."

"Maybe you'll have the chance, my dear friend," Chathu said, still laughing.

They returned to the main hall. The prisoners watched them with eyes wide with terror. Some of them had voided their bowels and bladders, and the foul smell of their fear hung heavy in the stale air. The translator was waiting for them near the door. *You have no idea of the day you're about to have,* Chathu thought as he smiled at him.

MORMINIU

I open my eyes at the sound of three discreet knocks on the door. I lie there, bewildered, trying to determine if the sound had been dream or reality. Three more knocks, this time louder, provide the answer. Blinking the sleep from my eyes, I glance to my left and am pleased to see that Valiria hasn't awakened. I drop my hand onto the sword I left next to the bed and call hoarsely, "Mmyes—" I clear my throat. "Yes?"

Totin enters noiselessly, eyes downcast to avoid looking at Valiria, and comes to my side of the bed. He leans over and whispers anxiously, "My lord, the Mothers are at the gate!"

Now I'm wide awake. I rise and think in amazement as I stretch, *The Mothers! What can be more unpleasant than waking to find a pack of priestesses at your door? Priestesses with unguessed magical abilities who are certainly ready to quarrel . . .* "Invite them into the Great Hall," I tell Totin. "Serve them tea and tell them I'm on my way."

The servant bows and exits as silently as he entered. I lean over the bed, propping myself on my left elbow to wake Valiria. Her pale face is so relaxed and full of contentment that I'm almost tempted not to wake her. Her lower lip pouts a bit, as if tugged down by its weight. Her breathing is light and even—*Graceful,* I think, gazing at this phrilira who sleeps with such dignity.

Eventually I sigh and lean forward to kiss her down-turned lip. She swallows lightly. When I kiss her eyes she awakens, looks at me with a gaze now bemused, then yawns widely. *Yes, it is still dark, but . . .* I think the explanation as I study her expression. She's puzzled, but her smile is happy.

"Are you going to stay there watching me, or are you going to tell me why you woke me up?"

I'd like to laugh. *Dignified and decisive, even in sleep. And always authoritative, but nonetheless sweet.*

"Morminiu?"

I kiss her and rise from the bed, laughing. The menace posed by the Mothers now seems far away. "They came from the House of Phriliras, Valiria," I say lightly.

"Excuse me?"

"A deputation of Mothers have come to talk to me. They're in the Great Hall now, drinking tea."

She buries her face in the pillows, making her breathing noisy. "Oooh, I can't see them!"

"I think it would be better if they don't see you," I agree.

"How can I meet their eyes? How can I explain it to them?"

"Maybe it's better to stay here and I'll tell you everything after I get rid of them," I say.

She lifts her head. "I'm not a criminal! I cannot hide forever."

"Of course, you could come to the meeting, but I don't know what good it would do. I think it's still too early for that."

She looks thoughtful. "Why didn't I feel them?"

"What do you mean?"

"I should have sensed their presence when they entered the house. I should have been on full alert by now, but I still feel comfortable and sleepy. I'm still in bed, when I know they're in the Great Hall!"

"Are you sure you should have felt their presence?"

"Yes! At least, if I haven't lost my powers."

"Or maybe," I suggested, "they didn't want you to know they're here, and blocked their presence somehow."

Valiria looks at me, suddenly silent. She rises and takes a few steps around the room, then stops with her back straight. With the same majestic air, she says calmly, "The Mothers wanted to keep me unaware of their presence, yes. They thought they would find you already awake, that they could meet only with you."

"Do you think it would be a good idea to play along with their game?"

Valiria pauses, as if listening. Then her gaze returns to me. "I don't know. What's certain is that this kind of mental manipulation is a serious crime in the House of Phriliras. They didn't have the right to block my senses. Now I perceive their presence clearly, and I can tell they are a bit anxious."

"Don't forget, we are not in the House of Phriliras, and you're no longer one of them," I warn her. "Therefore they have the right to manipulate you, as long as they think that we might hurt them in any way."

She nods decisively. "Very good, Morminiu. Wait for me. We'll go together to this meeting."

When we step into the corridor we look at each other, and I realize I don't know what it means to be prepared for such a meeting. The Mothers are all exceptionally gifted; they don't represent a state power for nothing. They dominate and influence kings and their counsellors. Thinking this, I'm breathing deeply to control my nervousness as we enter the Great Hall where five Mothers wait.

Three are seated on a couch, with the other two standing on either side. These two are young, tall, and slender. Under their long robes I can see the outline of their bone-plated combat boots. They keep their arms crossed over their chests, their hands tucked within their sleeves. Above high, sharp cheekbones, their eyes study us. If I'm not wrong, these are the bodyguards for the other three.

We stop in front of the couch and I bow respectfully to those seated there. Though they are older, they still look far more dangerous than their guards. One of them is very wrinkled, with a scar running from under her ear and over her chin toward her neck. Her lips are a thin line, stretched into an ugly grin. Her whitish-blue eyes measure me as if I'm a piece of meat. The other two are ageless. Their eyes tell me they are not young, but no wrinkles mar their clear, aloof faces, and their hands are fine and elegant. Both look amazingly like Valiria.

We sit on the couch across from them. On the little bone table between us rests a tray holding seven cups painted with a floral motif, a teapot, and a few small dishes of spices. All untouched. They're probably afraid of being drugged.

"Ladies, I'll be the first to taste the tea," I say expansively, then add, "Though it may seem rude, in the Southern Swamps it is customary for the master of the house to taste first, to prove his good intentions before inviting his guests to partake. This shows he is taking his hosting responsibilities seriously."

"We don't doubt your good intentions, My Lord Hitissh," the wrinkled phrilira answers sardonically. "The only thing we doubt here is her." She points to Valiria with one long fingernail, sharpened like a blade. She quickly withdraws her hand, curling it like a claw, and I struggle to stop myself from shivering. I don't like her!

"I beg forgiveness, Your Holinesses." Valiria inclines her head just a little, keeping her eyes on them. "I've been rude. I'll assume the hostess responsibilities alongside my husband."

A shadow passes over the three Mothers' faces at this sinful news, but otherwise they sit still. Such sacrilege seems so great and so unheard of that they don't know yet how to react and what to feel. If Valiria had merely taken refuge in my house, there would still be a chance that nothing had happened between us, that Valiria might still be undefiled. They might have taken her back to her High Priestess duties. But as a wife, Valiria has obviously lost her virginity; for the first time in millennia, in the existence of the House of Phriliras, the divine chain of High Priestesses has been broken. As the implications of her words sink in, I can only hope that Valiria has moved beyond guilt and will not give in to them.

She smiles, takes my hand, and says, "Morminiu, these are three of the thirty Mothers in the Council." She ignores the two standing on either side of the couch as if they don't exist, and that reinforces my belief that they're only guards.

Then, with a twinkle in her eyes and a warm smile on her face, Valiria goes on: "Her Holiness" —she indicates the wrinkled phrilira— "is called the Mother of Pain and she is the Consciousness of His Grace, the heir, Taharissh Chathu."

I hide my surprise and smile at her courteously, and she returns a sour smile. Her small eyes, like wounds in their folds of flesh, watch me unblinking, with the perseverance of a brops.

"And Her Holiness the Mother . . . " She pauses at the phrilira in the middle, seemingly the youngest of the three. She is a bit chunky, but otherwise she could be taken as Valiria. "Hmmm." Valiria clears her throat and resumes. "I want to say she is the Mother Who Walks Through the World's Structure. I used to call her the shorter Structural Mother, or Mom." Valiria looks at me. "Morminiu, in other circumstances I would've introduced her to you as the closest and dearest phrilira to me, and we would have been discussing my future. But now she is Her Holiness the Structural Mother and we will probably discuss my future, but surely in a different tone."

"I don't think there is much to be discussed," the third phrilira interjects in a sad voice.

"And Her Holiness," Valiria says of her, "is one of the most holy and worshiped Mothers: the Mother Who Studies Development of the Echo in Our Consciousness. I used to call her the Echo Mother; whenever I had problems, I would go to her to solve them, and to be comforted. She is the mother of my mother."

"Your Holinesses, I'm more than honored by your presence in my house. If I'd known this was a simple courtesy visit to see your daughter, granddaughter, and whatever else she represents to you, I'd have invited you for breakfast," I say smoothly. "But we all know there is an extremely important matter we must discuss. And that keeps us from having breakfast, doesn't it?"

The Mother of Pain turns her eyes slowly toward me,

as if I have lost my mind. Her mouth flattens into a thin line that almost vanishes within her wrinkled face. I don't know which one of them is the leader, so I address her.

"Let's put aside etiquette and talk straight. I notice you don't like it anymore than I do. Therefore, Your Holinesses, how may we help you?"

The Mother of Pain continues to keep her mouth clenched as she leans back against the couch. Valiria's mother leans toward the little table, lifts the teapot, and pours the greenish liquid into one of the cups. Then she peruses the spices, and sprinkles one that is very sweet and flavorful on the surface of her tea. Beside her, Valiria's grandmother rises and walks to one of the room's corners, apparently studying the sphere-fish furs that wrap the pillars. Everything is happening in slow motion, as if the Mothers are moving through liquid. It reminds me of a puppet show seen while inebriated with Crevex, the drug made from the bone butterfly's excreta. I'm alarmed, but I control my anxiety and I try to maintain control of the situation.

I feel one of the sharpened fingernails belonging to the Mother of Pain spiking my left hand to the arm of the couch where I sit and I turn my eyes from the Echo Mother to her, but I cannot move as fast as I'd like. And then I'm amazed that she is not beside me; in fact, she hasn't moved from her place, and nothing actually touches my hand, but the pain of the wound-that-isn't worsens. I strive to appear unperturbed and ask her, "In fact, what is Chathu's Consciousness doing in Valiria's line?"

"Now you're being rude, young Recipear," she answers in a hoarse voice, and begins to laugh.

"Why hasn't His Majesty's Consciousness come?" I press.

"Because His Majesty didn't allow her to—it seems you've got royal approval."

"Then what are you still doing here?"

"Now you're more than rude!" Her voice is like the

squeaking of an unoiled door and I feel my hands imprisoned on the couch's arm and seat cushion while an unseen, unstoppable force tears at my nails.

I look desperately to my right, wanting to tell Valiria to run, but nobody pays me any attention. The two bodyguards suddenly look bigger and more threatening, though they're still standing benignly.

As I swivel toward Valiria, her mother says, "We've come to take you home."

Then the Mother of Pain's squeaky voice announces, "You cannot leave whenever you want. You belong to us!"

The invisible power tears my nails from my fingers, then continues to scrape at my fingertips, skinning them. The pain overwhelms me, and as my head sags sideways onto my right shoulder, Valiria finally notices.

Frowning, she turns to the Mothers. "Leave him alone!"

The pain vanishes instantly and my body sags back onto the couch. I'm sweating profusely and panting. The Mother of Pain looks hatefully at Valiria, who confronts her with glaring eyes. I can see the concentration on her face. I try to rise, but the Echo Mother's voice strikes me and throws me back onto the couch: "Morminiu!"

My own name bears weight, pinning me again on the couch, with no possibility of helping my wife. The word strikes me, sinks deeper and deeper into me with resonant knockings that disappear in concentric circles, like ripples. I try to breathe, but fright overwhelms me—amazingly fast, my name has reached my greatest depths and now it's coming back, but instead of feeling small and faraway, it is bigger and heavier than ever, growing in all aspects as it nears. I'm certain it will rise directly into my throat and smash me.

Then I realize—Echo Mother—the Echo Mother is playing with me! It's all an illusion, like the nails torn out by the Mother of Pain. But immediately, the idea is loose, travelling through the room with formidable speed, and I feel the word Morminiu still rising toward my throat, attracted to it like metal to a magnet. The idea spins around its center, somewhere outside the palace, in the plaza, in the Carami, before turning back to me with edges sharp as blades, thrusting toward my name. I begin to scream—or at least I believe I scream—and the scream spreads around me like a shock wave. And now I know its echo will return and tear me to rags, will disembowel me, will hack me into pieces!

And for the second time I am released. I open my mouth wide, gasping for air, and my gill slits move spasmodically.

Valiria floats somewhere above her armchair, her eyes shut and her arms outstretched, the palms of her open hands facing outward. The Echo Mother crosses her two forefingers in an X before her, her forehead deeply furrowed in concentration. The Mother of Pain presses her hands together, clawed fingers laced, and touches her forehead as one would in an attitude of veneration, only her expression is malicious and her mouth murmurs incantations. Only the Structural Mother is still, watching her daughter without emotion.

"Help her!" I shout. "Help your child!"

She ignores me. I try again to get up, but one of the bodyguards hits my legs with a staff I never knew she had and didn't see coming. As I fall back, the other guard punches my spine. The pain this time is real, spreading through me like burning oil, first down my spine and then in all directions, along my entire skeleton. I gasp and all the air leaves my lungs.

Hoping there will be no second blow, I leave my head on the back of the couch and open my mouth wide, sucking in air. My body feels ready to unravel.

I see, without having the power to react, the wall tearing in several places. Through the rifts roll the mercenaries I bought from Mahop, amazingly nimble for their size. The physical blows to my body have signalled to them that it is time to intervene. Two reach the Echo Mother, breaking her concentration; others run for the women on the couch and the bodyguard priestesses, their swords held already. But before they can cross them with the fighting staffs of the guard priestesses, their blades blacken, rust instantly, then crumble into coarse dust. The two guard priestesses move in sync, as if one is the reflex of the other, and the foremost mercenaries, too surprised to react quickly enough, fall under the lightning blows of their fighting staffs.

The mercenaries behind them have recovered; they lift thin, deadly daggers that also rust at the moment of impact with the priestesses' staffs. The phrilira swing their staffs overhand, striking skull, then neck, then face, and the mercenaries topple to the floor. Everything is happening so quickly that I'm not sure what I've seen, that I'm not still hallucinating.

Sharp little wooden throwing stars fly toward the two warrior priestesses from my mercenaries on the far aside of the room. The first of them crumble an arm-length from the philiras' faces, as does the wave. Only then do I detect the flashes from their tracheas—basai blades! The priestesses have been modified and armed with implants by Chathu's people!

But already another wave and another and another is spinning toward them and the priestesses cannot breathe rapidly enough to deflect all of them. Instead of falling pierced by numerous throwing stars, however, the priestesses smile widely, watching the stars turn into a rain of flowers.

The Structural Mother, I'm telling myself as, with a supreme effort, I pull myself off the couch, stumble forward, and fall over her. My body's weight crushes her into the couch; she tries to push me away, but not even I have the strength to pull myself up with limbs gone inert. I don't know what their guards have done to me, but I only hope I'll not remain crippled. Though I cannot see it, there is a big hubbub going on in the room behind me, now that the witchcraft has stopped.

After a few minutes, my guards lift me carefully and lay me on the floor. Valiria bends over me, looking worried. She touches my arms, then my legs, after which she returns her attention to my shoulders and walks her fingers bit by bit to my neck. She signals to two soldiers to help her turn me facedown. After a few seconds of prodding she finally finds the tender spot where I'd been hit. Her probing fingers, though gentle, conjure pain. I cannot move my tongue, so I have no way of telling her she has found the spot, but she seems to know what she's doing, because she grips my shoulders, puts her knee against the exact spot, and pulls forcefully. I feel a cracking sensation inside my body, like my joints are breaking. She walks her fingers along my spine, pressing, massaging, or simply cracking vertebrae; finally I begin to feel my muscles twitching. This makes me happy, though the sensation itself is completely unpleasant.

My mercenaries lift me from the floor and settle me gently in one of the armchairs in front of the Mothers, arranging my limbs as if I'm a puppet. It will be some time, I suspect, before I'll have recovered enough to move on my own.

The three Mothers are kneeling on the floor, their heads bent. They are being held there by three of my mercenaries, each with one foot positioned against a Mother's back and his fingers wrapped around her neck. They would only have to squeeze to end their captive's life. After experiencing what their guards did to me, I'm sure they are capable of doing similarly frightful things, of effortlessly killing a phril with only the pressure of a single finger. That is power!

Lying on the floor in front of them are the still bodies of their warriors, their heads resting at unnatural angles. "The bodyguards are dead?" I manage to articulate.

"Yes, Morminiu. They resisted to the end. I couldn't save them," Valiria answers.

"They have done well, my boys," I say, looking proudly at my mercenaries. I cannot distinguish the slightest expression beneath their yellowed bone masks, or in their eyes behind the visors. Nor can I catch any movement of the thin hose that snakes out of their masks to disappear under their carapace. I can't know if my appreciation has any importance to them or not.

"We were lucky to have them," Valiria agrees.

I don't understand what she means. "Lucky?"

"Now, I'm sure they're not phrils," she says as if she feels she's stating the obvious. "And more, that there is nothing phrilic about them. Otherwise the Mothers would have manipulated them, as they did to you."

"Ah. Something we'll discuss later," I say, indicating the three Mothers. But I sigh. I owe my life to Mahop ten times over, and still I have here a conflict of interests. "What shall we do with them?"

Valiria is silent, her face calm as she gazes absently at her three relatives. Then she rouses herself and tells me, "I don't know; it doesn't depend on me. The master of the House will decide their fate. This is the most correct thing." And she leaves.

I turn my eyes to the prisoners. *Tough decision!* I command in low voice, "I want to see their faces."

The mercenaries release their necks, pull their heads up, then return their fingers to their position around their necks.

"What you've done here is murder and you'll not remain unpunished," croaks the Mother of Pain, indicating the two bodies.

"Mother of Pain," I interrupt, my tone musing. "I wonder about what must be a shortened name. Valiria told me about the Mother Who Studies Development of the Echo in Our Consciousness and its diminutive, Echo Mother. And I'll take this opportunity to thank you, Your Holiness, for the miraculous experience I had. It will no doubt be food for my spirit for a long time."

The Echo Mother's face is like stone. She doesn't look at me, but stares blankly into the middle distance. I don't think she is feeling remorse, but rather a failure of consciousness. I turn to the one most entitled to feel remorse.

"Then Valiria presented me with her good and holy mother, the Mother Who Walks Through the World's Structure. I didn't quite gather where it is that she so piously walks, until I saw those solid metal swords turned to dust, and the little stars turned into flowers in mid-air. Yes, the Structural Mother . . . Now, I don't know if she didn't touch me or Valiria for a certain reason, or because that was the plan."

Defiantly silent, Valiria's mother meets my gaze, her face emotionless. I think it was the plan to let the other two take care of us. All I know for sure is, I'll never willingly step into the House of Phriliras, with so many weird Mothers lurking at my back.

"But what shall we do with the Mother of Pain? What is the full form of her name? The Mother Who Studies the Development of Pain in the Mind? Or the Mother Who Plays with Pain for Her Own Pleasure? Oh, no, no—for the Pleasure of the Heir Prince."

She grins: teeth showing through the slash of her mouth. Though she seems the most straightforward—what could be more explicit than a Mother who produces pain being called the Mother of Pain?—she's still the most mysterious of all. How does pain figure in a caste society of the type the phriliras follow? Why is she so wrinkled? What's her story? What is her role regarding the Taharissh Chathu—or, what is her relationship with the even more mysterious prince?

"Tell me," I ask aloud, "what shall I do with Your Holinesses?"

"You'll pay for your crimes," the Mother of Pain says, persisting with her previous train of thought.

"Did you have the King's permission for your visit?"

"The heir Taharissh Chathu's permission is enough," she replies.

"Did you have the King's Trust's permission for your visit?"

She ignores me. "Give up Valiria and we'll forget about

your crimes."

"Am I to understand you had neither the King's nor the King's Trust's permission? That this was, in fact, a kidnap attempt?"

"If you surrender her now, we promise you won't die at the hand of a member of the House of Phriliras. You have plenty of enemies already; plenty of reasons for counting your days and thanking the Sky Father for every day you're granted life." The Mother of Pain's rusty voice falls into the monotonous pattern of a foretelling.

"I think we have a lot to talk about," I counter. I look to my bodyguard. "Take the other two Mothers outside the palace and release them. If you're smart, you'll keep away from us," I tell those two. "And if you have any compassion, maybe in the future you'll think of Valiria as your daughter and granddaughter, and not just of her function." I turn to the Mother of Pain as the other two rise to follow the mercenaries. "Your Holiness, you'll keep me company for a while."

"There is only one place where I'll keep you company," she growls, and I immediately feel invisible hands pressing my eyes into their sockets and fiery fingers strangling me and burning my gills.

It lasts for only two or three seconds, ending as brutally as it started. The Mother of Pain's head hangs limply. The mercenary places her on the floor and resumes his position, waiting. The other two Mothers fight to come back into the room, but the strong arms of my mercenaries push them forward.

"Hitissh Morminiu, you don't know what you have just brought down on you, right now!" the Echo Mother shrieks. "You don't know the terrible fate you've just sealed!" Her voice fades with distance, then vanishes as she's thrust through the front door.

My breathing slows. I look again at the three bodies and shake my head. *I didn't have a choice,* I tell myself. *My mercenaries are professionals. They were hired to protect me. If they could have saved me while leaving them alive, they would have done so. They proved they are capable of that. If they're dead, that means they had no choice.*

I begin to feel my muscles again. I walk hesitantly, but at least I can stay on my feet. Valiria is standing in the middle of the bedroom, her gaze empty, her eyes red and glistening. Taking refuge in our bedroom, far away from others' looks, she succumbed to her emotions, and found some relief.

I sit down heavily in a chair and sigh. "What should I have done with them, Valiria?"

"I don't know, Morminiu."

"Why did you leave?"

"I could see in their minds what they'd prepared for me," she says, her voice tight, fighting tears.

"Tell me," I urge.

"Do you remember when I told you in the Altar Cave that traitors are banished to the Great Desert and left to die?"

"Yes, and I told you if that is so, we'll be leaving together."

"Well, the Mother of Pain had prepared for me a purification through pain. They wanted to torture me to purify my flesh, then force me to mate with that unknown phril. After the birth of the new High Priestess, the Mother of Pain would then have taken what was left of me into her charge. I probably would have been tortured to death, long and slow—prolonged pain as only she can produce."

"The Mother of Pain is dead now," I tell her flatly. I shake my head. "I cannot imagine a holy caste like that of the phriliras can preach faith and life through birth, yet can also torture!"

"Have you killed them all?" she asks me, her voice high with trepidation.

"No. I released the other two. Even the Mother of Pain was killed by a mercenary only after she attacked me."

She begins to cry again. I rise from the chair and sit next to her on the bed. I take her in my arms and caress her and kiss her. But the Mothers' threats don't give me peace.

"My own mother," Valiria chokes, "my own flesh, the mother who gave me birth—she is the one wishing such a terrifying end for me!"

"Maybe she didn't know what the Mother of Pain had in mind."

"She knew!" Valiria cries and I have to hold her tighter, so she won't fall from my arms.

ANTIQUE HONOR RECIPE: BLACK TRAUM IN RED SAUCE

Sometimes our pride is so hurt that we feel the need to make it public, to announce it, to have everybody watch our revenge. We want to make a show of our enemies' humiliation and always, since ancient times, the only thing we believe can restore our honor is blood.

Although they have been forbidden for centuries, I'll be bringing back a series of dark Recipes. They are declarations of war that a real phril would make before confronting his destiny. One of the oldest Recipes has its origins in the Great Migration age, when the blood raged more ardently in warriors' veins. It is the Recipe of the Black Traum. Here is its story.

INGREDIENTS:

1 BLACK TRAUM.
HOT SPICES DERIVED FROM SALLOW BUTTERFLY WINGS.
POLLEN OF RED DUSK FLOWER BLOSSOM.
RED SWAMP WINE.

PREPARATION STORY:

Situate your friends near a stream. Ensure they are seated next to you, so that no one is overcome by thirst. Pour the swamp red wine into their pots.

Drive the traum onto the gathering wheel and look into its wide, scared, glistening eyes. If you don't want to go through with it, this is your last chance to change your mind. If you still want to continue, speak your enemy's name and quickly thrust a thin, sharp knife into the jugular vein of the animal, then withdraw it quickly. Blood will spurt, black at first then turning foamy.

Fill a clay pot from the stream and slowly tip it over the wheel, letting the sweet liquid flow into its gathering channels. Set this aside; you'll use it later. Now is the moment to combine your friends' wine with blood and whisper to each of them the name of the one you have condemned.

The drums should start at this point, the musicians first beating a warning rhythm, their hands barely touching the skin stretched over the bone stumps. From there the rhythm will intensify gradually in an angry crescendo that will strike like the storm upon your Course. This is the purpose of the drums, to maintain tension till the end.

Return to the gathering platform, where the traum, already weakened by blood loss, waits trembling in fearful ignorance— exactly like the phril that pushed you to do this. Take the sword in your hand and tell your friends what you'd do to your enemy, and specifically how you'd do it. Then turn and thrust the sword into the traum's front calf. Its roar will act as background to your story for, from that moment, it will assume your opponents' role in your story.

You have to handle the sword skillfully, or you'll grow tired and everything will end before you have accomplished your purpose. You won't have the strength to keep your vow, and now there is no pulling back. You were warned of this before.

Stab your sword countless times into the chosen calf, then cut it and hack it as the drums' rhythm intensifies. You'll feel your fatigue mingling with the blood flowing into the channels and your hand will move faster and faster, cutting and hacking until you are one with the elemental furies that indiscriminately and passionately sweep aside everything in their way. And then, you'll stop. You have to regain and hold your passion. You have to do it willingly; feel it and never forget it and, if it ever happens to take this path again, to be aware of the mountain you have to climb. Because at every crossroads you need to stop, wipe the blood from your eyes, and see where you have gone.

Stop. At this moment, the traum will have fallen on its side, its strength gone, capable only of moaning gutturally. The wheel has been filled with chunks of the flesh that was flung in all directions and you risk clogging the gathering channels. The calf is probably minced, ready for the next step. You didn't think you only had to thrust your sword and leave, and let your friends, who supported you and stayed by you in your thirst, watch a body die while you ran away, did you?

It is your decision if you leave the traum alive to die slowly while watching you cook its calf, or cut short its misery. This will be your decision later—how much suffering do you need?

Take the meat you have minced, shave off anything still left on the bone, and toss it all into the wok. Sprinkle over it the hot spices of sallow butterfly wings. They should be so hot that they make your eyes water. That's good—until you understand your enemy's torment you can't possibly grasp what you've done. You must empathize with him to enjoy his pain.

Choose a chunk of meat, hot and raw, and set it aside. Pour wine over the rest, and then fill the wok with the traum's blood and place it on the fire. While your Course cooks, set the chunk of meat in front of your friends. They must see you as you work.

The drums should have stopped by now, the climax of rage passed. Your friends are probably on their third pot of wine at this point, into which they have been shaking a few drops of blood, in order to be at the same stage as you. In utter silence, you must now thrust your teeth into the raw meat and take a bite. It will sting and be difficult to swallow, but all enemies are like that—hard to swallow in their lifetime, even harder to swallow after death. By the time you finish eating the chunk, the traum will probably be dead, if you didn't end its suffering earlier.

When the blood has been absorbed completely by the meat in the wok to form a thin and crunchy crust, toss red dusk flower pollen over the mixture. Ensure that you use a red blossom, which tastes sweeter and has a stronger fragrance. Now is the time to pass over your remorse and enjoy your deeds.

Spoon the prepared food into wooden dishes for your friends. It must be eaten with the hands and washed down with pure wine. If you're not enjoying it even now, then you haven't made a good choice—your enemy's life is worth sparing. But if you like what you taste, nobody will stand in your way.

(*from* The Recipes of the Ancients, a special chapter in The Teachings of the Recipearium Revolution by Grand Master Recipear of the Green Kingdom, Morminiu*)*

XIV. GREEN KING'S COURT

For a moment, as Morminiu entered the throne room, the voices hushed, and all eyes turned toward him. He bowed politely and continued on his way. He wore a green waistcoat of aquatic spider fabric over a long, black, embroidered lace shirt, their deep colors accented by the blood-red sash wrapped tightly around his waist. Over all hung a cloak embroidered with Mormont House's devices: a skull in green silk, crowned with a little red circlet. The skull symbolized the depth of unknown forces, the mystery from beyond, the magic and the black beauty of life, the Meaning. The red circlet represented spiritual power. An oval—as the obviously rounded skull could be interpreted—wrapped with a circle, in the old written language, was the letter M. An old letter stressed with red represented more than a letter, however. It was a mystic, secret formula, with a power and a significance bound only by the person daring to use it. Few still knew how to manipulate the letters in this way, so the sight of such mystic formulas imposed respect and fear. Underneath the cloak, he wore his dark sword, its hilt wrapped in red fabric to signify defiance— the sword requested blood. Translation: revenge.

As he advanced with slow and determined steps, the courtiers drew back before him. Their faces were unreadable, but he could sense their envious respect of such power. A few younger ones pushed forward and welcomed him, inviting him without touching him (showing obedience toward a superior) to sit in one of the empty armchairs.

The throne room was very long, very tall, and impressive not only for its size, but its splendor. The walls were covered in gold leaf, and painted with historical scenes. Here and there from the ceiling hung huge candelabras bearing hundreds of candles as thick as an arm. More delicately-crafted candelabras hung even lower, their slender candles dripping white beards of wax. A statue of Father Sky stood against one wall, reaching almost to the ceiling and masterfully rendered by a well-known sculptor. Morminiu had learned that the statue was present in the throne room more for artistic appreciation and Perpetuation Guild courtship, than for religious fervor.

At the end of the hall opposite the entrance was the throne, a pretentious combination of shells blackened by age and use, and sacred formulas rendered in gold leaf. An impressive arch of sharp, curved fangs formed the back of the chair, making it look rather like a beast's gaping muzzle with its tongue extended—the chair's flesh pillow, a dirty red. The whole thing was three phrils tall and rested on a dais that added even more height. Those entering the room were forced to walk its entire length to reach the throne which, because of its size, gave the mistaken impression that it was closer—until supplicants began the seemingly endless journey toward it between two rows of courtiers. Worse, because etiquette forced the supplicant to look only at the sovereign as he approached, his head would be tipped completely back by the time he arrived.

Harissh Tahmimh, one of Morminiu's few friends, joined him immediately and initiated a comfortable discussion. Their circle grew as young nobles, attracted by the kingdom's only living hero, joined them to satisfy their curiosity and admire their role model.

A fanfare announced the arrival of royalty and everyone rose, turning toward the throne. A door to one side of the throne opened and the King entered. The fanfare continued until he'd seated himself on the royal chair, looking like a doll on a giant's throne. The courtiers' carefully cultivated masks displayed only respect for the royal institution, for the power it represented.

Eventually the fanfare stopped and the King spoke. "Today our soul is wasted."

The King hadn't given permission to sit, so everyone remained standing in utter silence, though many curious eyes turned to Morminiu. He remained expressionless, eyes on the sovereign.

"Today our dearest friend, Comtap, has died."

For a few seconds more, silence drummed in their ears, then mouths opened in an explosion of speculation. Morminiu puckered his lips in consternation. The King rose from the throne and his lanky silhouette emanated a surprising greatness. *He indeed looks royal,* Morminiu thought absently.

The heir prince approached the throne, but didn't dare step onto the staircase leading to the dais.

"We'll go into the garden to honor his spirit," the monarch commanded in the oppressive silence that had fallen. "The servants will take care of your ladies," he added, and withdrew. This meant the phriliras weren't allowed to assist in the ceremony. This was his right, the only one who could overrule it being the master of Comtap's House.

They gathered in an amphitheatre in a clearing amidst impressively tall "plants that feed on shadows" palms in the royal gardens. There, in the middle of the amphitheatre, a pyre had been built. Tall pillars bearing torches had been erected all around the amphitheatre, representing the protective circle within which the soul of the dead was held, to prevent it from losing itself, or being assimilated by the plants. Pits had been dug as well, in which burned fires for the fulfilling of the ritual. A leather mask had been placed on each chair, so the freshly exited spirit wouldn't be able to distinguish the faces of those gathered.

The King reappeared, surrounded by his personal guard, as was the right of only the master of the House; etiquette demanded that guests trust their host with their safety and enter alone, though armed. Yet the King waved his guards back and lost himself among the courtiers.

They put their masks on. The dancers began the ritual movements around the fires, occasionally shouting, "Oouuu!" for this was the dance between silence and calling. The nobles watching the movements grew more and more tense; when one of the dancers ignited himself, they all jumped, startled.

The flaming dancer threw himself over the Taharissh Comtap's body, which was lying atop the pile of dry, oil-splashed wood, and flames spread quickly over the pyre. The spasms of the dancer in his violent death mimicked a Tasting, and the sacrificed phril would act as a guide spirit to help the spirit of the dead phril, blinded by a pagan death, find its way beyond the circle to seek a new home in the body of a spectator. There would be no choice, either for the two dead phrils, or the living spectators. This was the Sacred Law of Transmigration. The King wished to pay for his crime of keeping Comtap from an honorable death by forcing the Court to honor the spirits of the dead.

The pyre grew to a huge torch. The dancers entered into a synchronized rhythm, and the courtiers started to mark the dance with abrupt shouts. The guide's dying howl rose over all. It suddenly grew in intensity, sending shivers through everyone present, then it fell silent forever. The spirits were free. The nobles intensified the staccato rhythm of their shouts, while the dancers moved faster, their choreography simpler.

Morminiu partially drew the mask off his face and looked around. Seeing everybody focused on the ritual, he continued to shout, but left half of his face exposed, in order to keep the spirit away.

Strangely, he perceived a fretting beneath his forehead. Something cool wiped the top of his head. Immediately, he felt Plabos' presence within him, something he hadn't felt for a long time. He shivered. What was Plabos doing back? What was happening? Then he clenched his teeth in an effort to stop a scream—his head had become a battlefield! Without, two icy palms clasped his skull between them, squeezing. Within, his master's fiery palms pressed in opposition to the external pressure. He felt the ice melting and running like sweat down his face. But immediately, a series of hammer blows struck his head. He had the impression that the hard bones of his skull had turned to cardboard and were buckling under the attack.

From within, corresponding hammer blows straightened the deformities made by the attackers. He fell on his knees and clutched his head. He wanted to scream, but couldn't; it felt as if his mouth were stuffed with wool, and he started to gag.

The knocks stopped as abruptly as they'd started, leaving behind only silence and peace. Then he jerked violently and fell among the chairs, his eyes opened wide. Something was drilling through his skull! It struck a shield, the impact reverberating through his brain and unleashing a storm of sensations behind his forehead; howling, tearing emotions pierced his brain.

He began losing control. His body spasmed and red foam blossomed at the corners of his mouth. He perceived faces gathering above him, at the edges of his sight, among them the King's, looking both worried and curious.

A powerful voice tore through the sponge of his brain to reverberate underneath the broken bone of his forehead: "He is my son!"

Silence again. Morminiu felt the weight lift from his mind, and he could breathe again. He inhaled deeply. He felt Plabos inside him, trying to relax him, soothing the wounds to his psyche.

Suddenly another howl ripped through the amphitheatre, and another body fell among the chairs, thrashing as if shaken by invisible hands. Those nearby drew back, made room around him, and all noise stopped—the drumming ceased and the dancers sagged to the ground, exhausted. The nobles removed their masks, revealing excited faces. The receiving body belonged to the King. Comtap had found his revenge.

"There is a traitor among us!" an angry voice blurted— Tathar. He climbed onto a chair to tower over everyone. His face transfigured by effort, by the flames, and by fury, he stretched his hand toward Morminiu. Those around the recipear immediately drew back. "A traitor and a criminal," Tathar continued, his hoarse voice sinister. He turned toward the heir prince. "Your Grace, arrest him!"

Chathu nodded silent approval, then turned his back and left. Everybody moved aside, making room for the guards. Morminiu rose on one knee, then he straightened his back and rose to his feet. His legs trembled and he felt dizzy—even more, he was exhausted. He couldn't react properly. He made the gesture to unsheath his sword, then dropped his hands. It was one of those moments in which one cannot speak, cannot justify oneself, though the silence was absolute. He felt as if, even if he were to scream, he would not be heard or understood. That accusing voice, though quiet now, had somehow overwhelmed any defense. He unbuckled his scabbard and moved hesitantly toward one of the young nobles.

"Harissh Tahmimh, I give this sword into your safekeeping. Please guard it as if it were my master, or my own body; keep it far from defiling hands. My enemies shouldn't feel any part of it but its sharp edge. I swear I'll be back for it; if I fail in this, will you swear to break it and bury its shards?"

"I swear," Tahmimh answered solemnly. He put his hand on the recipear's shoulder in a gesture of friendship. "Have faith, Morminiu." He took two steps back and held the recipear's gaze as the guards surrounded him.

They took him to the dungeons. He stopped only once, in front of Tathar, meeting his stare. A strong scent of dusk flower rose from the Harissh's clothes like an accusing scream. His nostrils flared as understanding came. "Tathar, you'll die in shame," he said. "And for sure, others will die the same!"

"Take him!" the noble growled, his eyes shifting nervously away. "Take him from here!"

Morminiu stopped the guards once again. "Your mouth smells of a phril's vulba."

In an eyeblink, the Harissh's sword was out and swinging toward the recipear. Morminiu dodged at the last instant, and the weapon bit deep into the back of the chair behind him. Only the King's moans and Tathar's panting disturbed the sudden silence.

It would have been dishonorable for a Harissh, and especially for the former Master Recipear of the Court, to kill the present Master Recipear of the Court in public. And worse, the victim would have been a noble at the height of his power, forfeiting the right to revenge in Tathar's defense. He would have been, at best, banished from the Green Kingdom. Only a hairsbreadth had saved the Harissh's reputation and Morminiu's life.

The King crouched on the throne. He looked sick. Much lower down on the dais, Chathu sat wrapped in his black cloak in his chair on King's left. The chair on the right was empty. As was another chair on the left, only one step lower than the throne. The empty chairs bore much significance: one meant the King's Trust was dead, and the other that the Master Recipear of the Court was potentially dead.

All nobles were seated as determined by their functions and ranks. Justice was one of the King's prerogatives, his jurisdiction extending throughout the Green Kingdom overall and, more intimately, over the nobles in their Houses and their domains. No phriliras were present; they were forbidden to assist in judgements. Their cases were judged by the Mothers Council.

The monarch made a sign to Tathar, who rose and strutted over to stop in front of Morminiu. Pointing theatrically at the recipear, he said, "I accuse you of treason against the King and the master of this holy House. While all of us were participating in the ceremony, you disobeyed the order and the royal wish. And when the spirits of the dead tried to enter you, you opposed and rejected them, defiling the Sacred Ritual of Transmigration. Such disobedience must be crushed in its first instance, Your Grace." The Harissh turned to the King as he finished.

"What do you have to say in your defense, Hitissh

Morminiu?" the sovereign asked him tiredly.

Morminiu weighed his words. "Of the first accusation, I have practised general obedience toward the royal institution. But I have not sworn total obedience because, much to my disappointment, I have not yet been asked to," he added quickly.

The King grimaced and avoided looking at him. Tathar took advantage of the moment and advanced victoriously, saying before the recipear could continue, "And this is an insult to the King. I accuse you a second time. Allegiance to the sovereign is implicit upon entrance to his court; it is not necessary that it be spoken. Especially when one steals a position of certain importance," the Harissh added, looking significantly toward the King. But, the monarch was looking elsewhere, as if not paying attention to the trial.

As Tathar hesitated, Morminiu quickly resumed. "All Your Lordship's statements are false. There are no laws concerning this in the Green Kingdom. The Oaths Law specifies that it be spoken, saying that an oath that is not spoken as part of established formula and ceremony isn't binding, and thus its breaking cannot attract punishment. With this the first issue is over, and I will only add my hope that eventually, His Majesty will allow me to offer the oath."

The sovereign had focused his attention closely on Morminiu. Tathar opened his mouth several times to interrupt him, but he stopped in time to preserve what was left of the dignity of his rank.

"As for the first accusation," Morminiu went on, "the Sacred Law of Transmigration states that neither the King nor the master of any House has the right to force a free phril to participate in a ceremony honoring a spirit. For the ceremony to be successful, the participants must offer themselves in good faith. That is why I—and probably all in this hall," he added cunningly, "—have interpreted it the way I did, not thinking even for a second, as Your Lordship has implied, that the King would break a law. I repeat, we interpreted our presence at the ceremony as being at the *invitation* of His Majesty. An invitation that we had the right to refuse without the possibility of offending anyone. And if I could refuse it in whole, I automatically could refuse it partially, as *di potesth minus, potesth plus.*" He stressed the judicial rule with the power of conviction. "Therefore, I have accepted that part of the invitation as implying that I might assist and passively participate in the ceremony, as my right and my freedom allow."

Tathar bit his lip and said nothing for a few seconds. Then he burst out vehemently, "Not in front of the King! Not in front of the supreme power! It is an insult!"

"Harissh Tathar," the King's voice thundered out, quite unexpectedly. The Harissh instantly fell silent, surprised. "The judgement is over. Don't you ever again dare to invoke the power of the throne to support your own purposes." The monarch glared at Tathar. "You may accuse only according to the law, not the royal power. If the realm's sovereign doesn't respect the laws, how could he ever impose them on his subjects?"

He had risen and once again dominated the court. He looked around the hall for several moments, his gaze touching each of the nobles. Finally he fixed his eyes on Morminiu and continued in a solemn voice, "Hitissh Morminiu, you're free. The judgement is over. You have been found innocent. You may resume your court functions." He looked around the court again. "I want to make a statement. This week our Court Recipear broke the Recipearium's record, preparing thirteen hundred Courses, of which two hundred were absolute novelties, and of high artistic calibre. I'm proud you're the Master Recipear of the Green Kingdom."

Around the room could be heard some approving murmurs. Most of the nobles bent their heads in appreciation. Morminiu bowed deeply to the King, then he took his sword that Tahmimh was holding out to him.

"One more thing," the King said, then added after a

moment's thought, "Or apparently two or three; it is hard, being without the help and reminders of my friend. Tomorrow I will bestow upon Morminiu the titles for the Sun and Siah domains, left in the Royal House's care after the deaths of their masters during the SCeders invasion. And of course, he will be elevated to the rank of Harissh."

It was obvious to everyone that his elevation was only a political maneuver, with no practical basis. The two provinces were situated on the northern border of the kingdom, their population fleeing at the beginning of the SCeder invasion and the land devastated by the SCeders during the campaign. The territories had remained something of a no phril's land; a limbo area.

"Also, tomorrow, Harissh Morminiu will be nominated as Chief of the War Council," the King added, prompting murmurs of surprise to ripple around the room and an increase in the general tension.

Even Morminiu, smiling at the first part of the announcement, opened his mouth in an O of wonder. The actual Chief of the War Council, the old general, rose to stand with trembling jaw, struggling to say something; finally, after a helpless look around, he reseated himself.

"The next announcement regards the outrageous grandstanding we have all just witnessed." He turned to glare at Tathar. "This phril, who for almost two decades never brought the smallest contribution to the Royal House while he was Master Recipear of the Kingdom, and who now has tried to use the royal power for his own purposes, is expelled from the Royal Carami and the Green Kingdom, without the possibility of ever returning, and his fortunes and estates are confiscated."

The hall erupted in a flurry of agitation. The Harissh Tathar fell to his knees in front of the sovereign, his hands upraised, begging for mercy. Ignoring him, the King stepped back to his throne. Tathar remained kneeling for a few seconds, eyes on the sovereign's back, then he slowly turned his gaze to

Morminiu. Leaping to his feet and drawing his sword in one lightning move, he lunged for Morminiu, who danced aside to avoid the blow, drawing his own sword. They paused facing each other, swords ready.

"Tathar! Stop right now!" the King roared.

But Tathar lunged, thrust, then swung like a madphril, putting all of his rage into his attack. Morminiu parried easily, moved smoothly between two blind strikes, and thrust his sword deep into the former Court Recipear's body. Silence fell over the hall. He withdrew his sword and Tathar fell onto his back, his eyes wide and empty.

Morminiu realized that if he had forgiven the Harissh and allowed him to leave alive, the phril's hatred for him would have grown tenfold. Now the conflict was definitively over, though the air was still heavy with the smell of revenge, and something else . . . The floral scent mingling with the stench of decay overwhelmed him for a moment, and he glimpsed in his mind's eye the masked presence, the black shadow that had always lurked behind Tathar.

Morminiu looked around, dizzy, trying to discern which of the present nobles might have played that infamous role. He saw only faces shocked and surprised by events. *One of these nobles bears this stink, the pestilential stench of a phril rotting alive* . . . He remained dumbfounded, and turned his gaze toward the dais.

The King was silent, standing as if turned to stone in front of the throne. Lower, the heir Chathu had risen from his chair, his black embroidered cloak open, breathing heavily as he stared at the corpse. He climbed down a few steps, stopped, and looked around the court as if coming to his senses before looking at Morminiu with eyes full of hate. Then he turned back.

Morminiu's mind supplied the logical conclusion to his earlier thought: *Pelhitza. It smells of pelhitza, of the sickness rotting the heir prince alive, so he must bathe in floral perfume to hide his terrible decay.* He stared at Chathu with sudden familiarity and for the first time he perceived him as a singularity, a mass of darkness.

The King had given the order to remove the body and clean up all trace of the battle. He lifted his hands to signal for silence, then resumed in a tired voice, "My final announcement: in a month, concurrent with celebrating the victory of my glorious ancestor, the great Chathron the Conqueror, the Royal Auction will take place. I'm waiting for your lordships' offers."

A surprised murmur crossed the hall, and Chathu glanced sharply at the King. The Royal Auction took place only once in a monarch's lifetime. It decided the official heir to the throne by naming the one who would Taste the sovereign. The auction ceremony was usually symbolic, since the heir was always the king's child, and the other nobles who bid were doing so only out of respect for the tradition. But the present king had had only one child, a phrilira who had automatically been taken by the Guild to raise and educate themselves, so she wasn't considered a potential heir. The closest relative was Chathu. At first glance, it seemed that the auction was following custom and the ceremony would be a mere formality. Yet, during a period in which all values had been turned upside down, nobody could be sure of anything.

When the hubbub died down, Taharissh Chathu stepped forward and said, "I'd like to have the honor of Your Lordship's collaboration, Recipear Morminiu, in the bidding preparations."

To accept would mean the reduction of Morminiu's status, as he had already said, to that of a simple recipear. It would be impossible to participate in his own name, through his rank. Morminiu turned to the King, then to the court. "Your Grace, here, in front of Your Lightness and Their Highnesses, I announce that I will make use of my right of vengeance against Taharissh Chathu; I cite the law that applies to everybody except the King and phriliras."

Chathu turned yellow. The King looked questioningly

at Morminiu and said, "Hitissh, nobody can seek revenge without a good reason. It is forbidden by law."

"I seek revenge for the attempt on my life in my own house a year and half ago, in which the Taharissh Chathu participated personally, together with Tathar; they may have succeeded, had not Your Majesty saved my life. Also for the other attempts on my life and to steal my work, throughout this very long year."

"If you can prove it, you're free to apply the law," the King conceded.

MORMINIU

Labyrinthine paths unfold throughout the gloomy semi-darkness of the park surrounding the Royal Palace. Dry leaves crackle underfoot like mummified skins. At the end of this path rises a decorative fountain in the shape of the Carami, water trickling from its mouth like the juices from a squashed bug. The fountain's bone is stained black with mildew. The city is somewhere far away, its noise damped by the thick vegetation surrounding the sleeping palace.

We haven't said a word since entering the park. The sense of great age here overwhelms me. It drives me back in time, to memories of my time before coming to the city. A life left behind five years ago seems unbelievably distant, as remote to me as childhood memories to an old phril.

We pass by the fountain and the King chooses a path that goes deep into the vegetation. He is no longer the elder, avid for life that I knew in the beginning. Curious, how many things can happen in a relatively short period of time. A quiet life and then, the fatal year. I remember Plabos' words: "Don't let time slip away; a kingdom can perish in a week." How right he was!

The King's earliest ancestors planted this forest. Sometimes I have the impression that he is as old as the trees, that he'd been planted with the first saplings. I think of Valiria; I can't see her aging. She is a different kind, pagan but beautiful, shameful but daring; she thrills me. There is change in the air. But even I, like all the others, would like a change that won't spoil the peace and the false security of nostalgia. A change that wouldn't change.

We stop in front of a crystal bell, suspended as high as my knees, that I could take into my arms. The old phril approaches it and sits on a rock a few steps past it, its surface polished by the many Kings who have rested there. I feel a wave of admiration when I realize it is a real stone—gray, cold, porous, brown moss in its cracks. I bend over and look inside the bell.

"It is my family's Hark," the King explains, gazing fondly at it.

Inside that enormously small space is enclosed a world. Fixed in the middle is a precious green stone, clear as crystal, like a solidified lake. Around it have grown huge forests in miniature, holding back a desert of menacing fangs no bigger than my teeth. On one side, on the edge of the world, hanging over nothingness, is a city swarming with life, developing, but somehow intrinsically. I can perceive growth within it, but I'm sure that it's been this size for centuries. I feel my eyes grow moist at the genius and the futility of it all.

"It was created by Chathron the Conqueror," the King says, his voice expressionless. His white cheek is crossed by the soft valleys of wrinkles. "It is my greatest satisfaction." He pauses, then quotes in a small voice, his face empty, "'Climb up the sun's rays / Toward the Sky's Daughters / Mobs of phrils changing their clothes / Worms remain, crawling in their flesh / Since the beginning and until the end.'

"It is the spirit of my family, created once with the Hark. At the beginning it was more optimistic. Over time it's been chiselled away, little by little—for nearly a millennium. The word 'end' used to be plural, but I erased that."

I sit directly on the ground and look straight at the Hark. I don't know what to say and, in fact, there is nothing else to be said. He has succeeded in communicating everything and now we sit like two quiet strangers, at the same time much closer than we could have been after hours of conversation. The forest is dead silent. No animal can survive in the shadows of "the plants that feed on shadows." We're alone. I remember the Hark in my house, abandoned and dirty. I couldn't find enough soul resources to restore it.

"It is said that Bartrabar, the last red-headed king, and Chathron stayed like this, thinking. After which Chathron chopped off his head. At the moment Bartrabar died, he conceived the Hark. It is said that the Hark has the red-headed king's heart at its core, green as a crystal, and Chathron's will to grow and develop. There have been centuries of creation," he tells me as if he is crushed under them. "Now it belongs to me, and after me to the emptiness. Before I leave this world, I'll give them freedom. The last piece of creation."

Although I understand him and I usually enjoy a period of philosophical detachment, I cannot forget that he's the King. I wonder what's he after. Why is he telling me all this? Yet I cannot help thinking that his creation will be the greatest.

"Your Majesty," I finally say.

"Yes, Morminiu?" He looks at me, surprised and attentive, as if he'd forgotten I was still there. Now he's waiting—he supposes I have something to ask and that this puts me on guard. If I hadn't done my homework, it would have.

"There is an important problem you should know of."

The King is quiet, attentive. *The land is swampy,* I remind myself; *I have to be careful where I put my foot.* "Recently I discovered something pretty serious. I didn't come to you right away because I wanted to run more tests and recheck things."

This time he raises an eyebrow and licks his lips in curiosity. I cannot say, but I think I've hit upon something else that he's expected.

"It is about the Green of the Gods."

"What about it?"

"It has some unwanted side effects." I hesitate, then remain silent and my eyes fall on the Hark. I remember Valiria and Donasa, Plabos and—not the last—Leomi.

Plabos left me at a certain moment, probably discovering something that forced him to choose. The problem is, only lately have I realized that he was led by power and ambition even after his death. The damned truth is crooked. Plabos, inside me, unconditioned by a system of mores, laws, common sense, money, and social positions, discovered his true path much easier, and decided to follow it. Just like that. In life, one would make sure to take the luggage as well. And for that we are forced to make compromises.

"Your Majesty," I resume before he loses his patience, "the tea can eventually kill you. You have only two possibilities: give it up and clean it from your system, or don't give it up and, sooner or later, die—"

"Happy!" the King says as if completing my sentence. For a few moments I can only gape at him in surprise. "I felt something odd in this tea," he tells me. "It's too beautiful to be true. Don't you know that Death is a beautiful phrilira you mate with in your last hour, until you pass away?"

This wasn't the reply I expected.

"I'll be Tasted soon," he tells me. "So none of your concerns will matter anymore."

"Unfortunately, Sire, they will. The Taster will get the addiction and its side effect from you and eventually die. There is no point in transmigrating into somebody else only to kill him. You'd only move the ending a bit further along. But you can be cured."

The King is quiet. He's at a dead end and he doesn't like it. Only the wisdom of age and the coming ending keep him calm. Here, my calculations have succeeded. At last he asks me in a resigned, quiet voice, "Then, I have only two solutions—be cured or die pagan?"

"There could be one more, but I'd rather choose being cured."

"Then I'll choose the tea."

I notice he doesn't mention the inevitable death that would follow and I shiver—no drinker of Gods Green has ever given it up. I think that Death has found the most appropriate ally and I envy her, for nobody has as much fidelity.

"The last solution, Your Majesty," I say heavily, "is to live . . . but differently. In the event that the dependence is incurable, and that is not the case here, this last option is a compromise to retain life and the Gods Green, too." He's still silent. "You would be planted on the muddy bottom of a lake with your feet thrust into a pouch of Gods Green root. The surrounding ecosystem will assimilate you, absorbing a good part of the poison and transforming it, giving you back your life. You will become a vegetable."

"That's humiliating!" he sputters and I know he's thinking of the unworthy phrils who must be planted to obey orders and not leave their posts.

I slowly bend my head and wait, surprisingly without fear, for the consequences. In a way I've made peace with myself. I should have done this long ago, but fear prevented me. But having revealed everything, I realize I didn't do my homework properly. The King is staring at the Hark with sadness on his face when in fact he should have immediately thrown me in prison. Instead, he's thinking. I notice, feeling invigorated, that the morbid atmosphere of the place and the monarch's resigned air don't depress me anymore. I feel free, ready to fight. And that's what I'll do, if he forces me. I cannot stand up yet, but I'm anxious to leave. Valiria waits for me at home, well guarded by my mercenaries.

"What do you want in exchange?" he asks at last.

"Nothing," I mutter with half of my mouth and only half of my soul. "I have to help you, it is my responsibility."

Silence, then, "You told me nothing of the High Priestess."

I need a few seconds to control my surprise before replying cautiously, "Now is not the time. The problem can wait."

"It won't wait, Morminiu. This is one of the problems that kept me from throwing you in the dungeon. Although, in a way, I appreciate you being honest with me."

My breath stops, but the King goes on.

"On the other hand, the problem is more serious than you think. It sounds familiar: religious war, machinations, conspiracies, mutinies, assassinations . . . " He studies my reaction. "We can handle the problem now; if we wait too long, we'll be in trouble. Now, if a High Priestess has taken this step, then the whole thing has deeper meaning than we can decipher. And you—do you want to stay with her?"

"I won't give her up for anything in the world, Your Majesty," I answer passionately, and he smiles.

Then he sobers. "That would mean overturning a tradition that has existed since the origins of the Green Kingdom."

Only now do I realize that he's been offering me the key to this discussion ever since the beginning of our conversation, when he told me the story of his family's Hark. "One that nobody believes in anymore," I answer hopefully.

"What about the phriliras?"

"Only those living in the House of Phriliras. And if even the High Priestess has crossed to the other side . . . "

"That would mean the fall of the Perpetuation Guild myth, as well, along with everything that upholds a world," he says.

"Not the fall, only the transformation, Sire. The world will keep spinning, as it's done for eons. The phrils in the countryside, less caught in the rigid and conservative systems that exist in the Caramis and, I dare say, with a healthier life and morality, long ago stopped believing in this kind of world."

"This kind of world," the King interrupts, half preoccupied, half amused, "doesn't belong to me. I didn't make it; Chathron and his heirs did. I only received it, and without a choice in the matter. Chathron died almost a millennium ago and I believe that truly, his motivations were corrupt."

He looks at me and sighs. "Morminiu, you're free to stay with the High Priestess. You will have my protection. Yet, I'll give you a piece of advice—she's much more ancient than Chathron. If the depth of the past doesn't make you dizzy, then keep her."

He's quiet again but I sense that the discussion is not

over. What else is there to say? I wait anxiously and eventually he continues.

"What happened at the Transmigration ceremony?"

I choose my words carefully and speak slowly, watching for his reactions. "Comtap's spirit attacked me, and for a moment I thought he attacked me, specifically, as odd as it seems."

"I never heard of a spirit attacking somebody!"

"Me neither, until that ceremony. But I can swear I've never received stronger or more painful blows than those. My skull turned into a papier maché ball, without any resistance in the face of such aggression."

"And in fact, who was he attacking?" the King asked curiously.

"Plabos," I whisper, and wait.

The silence is heavier than ever. The sovereign's face goes gray and he glances at the Hark. He touches his lips with his fingers then raises his eyes toward me. "Morminiu, I've never told you, but I think you should know—Plabos had been banished as a result of a plot. Comtap was behind the whole thing." He pauses, watching me, and adds, "Plabos and Comtap were brothers."

I'm astonished. I never knew. Plabos should have warned me!

"Plabos was the elder brother, more gifted and with a promising, bright future. Comtap had no chance of inheriting the House, so their father gave him to the court for education and, eventually, a public position. And that made him hate Plabos. In time, both of them being very ambitious, they became the most important phrils at the court—one was the King's Trust, the other Master Recipear of the Court and, through this, sometimes the King's adviser. Somehow, rival positions. So, in the end, Comtap had his revenge. Tathar helped him joyfully, hoping to get the Master Recipear's position. Comtap used his greed to reach through him to Taharissh Chathu and involve him in his plans for revenge. Because there were many demanding Plabos' head, I eventually banished him from the court."

He sighs. "I'm sorry I brought you to the ceremony and put you in danger. If I made the first mistake with Plabos, I should've taken the opportunity to protect you, at least."

"That's why Your Grace helped me so? To pay for the injustice done to Plabos?"

"In the beginning, yes. But later, you proved to be even better than the Master, and everything came naturally. Now, I only have one question: how did Comtap forgive you?"

I think on this, analyzing everything that had happened. I come to only one conclusion, and I don't know how clever it would be to reveal it. But now, after all the King has said, I have no more reasons to hide. So I tell him, "In that moment, I found out that I'm not only Plabos' disciple, but also his son."

The King breathes deeply, then rises. I sense he is thrilled. The future has already started to be written by the past. I keep from grinning and follow him.

ADVICE.   *The most difficult is the ending of a work. One could just say, "That's it!" But everyone knows that something must always follow. History has taught us that there is no beginning and no ending. So I can only say to you: Pay attention! The future crumbles around you. You don't have time to see its end, because it is already the present, and another future is coming to crush you under its weight. Anyway, you are your time to Taste and savor. You only have one future.*

(from The Teachings of the Recipearium Revolution by Grand Master
Recipear of the Green Kingdom, Morminiu)

XV. THE PHRILOLIR HOUSE

"I cannot believe that we finally did it," said Morminiu, looking into her eyes.

"What?" asked Valiria, looking back to him from the table full of instruments.

"That we did it in that room, that you had those gross spiders crawling all over you, that we've used all those bizarre things, that it's been so wonderful, that you are so beautiful, that I'm so lucky. I can't believe it!"

Valiria lowered her eyes. She felt two tears tracking down her cheeks.

"Do you believe in us?" he asked her, raising her chin.

"With all my heart, with all my desire."

He took her in his arms and lowered her onto the table. "I can't stand the thought of seeing you grow old. I want to feel you day by day, moment by moment, to perceive you through all my pores yet clench my teeth, get ahold of myself, and be satisfied with so little. I want to do to you all that can be done in the world, at once, with a single gesture, to taste all of you, to pour my love over you all in an instant, yet I'm unable to. To be so near, but hidden behind an absurd barrier—that's cruelty!"

"Still, I was thinking we could do it the other way

around."

"No way. You're not ready for something like this. Valiria, be realistic. For entire generations, in fact for millennia, it hasn't been done. You don't have the education, through birth or blood. But we—for this we discipline ourselves for a lifetime. From the first rays of sunshine to the last. Add to this the experience of all my ancestors sent into their heirs, strengthening me. It's essential. The pain would destroy your spirit too quickly."

"We'll be going against the world," she murmured.

"We'll put the world back on its natural track," he corrected her.

"Morminiu, let's wait until the Royal Auction. There are only a few days left. I have a feeling."

"What, exactly?" Morminiu prompted.

"Important things will happen at the auction. You could be the main player."

"I'm not interested anymore, Valiria. None of these things interest me anymore. I'm ready for today, that's enough. But it is also important that you—"

"I know, I know, Morminiu." She pressed her fingers over his lips. "I told you, I have already begun my education— or my training, as you called it; with you, it's been more like a refinement. Don't be afraid, I wouldn't take any chances; that would be crazy! Now if you're ready, let's do it," she finished in a low voice.

She moved away from the table to her place, where she watched his final preparations for a few minutes before asking him, "I haven't seen the mercenaries today. Did you get rid of them?"

"Yes, although I don't believe I did the right thing. Anyway, if you change your mind, I can reinstate them immediately."

She shook her head. "You did the right thing. There was something evil about them, I felt it. They weren't a good presence in the house."

"Still, I hope you're wearing the Aura," he said, casting a worried glance her way.

"Of course," she lied, keeping her tone natural.

He looked around the Ritual Hall, checking the preparations, then nodded his satisfaction. "Everything's ready." He smiled and came to her. "It is not necessary to say good-bye."

"And yet, I'll miss you!"

"I won't give you the chance."

He looked as if he wanted to say something more, but gave up and walked to the fireplace to start the fire under the cauldron. Then he undressed, exposing a body shaved clean of all possible hair, and climbed onto a chair beside the cauldron to step into the water.

As if by magic, the music began. *Tanghshu.* Boiling swamps. *Tanghshu.* Enormous roots of a seqolosal housing a whole village, its trunk rising high above the roofs. *Tanghshu.* Poisonous spiders . . . birds grinning, slavering, from the center of their nets. *Tanghshu.* Harvesting sequ in the red light of dusk, accompanied by the chorus of the harvesters' deep voices.

Morminiu smiled as Valiria carried a bucket of mud over to the cauldron. She set it down on the floor and looked anxiously at the spices arranged on the table.

"Not there," he corrected her gently.

"I know, I know. Let me focus."

She walked hesitantly toward the table. Selecting a root from a pile on one corner, she cleaned off the soil dried on its fibres and scraped off its outer layer, her movements growing more and more confident. She set down the root, now clean white and damp with juices, and repeated the operation on a few more roots. Then she diced them and threw them into the water, scattering them over Morminiu's body.

"Don't forget about my books," he reminded her. "They'll be our children's heritage. And . . . don't ever reveal the secret of the fulguses."

Valiria nodded then looked around, again hesitant. The room's lighting had dimmed to simulate red dusk. She felt a small thrill of panic.

"Now," he whispered.

She leaned over and lifted the bucket of mud from the floor beside the cauldron and poured it into the water. *Boiling swamps. Tanghshu. Bloody dusk* . . . He was panting, his lungs swelling and deflating with the rhythm of the song he sang, his powerful voice deep and trembling. Big drops of sweat blossomed and trickled down his face. He released his first howl. Valiria whirled to grip the edge of the table with shaking hands.

"Look at me!"

She clenched the table edge, afraid to comply.

"Don't turn your back on me, please!"

She turned and looked at him. Morminiu resumed his singing in a weaker voice. His second howl sent Valiria to her knees.

"Stand up . . . stand and fight!"

The third howl. Tears gushed from Valiria's eyes like twin springs. More of the song. A howl. Song. Howl. Murmuring and panting. Valiria's body trembled as if it were formed from jelly. His howls ended in groans. *Tanghshu.* Valiria sobbed, her body shaking violently, and put her hands over her ears.

Watching his dusk-darkened face as he groaned and howled like a stabbed animal, she felt nauseous. She fought an urge to vomit and succeeded only after she'd bent over the floor, clamping her mouth shut and looking at him. He was in pain, praying, but watching her. She focused, imagined the gastrophiza, conjured an image of *her* gastrophiza. *Concentrate* . . . The urge to vomit turned into a jugular spasm. Her stomach wrinkled and crawled up her throat. *Huge worm licking her throat . . . Vomit . . . Jugular spasm . . . Vomit. Her stomach, lying on her tongue. Jugular spasm. Vomit. Jugular spasm. Jugular spasm.* The imagined gastrophiza worked madly.

Jugular spasm— Her tensed facial muscles relaxed. The danger had passed. For the moment.

Howls. Morminiu had his arms stretched upward, shaking like sticks. Then he fainted. Valiria reeled in the sudden quiet. Her face was wet. *Tanghshu. Dementia. Vomit. The image of the gastrophiza*— This time she moved faster, crawling to the table where she paused and leaned her head against its cold bone. She cried quietly.

"It is important to resist as long as possible. Then my spirit will find the way out faster. But if I give signs that I'm losing my mind, kill me. One clean cut. Like this!" Morminiu's voice came back to her, like an echo bouncing from the corners of the room. *"Like that! . . . Like that!"* The sword's blade shone sinister on the tabletop.

"Did he die, or the madphril?" She shivered and bit her lips in despair. "Forgive me, Morminiu, I didn't have the strength. I didn't have . . . " She lifted the sword and turned it clumsily. "Whatever it may be, we'll be one."

A groan. She started violently and dropped the sword. Morminiu looked at her with dying eyes. Then he shouted desperately, "Valiria!" His eyes went so wide, they looked as if they'd pop out of their sockets.

She snatched up the sword. At the same moment, the hall's door slammed back against the wall. The lifeless body of Totin, the house phril, fell into the room. Three phrils in black cloaks rushed in after him. They stopped for a moment, surprised by what they saw, then one of them shouted, "Blasphemy! Treason!"

She recognized Chathu. And next to him, Bahara and Mahop.

"Make sure he sees what I do to the whore," Chathu told Mahop.

Valiria ran for the marketeer, but the Taharissh caught her and flung her to the floor. Mahop went to the cauldron with his sword in his hand. He was wearing a cloak bearing the noble's device, she noticed. He studied Morminiu a moment, then his shoulders shuddered. Morminiu, his face purple, stared back at him with bulging, crazed eyes. The howls wouldn't stop.

"Let him be tortured some more!" Chathu cried, his expression excited.

Mahop clenched his teeth and thrust his sword into Morminiu's nervous belt, then sliced across, cutting him in two. Morminiu's head toppled back, then slipped into the mud.

Silence. *Tanghshu. Red dusk. Boiling swamp. Tanghshu* . . .

Chathu yanked Valiria to her feet, looking at her with hate. She swayed, fighting for consciousness. Behind him, Mahop was leaning against the wall, puking. Dark spots clouded the edges of her vision as the marketeer straightened and ran from the room. When the Taharissh unbuttoned his cloak and his carrion stench flooded the room, she fainted.

She came to with the Taharissh joined with her soft body, Bahara supporting her from behind to keep her at the proper height. Instantly she brought up the sword she still clutched and nailed him to the wall. Chathu hit her hand and Valiria dropped the sword. He slapped her once, twice, then grunted in panic and released a hoarse roar of shock as the High Priestess turned to stone, imprisoning the Taharissh in her stone coldness. He struggled futilely, growing weaker and weaker until he hung motionless from her statue-hard body. Only then did Valiria begin to soften.

❧❧❧❧❧❧❧❧❧

The doors opened and the Sheriff burst into the royal apartment. He strode toward the King's desk and knelt. "I beg forgiveness for this intrusion, Majesty. The SCeders are at the city's gates."

The sovereign, halted in the act of seating himself behind the desk, gave the officer a stunned look as he sank into his chair. Breath whistling as he fought for calm, he ordered, "Send for Morminiu."

"Harissh Morminiu is dead, Majesty."

"*What?* When did this happen?"

"Only minutes ago, Hitissh Mahop arrived at the palace. He wanted to let you know in person."

"He was there with Chathu," the King immediately concluded, and ground his teeth in anger. "Kill him. Kill them both!"

<hr/>

The SCeders were drawn up in front of the city's three commercial gates, which had been barricaded with tables and barrels and wall planks from the market stalls. Behind the barricades waited a few hundred soldiers. Word ran through the streets like wildfire as Valiria ran toward the east side of the city: the barbarians were preparing to attack.

She stopped at a mouth, an exit from the city that Morminiu had shown her, unused since the age of the red-headed phrils. He had cleared it and made sure it still gave access to the exterior. Here, away from the city's core, it was quieter, the sound of fighting and the smell of smoke fainter.

Waking up from her stony condition, she'd noticed with amazement the strength and coolness with which she faced the situation. She had removed the corpses from the hall and resumed the ritual. After she swallowed the last bite from Morminiu, she gathered and tucked into the recipear's rucksack the processing unit and the memoric store loaded with all of the data gathered by Morminiu and the fulguses, and left the palace.

The whole city was in panic, with terrified phrils running in all directions, though most headed toward the known gates in the south and the north. The eastern gates were the oldest, and mostly forgotten; they opened on the mountain slope against which the Carami rested. It would be the first time she'd ventured outside the Carami. She would climb up the mountain to the ridge, beyond which, Morminiu had told her, he had erected a small temple dedicated to her. He'd named it the Phrilolir House. She'd loved the name when he told her.

The cold air hit her when she stepped outside into the combined shadow of the Carami and the mountain, so the light didn't bother her. Nevertheless, she donned the lens Morminiu had made. More relaxed with their protection, she began her journey.

At a certain moment she said loudly, "The next name of the ⚠ has been revealed to me as KAVOH. I cannot remember the other name of ⚠ ."

A shiver shook her and her eyes filled with tears. A new era had begun. The name had been revealed to her! "The House of Phrilolir," she said in a voice taut with effort. "Thank you, KAVOH." She began to cry happily.

MORMINIU

Suddenly I awake, dizzy, with chaotic thoughts and sensations swirling through my mind. I'm slipping through a tube that is dilating at my passing. I know I'm rubbing against the walls, though I don't feel it. It's dark. Eventually I'm expelled like a cork through a small orifice, and I remember everything. My first thought is, *Valiria!* After that, I wonder about me. "Morminiu, my boy," I tell myself, "you've been reborn! But where?"

The dark is all-embracing. Uncertainty fills me. I need landmarks to keep my bearings, my balance, otherwise I'll puke. The problem is, I have no way to puke, because I have no body—I just know it!—and this disheartens me. I am in the Total Darkness, floating in nothingness. I'm moving—I know that immediately, without thinking of it. The answers to problems come instantly, as they occur. I make no effort to move and I don't know where I'm going. Moving doesn't make any sense—in all directions lie only darkness and nothingness.

I perceive a multiple presence. Plabos! A thrill shivers my hair—or my sensation of hair. "Plabos, is that you?"

I see him. He's approaching, darkness against darkness, but I see him. Behind him is a whole procession. It looks like a swarm of golden butterflies and the thought that I've been reborn into a cesspit amuses me, to the consternation of the others.

"Master, I missed you!" I say when he draws near.

"Forgive me, boy. I intended to come back, to see what you were doing. Now I understand. Without advice, inexperienced in a royal city full of temptations, you gave up. I'm the only one to blame."

"No, Master, it's not that."

"What, then? You didn't die pagan!"

"What makes you say that?"

"We've suddenly been thrown from the Otherside

back into Darkness. The Otherside is no more. And even the Darkness is not the one we knew. It's different! What happened, boy? Is this your death?"

"No, Master, relax. I'm just a little bit confused. You know, I'm new around here, plus the shock of the reunion . . ."

"I know how it is. It took me a very long time to get used to it. And I saw the ancestors' spirits only after a very long time of adaptation."

"Let me catch my breath. I've been Tasted and I transmigrated. I did it!" The others don't respond to my enthusiastic words, as if I'm a bit too effusive. I ignore them, continuing to connect things. "Now I am in her conscious. That means the process is working. Everything was a lie, all the histories. We've been blindfolded. Here is the Truth!"

"What are you talking about? What Truth?"

"You know the phrilolir myth? Of course you know it. It is not a story. Everything it says is real. But in one way or another, our ancestors took the wrong path and turned the reality into a myth, living a millennium of lies. Who could've done this to us?"

"Morminiu, boy, we're losing our temper. We've got other things to do. We need to exit the Darkness and you must help us. Where are you and which is the way to the subconscious?"

"I'm in Valiria, the High Priestess of the Perpetuation Guild. And the way to the subconscious is completely unknown to me at this moment."

"Are you crazy? You're in a phrilira?" Plabos snaps. His words hit me hard.

"Yes. Together we will remake the phrilolir."

"The phrilolir is just a story. You broke the Sacred Law! You doomed us all! Centuries of tradition, lost from a madness!" Plabos moans. His words hit me more and more violently.

The others repeat, "Are you crazy? What have you

done to us? Get us out of here. You're crazy!"

The words are hard rocks that smash me and squash me. I'm crawling through nothingness, but I have no way to hide. Suddenly I fall, slip through a hole, as if a trapdoor opened under me. I plunge into chaos! Bright light and mad colors shock me. I close my eyes and remain floating, waiting to recover.

I open my eyes again and look around in wonder, because I'm lying in grass, grass that is a healthy, raw green, caressed by real sunlight. I'm in the vicinity of a swamp and the landscape is somehow familiar to me. The Southern Swamps. Home! I start to cry.

"Welcome to Valiria's conscious. She prepared this space for you, so you wouldn't feel alone."

But, she's never been outside, never mind in the South.

"No, she hasn't. But you have, and that's enough."

And does she see all this now? I ask, full of hope.

"No, not yet. You must find your way to her. I'm here to help you."

I lie in the soft grass beneath the sun and wipe tears away. After so many months of shadow, the warmth of the sun overwhelms me. It feels good, now that I've released my soul through crying.

We'd like to become the phrilolir, I think, and my thoughts are heard.

"Yes, you'd like it so. But you don't know how. For this, you must look into her subconscious. The path is surely there."

Everything bursts like a foam bubble. I wake up on stone pavings, near walls gnawed by age. Purple dust floats in the air as if suspended there.

"It seems you'll have to find your way through the labyrinth to the phrilolir at its end. My power ends here. But every time you feel tired, call on me," the consciousness voice tells me.

I enter the labyrinth—a long, endless corridor without branches. *If what I see is real, then I only have to walk the corridor to its end,* I think, and take a few steps forward. I notice I walk without advancing. I didn't imagine the subconscious would be like this. Somewhere there must be a key to help me open it.

I look around and notice immediately a row of caskets along the wall, for as far as I can see, and beyond. My first impression is that they are some kind of decorative element, but when I get closer I see that they're actually images—images from history, known and lesser-known scenes from the past, and from legends, myths, and fairy tales. The first casket displays the Green Kingdom's last victory over the SCeders. There is where history has ended for me. I touch one of the images. It slides silently then stops, waiting for me to push it aside with my hand. Behind it another image appears, another historical scene.

Without any apparent connection, I remember the King's advice: "Valiria is much older than Chathron. If the depths of the past don't make you dizzy, then keep her." I smile. I understand immediately the rules of the game. I can advance through the labyrinth only by discovering history. I need to remake the natural order of things to the end, to what would be for me the beginning, the origin of phrils and phriliras. To the phrilolir. Perhaps this way, if I find the mistake, I'll know to undo it and avoid repetition of the lie. The phrilolir must remain what it is, because we are the phrilolir. In the end or at the beginning.

I sigh happily and begin the reconstruction.

EXCERPT FROM
THE PARALLEL CHRONICLE
ARINTH HISTORIOTH
(THE ROYAL STORE, F.D. 54890)

1. The chronicler profession forces me to industriously fulfill at least one mission—the narration of all aspects of court life and the deeds of the great sovereign, the Green King Chathron Cath XVI—as all the chroniclers before me have done, as has been the custom for the past four centuries, having been brought from the lands beyond the seven kingdoms. I will, however, add one more thing.

2.1.   Parallel with the chronicle of Chathron XVI's reign, I will write about the beginnings of the Green Kingdom in that troubled period that, although covered in the mists of time and morphed into legends and glorious war stories, is still uncertain in its facts. Perhaps this is because the period has not interested chroniclers, who feel that the tales of past glory are enough for the people—but in facts there is meaning, and a clearly marked road that can be followed again or avoided.

3.1.   One must also remember that each chronicler writes what is allowed in that chronicler's period, because the times were not always peaceful and flourishing, fruitful for the arts and the rigorous thinking required for science; and not a few periods had three or four history chroniclers, while others had only one, respecting the princely custom of keeping a chronicler as a figure of the court. In the same way that other artists and especially unofficial scribblers grew in number during the ages of free expression, because genius emerges especially during the hard times but cannot express itself where there is no freedom of expression, the ages marked by strict regimes produced fewer chroniclers, and even the value of those few suffered.

4.1.   Only the recipears have always been favorites of the faith, their freedom untouchable as long as they worked within society's norms, no matter its ethics. Because any kind of regime could be initiated by the sovereign, in the Gastronomic Arts the regime was established only by the Master Recipear of the Court, and in accordance with his skills and his freedom of spirit, the Recipearium practice might be in total contradiction to the intellectual and social darkness of the society.

2. I have chosen to write about this subject too, not because it has any importance to me, but because it seems meaningless to again write about a period already covered while there are whole centuries left in oblivion; on the other hand, to begin with a random century chosen from those unchronicled seemed risky to me, the danger lying in the lack of raw facts to accurately filter the period through contemporary eyes. It would require starting from a selected moment and rebuilding certain realities on which I could rely, or locating another possibly bold chronicler to aid in digging up and bringing to light those dim ages past, without filtering them through his present.

2.2.   There could be opinions, such as: the past doesn't, in fact, stop at the point I chose. They are certainly right in terms of time and chronology; but all that exists at this hour does have some connection with the ancient civilization located here, and I think that only after our history is written and known can others start digging up special pasts, with no implication in the future. These would have interest only for the researcher's eye and spirit, in completing a picture of a culture that holds no interest to the masses, but is only an accounting of the people's heritage.

3. I will speak about an age for which I have few resources, and most of those oral, gathered from people of that time and organized into a volume from which one must separate fairy tale from reality. This is possible only by comparison with the present and especially by confrontation with the few written resources bearing a strong common characteristic, such as the scarcity of information.

2.3.　　We can draw a conclusion even at this stage, that during this period the phrils didn't have time for writing or practice of the Recipearium, being much too busy with warfare during a time of cruelty, trickery, discord, and rebellions, a time when everything happened twofold: war and peace, war and peace.

3.3.　　Internal peace was harder and bloodier than war, while externally, the enemies, called at the time the *green plague,* were like an excessively violent fire, unquenchable only through compromise and tributary peace.

4.3.　　The age's fury was felt at its strongest in the Royal Carami, the nerve center of the young kingdom, born overnight, and still not precisely drawn. It was a juncture where ambition subdued nobility, and these interests had thrown honor into the shadows; virtue was often repaid with the shameful death of assassination. The laws were silently repealed and replaced by the chaos of personal justice. The unworthy Rule of Assassination is reminiscent of those times, shamefully still in practice today. It is said that only thus could balance be maintained in a society of strong individuals and weak ones, a society where the balance is only apparent and where this rule represents a valve to release pressure that would otherwise endanger the balance of the power.

4. Only the strong personality of Chathron the Conqueror succeeded in maintaining the fragile fledgling kingdom in the face of its internal strife.

2.4.　　Only the Green phrils' spirit of unity in the face of external dangers and the political wisdom of the Perpetuation Guild made possible the existence of the state and the regularization of its society, as well as its relations with neighbors in a region obviously hostile to the new reality.

5. Two-thirds of the actual territory of the Green Kingdom before our invasion belonged to the red-headed phrils; the other third was divided into no less than four realms, with the exception of the Southern Swamps, which have never been reclaimed. The red-headed phrils, or the Reds for short, were

not a numerous people; to my amazement, I learned that they retreated completely into the Caramis and their dependency on the monster-cities was their main characteristic.

2.5.   I found no information on the logistics of their food supply, though there must have been some system, since none of them worked the land or raised animals for food. It is also a mystery how a society of tribes isolated in their own Caramis could still obey a central power which was even then the same city as our own capital—the Royal Carami. How could they also maintain permanent lines of communication between them, despite their obvious physical isolation? For instance, other cities learned immediately of our siege of the capital city and sent reinforcements to attempt to break the siege, all without any living being leaving the city, as resources of the time assure us.

3.5.   Like all other peoples on the continent at the time, they didn't know of the practice of the Recipearium. That was one of the great revelations that brought peace and brought us to the attention of our neighbors, near and far. For all intents and purposes, we brought the Truth to these lands, for what is the Recipearium if not the Truth?

4.5.   This thing overturned the value system for all of the many peoples on the continent, following so many religions; wherever you went, their object was the same—the Faith. And the phrils, lacking the Truth, were the instruments of the Faith, which they didn't feel, but served by serving the phriliras; once the revelation was made, the effects spread rapidly, restructuring every society from its foundations up. This thing, ably woven by the Perpetuation Guild, put an end to the wars and turned the young Green Kingdom into a place of pilgrimage. The Recipes became the coin of trade in a blossoming commerce that for the first time turned art into a business. Because of this, things tended to take an ugly upturn; yet, very rapidly, a new system of thought was imposed on our society, it being natural that a single nation come to the forefront and the other thirty be assimilated and expected to adapt to the other's lifestyle, including the continental relationship system of laws.

6. There are no resources that tell us where we came from; we know that we came from somewhere to the east, but nobody can precisely point to the place of origin. At the relevant moment we were an overwhelmingly large migration wave, being equal in numbers to the Reds, who were still a settled population; moreover, we came with new fighting skills, paralyzing the armies of that age, allowing us to crush any resistance. Chathron the Conqueror's policy was simple: in any community there are three points of existence—the maximum, in which society has reached the balance between the number of the phrils and resources, the tendency being that of stagnation and spiritual evolution; the minimum point, meaning that there is a level of development in which progressive tendencies vanish, making room even for suicidal syndromes; and the tension point, representing the extent of a community's expansion, the moment at which appears an overwhelming will for survival, and the capability to perform miraculous deeds.

2.6. Chathron knew he had no choices, therefore he preferred to eliminate the entire Red population, the society of which had reached their maximum point. If he had followed the principle of leaving his surviving enemies alive after their defeat, since their society had been regressing and would enter dissolution by itself, the choice would have been a mistake for that particular type of war—invasion—because the survivors would have assimilated into our society and then recovered, reorganizing themselves into a normal society that might possibly have usurped our supremacy; if he had killed as many as possible while still taking prisoners, they would have reached the tension point, where their children became much too dangerous through their exaggerated survival instinct. The only solution was the extinction of the entire population of Reds, to avoid any further possibility of a civil war.

Different sources, especially from the oral tradition, say

that the Reds still actually exist, their last survivors retreating in front of the Green blades to disappear deep into the swamps of the south. The hypothesis has never been verified, because the swamps cover an area equal to that of the rest of the country. What's more, it is an extremely wild region, and no phrils have been able to enter the territory for longer than five days. The last dwellings are on the swamp's banks, extending into the marshes just a little through the sequ plantations. Specialists affirm that no community could survive in that rotting desert's conditions. In conclusion, even if a surviving tribe had retreated into the swamps according to the legends, its fate would have been sealed anyway.

7. After conquering the Red's kingdom as well as some of the neighboring territories, the main problem was the administrative organization of the country. The lands had been shared between the tribes. But, until the final sharing, we'd been forced to resort to force at least three more times, to defend our new territories. The internal fight for these lands was bloodier than the wars; only the alliances between the tribes manipulated by the Perpetuation Guild and the strong hand of Chathron succeeded in stopping the cruelty unleashed between those who marched to take over their lands.

2.7.　　　As there was no clearly defined hierarchy and the only leading organism, after Chathron, was the War Council, it had come down to tribal policy. The noble titles derive in fact from the tribal names; thus, the strongest and the most numerous tribes were the tahrays, their leaders called Tahrayisi, transforming over time to the current Taharissh; next in importance, the hrays, with their leaders the Hrayisi, became the current Harisshes; and the hirays, led by Hirises, became Hitisshes. Each warlord had the right in the council to a certain number of votes according to importance of the tribe he led—that was the tribal policy. Chathron proclaimed himself king and chose as his seat of power the Reds' Royal Carami, whose palace he transformed and developed over time, adapting it to the needs of his court.

3.7.　　Three things dominated the youth of the Green Kingdom: the Carami, the Recipearium, and Religion. The Carami, meaning the city, was truly a discovery for the Green phrils; supposedly because, being nomadic until that time, they lacked written resources. Though I personally believe, according to the evidence, that they had not been nomads, but only a segment of the population deposed from their birthplace, and pushed for decades in this direction, where they finally settled; the evidence indicates that the Green phrils brought the sequ and monumental architecture to this continent, inexplicable customs for a nomadic population.

Still, despite these things, the sources speak clearly about the novelty that the Caramis represented; it is true even now that we cannot explain their origins, despite being accustomed to their existence. We, or any other population on the continent, have no record of a newborn Carami being discovered, or a new Carami arriving from elsewhere, although it is certain that the city's organism develops in time, grows, and modifies its structure imperceptibly.

At that time, the lower level of the Royal Carami was still underwater. The Reds had lived in areas formed naturally that randomly appeared without any phrilic intervention. We can say that only then did the city's civilizing period start: the water was slowly drained out over two or three centuries, the interior was systematized, and its growth guided through artificial constructions with materials found in the creature itself, so they would be incorporated faster and more easily into the whole. After only five centuries, the Carami's system specialized, self-generating in its turn the necessary structures for the course of a normal urban life.

4.7.　　The Recipearium was the second dominant change, because the changing of the medium required the adaptation of the Recipes, of the gastronomic concepts, of the artistic philosophies, and even of the consumers' metabolism. The war provoked the death of a significant number of recipears and with them went a great cultural loss, a fact that determined strong movements among the artists who were confronted with the new medium and with the empty spots left by the deaths of some key figures. The new wave of recipears born in the first century, their growing importance on a social level, and the desperate struggle for adaptation and the making of a new reality, led to the Gastronomic Revolution, which peaked with the birth of a hierarchy in the class of the artists. Initially it resembled a tribal hierarchy, with the most important recipear being the royal court's, then one for each tribe, based on the importance of the community he represented—strengthened with the adoption of the commercialist philosophical system, about which I spoke before, and about which I'll refer to in detail in a special chapter. Before entering the matter of religion, we have to notice the specific relationship between the phril and the phrilira.

8. According to the Recipearium, phrils are different beings from phriliras. The physical makeup, as well as the moral and psychic, lead us to the same conclusion: there are two absolutely different entities, united on the social plan through who knows what game of chance; on the other hand, the philosophy urges us to believe that in fact they are not only beings of the same nature, but even of the same being. The central school, from which have grown all the other streams, including any defunct contrary orientations—I am speaking about the Originist School—sustains the idea of the existence of a primordial being, the phrilolir, from whom the contraries that have split and separated originated.

2.8.   As for now, the Recipearium represents the Truth, and the philosophy never had the pretence that it is the keeper of the Truth, but only the seeker. I tend, like all my ancestors, to approve the evidence, because the practice of the Recipearium finalizes in something solid, though inexplicable; something relatively touchable, something that is totally contrary to the Originist theory. Still, the fact cannot pass unnoticed that these two hypotheses—the gastronomic one and the philosophical one—although contrary to each other, have never been denied totally, and that the phrils keep them both in their contrariness in a natural relationship, believing at the same time that the phril-phrilira relationship is very normal, with all the obvious opposability of the nature of the two beings. This polarity in fact offers the substance of the phrilic family existence; on one hand we have the phrilira with her overwhelming religious spirit, with a way of thinking and a kind of mystical reasoning, spiritually part of the phriliric society and physically, to the phrilic society; on the other hand we have the phril, impotent from the religious point of view, with a practical, logical way of thinking, spiritually owned by the Recipearium, which is the opposite of the Religion, and physically, to the society in its entirety. This is their only common ground, what keeps the two beings together both in society and in the instinctive perpetuation of the species.

www.ingramcontent.com/pod-product-compliance
Lightning Source LLC
Chambersburg PA
CBHW051241260626
47162CB00002B/540